BLIND TURN

CARA SUE ACHTERBERG

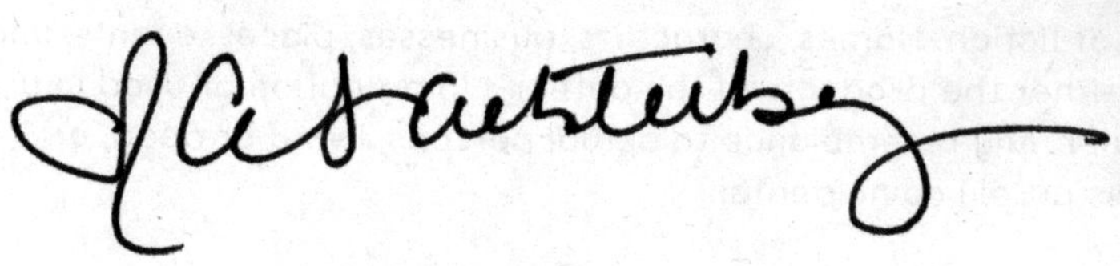

Black Rose Writing | Texas

First printing

This is a work of fiction. Names, characters, businesses, places, events, and incidents are either the products of the author's imagination or used in a fictitious manner. Any resemblance to actual persons, living or dead, or actual events is purely coincidental.

ISBN: 978-1-68433-610-4
PUBLISHED BY BLACK ROSE WRITING
www.blackrosewriting.com

Printed in the United States of America
Suggested Retail Price (SRP) $20.95

Blind Turn is printed in Georgia Pro

*As a planet-friendly publisher, Black Rose Writing does its best to eliminate unnecessary waste to reduce paper usage and energy costs, while never compromising the reading experience. As a result, the final word count vs. page count may not meet common expectations.

Cover photo by Nancy Slattery

For every writer who hasn't given up.

Acknowledgments

Where to begin? If you knew the history of this book, you'd brace yourself, knowing the people and factors and fate that had a hand in this book are vast and messy.

I have to start with my former literary agent, the first agent to love this book and sign me for it—Tina Schwartz. Her belief and outright affection for this book buoyed me long after we'd parted professional ways. Her efforts and her advocacy for this story deserve more than my thanks, but it is all I have to honor the spark she blew into a flame, even if the fire was six years down the road.

Next, I must thank all the readers of all the different versions of this story. I am telling you flat-out that I'm certain I am missing a few. There were so many beta readers and critique partners and kind-hearted friends and almost-agents and would-be publishers to keep track of, nevermind the number of times I started over and required all of their eyeballs once again. The lists and post-its and notes on my phone are jumbled and unreliable, but in no particular order, I would like to thank:

Mom and Dad, There is never enough space to thank you for your constant support and absolute belief in my abilities, despite having born witness to my messy teenage years.

Margot Tillitson, my speediest reader, favorite mother-in-law, and wise encourager.

Margie Geasler, for your smarts and for telling me that 'this is the one!'

Leslie Johnson, my full-time fan, occasional grammar consultant, and long-time friend.

Candace Shaffer, editor extraordinaire, who perfected her craft on this story time and again; I can never pay her for the hours she spent picking it to pieces and noticing every single detail.

Gina Moltz, for many reads, much hashing of the story, but for always, always being enthusiastic and encouraging.

Heather Marsiglia, a reader I never met who nonetheless, generously offered her time and thoughts.

Dahna Clarke, my former neighbor and fellow down-hiller, for reading this in its YA phase; I'm so grateful this story allowed us to reconnect after thirty+ years.

Susan Robinson, you read this one so long ago and so many versions ago, I'd bet you don't even remember reading it. Thanks for being my toughest critic; I wish I could clone you.

Lisa Weigard, for never giving up hope in the story or in me.

Adelaide, whose supernatural grammatical skills were not inherited and who read this manuscript and was paid per error she found. See? It finally got published!

Carly Watters, my current agent, who unleashed me to find a publishing home for this manuscript. I owe you a debt for the hours spent on this manuscript and for teaching me that every chapter has to have at least two real plot points so the reader doesn't get bored. Excellent advice that kept me from wandering in the swamp of my own verbiage.

Steve MacDonald, for patiently answering my legal questions and translating the confusing system into words I could understand and then assuring me, "But this is fiction, so you could probably leave that out."

Jacquelyn Mitchard for doing her darndest to acquire this book despite her publisher's ultimate no. You gave me legitimacy at a moment in my career when I needed it most. Your belief in this story was one of the main reasons I've never given up on it. "If Jacquelyn Mitchard loves it, I'm for real."

All the judges on twitter pitch wars, the editors who almost bit, and the publishers who passed, you sharpened my aim and helped me see that while it wasn't my time yet, I was getting closer.

For Reagan Rothe and Black Rose Writing for finally (finally) giving Blind Turn a publishing home.

For my husband Nick, who has listened to the long and winding road of this novel for more than seven years and never once asked to read it or doubted its future. I love you for that (and lots of other reasons).

BLIND TURN

“Forgiveness is the act of admitting we are like other people.”
– Christina Baldwin

1
LIZ

"You need to take this." Avery shoves my cell phone at me. "I'll deal with the party."

"Who is it?"

I glance at my watch. Eleven-thirty. I rarely work on Sundays, but it is Edna Mae's 100th birthday and her entire family is here for a birthday brunch, as well as a reporter from the paper. She probably doesn't even know the party is for her, but I wanted to be on hand to be sure it went okay. Her great-grandchildren have just blown out her candles and a cheer goes up.

"He kept calling," Avery says. "He says it's an emergency."

The residents break out with an enthusiastic but out of tune rendition of *For She's a Jolly Good Fellow*. Their time-worn voices always center my heart, reminding me that life wasn't always so complicated and on-demand. One time when my daughter Jess was maybe eight, she heard them singing and asked, "Don't they know she's not a fellow?"

I take the phone and slip into the hallway, pulling the door closed behind me. The call is from Jake, my ex-husband. I have not talked to him in weeks; parenting is mostly a side gig for him, something he squeezes in between fishing season and the latest bimbo.

"What do you need, Jake? I'm busy." I glance back through the narrow window in the door to watch Avery lean down and kiss Edna Mae on her crinkly cheek, leaving a faint red trace. Edna Mae smiles, pats her arm.

"It's Jess."

It is the sound of his voice that frightens me. Instead of the cocky boy-man he has become, I hear a scared kid, the one who proposed to me because he didn't know better.

"She's been in an accident," he says. "It's bad."

I hurl questions at him as I sprint to my desk, grab my purse, and run for my car. "Is she okay? Where is she? What happened? Why didn't you call me sooner?"

"I'm calling you now. She's at Memorial. They're checking her; they said the injuries aren't life-threatening..."

The phone goes quiet and I think it has cut him off, but then I hear him talking to someone, muffled voices, Jess' name.

"Jake?" I shriek as I open my car door.

"She hit someone," he whispers. He says nothing more. I wait for him to explain, but all I hear is the buzz of a hospital corridor. He takes a breath, and I can hear it catch on the inhale. *Is he crying?* He exhales loudly, slowly.

"She hit someone? What do you mean? With her car?"

I have always operated at a much higher speed than Jake Johnson. He's a good old boy from Texas, a guy used to taking his time, never in a rush to say anything he doesn't need to say. As he has done for the better part of twenty years, he ignores my questions.

"Lizzie," he says. "It's real bad."

"I thought you said her injuries weren't life-threatening?"

"It's not her, it's the guy she hit—he's dead."

"What?" My world teeters sideways. Skidding to a stop. For a moment, just a moment, I thank God it was someone else and not Jess. And then I dig in my purse for my keys, toss out receipts, mints, and earbuds, leaving them where they scatter on the pavement. Finally, my keys.

"She was taking Sheila home," Jake says, as I slam the door behind me and crank the engine. "She hit some guy on Elm."

"I don't understand! You're not making any sense!" I scream as I back blindly out of my spot, slamming on the brakes when a nurse jumps out of my path. I wave an apology, and she scowls. I take a breath. "I don't understand," I say again, calmer now as I carefully back out of my space. "Is Sheila okay?"

"I think so. Nobody said. The guy was walking on the side of the road."

"Then how did she hit him? That makes no sense," I insist. I wonder if Jake got all the details or if he was only half-ass listening, as usual.

"That's all I know, I just got here. I'll call you when I know more."

"I'll be there in ten minutes."

The yellow light turns to red as I press the pedal to the floor, my dragging tailpipe banging through the dip in the intersection. The entire way to the hospital, I chant, "No, no, no, no," as if I can change whatever has already happened.

Sixteen years ago, when I found out I was pregnant with Jess, I thought my whole life was ruined by the reckless choices of one night and a cute boy. It was the Senior Formal. I had used all my babysitting money to buy the most exquisite dress—periwinkle blue with tiny shimmering sequins and a matching shawl made of translucent fabric that winked silver. I can still remember Jake's face when I opened my front door and spun for him. "Damn, I didn't know you could look like that," he said.

He never left my side that night. Instead of cutting up with his buddies, he kept his eyes on me. When the dance ended, we drove to the quarry in his pickup truck. There was no discussion, no debate. We knew what was going to happen. Why we couldn't stop for a condom at the Quikmart, I do not know. But we were teenagers, invincible, on top of our world. I remember thinking afterward, as we sat on the hood of his car and watched the moonlight slide across the water, that even if I ended up pregnant, it would be okay. I loved Jake.

My Honda's tires squeal as I turn onto the hospital campus. For one crazy second, I am jealous Jake got to her first. I should be glad he is there. Glad someone is with Jess. Maybe Sheila is with her, too. Sheila is her best friend, not the friend I would have picked for her, but Jess isn't three anymore, so I don't have a say about much in her life. Sheila's bottle-blond hair and runway wardrobe are years ahead of this tiny East Texas town where the hem length restrictions are spelled out in the school handbook, and when the cashier at the Gas & Go dyed her hair blue, it was nearly front-page news.

I park the car in the loading zone and race inside. "No, no, no, no," I whisper as I run.

I haven't been here since the day Jess was born. I remember these faded pastel walls, the antiseptic smell. All I wanted was my mother that day, but my father had already whisked her away to Arizona and an alternative life that did not include daughters who disappointed him. They raised us Southern Baptist and while they would never have condoned me having an abortion, they couldn't face the idea of a baby either. An illegitimate granddaughter for the head deacon? Not in Jefferson. I married Jake, and I told my parents I loved him (and I believed I did), but a sin was a sin.

At the reception desk, the nurse speaks in soft reassurances to someone on the phone. I ask where Jess is, but she holds up a finger to shush me.

"Lizzie!" I hear Jake yell. He rushes down the hallway towards me. For once, the prodigal father comes through.

"She's all right," he tells me and my knees buckle. Jake leads me to the nearest chair. "She's in and out, and not making much sense when I saw her. She hit her head good, but the CT scan shows it's just a concussion. The doc said she's in shock, but she'll be fine. Just fine."

Fine is what I want to hear. It is what I want to believe, but I know it's not true. Nothing can be fine if a man is dead.

2
LIZ

Jess' swollen face is surrounded by a sea of white—pillows, blankets, and the halo of white gauze covering the stitches that closed the wound on her head. There are butterfly bandages securing the cuts on her face and faint purple around her eyes that will surely deepen in the days ahead.

"She's still a bit out of it," the nurse tells us before leaving us alone in the room.

Jake and I stand side by side in silence. Jess looks impossibly small, not the same girl who fights with me about curfew and tube tops, who takes all AP classes and has her sights set on a full-ride to a big college, anywhere but Texas. Not the powerful girl who holds the school record for the 400 and hopes to be captain of the track team, even though she is only a junior. No, she looks like the tiny girl who slept in a princess tiara and made me read the entire Harry Potter series to her when she was only seven.

"Did the police say what happened?"

"They're still piecing it together," Jake says. "But it looks like it was her fault, and there's something else..."

"What?" I cannot imagine it can get worse, but then it does.

"The guy she hit.... it was... it was Coach," says Jake. He blinks his eyes trying and failing to hold back tears as he runs his hand over the weekend stubble on his face.

"Coach Mitchell?" A shiver goes through me.

"No," Jess mutters, her eyelids fluttering as she stirs.

"Jess?" I lean closer and take her hand. She opens her eyes, looks at me, then at Jake, and furrows her brow.

"You're in the hospital, sweetie. You've had an accident."

She stares at me for a long moment, and then she says, "Your mascara is running."

I laugh with relief and turn my head to wipe fresh tears.

She looks at Jake. "Why are you here? Where am I?"

He grimaces but says nothing. Typical. He will leave it to me to tell her. He has always liked the fun parts of being a dad, but the dirty diapers and timeouts and curfews, he leaves to me. I have done the sex talk, the drug talk, the peer pressure talk, and the internet safety talk. As soon as she rounded the corner to adolescence, he never had time. I was the one subjected to her impatience and indifference. I used to think it was because his own father left when he was a baby, but that's not it. Jake doesn't like to upset people and more than anything he never wants to disappoint. Somehow I was the exception to that rule. He started disappointing me two days after we were married when he couldn't say no to a fishing trip down at the Gulf and left me alone and hormonal with boxes to unpack. But at least he didn't disappoint his buddies. "They're countin' on me," he said. "I'll make it up to you." Maybe he did that time, but wilted flowers from the Quikmart and dinner out at Jeb's can only take you so far.

"You had an accident," I tell Jess, touching her arm. I want to wrap myself around her, cushion the truth of what is coming, but I hesitate. Jess avoids my touch these days, rolls her eyes when I tell her I love her, hates when I call her my baby girl.

"What?" Her forehead wrinkles and she frowns. "Where's Sheila?"

Sheila spent the night ostensibly so they could work on homework, although when I got home at ten after staying late to set up for Edna Mae's party, Jess' car was not in the driveway. I should have stayed up and waited for them, held her accountable, but I was not up for another battle. High school is half over, and if I spend the next two years fighting with Jess, she will never come back. Instead, I've called a truce in my heart. I have had enough of fighting on every front—Jess, my father, my boss, Jake, even the cashier at the Quikmart who can't do simple math. I am not sure when everything got so out of control, but lately, my life is one episode after another of Liz against the world. I want to be on the same side as Jess again. So I let a lot go and trusted her to make good decisions—to *not* be the girl I was in high school.

"I think Sheila's fine," I tell Jess. "A broken arm, maybe, I heard. Jessica, what happened in that car?"

"Lizzie," Jake says. "She needs to rest. We can talk about this later."

I look at him perched awkwardly on a chair too small for him, like when he went to his one and only parent-teacher conference at the elementary school and said exactly nothing. His knee bounces and he wrings his hands. Once again, I am single parenting even though there are two parents in the room.

Jess doesn't answer me. She touches the bandages on her head, running her long thin fingers across the gauze.

"It's just a few stitches and a concussion, but the doctor says you'll feel pretty beat up for a while," I tell her.

"Did they shave my head?"

I nod. "They had to, to put in the stitches."

For the first time, she looks stricken, tears threaten. "What about Homecoming Court?"

Jess and Sheila were both nominated for Homecoming Court. We have been dress shopping for weeks and haven't found a dress we can agree on.

"Can you tell us what happened in the car?"

"My car?" she asks, and it is clear she doesn't remember the accident.

Jake shifts in his seat; he looks at me and not Jess.

"You don't remember? You hit someone with your car," I tell her, hoping it will bring the memory back.

"I did not," she says and for a moment she is four again, hands on hips, frilly yellow dress, red Jello powder spilled down her front denying she has eaten it. "I'm sure I'd remember something like that."

Jake says nothing. He studies the ugly faded painting on the wall opposite the bed. Ducks skim the surface of a pond, preparing to land or maybe get shot depending on if they are landing here in Harrison County where 90% of the population owns a gun.

"That's not possible," Jess insists again.

"The doctor says you're in shock, but maybe it will come back to you."

A policeman raps on the door and peers through the tiny window. I wipe my face and go to the door. I open the door a crack and look at the policeman standing there. "Can't this wait?" I ask. "She's barely awake."

"I'm afraid not," he says.

I hear Jake say, "It'll be okay. Everything will be okay."

Why he thinks that is beyond me. There is no way in hell this will be okay.

The police officer with pimply skin and a serious face approaches the bed. He takes off his hat, his pink scalp sweating through his close-cropped hair. He sits in a plastic chair, scooting it closer to the bed. It screeches on the linoleum. He pulls out a tape recorder.

"I'm Detective Pittman." He nods at Jess. "I need you to tell me what you remember about the accident."

I sit down beside Jess, take her hand. Jake gets up and paces the room.

"I don't remember having an accident," she says.

Detective Pittman sighs and looks at his notes.

"You were on Elm Drive, going south. Do you remember where you were going?"

She drives that route every day, taking Sheila to school in the beat-up Toyota Jake gave her. Sheila has a shiny red Mustang, but her mother won't let her drive it to school. She worries someone will ding it in the parking lot.

"I was driving Sheila home," she says. "I remember that much."

The officer frowns. "Did you take any medications today?"

Jess shakes her head.

"How about drugs or alcohol?"

"No."

Jess is an honors student and a varsity athlete. While she and Sheila get into their share of trouble, she wouldn't do anything to jeopardize her chances for a college scholarship. She is more than aware it is the only way she can go anywhere except the community college if Jake and I are left to pay for it, or more likely, me.

"Can I talk to Sheila?"

The officer ignores her question. "Were you using your cell phone?"

"I don't use it when I'm driving." She looks at me and scowls. Once, I ran a stop sign while arguing with Jake on the phone. If the other driver had pulled out a moment sooner, we would not be here now. Jess brings it up every time I tell her to be careful driving. The detective writes something on his pad.

"So, you remember nothing about the accident?" he asks again.

"No," she says again, crossing her arms over her belly, hugging herself.

"You don't remember hitting a pedestrian?"

She shakes her head. "No. I just told you I don't remember anything." I can hear the impatience in her voice. *She doesn't get it,* I realize.

Detective Pittman does not tell her what he knows, what Jake and I know. Instead, he says, "I may need to speak with you again. You'll be at your mother's house?"

"I guess so."

We all watch him make more notes; his pen presses hard into the accident form making triplicate copies. With a heavy sigh, he closes his pad and stands up.

"So, what happens now?" I wipe my eyes with a wadded-up tissue that comes apart in my hands.

Detective Pittman puts on his hat. "The investigation is ongoing. I really can't say. We may need to talk to Jessica again. The DA, too, probably."

"Will you charge her with anything?" asks Jake.

Charges? My baby girl?

"That's not up to us. We just pull together all the information. With something like this, the District Attorney's office will make the call."

"What could they charge her with?" Jake asks.

"I told you, sir, I wouldn't know; that's not my call."

"You don't know, or you don't want to tell us?" I ask. A flush of anger, or maybe fear, colors my face. This is only the beginning, I realize. This accident is far from over.

"Lizzie, he's just doing his job." Jake takes my arm, and his touch infuriates me. I push his hand away, busy myself looking for a new tissue.

The officer taps a finger to his hat. "Ma'am," he says and moves towards the door.

Jake shakes the officer's hand and closes the door behind him.

"You okay, kiddo?" asks Jake.

"What happened to the pedestrian? Is he hurt?" Jess asks.

Jake looks at that stupid duck picture again and says, "I don't know." He is a terrible liar. Maybe if he were better at it, we would still be together.

I abandon the search for tissues and pull another stiff one from the box on the counter. After I blow my nose, I tuck the blankets around Jess; she cringes when I kiss her cheek.

"I'm just going to make a call."

Jake follows me into the hallway. "Do you think we should call a lawyer?" he asks.

"I'll handle it." I scroll through my contacts as I walk away. I know just who to call. I never thought I would be calling him, but luckily I kept his number just in case.

3

LIZ

When I get back to Jess' room, Jake is finishing a Twinkie and offers one to me. I ignore him and sit next to the bed in one of the orange plastic chairs.

"I really *don't* remember what happened," Jess says before I can say anything. "I don't," she says again. I am not sure if she is trying to convince herself or me.

Jake leans against the counter, bumping the box full of plastic gloves to the floor. I wait. I will not be the one to tell her. When Jake looks at me, I look away. Jake puts the gloves back on the counter and sits on the edge of the bed.

"Jess," he begins, "This is real bad." He scans the ceiling, takes a breath. My anger softens as tears rim his eyes. He looks back at Jess with such tenderness, I want to reach out and take his hand, but I don't. Finally, he says, "The person you hit is dead."

"What?" screeches Jess, shock rippling across her face. She looks at me, imploring me to tell her it isn't true, that it is a mistake. I get up and sit on the bed too. I put my arm around her, pull her to me and she lets me. I reach for the right words but find none. Jake's eyes meet mine. He reaches for Jess, rubs the back of her neck. Jess shudders in my arms, sobbing.

I want to fix this. I want to save her from what is coming, even though I don't know myself what that will be. I can hear our tiny town whispering about my daughter, eagerly sharing our tragedy. Telling the story, filling in the blanks that even Jess cannot. In a small town, people mistake proximity for intimacy, believing they know you when all they know is where you live and shop, how often you go to church, and whether you wear makeup to the post office. I hug Jess tighter as if I can keep her safe from their judgment, knowing I can't. Just like I couldn't escape it seventeen years ago when I walked around town hiding the bump under my t-shirt that would be Jess. In Jefferson, Texas, teen moms were the ultimate failure. My parents moved away to a retirement community in Arizona a week after my wedding rather than face the failure my father perceived was his own.

After they left, I drove Jess there once a year. We spent more hours in the car getting there and back than in their home where my mother would fawn over Jess and my father would disappear into his wood shop. My mother passed from pancreatic cancer six years later. She had never told me she was sick. At her funeral, my father said, "I thought Jesus would heal her," as if he was truly surprised.

Jess' muffled voice speaks into my shoulder. "Who was it? Who died?" Her words hang in the air, the marker dividing our lives into before and after. I know my answer will change everything.

"It was an accident," I say. Jake nods, silenced by the tears streaming down his face.

"Just tell me!" demands Jess removing herself from my grip.

"It was Coach Mitchell," Jake says quietly, but he looks at me, not Jess. Coach Mitchell was the one he turned to when we found out I was pregnant. He was the only adult in his life at that time who did not tell him to pay for an abortion and walk away.

"Coach Mitchell?" Jess shrieks. "They think I killed Coach Mitchell?"

"Don't say it like that. It was an *accident*!" I tell her. "It was an accident. It was. It was an accident." I say it again and again as if by labeling it, I can make it so.

Jess pushes me away and tries to get up, but pain forces her back down. She collapses against her pillow and covers her head with the sheet. A memory crosses my heart of her hiding in the bathtub after she has spilled an entire bottle of milk across the kitchen floor.

This would be devastating if it was anyone, but this is Texas. Coach Mitchell is the football coach at Jefferson High where Jess goes to school, the same school where Jake and I met. He was Jake's coach the year they won the state championship for the first time. The team has won it five more times since. He is as close as you get to a celebrity in this town, but to the football players, he is a god. More than that, he is a good man. I push the grief that rushes at me aside, focus on my daughter.

Jess pulls the covers off her head and says, “I don’t even remember being in the car! Where’s Sheila? I need to talk to Sheila.”

Jake gets up and sits in the chair where the officer was sitting; he puts his arm on the bed rail and looks at Jess even though she has pulled the covers back over her head. “Hey,” he says. “We’re gonna sort this out. The important thing is you’re all right.”

I walk to the window and stare out at the darkness, wishing this nightmare was not ours. I want to keep her here, safe with us in our little circle of three. Once we leave this room, everything changes.

— — —

It is late when Avery calls and offers to come to the hospital. I tell her no, but not because I don’t want her company. I would love nothing more than my friend beside me to hold my hand and complain about the coffee and help me see where we go from here. Avery is very good at keeping me grounded and grateful. But her life is too complicated and too many people depend on her who would not understand her absence at this hour of night. Besides her three-year-old, Kimba, she also cares for her twenty-six-year-old brother Curtis, who is autistic, and her mom who struggles with the debilitating effects of ignoring diabetes until she couldn’t. So, I say, “We’re fine.”

“Bullshit,” she says. “I can come over as soon as I get Kimba settled and check Ma’s sugars.”

Her kindness brings my tears. When I can speak, I say, “There’s nothing you can do and I’ll just worry about you being away from your family.”

“You know I might show up anyway, right?”

“I know, but please don’t. I’ll save that offer for when I really need it.”

She makes me promise I will call first thing and says she will let Morningside know what is going on.

"I love you, friend," I tell her.

"Back at you. Hang in there, boss."

— — —

All night long, the nurse comes in and wakes Jess, again and again. She is supposed to rest, but not actually sleep. The hourly checks are a form of torture. Each time, the nurse snaps on a new set of gloves before she touches Jess like the awful thing she has done is contagious. She peers into Jess' eyes with a tiny flashlight then takes her blood pressure. She adjusts her blankets and tells her to rest. I watch her work and wonder if she went to Jefferson High. I wonder if she knows what my daughter has done.

4
JESS

The nurse tells me to get some rest, but that's basically impossible since she comes back and wakes me every hour. She shines a light in my eyes and asks dumb questions about what day it is when clearly it is night. This shit goes on all night long. Mom pretends to sleep, but Dad watches me. He hasn't given me this kind of attention since I was a little kid and he'd take me fishing on his boat. He always made me wear a life vest, but he also tied a rope to me just in case. "Your mom will kill us both if you drown," he used to joke.

It's weird to have Mom and Dad in the same room. Ever since I got my license they don't have to see each other, and they're happier that way. It's been kind of nice not to have to pretend I don't hear them fighting about the same stuff—responsibility (Dad's lack thereof), or unreasonable expectations (Mom's).

Mom has never liked his girlfriends, his dogs, or his dinner choices. Dad always says Mom is uptight. "Even her spaghetti is in knots," he would tell me. I'd go home to Mom's and study the spaghetti whenever she served it. It wasn't until later I realized what he meant. My mom likes things a certain way. Avery says, "Your Ma is too smart to abide fools; that's why she'll never have a man." I'm pretty sure she was half-looped when she said it, but it seems accurate. Your friends know you best. That's why I've got to talk to Sheila. Find out what the hell happened in that car.

I don't care what that cop says, I could not have done what they're saying. I'm an excellent driver. I'm one of the only kids who actually paid attention in Driver's Ed. I got my Intermediate license when I was exactly 15 and a half, but I've been driving for years with Dad. Once I was tall enough to reach the pedals, he had me back the boat trailer into the lake so he could unload the boat. Backing up a trailer takes skill. I'm careful. I take driving seriously. How in the hell could I have hit Coach Mitchell? This makes no sense. I'd remember it if I had.

Sheila's a lunatic behind the wheel. She sideswiped a mailbox one time, and we told her mom someone hit the car in the mall parking lot while we were at the movies. She once got a warning for doing sixty in a twenty-five. Charmed her way out of the ticket with tears. But I'm a careful driver. I couldn't have hit Coach. Not possible. Something is seriously screwed up here.

When that policeman came into the room earlier, though, he looked familiar. I had a weird Deja Vu moment or something, and the last time the nurse woke me I was having a dream that scared the shit out of me. I can't remember the dream, just pieces—flashing lights, the shine of a badge, Sheila yelling, the smell of burning rubber. And a horrible thud that woke me up even before the nurse turned on the lights. Was it a real memory, not a dream?

I just wish I could go back to before this happened and change things. None of this makes sense. I didn't even party last night. Sheila and I had planned to meet Jason at a party, but the cops broke it up right before we got there. We hung out at McDonald's til it got late and then I went home because it was pretty clear Sheila and Jason needed to get a room. Most of the time it doesn't bother me when they're sucking face right in front of me, but I had homework, so I left. I spent the rest of the night working on my history project and then watched YouTube videos waiting for Sheila to not show up. She said she was spending the night, but that was just so I'd cover for her if her mom called. I don't have to imagine what they did with the rest of the evening because Sheila gave me the play-by-play in the morning. Everything with Sheila is Jason this and Jason that, but I put up with it because she's in love. That's how love can be, I guess.

And he loves her too. Sheila and I made the homecoming court this year thanks to Jason. He got all the guys on the football team to vote for us. I still don't have an escort, but Sheila says that Jason's working on something as if I'm a charity case, which compared to her I kind of am. Some people ask their dad to walk them in, but I haven't done that yet because there's a good chance my dad wouldn't actually show up and even if he did, he'd probably be covered in grease or drunk.

After Sheila me about what she and Jason did up at the lake, most of which I think she embellished because that's kind of what she does, she copied my chemistry homework. And then I drove her home. That's the last thing I remember. No matter how hard I try. Just putting the car in reverse and Sheila talking about how her mom would probably be pissed because she missed church.

It freaks me out that I might get arrested. How can you get arrested for something you don't even remember? Will they put handcuffs on me?

Mom reaches for a tissue from the tray table at the end of my bed. I've never seen her like this. She cries at Disney movies and sometimes just before her period, but it's never like this.

Sheila has probably talked to Jason by now. He's the captain of the football team. Coach is the only reason he hasn't quit high school to work with his dad's plumbing business. If Coach Mitchell is really dead because of something I don't even remember doing, Jason will hate me. But then, so will everyone else at Jefferson High. My life would pretty much be over.

"I'm going call work and let them know I won't be in," Mom says and Dad nods. He doesn't have to call his work because he's the boss of his sorry-ass garage.

It's hard to imagine my parents have ever been friends, even harder to believe they were ever in love with each other. If Mom hadn't gotten pregnant, she wouldn't be stuck in a dead-end job saving what little money she has for annual trips to Minnesota to see her sister. I mean, I love Aunt Kate, but Minnesota is even more boring than Texas.

Dad, though, he would probably still be doing what he's doing, happy in his crappy trailer park, working on his truck or out on his fishing boat, but I know Mom gave up everything for me. She could have gone to college and gotten out of Jefferson. Instead, she's stuck in that crappy job at the nursing home in this crappy town. When I was younger, I thought if I could be the perfect student and model daughter, my parents would have less to fight about. It turned out they didn't need any excuse to hate each other.

Dad sees me awake and scooches his chair closer.

"How ya doing?"

Is there a dumber question to ask me at this moment?

I shrug.

"It's like your mom said, it was an accident. You have to remember that. That's what's important."

Miracle of miracles—they agree on something.

"Can we not talk about it?" I ask him because I can't talk about it. I can't think about it. It cannot have happened.

5
LIZ

On my way to the coffee station in the waiting area, I run into Sheila's mother, Janet.

"How's Sheila?"

Janet has never been friendly with me, probably because I have never been one of the moms who volunteer with the PTA, chaperone the school trips, or work the concession stands at sporting events. It is not just that I am busy working, which I am, it is more because I feel so out of step with the other moms. I had Jess when I was eighteen. The other moms are older than me. Their confidence and comradery are intimidating, and it is hard to find anything to talk to them about. The very few times I have tried, the awkwardness was painful. They never seemed to need or want me there, so I just stopped trying.

But now, seeing Janet, I have the urge to hug her. She looks worn through, instead of the pulled-together shiny-bright woman I have always known. She won't meet my eyes and turns to press the elevator button, but my question stops her. She adjusts her purse strap, glances over at the nurse's station. "Her arm is broken. Thank God, it's not worse."

"I'm so sorry. Jess is banged up pretty bad, too. Concussion. She can't remember the accident. She's been asking for Sheila."

Janet's thin lips curl and she sets her jaw and still will not look at me as if she cannot bear the sight of me. After a few chilly seconds, she says, "I think it's best if the girls don't talk."

"Why? They've been in a horrible accident. They need each other."

"A man is dead. I think what we need to do is let the police sort it out."

A man is dead. An image of Coach Mitchell appears in my mind. Smiling, congratulating me, shaking Jake's hand in this very same hospital the day after Jess was born. The elevator doors open, and Janet gets on without a word. I wander back to Jess' room in a daze. A few moments later, a new nurse comes in with paperwork, followed by a doctor.

He nods to Jake and me, then sits on the edge of the bed. "I'm Dr. Alstair. I'm just going to take a look at Jessica." The nurse hands him his own set of gloves and he pulls them on. He looks at her chart. "She seems to be doing well, considering."

No one says a word. Silence echoes through the room. The high-pitch squeak of nurses' shoes fades down the hallway. A delivery truck backs up outside. Jake cracks his knuckles, and I bristle at the sound. Jess says nothing, stares out the window. *Is she doing well?* Jake stretches, then leans back in his chair, making it creak. None of us are doing well, but that is not this doctor's concern. He is focused on the physical being, not the hearts that are shattering all over this room.

Dr. Alstair does the same routine as the last doctor. Shining the light, making Jess track his finger and asking simple questions like, who is the president and what day it is. Then he signs a paper and hands it to the nurse.

"The nurses will go over the concussion protocol with you. As long as she is stable all morning, you can take her home this afternoon. Come back in ten days to have the stitches removed or go to see your family doc," he says. Then he looks at Jess, shakes his head, just slightly. *In what? Pity? Anger? Judgment?* Or am I only projecting what is to come? "Good luck, young lady." He shakes Jake's hand, and I watch his white back go out the door.

Later Jake goes to the cafeteria and comes back with lunch. Neither Jess nor I can eat, but nothing seems to get in the way of his appetite. He has just balled up the empty wrapper to his sandwich when the nurse comes in.

"I'll need some signatures," she says and hands me papers. "You'll want to bring your car around to the back entrance."

"Why can't we go out the front?" I ask.

"I think it would be better if you went out the back. There are reporters out front and a lot of people in the lobby."

"They're here because of Coach," Jake says. It is not a question. "I'll get my truck. I'll call you when I'm at the door." He doesn't look back at us.

I feel as if the twenty-four hours since I arrived at the hospital have been a slow grind up a rickety roller coaster track and we are perched at the top now, about to go down, unsure whether the track will hold or the seatbelts will work, or whether I can even watch.

— — —

Driving home, we sit three across in Jake's tow truck. Its steady, insistent grumble would drown out our conversation if we had anything to say. I hate this time of year, the days growing shorter, the cold seeping in at night. Cars flash by, drivers hurrying home from school or shopping, their day just like any other, but today, everything looks foreign. Dangerous. We pass a woman jogging, and I tense up until we have passed her. Jess says nothing; she just stares blankly out the windshield, unmoving. I reach for her hand, but she pulls it away, tucking it between her knees.

We are almost to the house and Jake says he plans to stay over. "I want to be here in case you need me. In case Jess does," he clarifies when I roll my eyes at his offer.

I do not need him hovering, acting like he can help when he can't. There is nothing to fix, at least nothing he can fix. Besides, his latest floozy is probably waiting at his trailer.

When I made the decision to keep Jess and marry Jake, I changed. I grew up. One of us had to be the adult. I thought once the baby was born, Jake would step up. He would stop running around with his buddies and be the husband and father I wanted, no, I *needed* him to be.

I think my conviction—the naive belief that he could be a better man—is what underwrote our divorce. I could not see past the man I wanted him to be, and I finally realized he didn't want to be that man. Jake is a great guy, the guy everyone wants to hang out with, drink a beer (or ten) with, take fishing. But they don't have to live with him. In the end, I became a shrew, and he moved out to Gillam, where there are no neighborhood associations, and no one goes to church on Sundays during fishing season.

"We will be fine, really. Besides, you'll need to open the shop in the morning." I say this even though I know he doesn't. His garage is the local hangout where all the other men who don't have real jobs and never grew up come to hang out and talk about all the things they will never do and whether the fish are biting.

As we turn onto our street, a truck speeds past us, swerving to avoid the news vans and reporters that line the street and crowd our driveway.

"What the—" Jake stops himself from saying any more, but he guns the engine, blaring the horn as he makes the turn into our driveway, scattering people like birds.

My heart races and I instinctively pull Jess to me; she stares out the windshield in shock. Jake jumps out of the truck and starts yelling and waving his arms. Camera's flash, but people back up onto the lawn, out of Jake's reach. One big guy who looks familiar steps forward and for a moment I think Jake is going to hit him, but then a police cruiser roars up the street. The policeman instructs everyone to move back. "Shows over folks. You need to step back to the sidewalk." I pull Jess from the truck and hurry her into the house. Jake follows us in.

Jess collapses on the couch and turns on the TV.

Jake looks at her and back at me. "I'll just hang around a little while."

I don't argue. Jake steps towards me. Lowers his voice. "This isn't good."

I bite back the sarcastic comment that would normally rise to my lips and wave him into the kitchen. There is no wall between the kitchen and living room, just a line of sagging pine cabinets and a stained Formica counter. This house is exactly like every other house on the street, except everybody else has at some point remodeled the interior which is straight out of the seventies-era all-one-big-room fad. So, it is not as if Jess can't hear us, but now we at least make an attempt at being discreet.

Jake sits at the table and gives me a knowing look, one that pulls me back to graduation day when I hid my growing belly under my gown and smiled at the people who avoided my eyes and whispered behind their programs. I shudder at the thought of Jess under such a microscope. Surely, Jefferson has evolved.

"Now what?" he asks.

"The lawyer will be here soon," I tell him.

"What lawyer? They haven't even charged her with anything. Shit, Liz, how're we gonna pay for a lawyer?"

"He's a friend," I tell him, although I am not sure that is true. I met Kevin Sharp when his father was a resident at Morningside. His father was an elegant man, a serious Scrabble contender, and his mind never lost a step; everyone on staff loved him. He adored Kevin, bragged about him incessantly, and yet Kevin rarely visited. He was always busy. Always had some big case. His father died of an aneurysm in his sleep, and Kevin asked me out the day he came to collect his father's things. It seemed inappropriate and I turned him down. I saw him two more times after that and each time he pressed his business card into my hand and told me to call him if he could ever do anything for me.

So I called him, and I am really hoping he can do something for me.

6
LIZ

Jake shakes his head, frowns. "Oh, I get it. This lawyer's some guy you slept with. That's how come he's gonna help us? How do you know he's even a real lawyer?"

I don't take the bait. Jake always looks for a fight. But this is different. We can't fight about this. I level my eyes at him and say calmly, "Right now he's all we've got."

The doorbell rings. Jake stands to answer the door, but I pull him aside. It's my house. He's the one who left and I don't need him offending Kevin before he's even in the door.

When I open the door, though, it's not Kevin Sharp, esquire. Lights flash. People crowd the porch, flinging their questions and waving microphones. "Are you Jessica Johnson's mother? Was Jessica texting when she hit Coach Mitchell? Was alcohol involved? Has she been officially charged with anything yet?"

I slam the door and turn to Jake who is right behind me. I am shaking and I can't form words. He hesitates, and for a moment I think he is going to put his arms around me, but then he touches my elbow and moves past me. "Where'd that cop go? I'll get rid of them."

Jess races for her room. As I dial 911, I can hear Jake. "Get off this property right now!" The reporters yell more questions, but Jake yells even louder, "Get the hell out of here!"

The people retreat to the sidewalk, but they don't leave. I can hear them. The dispatcher who answers my call says she will send a car.

"They moved back, but they're not going to leave," Jake says.

I am still holding my phone. Frozen. I look up at Jake, and my tears start again. I can't seem to stop them. He takes a hesitant step toward me, but I wave him away and instead go to my room to change before our meeting with Kevin. I am still wearing my work clothes and my name badge from Morningside. *Hello, my name is Elizabeth Johnson, please let me help you.* I'm glad Jake is here, but I wish he would leave. I do not want to depend on Jake Johnson. I don't want to need him.

I wash my face and change into a clean sweater and jeans. There is no point in makeup as my tears come and go at will. *Was Jessica texting when she hit Coach Mitchell?* Why would they ask that? Why would they think that? Jess gives me holy hell whenever I use the phone while driving. I put my phone in my purse in the back seat when I'm driving just to appease her.

I call my sister Kate. I tried to reach her from the hospital but only got her voicemail. I vaguely remember her telling me something about a camping trip. She must be home by now. Through my tears, I tell her all that has happened.

"Should I come?" she asks.

"No, no. There's nothing you can do. I don't know what will happen yet. Jess seems most upset that they shaved some of her hair and she can't talk to Sheila. She doesn't believe that she did this. Frankly, I can't believe it either...Coach Mitchell is dead, Kate. Because of Jess." My voice breaks and tears engulf me.

Kate waits.

"I feel so helpless. I don't know what to say or do. It was an accident. Won't people see that?"

"You do remember this is Jefferson, Texas we're talking about?"

I know what that means. These people only see in black and white; gray is too complicated. And what if they're right and this is Jess' fault?

"I wish we knew what really happened. She wouldn't have been texting. I just can't believe she could have done what they're saying."

"She's a teenager, Liz. I know you think the sun rises and sets because of her, but she's just a kid. Kids do stupid things. Even smart kids."

She's right. I know, but her words make me angry. Jess isn't like other kids.

"She wasn't texting."

"I hope you got a good lawyer."

I don't say anything. All I know about Kevin Sharp is he is partial to banana pudding. His father always asked for it when he knew Kevin was coming to eat with him.

"You did get a lawyer?" Kate asks.

"Yes. I have a lawyer. He'll be here any minute."

"Do you need money?"

Kate doesn't have money to throw around. She lives hand to mouth as much as I do, but I have no doubt she would put herself in debt for her only niece.

"I'll figure something out. Kevin is a friend, so I'm hoping he'll cut me a break on the fees."

"What kind of friend?"

"Not that kind of friend."

"Too bad," says Kate, and I can see her smirking right through the phone line. She has been after me ever since Jake and I divorced to find a man. I do not know why it is so important to her I find a man. I asked her once, and she said, "I just think you're not the kind of woman who's happy alone."

"I have Jess."

"Jess is not staying in Jefferson. Not in a million years."

She's right I know.

"Hey, this is really bad timing," she says, "But when I got home, there was a message from Dad's nursing home. He's getting worse."

"I can't deal with him right now."

"I know; I shouldn't have brought it up. We can talk about it in a few days."

"Just don't tell him about Jess."

"I wouldn't. Besides, there's no point. Last I talked to him, he thought I was still in high school. Asked when I was coming home."

Most days it is easier to pretend he doesn't exist. I haven't been to see him since Mom died. I don't owe him anything; I remind myself.

"Hang in there, Lizzie. Let me know if you need me."

"I will," I tell her, even as I am certain I won't ask for her help. If my father taught me anything, it's how to take care of myself.

— — —

At 5:00 the doorbell rings. Jake checks out the window and then nods to me. I open the door. Kevin is wearing a suit that probably costs as much as my monthly mortgage. His tie is loosened, and his coat unbuttoned. "Liz, it's so good to see you." He gives me a broad smile, which fades quickly as Jake steps into view. "I'm sorry about the circumstances, though."

"Thanks for coming," I tell him and wave him in.

"You must be Jessica," he says when he sees Jess on the couch with her arms crossed, furious that we forced her to come out of her room for this meeting.

"Brilliant, Sherlock," says Jess so quietly he can't hear her.

"We're really grateful you're here," I tell him and shoot Jess a warning look.

"I'm Jake, Jessica's dad," says Jake offering his hand. "Thanks for doing this."

"I'll do what I can." Kevin takes a seat on the recliner facing Jess. "Liz was always so good to my dad at Morningside. It's the least I can do."

Jess rolls her eyes as she pulls the afghan Kate made for her around herself. I am just grateful she doesn't put it over her head.

"Your dad was pretty special," I say as Jake and I sit on the couch on either side of Jess. "Would you like some coffee?"

Kevin takes a folder from his briefcase. "No, I'm good. Coffee this late in the day will keep me up."

"Tea, water, soda?" I ask, and he shakes his head.

He opens the folder and spreads out a few papers.

"At this point, they're still investigating, but, to be honest, it's not looking good. I would expect them to bring charges very soon."

Jess sits up, and I reach for her hand, but she pulls it away. I watch Kevin leaf through his papers.

"Define 'not looking good,'" says Jake, leaning forward his elbows on his knees.

"It's a given they'll charge Jessica with Inattentive Driving or Reckless Driving. But it's possible they'll also go for vehicular manslaughter or criminally negligent homicide, which is a felony."

I gasp.

"There's not much precedent for going there, but the current DA is ambitious. We should be prepared for anything."

"What happens next?"

He glances at Jess, then back at Jake and I. "If they're going with the more serious charges, they'll arrest her. We'll go to the magistrate's office for a preliminary hearing. If we're lucky, it'll just be reckless or inattentive driving, but that's kind of unlikely since there's a death involved."

"What's the difference between reckless and inattentive?" asks Jess.

"Inattentive means you just weren't paying attention. Reckless means you were intentionally driving recklessly."

"I wasn't reckless," she says and I nod. Jess is not reckless. Kevin ignores her comment.

"They still haven't determined if texting was a factor."

"But she wasn't texting," I insist.

Kevin looks at Jess, who looks at the coffee table.

"The police are pretty sure she was," he says.

"Jess doesn't remember what happened," says Jake.

"She may not remember the accident, but the timestamp on her phone shows she received and read a text at 10:25 am, which was only moments before the car struck Mr. Mitchell."

"That doesn't mean she was the one who opened it," Jake and I both say at once.

"That's the fuzzy part," says Kevin. "I'm not sure if they can prove she opened it, but they sure think she did. They have a witness who corroborates it."

"Sheila," I say.

"Sheila probably looked at it. I don't text and drive," Jess says. "I'm not that stupid."

Kevin looks at his papers. Makes a note. His accusatory silence prompts Jess to insist, "I never text when I'm driving." She looks at me for confirmation and I nod again.

"She wouldn't." I fight the tears gathering; the narrative seems to be spiraling out of control, like a top released from its string.

"Okay, let's say, for now, you weren't texting. What do you remember?"

Jess twists her left wrist with her right hand; she stares at the patterned afghan covering her legs. "Nothing really. I was taking Sheila home, but I don't remember anything else until I woke up in the hospital. But I would not text and drive. I don't do that."

"You don't remember receiving and reading a text?" Kevin asks.

"She already said she doesn't remember anything," Jake answers for her.

Jess bites her lip, gets up and goes to the window. She pulls the curtain aside and stares out into the street. What is she looking for? A getaway car?

"What do we do?" I ask Kevin.

"I'm not sure yet. Like I said, we have to wait for them to make a move. For now, don't let Jess talk to anyone. Whatever she remembers or doesn't remember, don't tell anyone before you ask me first. If there is going to be an arrest, it will happen quickly."

"Will they just show up and arrest her?" asks Jake. Jess is still frozen at the window.

Kevin shakes his head. "Hard to say. They could, but I think I will know about it before it happens—if it happens. I'll walk you through it."

"Thank you," I say at the same time that Jakes says, "Damn," and shakes his head.

Kevin is more handsome than I remember. I am not naïve enough to believe he volunteered to help us just because he is such a nice guy. Nice guys don't wear quite so much cologne. At least in my experience.

He gathers up his papers. "There will be services for the coach. They are expecting a big turnout."

"We knew him. He coached Jake when he went to Jefferson."

"I'd like to go," says Jake quietly. Coach Mitchell has been a father figure in Jake's life. He never knew his own father. I touch Jake's arm. Kevin averts his eyes.

"That makes it tricky. Send a note or flowers but be careful not to apologize. You don't want to give the impression this was Jessica's fault."

"But what if it was?" I whisper.

"All that matters is who the law says was at fault."

"Do you need me anymore?" Jess asks abruptly, turning from the window and dropping the afghan at her feet.

"I think I've got all I need from you," says Kevin.

"You feel okay?" Jake asks.

"Pristine," she says, before disappearing into her room.

When Jess goes to her room, I finally ask the question I have been afraid to ask.

"How much will this cost?"

Kevin shakes his head. "Let's not worry about that now."

"It can't cost nothing. Look, we don't have a lot, but I can get a loan," Jake says. I find that hard to believe, but I suppose he might be able to get a second mortgage on his shop.

"Or I can," I add.

"We can sort that out later." Kevin smiles at me as he stands to go.

I don't know what that means and I have to wonder–how far would I go to keep Jess safe?

7
LIZ

I knock on Jess' door softly, but there is no answer; so I open the door and creep to her bed. She is so beautiful, even with black eyes, a swollen cheek, and her bandaged head. She is the best version of me and Jake, as if God used only our good parts to create her. But she is better than us too. She has a drive and a ferocity that will help her survive this. Maybe all these years arguing and battling with me and her father were only to hone her skills so that when the real test came, she would be ready. Because she will need steel in her bones to take on the judgment of this town, no matter what the police decide.

She stirs. "Hey, baby," I say.

She rolls over and scans my face. I watch the memory of yesterday register, stealing the brief peace she found in sleep. She bites her lip and looks away. I wish I could tell her everything is okay; I wish I could protect her from whatever is ahead or change what has already happened. The bandage on her head has shifted, and a few stray hairs stick to her face. The nurse said to keep the wound covered. I reach up to adjust her bandage, but she scowls at me and moves away.

She crawls out of bed and stumbles to the bathroom. I stand in the doorway as she drinks from the faucet. The water dribbles down her t-shirt.

"Kevin called. He wants us to meet him at the police station."

Jess lunges for the toilet and heaves. She has always had a sensitive stomach. Despite her tough exterior, it gives her away. She throws up whenever she is upset or nervous. Track meets and tests will send her running for the bathroom. I kneel beside her and hold what is left of her long, thick hair out of her face. Her hair is the same strawberry blond as her father, and she has his freckles too. When the heaving finally stops, she leans back against the tub and covers her face with her hands. The gold nail polish on her fingers catches the light and sparkles. Will she ever be that girl again? The girl who paints her nails gold and dreams of being the Homecoming queen?

"Why don't you take a shower. Your father went home to feed the dogs and put a note on the shop. He'll be back to go with us. Just be careful; don't get your bandages wet."

She touches her head, nods.

"Am I going to jail?"

"No. This is just a hearing. We'll find out what the charges will be."

"But they could put me in jail. I read that."

"Where?"

"Online."

"They won't put you in jail. If we have to, we'll post bail." Kevin has explained all about bail to me and Jake this morning on speakerphone as we huddled in my bathroom so that Jess wouldn't hear us. He gave us the number of a bail bondsman, and Jake called him. I just hope Jake's shoddy credit history doesn't hurt us.

"You don't have a relative you could call?" Kevin had asked.

"I never met my dad. My mom's been dead for years. Smoking cancer," Jake told him. "Not that she'd have helped us if she were alive."

He is right. His mother had her own problems, any number of which would have killed her if the lung cancer had not done it so swiftly.

"I have a sister who would help," I told Kevin. "She owns her home and she would do anything for Jess."

"You'll want to touch base with her then."

I called Kate before I woke Jess.

"Absolutely. Anything you need. I'll do it," she said, as I knew she would.

— — —

A half-hour later, Jess emerges, a plaid wool cap pulled over the bandages and her hair in a low ponytail. If not for her black eyes, she would look cute with her color-coordinated sweater (one I have not seen on her in years) and skirt. I am making scrambled eggs, but doubt she will eat.

"Did Sheila call?" she asks.

"No," I tell her. Despite my feelings about Sheila, even I wish she would call. "I spoke with her mother at the hospital, though."

"You did? Why didn't you tell me that?"

"She has a broken arm; she's fine. But Janet didn't think it was a good idea for you to call her."

"Why?"

I place two pieces of bread in the toaster, stare at the red coils heating up.

"Honey, I think Janet was just upset. I'm sure you'll hear from Sheila soon."

"But I don't understand. Why doesn't she want me to talk to Sheila?"

I pull the saltshaker from the cabinet and sprinkle salt on the eggs.

"What did Mrs. Richards say?" Jess asks again.

The eggs are sticking. I lift the pan off the hot burner and turn to her. "Just what I told you. She doesn't think you and Sheila should be talking. At least not until the police sort this out."

I set the eggs down, poke at them with the spatula, try to salvage them.

"That's ridiculous." She retreats to the couch. "Why can't I have my phone? I need my phone."

"The police will probably keep it for a while. They took everything in the car. They're trying to recreate the accident."

"How could my phone help them do that?"

I put the eggs on the counter. *Was Jess texting when she hit Coach Mitchell?*

"They are just doing their job."

"This is crazy!"

I say nothing, get out a plate, and put some of the eggs on it.

She pulls Kate's afghan over her head. I go to the window and peek around the curtain. A news van parks at the curb, and two women with notepads get out and question Mrs. Katz from next door. Mrs. Katz is wearing a housecoat and searching for her newspaper amidst the overgrowth beside her mailbox. She has a lot of cats, which is something that always makes Jess and I laugh—Mrs. Katz and her cats.

Jake pulls up in his tow truck. The reporters hustle over to talk to him. Jake is bigger than any of them. Tan and muscled from the hours he spends working on cars and fishing in all weather. He wears work boots, blue jeans, a flannel shirt, and a grimy baseball cap with a Pennzoil patch. He looks down at the reporters in their skinny jeans and bright wool jackets. He shakes his head and when the man with the camera turns it on him; he gives him the finger. I return to the kitchen and pour Jake a cup of coffee.

"Hey," he says as he drops his keys on the counter. "How is she?"

"Ask her yourself." I nod toward the couch where Jess is still under Kate's afghan.

"Hey kiddo; how're you feeling?"

Jess says nothing.

Jake picks up the leftover eggs and starts eating right out of the pan. I hand him a plate. He places it on the counter and continues eating from the pan. He waves me to the bedroom, and I follow.

"The newspaper says Jess was texting when she hit Coach Mitchell," he says.

"She couldn't have been."

"If she was texting when she hit Coach, that makes this more than an accident. One guy called it murder."

"Jess didn't murder anyone. That's crazy."

"I don't know. You should hear what they're saying on the radio."

"They're talking about Jess?" My heart races. Are people talking about my daughter as if she were.....what? A murderer? A villain? Jess, who was nearly in tears when she accidentally cut a worm in half with her spade while planting petunias for my Mother's Day last year. The room spins. I sit down on the bed. When I look up at Jake, he is still holding the frying pan, tears on his face. I am stunned by his tears. I touch his arm, reach for him. He turns for the door.

"We've got to get down to that courthouse. I'm gonna pull my truck around to Canyon Street. Bring Jess through the Kline's backyard, and meet me.

"That's crazy!"

He pauses in the doorway. "Yeah, well, you got a better idea?"

I don't, but I feel like we are criminals as we race across our backyard and duck under the little stand of trees that separate our tiny yard from the Klines. We are silent as we drive to the police station. Kevin is there when we arrive.

He leads us inside and we meet with a police officer in a small, sterile room with a metal table and three chairs. There is a sign that says, '*no smoking*' in five languages. "Jess, this is officer Hernandez. He will read you your rights."

Jess' eyes widen and Jake steps up and puts an arm around her.

"Jessica Johnson, you're under arrest for reckless driving and criminally negligent homicide...." As the officer recites the familiar words, tears roll down her face, but she meets his eyes and nods when he is through. "I understand," she says when he asks.

Thankfully, they don't put handcuffs on Jess. The officer opens a door on the other side of the room revealing the same courtroom where Jake and I dissolved our marriage. He holds the door open, waiting for us to enter. Jess hesitates, so Kevin takes her by the arm and escorts into the back of the courtroom. The judge is listening to the crimes of a small scruffy man wearing a Superman t-shirt. When they finish his case, he is led away in handcuffs. The officer standing by the door mutters, "So much for those superpowers."

A side door opens and an Assistant District Attorney comes in. It is not Bill Monroe, the ADA whose kids Jess has babysat every Friday for the last four years. I don't know why I expected it to be him. Of course, he would have to recuse himself.

The judge announces Jess' name and Kevin tells her to stand. He stands on one side of her and we stand on the other. Jess is white-faced and grabs my hand. She is shaking, and I try to anchor her.

The judge reads from a piece of paper in front of him. "Jessica Katherine Johnson, you are charged with reckless driving, a misdemeanor, and criminally negligent homicide, a felony." He looks over his bifocals at the ADA.

"Ah, ADA Filmore, what are your bail recommendations?"

"The defendant is a minor in good standing in the community. The state recommends bail be set at $10,000."

I hear Jake let out a breath beside me. Ten thousand means we only need to come up with a thousand to make bail. We can do that. By now Kate has already wired $500 to my account and Jake and I can scrounge up the rest.

It takes a few hours to get through all the legalities of keeping my daughter out of jail. Kevin stays with us through all of it. He is kind to Jess, bringing her soda and candy from the machine while she waits in the same tiny room where they arrested her.

Finally, everything is finished, and we can go home. Jake drops us off at the Kline's side yard and then drives to the front of our house as a distraction while Jess and I go in the back. When we are in, I flash the lights and Jake toots his horn goodbye. He will be back in the morning. He wanted to stay, but I insisted he go home. There is nothing any of us can do now but wait. Jess will have a preliminary hearing in one week when we will find out what the state knows, and a judge will decide whether there is enough here for a trial. That is also when Jess will have to plead guilty or not.

— — —

Kevin calls late in the afternoon to check on us.

"How're you holding up?"

"Not very well," I confess. Jess has been locked in her room for hours and I have been reading online about criminal law, boning up on the definitions of misdemeanors, felonies, criminally negligent homicide, and reckless driving. With every word I read, my heart sinks further. My daughter is in deep, deep trouble.

"Is there anybody you can call? You really need a support system right about now."

I sigh. Graduating pregnant, while maybe not so uncommon elsewhere even then, didn't happen in our conservative town. My friends who didn't shun me took off for higher education and more progressive cities; the friends who did stay avoided me altogether, none of them willing to risk the judgment of the First Baptist Church deacons of which my daddy was one. After Jake moved out, I became an army of one, determined to prove to everyone that I could handle the life I had created. I worked and took care of Jess. There was little room in my life for anything else. I considered calling Avery, but the woman worked too many hours–paid and unpaid. She did not have time to come hold my hand. I wouldn't ask it of her, even though I knew she would. In a heartbeat.

Which leaves Kate. She would get on a plane in the next hour if I asked, only I won't. When my father told me, "You've made your bed, now you can sleep in it," I made it my mantra. I did not need him or my mother or in the end, even Jake. I have proved that again and again; I can take care of myself.

"Not really. No. My sister is in Minnesota. I've been talking to her a lot."

"I am headed out soon and need to grab some dinner. Can I bring you and Jess Chinese? You like Chinese?"

"I'm not hungry."

"When was the last time you ate?"

"I can't remember."

"Exactly. You need to eat. What about Jess? What does she like?"

"Dumplings."

"I'll get her some."

Later, after Kevin arrives with dinner, I knock on Jess' door to see if she is hungry, but she says no and shuts the door in my face. I know she is scared. I wish she would talk to me.

We sit at my worn kitchen table under the harsh glare of the overhead light. I put the Chinese food on plates and watch as Kevin eats his lo mien with chopsticks. I hear myself talking endlessly, trying to convince him Jess is a good kid. That this is an isolated incident, a simple mistake. I want him to know Jess is worth defending. But periodically, as we talk, I am struck by how surreal this is–offering him a glass of wine, making small talk, while my daughter's name is likely on the lips of everyone in town, blame and judgment coloring their words. People are devastated. And some are surely angry. Coach was an icon here, beloved by all. And he is gone. Because of my daughter. My precious child. I cannot imagine a scenario in which Jessica is not at fault. It was her car. And yet, she is a good kid. She would never hurt someone. *But they will forgive her, won't they?*

I try to keep the conversation focused on Jess. I tell Kevin how she has always been an honor student. How she wrote an essay on safe driving that won a contest last year. How she badgers me about using my phone in the car. He listens, but I feel like I am selling something—my daughter's goodness. I want him to know she would never text and drive. She is not that kind of kid. But do I know that? I know her less and less lately. He nods, listens politely. Finally, he says, "I get it, Liz. She's a good kid."

"She is," I say, nodding. "I just want you to understand that."

"I do." He smiles. "Look. The fact that Jess is a good kid will work in her favor, but the thing is, and this is hard to hear maybe..."

I nod for him to continue.

"Good kids make mistakes. I will do what I can for you. For Jess."

I look at him then, wanting so much to believe this virtual stranger can help us. How can one moment, one split second, alter a lifetime, split it decidedly into before and after?

8
JESS

A reporter sits in her car across the street, the glow of a cellphone lights her face. Maybe she's not a reporter, maybe she's just some woman checking her gps directions. Maybe I'm paranoid. I watch the activity bus lumber down the street; it pauses on each block to spill out the kids who stayed after school for sports. Kids pour down the sidewalks now, heads down, hoods up, or laughing and teasing each other. Some of them look pointedly at my house. They know who lives here. They've all heard by now.

Kevin Sharp is in the kitchen with Mom. From the sounds of it, they're having a dinner date. Kevin Sharp looks sharp. Not sharp as in good-looking sharp, but full of hard edges and defined features. Even his nose is pointy. His dead father used to live in the nursing home where Mom works. I don't really remember the old guy or Kevin Sharp, who seems to have the hots for my mom, pathetically, but I guess that's why he's here. I've conveniently gotten myself arrested and now he has an in.

Mom was all over him today, twisting her blond hair between two fingers like she does when she's stressed. Asking him stupid questions, thanking him over and over again. I could tell Dad was annoyed. Kevin Sharp is the anti-Jake Campbell. He wears cologne and cufflinks, talks like he's not from Jefferson, and drives a BMW. I can't imagine any scenario, besides my current nightmare that would have the two of them spending a day together as they did today. I can't tell if Mom likes Kevin or just wants him to like her, so he'll help me. I notice she put on makeup before he came to cover the circles under her eyes. I also notice that she laughs at his stupid jokes and agrees with him a lot more than she agrees with anybody.

The girl in my mirror has two black eyes, one darker than the other, but both puffy and yellowing at the edges. I unwrap my bandage, unspooling it from my head to reveal stitches that look like Frankenstein's. The bare spot on my scalp, where they shaved my hair, has freckles. They are bigger than the ones on my nose. Weird.

I look like the villain I seem to be. I hurt all over like someone has tossed me around in a rock tumbler like the one I got for my birthday when I was eight. I turn off the light and creep back into my dark bedroom. I don't want the reporters who come and go outside to see me. Sleep is impossible because I can't stop thinking of Coach. I'm standing on the sidelines at the football game watching Sheila cheer as Jason runs up the field, Coach Mitchell high-fiving him as he passes. Then gym class sophomore year with Coach Mitchell. I knew him because of my dad, but that only made me more nervous. I might be able to run, but not many other physical feats come naturally. Plus, we had to change into gym uniforms and there was that whole awkward getting-dressed-as-quickly-as-possible-without-looking-at-anyone-else experience. But it turned out gym was fun. Coach Mitchell made it fun. He didn't favor the jocks, and he never made you feel bad if you couldn't do pull-ups. Everyone loved him, including me.

Coach Mitchell can't be dead. That isn't possible. There has to be some mistake. At the police station today it was like I'd wandered onto the set of a *Law & Order* episode. I kept waiting for that scene change music, *da-da-da-don*! Never in a million, jillion years did I ever think that I would be arrested. At least they didn't handcuff me. Mom kept saying that as if that meant it wasn't so bad.

The conversation in the kitchen moves to the living room, it's louder now so I turn on my fan. What could they possibly have to talk about for two hours? *Did she? Didn't she?* I couldn't have. I hear mom laugh. I need to get out of this house. I need to talk to Sheila. Why hasn't she called? I called her from Mom's phone five or six times now. It always goes to voicemail immediately. It's crazy that I can't talk to her. I've talked to her every day since sixth grade. I wish I could go for a run, but my head throbs relentlessly. If I put on my sneakers and started running now, I might never stop. Just like Forrest Gump.

I open the drawers of my desk looking for my old MP3 player and spy the flyer for the homecoming dance and a form to order letterman jackets. I lettered in track last year. All I need now is the jacket to put the letter on. Mom says the only way I get that jacket is if I give up cable for three months. I'm debating it.

But she killed a man, I hear my mother say. Or do I only imagine it? How important is a letterman jacket, now?

I whisper, "I killed a man. I'm a killer," but then I say it louder. I sound like an actress on the set of a movie or one of those crime novels Mom likes to read. "I'm a killer," I say one last time and then wad up the homecoming dance flyer and toss it at the trash can. I miss.

How could Coach Mitchell be dead because of me? There has to be some kind of explanation. If I hit him, why can't I remember it—why? Did he not see my car and step into the road or something? Did I swerve and try to miss him or did it happen too fast? Even if it was an accident, like Mom keeps insisting, and even if I can't remember it—it happened. There's no way around that. That's the bottom line. He's dead. For real. He went for a walk, and now he's dead. He was probably thinking about what he would eat for dinner, or maybe about the game the night before, or maybe he was talking to his dog. The police said that's what he was doing—walking his dog. Dad talks to Willard and Homeboy all the time. I wonder if the dog died, too. Nobody said if the dog died.

My stomach heaves, and I run for the toilet. My room has a door to the bathroom, but the bathroom has two doors and the other goes to the living room. I keep it locked unless someone's here. Thankfully, Mom never thought to unlock it for her date. All I need is concerned Mom and ass-kissing Kevin in here.

I retch again and again. The orange juice I drank earlier burns my nose. Finally, there's nothing left, so I lie down on the cool vinyl floor. I press the side of my head against the grimy floor and study the dust and hairs clinging to the side of the toilet. I cleaned the bathroom on Friday when Mom told me to, but I skipped the floor. It's not like she ever comes in here. No one uses this one except me and Sheila, and Avery when she hangs out with mom to drink wine and talk about Morningside or that guy she dates who's in prison. Sometimes she brings her little girl, Kimba. Sheila and Avery and Kimba don't care if my bathroom floor is clean, so what's the point?

I had to do my chores on Friday before Mom said it was okay for Sheila to spend the night like I was still ten years old. Mom has this crazy drive to make me a good person. She thinks chores and community service and A's will make us good people. Perfect people. Why she cares so much about what this town thinks of us makes no sense to me. And now it doesn't matter, does it? All that for nothing. I'm leaving, anyway, and when I finally get out of Jefferson, I will not be back. You can count on that.

I hear the front door close and Kevin's wingtips click down the steps. My lawyer. Who'd have thought I'd ever need a lawyer. Crazy. This is all crazy.

She killed a man.

I only had Coach Mitchell for gym sophomore year. When I was a freshman, we had a long-term sub. Coach Mitchell took that year off because his wife had cancer. The school did all kinds of fundraisers to help pay for her treatment. The track team sold poinsettias to raise money. Dad donated free oil changes for the silent auction.

Mrs. Mitchell got better. That was the town's miracle. And Coach Mitchell went back to coaching the football team, and last year they won States. At the awards assembly in the spring, he cried when he thanked everyone. He was a good man.

And now he's dead.

She killed a man.

I wonder if now Mrs. Mitchell wishes she hadn't beat cancer. It took a whole year to save her life and only seconds to take her husband's.

I hear Mom's shower turn on, the pipes groaning into action. My clock radio glows 10:45 pm. I creep to the kitchen without turning on any lights. Mom's phone is on the charger.

Sheila answers on the fourth ring. "Hello?" Her voice is uncertain and breathy. I wonder if she thinks I'm my mom calling her.

"Hey," I say. "It's me."

The line echoes with silence.

"Sheila?"

"You shouldn't call me." Her voice is urgent, angry.

"Since when?"

Another long silence.

"I can't talk to you," Sheila hisses, but then I hear her sniffle. Is she crying? "I can't believe he's dead."

"I know," I say. "It's crazy. What happened?"

"This isn't my fault. Jess, you were driving. You didn't have to look at the phone. This is on you. All on you."

Her words make no sense, but more than that, her anger stuns me.

"Why are you angry with me?"

"Jason is ripped up. It's like he's blaming me. *You* did this, not me!"

I don't know what to say. She's talking to me like she hates me; it chokes my words in my throat. "I'm just...I'm so sorry. I wish I could go back..."

"Sorry's not enough for this. There is no going back."

"This is messed up. I can't remember any of it. I never saw him. Why was Coach there?"

"Jesus, Jess! How could you not remember?" Her shrill words hang in the air.

What is happening? How did my life go so completely off the rails? And Sheila, the one person who has always had my back, how could she say my name with such fury, a repulsion even?

"I'm sorry," I say again. Lame. I am lame and pathetic. I can't catch my breath, but I need to ask her. I need to know. I know she is mad, but she was there and she's all I've got.

Sheila sighs. I can picture her now, dabbing at her eye makeup, even when she's upset she stays beautiful.

"Jason's really mad. I told him I didn't have anything to do with it. You can't tell him."

"What are you talking about?"

"You can't drag me into this."

"What do you mean? How are you not involved in this? You were there and I don't remember the accident," I say. "I need you to tell me what happened."

"Oh, C'mon, now you have amnesia? You were there, don't pretend you weren't. You were driving."

"I'm not pretending. I don't remember."

"You really can't remember?"

"Honest."

Her voice perks up suddenly. "Oh, well, even if you did, I can't talk to you anymore. My parents got a lawyer and he said not to talk to you. Jason would be furious if he knew I even answered this call. I can't talk to you."

"But I need you. I don't have anyone else." I sound desperate and I am. "You can't just decide not to talk to me. We always talk. You're my best friend."

"You don't see how big this is. You don't see how screwed we both are. Coach is dead. It was *your* fault; this is so fucked up," she explains as if she's impatient for me to get it.

"But why did it happen?"

"God Jess! I don't know. You looked at your phone! You hit him!" she shrieks.

Her words strike me like a fist. I touch my heart where the pain is worst. I try to speak, but nothing comes out. Before I can pull my thoughts together, she dismisses me.

"Just don't call again. I can't talk to you." Sheila's voice is clipped but certain.

I whisper, "But you're my best friend. I can't do this without you."

The phone goes dead; I put it back on the charger and stumble to my room. I crawl in my closet, shoving the piles of shoes on the floor out of the way. I press myself against the back wall and try to pull the door closed. It's one of those folding doors. If I open or close it too fast, it comes off the track, and when I was little it used to pinch my fingers and give me blood blisters. Now the door gets hung up on the shoes, so I grab the first shoe I can reach and fling it out of the closet. It hits the dresser. The perfume bottles rattle and a framed picture of me and Sheila from last summer falls to the floor.

The next shoe leaves a ding in the wall. I keep throwing them one by one. A stiletto from last year's Spring Fling catches the top edge of my Marion Jones poster and leaves a tear. I throw shoes until there aren't any left to throw. I yank the closet door closed and cry big, snotty sobs like when I was little and didn't get my way.

I wish I could die. My skin is too tight, and I pull at it. The buzzing in my head is deafening. It's hard to breathe. I kick at the closet door, but the latch holds it closed, so I kick harder. The sound in my head grows louder. It rumbles through my body and barrels out my mouth. I don't recognize the sound. It's like it's coming from someone else. I scream and sob, kicking at the door that finally gives as the cheap wood splinters.

9
LIZ

After Kevin has gone, I take a shower. I haven't had one in two days, but more than that, my desperation feels dirty. I will do whatever it takes to save my daughter. Even if it means cozying up to Kevin Sharp. And that makes it okay. *Doesn't it?* As the water rushes over me, I sink to the floor of the tub and sob.

Toweling off my hair, I can't get past the feeling that nothing will ever be the same. From now on. Not for Jess, not for me, not for this town. I am about to click on the hairdryer when I hear thumping sounds coming from Jessica's room. I pull on my robe and am halfway across the living room when I hear an awful keening, like a wounded animal. Next comes the sound of splintering wood. I fling her door open. Jess is curled in a fetal position among the wreckage that used to be her closet door. I try to reach for her, but she kicks at me. I pull the broken closet door out of the way and beg her to stop. It is as if she can't hear me. Her foot catches me on my collarbone. The pain is instant, but I grab at her and dodge her kicking feet. Finally, I get ahold of her foot and drag her out of the closet across the carpet, still kicking, still screaming. Now she yells, "Just leave me alone! I want to die! Just leave! Leave! Now!"

She smacks at me, but I kneel next to her and wrap my arms around her. She pushes against me, trying to get away, but I roll to my side, still clutching her. Finally, she relaxes in my arms, sobbing. We lay spooned together, both of us crying, our tears in tandem.

"Why did this happen?" Her voice is hoarse.

"It was an accident," I tell her. She needs to believe this. I need to believe this.

She goes quiet, just her breath catching in hiccups through her tears. She whispers, "Accidents happen when you spill your milk or trip over your shoelaces; not when you kill someone with your car. This isn't an accident."

I hold her and let her cry. "We will get through this," I tell her.

A memory comes to mind. My father knocking on my bedroom door, asking me to come downstairs because I have a visitor. These are the first words he has spoken to me since the day I told him I was pregnant and I planned to marry Jake. In the living room is a nice couple, probably in their late thirties. They look vaguely familiar; they are members of our church. It takes me a few minutes of polite conversation to realize why they are here. My father wants me to give my baby to them.

"The baby would be an answer to prayer," the wife says.

"She would never want for anything. We have a beautiful home, plenty of money, the nursery is already set up," the husband says.

"It would be the most amazing gift," the wife tells me.

"God works in mysterious ways," says my father, smiling, as if my pregnancy is a good thing, not the abomination he called it only a few weeks prior.

I pull Jess tight against me until mercifully, she falls asleep. She is not a mistake or an abomination or a killer. She is my daughter. And I will not let this take her from me.

— — —

The smell of bacon draws Jess to the kitchen, just like it has most Saturday mornings all her life. Only it isn't Saturday. And everything is different. She sits at the counter with her comforter wrapped around her. I put the plate of bacon in front of her. She picks up a piece and nibbles at it.

"There are still people out there," she nods towards the front of the house.

I turned the ringer off the house phone, but the reporters still call and my voicemail is full.

"They will give up eventually."

I say this, and yet I fear they won't. At this very moment, people all around town are talking about the accident. They are saying my daughter's name in hushed tones, shocked. Or maybe not. After all, she is a 'child of sin.' For seventeen years, I have worked to prove my father, my church, and my town wrong, but here is the evidence. I have never thought of Jess as a mistake. What I did may have been a sin, but this child Jake and I made is not. A lot of time has passed. Maybe I am being paranoid. Maybe people are more understanding now.

Although the way the town turns out for the Friday night football games, I am pretty certain what Jess has done, accident or not, will not be easily forgiven or forgotten. Coach Mitchell was a great man. There is not a person in this town who didn't love him. Myself included. But I can't think about that now. Now I have to think about protecting my daughter.

She picks up another piece of bacon. The comforter slips, and she pulls it over her shoulders again. My cell phone rings and we both stare at it. Jake.

"Hey," I answer.

"How is she? I've just gotta run the dogs a bit and then I can come right over."

"There's nothing you can do here."

I wipe the counter, rubbing the same spot repeatedly, trying to quell my annoyance. I know Jake wants to be the knight in shining armor, riding in to save the day, as if he could. Maybe if it was just a noisy muffler or a leaky exhaust, but this is his daughter and her heart is breaking.

"Let me talk to Jess."

I know Jess can hear him ask, so I look at her, raise my eyebrows. She shakes her head and picks up another piece of bacon.

"She can't talk right now."

Whatever he says is drowned out by his dogs barking. I have to hold the phone away from my ear. A smile momentarily crosses Jess' face as we listen to Jake yell at the dogs.

When Jake moved out, the first thing he did was get those hound dogs. He was upset when I told him to leave, but once he discovered the trailer park in Gillam, he acted like leaving was his idea. At that point, it was past time and I think we were more relieved than anything. We had been weighed down with the shame of failing just like everyone predicted and the guilt of what it would do to Jess. We had no choice, though; we were grinding each other's hearts into dust.

I take the phone to my room. Close the door. I need to talk to him about what Kevin told me last night.

"Kevin says if the DA has a solid case, we will have to consider a plea bargain."

"What does that mean?"

"It means Jess pleads guilty to a lesser charge. It could involve a hefty fine, so we need to figure out how much money we have, get appraisal letters together, stuff like that."

"You really think this would go away with just a fine?"

"No!" I hiss. "But let's assume the best for now."

"What does that mean?" Jake asks, clueless.

"It means we know our daughter didn't kill Coach Mitchell."

"Do we?"

"Jake! If you don't believe in her, who will?"

"Look, I'm not saying she did anything on purpose, but if this accident is her fault, there will be consequences and right now I can't figure who else could be at fault."

"The state has to prove she did this without a reasonable doubt. All we have to do is prove there's a reason to doubt that Jess would intentionally do this."

"That doesn't sound simple. And since when did you become Nancy Drew?"

I pull the curtain aside from my bedroom window, checking for reporters, and ignore his dig. "Until we find out what kind of case they have, we can't do much. But we need to figure out how we're going to pay Kevin."

"You sure he knows what he's doing?"

"Yes. He does." Kevin deals mostly with divorce these days, but he used to handle DUI cases. He has already told me we might want to get another opinion.

"Maybe we should consider other lawyers. You know, ask around instead of just going with some guy who's got the hots for you."

"Just call your bank and find out how much money you can access and how much you can borrow. Call your lender and find out what your trailer is worth."

"Whatever I have ain't worth enough to put a dent in anything."

I sit down on my bed, glance at the novel I was reading only two days ago. It looks foreign to me. "Just do it, Jake. For once, step up and do what you're supposed to do."

"What the hell does that mean?"

"It means Jess needs you to act like a real father right now."

"That's exactly what I'd like to do if you'd let me come over there and help."

"There is nothing you can do unless you've got a million bucks squirreled away somewhere to pay for a Dallas lawyer. If not, then you will just have to trust Kevin."

"That's not fair. There are other options. What about a public defender?"

"We are not going to use a public defender. So far, Kevin is doing this for free, but if this drags on we have to pay him."

"Nothing's free, Lizzie, the guy will want something."

"Leave it, will you? I am doing the best I can." I hang up. I don't need his help. I don't know what Kevin wants, but I think he can help Jess. And that is all that matters here. I glare at my phone, waiting for Jake to call back. For once, he lets it go.

"If you weren't so busy living out your eternal childhood, maybe we could afford a real lawyer," I say to the silent phone.

When I return to the kitchen. Jess is still at the counter. "You ate *all* the bacon?"

She shrugs and heads to her room.

I poke my head in later to check on her, and she is cleaning up. Her clothes hang neatly in her closet. She is lining up her shoes beneath them, wearing earbuds and humming *The Yellow Submarine.*

I would like to live in a submarine. That way nothing could surprise you. Little blips of the radar would alert you to danger ahead. Nothing new could come out of nowhere and side-swipe you.

10
JESS

I clean up my room, not because I know it will make my mother happy, but because I'm hoping it will help me keep my shit together. My mind is still spinning and since I can't run, I need to do something. I found an article about the accident on a website for the local paper. Reading it makes it pretty clear my life in Jefferson is toast. Mom keeps saying people will understand that it was an accident, but she's living in la-la land because clearly, that is not gonna happen.

BLUE89: Coach M was a great man. He changed my life. That girl who killed him should get the electric chair.
CATGIRL: Put her in prison and set an example. All teens do this. They're all idiots.
MINNIEMOUSE: I'm sick of disrespectful, selfish teenagers always on their phone, never paying attention to what's around them. She needs to be made an example of – I hope they lock her up.
PISH1282: She's just a stupid teenager. They do dumb things all the time. Have a little mercy.
WALTERF: What kind of mercy do you want to extend to the Mitchells?
BAMBI: I know the girl who did this. She goes to Jefferson and she's a stuck-up bitch. I'm not surprised she'd do something like this.
68573: I heard who it was, but I don't know her. Glad I don't. Anybody know what the charges are?

WALTERF: Should be first-degree murder, but I heard it's vehicular manslaughter. At least when she's convicted they'll lock her up and get her off the streets before she kills anybody else.
68573: They should give her the death penalty. That's what she deserves. Eye for eye, or in this case stupid girl for great man.

People want me to die. Well, that's fine. That would be perfect.

— — —

The rest of the day goes by in a blur. Mom and I watch a movie. I couldn't tell you what it was about. I just keep thinking about dying. Do you just stop being? Or would you float around somewhere still feeling awful about the terrible thing you did and watching everyone? I wonder if I died if anyone other than Mom and Dad would cry at my funeral? WALTERF and BLUE89 would probably celebrate. Still, the death sentence might be better than prison. I don't think I could survive in jail.

I go to bed, but I can't sleep, so I get up and google, *'How to kill yourself.'*

Most people recommend if you don't have a gun, jumping off a tall building would be quick. There aren't any tall buildings in Jefferson, except the fire hall, but probably the firemen would stop me before I got to the top. Besides, I'm kind of afraid of heights and I hate that feeling when your stomach drops out from under you going downhill on a rollercoaster. I'd probably make it to the roof and throw up. I don't think I could do it. Carbon monoxide poisoning was also suggested, but we don't have a garage. Besides, I don't have a car anymore.

I could never slit my throat. Hanging yourself sounds simple, but there isn't anything to hang from except the curtain rod, which always falls down when I slam the door too hard, so it's probably not really an option. I could take a bunch of pills. Mom has sleeping pills she never takes because she worries she won't wake up if something happens, like a fire or a burglar. But the advice online said you have to know how many to take or you can just end up a vegetable or brain-damaged.

— — —

On Thursday, the reporters out front finally give up, but no one says anything about me going to school, which is good because I'm not going. Dad shows up with McDonald's for lunch and argues with Mom. I binge-watch stupid shows I've seen already, anything to try not to think. Mom goes over to the school and gets my homework, but it sits in a pile on the counter untouched. What's the point?

— — —

Friday morning, early before Mom is up, I pull on my sweats and running shoes. As I open the front door, Mom calls from her bedroom.

"Jess?"

As soon as I hit the sidewalk, I start sprinting. My brain feels like it's slamming around my head and the pain is loud, but I welcome it. I want to hurt. I concentrate on putting one foot in front of the other. I can hear Mom calling me from the porch, but I keep running.

I finally pull up to a slow jog on the other side of McClain Avenue. The trees line the road on either side, leaning together to form a tunnel. This time of year, it's yellow and gold and brown, but in the spring it's green. The familiar branches look foreign, like I didn't just run down this road a week ago. How did this happen? I can't stop seeing the words on the computer screen. *She should get the death sentence. At least they'll lock her up*. I wish I could talk to Sheila. I tried calling again, but she didn't pick up. I can't imagine my life without Sheila.

I remember the day I met Sheila. It was like someone switched on a light. I'd always been a good student, mildly popular, at least nobody hated me. I had a few friends, but when you get to middle school it's every girl for herself. On the morning of the first day, I was in the hallway talking to Mr. Henry, the science teacher. I knew him from Morningside; he plays his guitar there on Sunday nights. He's kind of a hippie.

I've never understood why Sheila picked me. She's probably the most popular girl at Jefferson High. Being Sheila's best friend made me popular, too, by proximity. That first day of seventh grade, though, no one knew her. She walked right up to me and said, "Hey, I like your flip flops." I was wearing these flip-flops I'd made at camp. They were green with pink sequins and shells glued to the straps. Sheila was tan, about the same height as me, and her hair was blond, sleek, and straight. Hair like I always wished I had instead of my sunburned brown hair that tends towards the frizzy side. Sheila wore bright pink lipstick, exactly the color of the tube my mother had taken away from me that morning. And she wore the shortest shorts I'd ever seen inside a school building. I looked at Mr. Henry to see if he would say anything about dress code violations, but he was looking over our heads at the students coming in the front doors.

"I made them at camp," I told Sheila.

"They're cool. I'm Sheila, I'm new here. Where's the office?"

I pointed down the hallway. "It's up that way. Where'd you move here from?"

"California," said Sheila with a smirk. God, she was so cool.

I walked her to the office, and she asked me who the most popular girl in school was. I told her I had no idea, and she said that was okay because soon enough it would be her. "Cool," I said. Then she asked for my phone number and wrote it on her hand. It didn't make sense that we became best friends. The only thing we had in common was we both needed a friend. I guess that was enough. I'd never been popular or thought I would be, but I nodded and agreed with everything she said. Looking back now, I wonder if I really wanted to be popular, or if I just wanted Sheila to like me.

It's still pretty dark when I arrive at the Mitchell's house. I've never been in it, but everyone knows where Coach lives. Every light in the house is on. There are five or six cars in the driveway. The whole family is probably there. At least Helen Mitchell isn't all alone.

Dad didn't say anything, but I know he went to the funeral yesterday. That's why he was so dressed up when he brought the McDonalds. He loved Coach Mitchell. He worked on his cars for free and went to every football game. When I was little, Coach used to bring me a lollipop when he came to Dad's shop, and once when Dad took me to a football game, he watched me do cartwheels on the sideline even though the game was going on.

I turn and sprint for home.

11
LIZ

The preliminary hearing is tomorrow. Jake, Jess, and I sit in Kevin's office and go over what will happen. The DA will explain all the reasons they believe Jess is guilty. They will share the evidence they have. They may even call witnesses.

"The only witness is Sheila," Jess says. "Will she be there?"

Kevin frowns, glances at me. "She might be. It's possible, but they will also question the police and the investigators."

"What do we do?" I ask.

"Well, I've got a couple of pretrial motions I will present."

"Like what?" asks Jake.

"I'm going to ask that they dismiss the charges because the victim, er, Coach Mitchell, was inside the white line."

"But there's no shoulder there," says Jess. "There is no way not to be in the road."

When Jess first started running, we walked the routes I would allow her to run. That was several years ago and now I don't know where she runs, but Elm was one of the roads I forbade her to run on specifically because there is no shoulder.

"If Coach was in the road, then it was his fault?" asks Jake.

"Well, not technically, but it could mean he contributed. I'm just trying to create some room for doubt. The burden is on the prosecution tomorrow to prove they have a solid case worth pursuing. It'll be up to the judge to decide if they do."

"And if they do?"

"Then we'll have a little time to consider what Jess' plea will be and whether there's a deal that can be made."

"A deal?" asks Jake.

"Then Jess would plead guilty to something lesser, right?" I ask. "Something that wouldn't require a prison sentence?"

Kevin nods. "Exactly."

"Is there a chance of that?"

"That will depend on the political aspirations of our current DA."

"What does his political career have to do with my daughter's life?"

"A lot. This could be, actually already is, a high-profile case. He could use it to assure his political future with the voters of this town."

"If he puts away the person who hit Coach Mitchell, people will vote for him," Jake says. I know he knows plenty of guys whose votes would be assured with a guilty conviction and prison sentence for Jess.

"That is kind of how it works," Kevin says and leans back in his chair. His eyes fall on Jess. She has been very quiet. "But I will do everything I can to keep us from getting to that point."

"We appreciate that," I tell him. "Is there anything we can do?"

"Jessica," he says and Jess startles. Her eyes give away nothing, but she bites her lip and circles her wrist with the thumb and pointer finger of her other hand. It is a habit she has had for years, as if she is sizing up her wrist for a bracelet. Or handcuffs. "Is there any reason to believe that Sheila would want to make you look bad?"

"What?"

"Is there any reason she wouldn't be telling the truth?"

"What do you mean? She was there. She saw what happened."

"And you trust her to tell the truth?"

"Yes," says Jess. But I don't. I do not trust Sheila to tell the truth when you ask her what color the sky is.

"All right, then. You all get some rest and I will see you in the morning."

12
JESS

I listen as the DA reads the police report and questions the police officer. The same guy with the buzz cut who came to the hospital. He was the first one on the scene so that was why he looked familiar I guess. They ask him a lot about the skid marks and about how far Coach Mitchell's body was from the car. It's like I'm watching a TV show. None of it is familiar even though I was there. Kevin asks a few questions, but no one seems to know for sure exactly where Coach Mitchell was when I hit him. They seem certain though that I hit him just to the right side of my bumper and grill and that he bounced off the hood and landed in the roadway before my car went up the embankment and landed on its side. I don't know any of this. I wonder why Kevin or someone—Mom?—didn't tell me. For some reason I pictured the scene being my car skidding to a stop and Coach Mitchell lying in front of it. I don't know why. I guess that seemed the least violent. But when the prosecutor makes the police officer and then the accident investigator explain all the details, it seems much worse.

"How fast do you believe the car was traveling when it hit Robert Mitchell?" Kevin asks as if the car did this on its own. He doesn't ask how fast Jessica Johnson was driving.

"It was traveling at least thirty-five miles per hour."

"And what is the speed limit on that road?"

"Forty."

"So perhaps, the defendant saw a pedestrian in the roadway and was attempting to brake."

"The skid marks on the road aren't consistent with that assumption."

Kevin hesitates. Looks at his notes. He reminds me of me when I'm put on the spot and don't know the answer. Finally, he speaks.

"Do you know if there was any oncoming traffic? Perhaps it was confining Ms. Johnson to the right side of the roadway and there wasn't any way to avoid the pedestrian in the roadway."

"We don't believe there were any other vehicles involved."

"You don't believe or you don't know?" asks Kevin.

"No other driver has come forward as a witness."

"So there could have been another car."

"It's unlikely."

"But it's not impossible."

"The witness in the car says there were no other vehicles present."

"But she's not here to tell us that."

The police officer glances at the DA who says, "She's next on my list."

Sheila is here. Now she can tell them it was an accident. That I couldn't have prevented it.

After Sheila is sworn in, she glances at me once, but there's no smile, no sign that she is on my side. Her parents sit on chairs behind the DA. Mrs. Richards holds her husband's hand. She sits up straight, her tan legs crossed, her heel swinging.

The prosecutor asks a bunch of questions about how she knows me, how often she's been in my car. Her answers make it sound like being my friend was hard for her. Like I was some charity case. Her words chill me. If the only real friend I thought I had, was just pretending to be my friend, what else am I wrong about? To hear her tell it, we weren't best friends, we just 'hung out sometimes.'

And then he asks her about the morning of the accident.

"And Jess was giving you a ride home?"

She nods.

"And when Ms. Johnson turned on Elm Drive, what happened?"

"She got a text."

"Did she look at the text?"

Sheila hesitates for only a moment, but her cheeks flush, before she says, "Yes," and she looks at me, raising her eyebrows, daring me to disagree. And I can't, because I don't know. But what I do know is that

Sheila is lying about something. She gets overly confident when she's lying. I can see it in the way she sits up and squares her shoulders, flings her hair back after she answers. That's her stance. That's her I-dare-you-to-doubt-me look. I have watched her shrivel freshmen girls and occasionally teachers with her brand of bravado. In a sick way, I'm kind of proud. Here is Sheila playing everyone once again. And she can do it. Except, this time I'm not on her side.

"So, while driving her car, Ms. Johnson opened and read a text message on her phone?"

Sheila nods. "Yes." The slightest smile plays on her lips.

The DA leans in close now, speaks softly as if her next answer won't be easy.

"And at that moment, when Ms. Johnson had her phone in her hand and was reading the text message? What happened then?"

"Objection!" yells Kevin. "The witness did not stipulate that the defendant had the phone in her hand."

The judge nods. The DA tries again. "When Ms. Johnson opened her text message, instead of having both hands on the wheel, was she holding the phone in her hand?" He is asking Sheila, but he's rolling his eyes at Kevin.

Sheila looks down. She doesn't answer, and the DA has to repeat himself. Finally, she looks up, irritated. "Yes," she says. "She was holding the phone in her hand."

Why is she lying? And I know she's lying. It's clear in the way she flicks her tongue over her lip before she speaks and in the cool veil that comes to her eyes. I have seen her do it enough. She is lying. Listening to the cop and the investigator testifying, I was convinced I did it. They have solid evidence that I was texting when I hit Coach Mitchell, but now watching Sheila, I know that's not what happened. But what happened? And why is Sheila lying about it? What's in it for her?

She relaxes now that everyone has swallowed her tale. Attention is the air Sheila needs to breathe. She is enjoying the fact that everyone, me included, is hanging on her every word. I can see her tonight out at the reservoir or in our booth at Johnny Mac's, telling this story, replaying it word for word.

"Who was the text message from?"

A smile escapes her mouth as she answers, "Casey Miller."

My heart jumps. Another memory flashes. *"Casey's gonna ask you out!"* It was the first thing Sheila said to me when she climbed through my window that Sunday morning. "Jason told me he was at the party last night and he was going to ask you out when we got there but then the bust happened. He asked Jason for your number!"

I remember being surprised that she was genuinely happy for me. She has never understood my crush on Casey. I've liked Casey since the day in fourth grade when he kicked a soccer ball at me and split my lip. He cried when the teacher made him apologize. I remember seeing him for the first time, really seeing him. He had these incredibly green eyes, and his hair was all tangled. I've liked him ever since, but he's always seemed more interested in soccer than girls.

"And what happened when Ms. Johnson read the text message?"

Sheila doesn't look up, she wipes her eye at tears that aren't visible. Even with this tiny audience, she is playing it. "She didn't see Coach Mitchell in the road with his dog. He couldn't get out of the way and she hit him."

I feel my stomach heave. Kevin is objecting and standing, arguing about something, saying Sheila is speculating. Memories are rushing at me in no particular order. The phone buzzing with a text in the center consul of my car. Sheila laughing, singing that song, "Jess and Casey sittin' in a tree...." Her earrings flashing in the sun. And then a horrible '*thud*.' I tell my mom I'm going to throw up and she gets up to lead me out.

Kevin sees us and asks the judge for a moment. I don't know what he says because Mom whips the door open and yanks me down the hall to the bathroom where I throw up and throw up and throw up.

When I'm finished, she produces a toothbrush from her purse and some tissues. "It's almost over. Do you think you can make it?"

I nod. All I want is for it to be over.

"You clean up and I'll tell Kevin we'll be right back."

When I come out of the bathroom, she is waiting with Dad and Kevin. Neither of them says anything as we go back into the room.

It's Kevin's turn now to cross-examine. I don't even listen as he asks Sheila a bunch of questions about the weather that day, about why I was driving her home, about what we were doing before we left. He asks her if she is dating the captain of the football team, and she lights up. He asks if they are sexually active and Mrs. Richards gasps, but the prosecutor objects and the judge makes Kevin move on. He asks about the time Sheila was suspended for stealing a pack of hall passes. The DA objects again, they confer with the judge, but it all sounds to me like the teacher on the Charlie Brown cartoons. I can't make out a word they're saying.

Then Kevin asks, "On the night before the accident, did you or did you not spend the night at Ms. Johnson's house. And I remind you that you are under oath."

Sheila rolls her eyes, glances at her parents, looks to the DA, finally answers. "I did."

"So you did not, in fact, spend the night in Jason Gebhart's car for the purpose of having sex and lie to your parents that you were actually at Ms. Johnson's?"

As Kevin asks this question, he has to raise his voice over the DA's loud objections, but he finishes his question. The judge admonishes him but then surprises all of us by telling Sheila to answer the question.

"I didn't spend the night in Jason's car," she says, shaking her head and smirking as if it's a stupid question. She's right. They didn't sleep in his car; they slept on a blanket at the reservoir. If they slept.

Finally, Kevin asks Sheila about her relationship with me. She confirms that we used to ride to school together every day, but only so she wouldn't have to ride the bus. I watch her perfectly made-up face as she says this, note the new eye color, wonder–*who is she*?

Sheila leaves and there are no more witnesses. Everyone waits while the judge looks over her notes. It seems like an eternity. Mom is squeezing my hand, and Dad has his arm around my shoulders. I can't remember a time when we were a tight unit like this. When I was little, there must have been some good times. They didn't divorce until I was five. I have one fuzzy memory of them each holding my hand as we walked along the beach. Every few steps they would swing me, and I loved it. But that seems like a stock memory. I might have made it up.

The judge clears her throat and moves her papers aside. She looks up and says, "It appears the state has enough evidence to take this case to trial unless a plea agreement can be reached first, and, gentlemen," she looks from Kevin to the DA and back, "I would think you could come to a speedy and mutually satisfactory deal. If not, I will hear testimony on this case on..." she puts her glasses back on and examines her calendar. "February 26, 2010."

That is more than four months away. That's half my junior year. Track preseason will have started. My heart sinks.

13
LIZ

The morning after the hearing, I find Jess in the kitchen making coffee.

"Do you think I did it?" she asks.

I shake my head. "It's not up to me."

"But do you think I killed Coach?"

I set down my mug and spoon and turn to her. "I do not think you killed Coach Mitchell. I think there was a terrible accident."

The corner of her mouth twists as she thinks about this. "I've never texted while I was driving."

"I know."

"So it doesn't make sense."

"It doesn't."

"Still," she says, but then doesn't finish the thought. She takes her coffee and whatever she really thinks and retreats to her room.

I spend the morning outside. I gather the branches that have fallen from the trees that separate our yard from the neighbors. I rake the leaves and stack the plastic chaise lounge chairs that Jess and Sheila left out. Was it only two weeks ago, they were sunbathing, trying to erase the straplines before Homecoming? Finally, I sit down on the concrete pad that never became our screened-in porch. Just like so many other plans that Jake and I never followed through on.

The door opens behind me and Jess pads out in her socks. She lowers herself to sit beside me, her legs dangling over the dying mums planted on the perimeter.

"Hey," I say.

"Hey."

I take her hand and for once she doesn't pull away. "You're going to survive this."

"How do you know?"

"You're my daughter."

She frowns, pulls her hand away.

"What if I did what Sheila said?"

"It was an accident. You weren't reckless. The judge will realize that," I tell her.

"I'm scared."

"I will be right beside you. Your father too."

"If they offer me a deal, I think we should take it. Even if I have to go to jail for a little while."

"You will not go to jail. I will not let that happen. We will run away to Mexico first."

"Serious?" she asks, and I see a tiny flicker of a smile.

I shrug. "I don't know. All I know is that this story is not over. And whatever happened in that car, you didn't mean to hurt anybody. Maybe you made a mistake, but that doesn't mean you should go to jail." It is the first time I have admitted that Jess is likely at fault. At least out loud. I have tried to raise her to take responsibility for her actions, and I still believe that she should, but does responsibility for an accident mean going to prison? Ruining her future before it has even begun?

"Maybe we need a real lawyer."

"Kevin is a real lawyer."

"But he said he can't represent me."

"He said we might not want him to, he didn't say he can't. Besides, leave that to your dad and me. We will figure it out."

She doesn't say anything more. We sit side by side watching a squirrel carry a nut from under the fence up the tree and then back again. Making preparations. Taking care of her baby.

Without a word, Jess squeezes my hand and then gets up and goes inside. She will have to go back to school soon. No matter what happens. She cannot let this derail her high school career. It won't be easy. I know the judgment this town is capable of. I have felt it all my life. Everyone looked the other way when Jess was born. Jake and I were an island of three until he left, and then I built a lifeboat with just the two of us. Me and Jess. And while it has not been easy, it has been good. Money is always tight and our circle of friends is pretty small, but that is probably my fault as much as anyone. I don't trust my footing in this town. I know times have changed and no one thinks twice about single mothers or shotgun weddings. But this is different. This is not just any accident. This involves Jefferson football. It is ingrained in the soul of this place. For the past twenty years, maybe longer, the high school stadium has been a shrine and Coach Robert Mitchell has been the god they trusted to bring their boys the glory.

I know people are angry. Jake has been hassled by some of his old football chums. He says it is nothing, but I knew him then and I know those boys mean a lot to him. Coach Mitchell means a lot to him. To his credit, he has kept that grief to himself. I loved Coach, too, and Helen, but I can't let myself see their side. I have to stay on Jess' side because I know there will be sides and they will divide this town if this goes to trial.

Still, I can't let her take the blame for an accident she doesn't even remember causing. This town can be angry, but I will not let them take my daughter's future. It is hard to imagine that one judge – a person who we have never met, will decide my daughter's fate. Kevin says if we don't take a deal and it goes to trial because Jess is a minor it won't be a jury but the judge who decides. She will listen to the testimony, look at the reports, and determine my daughter's future based on one moment in her life, completely disregarding the millions of moments leading up to it.

When I talk to Kevin that night, he is insistent that we need to consider a plea agreement.

"We don't want a trial if we can avoid it. The quicker we wrap this up, the less time there is for it to fester, for public momentum to gain speed."

But public momentum has already been barreling along in the form of editorials in the paper, social media campaigns online, nasty emails, and hate mail. And it is only the beginning. As football season wraps up and the team loses, and it looks like they will, there will be one more reason for this town to want Jess' head. Never mind that this year's team was never going to win even with Coach Mitchell marching the sidelines.

— — —

On Thursday, Kevin calls to say his initial meeting with the DA did not go well.

"They are determined to make an example of Jess. I think it might be time to call in reinforcements." He says the DA must see the political opportunity before him and it is making him heavy-handed with his deals. He will not consider anything that doesn't include prison time.

Kevin has sent me the contact information for several trial lawyers, but beyond the fact that we can't afford them, I am convinced the best person to represent Jess is Kevin, despite his protests and Jake's doubt. I still have no idea how I will pay for him. Jake says one of the guys who hangs out at his shop got out of a drunk driving rap with a public defender, but he doesn't understand. This is not some drunk driving asshole between jobs, this is our daughter. We cannot take a chance on a public defender.

I call Jake after I hang up with Kevin and tell him what Kevin has said, except for the part about him not being the best lawyer for the job.

"We are going to have to come up with some money to pay him," I say.

"Why can't we just use the public defender? We pay taxes."

I sigh. "This is our daughter. We cannot use the public defender."

"Everyone always said you thought you were too good for this town. Nothing wrong with the public defender for everyone else, but no, not you. You gotta bankrupt us both just to get some fancy lawyer. Jess didn't do anything wrong. We don't need Matlock. And I'm not paying for it. You need some fancy lawyer—you pay for it!"

"There are so many things wrong with that statement that I don't know where to begin, but don't worry. I will pay for it. You won't have to give up your six-pack a day habit, or heaven forbid–actually work for a living!"

It did not get any prettier from there. It was one of our nastiest fights to date, but he is wrong. We cannot trust Jess' future to someone we don't know. Not that I know Kevin. I don't, but I trust him.

— — —

That night I can't sleep. I lie awake and wonder if all of this was inevitable, if my father was right. If all I have done for Jess as her mother was pointless. I worked so hard to raise her well so that she would be a good kid, the kind of kid my father thought I would be. Even if she did this, isn't she still a good kid? Does one monstrous mistake make you a bad person?

All that work and worry—what was it for? When she was little, I could hold her hand, pull her to safety. I could make her wear sunscreen and eat her vegetables and write thank-you notes, but I am powerless now. For the last few years, I haven't been able to reach her. I keep saying she would never text and drive, but how do I know? She never tells me what she's thinking or feeling, and I sometimes wonder if the things she does tell me are only half-truths, tossed out like crumbs so I will back off.

But she is my daughter. That is all that matters. I will do whatever it takes to save her from what is happening—even if that means cozying up to her lawyer or playing nice with her father. She is all I've got. And yet, right now, I cannot take another moment of her silence. Besides that, I need to get back to work. We need the money. Now more than ever.

As soon as it is daylight, I call Jake. My call wakes him, and he sounds like he has company, but I don't care. He wants to help, now he can step up and help.

When I hang up, I hear the television. Jess has spent her entire week watching endless crap television. She lies there like a zombie on the couch, cocooned in Kate's afghan. She won't even look at her homework and I don't have the heart to force her. It is as if our entire lives are frozen in place until February.

"I don't want to go to his place," Jess says when I tell her that her father is on his way.

"You need to get out of this house. Get some fresh air. Maybe you can get started on all that school work."

She frowns but throws off the afghan and trudges towards her room.

"Pack plenty in case you're there more than a few nights."

"I'm not staying in that trailer park for more than a few nights. Besides, Dad won't want me there because then Amanda won't sleepover."

Amanda is Jake's latest bimbo. He likes them young and stupid.

"He said you can stay as long as you need to."

"Good, I'll be home tomorrow then."

"We'll see," I tell her.

— — —

It feels like it has been months, not days since I was last at work. The quiet, clean halls reassure me that the world is not completely out of control. Avery steps out of a supply room and falls in behind me like a shadow. When we get to my office, she follows me in and closes the door.

"How's Jess?" she asks.

I shake my head. "She isn't good."

"I'm so sorry, Liz. This sucks."

I toss my purse on my desk and flip on my computer. "You're right. It absolutely does suck."

Avery sits down in the chair opposite my desk. "You should know something."

"What?"

"Aaron wants you out."

Aaron is the regional manager for our home and two others. He has never liked me. Or maybe I imagine that. I was hired by his predecessor. All the other managers Aaron has hired since he came on board are men. He always passes me over for the General Manager job at Morningside. When I asked him a few years ago why he had once again turned me down when the job opened up, he said I needed a college degree. I offered to go to school and get a degree if Morningside would pay for it. We haven't spoken of it again. Which is why I am still a day manager, despite the departure of two different general managers.

"How do you know?"

"I heard him on the phone."

"Here? Aaron was here?"

"He filled in for you yesterday because no one else was available."

"Who was he talking to?"

Avery shakes her head. "I'm not sure who he was talking to, but he said the sooner it happened the better before the residents begin to talk."

"About Jess?"

"Yeah. You know how old people can be. They blame every kid's bad decision on the way they were brought up."

I pick up a pencil and nibble on the eraser. "There's something to that."

"She's a kid," said Avery. "Kids do stupid stuff. This is not on you."

"Maybe some of it is. Jake is never around and I leave her alone too much."

"You have to work to support her. Jess knows that. Besides, I know her. You raised a good girl. Don't let all this shit tell you anything different."

"Do you think I should leave?"

"Hell no. Who would I have to bitch too?" Avery gets up and opens the door. She has to get back to work. She looks back at me and winks.

I smile. "Thanks for the heads up on this."

"You know I've got your back. Always," she says. Then she raps the doorframe and takes off.

After she leaves, I dial Kate. I need to hear her calm big-sisterliness.

"How's Jess?" she asks after I have told her about Aaron's threats and she pronounces him a power-hungry prick who must have a 'very small life.'

"I can't tell. One moment she is an angry, sarcastic teen and the next she's a little girl in tears."

"She's probably a little of both right now. She wants your help, but she wants to be able to handle this herself. Being a smartass is her defense. You sure you don't want me to come?"

"There's nothing you can do," I tell her, but I wish there were.

"I know it's still not a good time to bring this up, but I kind of have to."

I have been so wrapped up in our world; I have hardly thought about my father.

"The home called."

She sighs and waits for me to ask about our father, but I don't want to know. I feel bad that Kate is dealing with him all alone, but right now I haven't got an ounce of energy to spend on him. I don't think my father and I have had a real conversation since I got pregnant with Jess. He told me he was ashamed of me and closed his heart. He had already banished Kate after she told him she was gay. He was a deacon at the time, and he immediately resigned from the deacon board at the church.

I told him I wanted to marry Jake and have the baby and be a family. I said it was all I ever wanted, but how did I know what I wanted? I was eighteen.

When I married Jake, Dad refused to give me away and sat stiffly in his chair at my wedding, only there because my mother made him go.

He is old and harmless now and doesn't remember what he had for breakfast, but he remembers that his daughters disappointed him. I send him care packages, stuff I know he will need like soft tissues (the ones subsidized nursing homes like Morningside buy are as stiff as cardboard), puzzle books, slippers, and the mints he has always liked.

Ever since Mom died, Kate visits our father regularly at least three times a year. She calls it doing her penance, but for what I don't know. He gave up on her the day she told him she was gay, but she has never accepted his condemnation. She still sends birthday gifts and holiday cards and keeps tabs on his health. She was the one who found the home he lives in now, even though I could easily have brought him to Morningside. I did not want him that close. Two state lines between us works best for me.

"He's really struggling," she tells me now. "One of us needs to be named a medical guardian."

"It should be you."

"Just think about it. You're closer," she says. "And you know how these places work."

"I don't know if I can deal with him."

"Age makes people nicer."

"I spend my days with old people, and I am pretty sure that isn't true."

14
JESS

I haven't been to Dad's trailer in months. I stopped staying over once I got my driver's license. Even before that, we hadn't been seeing much of each other.

Dad's trailer is jacked up on one end by cinderblocks. 'Redneck stilts,' Dad calls them. "Just like them houses at the gulf." There are so many of what Mom calls his *toys* littering the lot it looks like a yard sale, except no one would dare come near the place with Homeboy tied up out front. He pees in the house, so Dad makes him sleep outside most of the time.

Dad drops me at the trailer and goes to his shop. He doesn't have cable, so the viewing options suck. I clean out his fridge, but there is nothing to eat, so I make coffee instead.

The caffeine makes me feel like I'm going to jump out of my skin and I pace the trailer like a nutcase, which maybe I am. Homeboy barks outside. Coach Mitchell was walking his dog when he died, but no one said if his dog died too. Willard is sitting only a few inches away, having tailed me on every loop of the trailer. He whines. I pull open a drawer looking for the dog biscuits I know Dad has. I should give one to poor Homeboy too. The first drawer I open has an empty package of dog biscuits. Dad buys the expensive bacon-flavored biscuits from the fancy pet store in Jefferson. They come in a package like Pepperidge farm cookies. I open the pantry to look for the backup pack I know will be there and find a carton of Amanda's cigarettes.

I pull a pack from the carton and grab matches from the bowl on the counter. Then I take the cigarettes and the biscuits, and Willard follows me outside. I climb on the picnic table and absently throw biscuits at the dogs; they try to catch them but always miss.

I light a cigarette and inhale. It makes me cough, but I inhale again. No one would imagine track star Jessica Johnson would smoke a cigarette. Or kill someone. Maybe the cigarettes will kill me. I smoke until my stomach hurts and my throat is raw. Each inhale is little knives cutting at my insides. Homeboy and Willard don't look much better. I've fed them the entire package of biscuits.

I go inside and pick up the phone. My dad is the only person I know who still has a landline. I dial Sheila. I can't accept that after all these years, she will just walk away from our friendship. But more than that, I want to know what the hell happened in that car and why she's lying about it. Otherwise, what is the point of going to trial?

When she answers, I don't bother with hello.

"I need to know what happened in that car."

Heavy sigh. "You were there."

"Obviously, but I don't remember. Maybe because I hit my head. Just tell me."

"I told the judge what happened, remember? You hit Coach Mitchell."

"That part I know, but what were you lying about?"

"I wasn't lying."

"Bullshit. I know when you're lying, and you were lying."

She sighs again, but I am determined. I need an answer. I will wait as long as I need to.

"I don't know what you want me to say."

"I want you to tell me what happened. I would not have been texting. Not me."

"You were all hot about Casey. Don't you remember that? He texted. We knew he was gonna. Jason said he would."

This news seems familiar, but wouldn't I remember something like that?

"But did I really open his text? That's the part I don't get. I don't remember doing that. I can't believe I would do that."

Sheila is quiet. It goes on so long; I wonder if she has hung up.

"This isn't my fault!" she hisses. "You were driving the car. You were the one all excited about that text. Not me!"

"I never said it was your fault. I am just trying to piece it back together and figure out exactly what happened. What is there to lie about? Why can't you just be straight with me? What the hell happened in that car?"

Silence.

"What is the matter with you? Why are you doing this?" I am yelling now and Willard tries to crawl under the coffee table. He doesn't fit.

"There is nothing wrong with *me*! I don't have a problem. You are the one with the problem, a big problem. Look, Jess, I can't hang out with you anymore. I'm not trying to be mean, it's just, you know. Coach. Everyone is blaming you."

It's like being smacked in the chest, or like that time I tried hurdles and landed on my face. I couldn't breathe and couldn't speak. This can't be happening.

Finally, I swallow my tears and beg. "But you're my friend. You can't just cut me out of your life. Real friends don't do that."

"It's impossible Jess, surely you get that?"

"No. I don't. I guess you're just as fake as everyone says you are."

"Maybe I am. Maybe that's all I know how to be."

"That's not true. I know that's not true." We are both crying now, and I just want it all to stop. I want this not to be happening. I want to go back to two weeks ago when we were texting pictures of homecoming dresses and talking about the hot substitute teacher in English. I want my life not to have been totally screwed by something I don't even remember.

"I gotta go," Sheila says.

"Wait! I just need to know what happened in that car!" As I'm yelling, I hear the dial tone. Sheila has hung up on me.

I need to know what happened. I have imagined a million scenarios, but none make sense. Even if it was Casey, I wouldn't have texted. I know better. But then why wouldn't I have seen Coach?

I dial Sheila again, but it goes to voicemail. "It's Sheila, do what you gotta do," says her familiar voice.

Why I expected more from Sheila Richards, I don't know. I am probably the only one who isn't surprised. But I know she can't mean this. She is just being dramatic, like always. It's because of Jason, I'm sure. She can't be friends with the girl who killed Coach Mitchell. And that's who I am now. A fresh sob erupts, and Willard hops up on the picnic table beside me, nudging me. I stroke his long ears. "I know buddy, I wish you could help too."

Nobody can help because no matter what happens, whether or not they convict me, I killed Coach Mitchell just as if I had stuck a knife in his chest. This town worshiped that man. From now on, whenever anyone sees me, they will think, "That's the girl who killed Coach Mitchell."

When Dad gets home from work, I stay in my room. There are cigarette butts all over his picnic table. I didn't bother to clean them up. They so don't matter. Not much does.

"So," he says, standing in my doorway. "When did you start smoking?"

I shrug. "Today."

"Any particular reason?"

I shrug again. "Seemed like a good idea."

"Well, it isn't. In fact, it's a horrible idea. Those damn things will kill you."

"Amanda smokes."

"She's an adult."

"Why do you care if they kill me? Maybe that would be a good thing."

Dad's face caves when I say this; he steps into my room, stares at me, a tear runs down his face.

"Everybody hates me," I tell him. "They wish I was dead. I do, too." My voice has become shrill, hysterical.

In two steps, he reaches me, kneels and wraps his bear-sized arms around me.

"Jess, don't ever say anything like that."

"But you loved him," I say, through the tears that betray me.

"I did," he says, calmly. He points to the spot on the bed next to me. "Okay if I sit?"

I nod. He wipes at his eye with his arm, then sits on the bed. The bed groans and sinks in his direction. I have to brace my feet to keep from falling on him.

"Whatever happened in that car was an accident. You were not trying to kill anybody. I know that and most anybody with half a brain knows that. Everyone is just in shock right now. You, too." Dad puts his arm around me and pulls me against his chest. He hasn't held me since I was a little girl.

"But what if I did it?"

He sighs a long thinking sigh. "Well, it looks like you did, but that don't mean you meant to hurt anybody. It was a mistake, a pretty awful one, but still not something you meant to do. It might just take people some time to figure that out."

I lean into him and whisper, "When will it get better?"

"I don't know," he says, "But it will. Promise."

15
LIZ

On Friday night, I meet Kevin for dinner after work. I arrive at the restaurant early and use the vanity mirror to touch up my lipstick. I should not be here. I am asking for the impossible. I should drive out to Jake's and apologize and get the name of the public defender that helped his friend.

At dinner, after we have ordered a glass of wine, made small talk, I plunge right in.

"I want you to represent Jess."

He frowns, looks into his wineglass, shakes his head slowly. "Look, it's not that I don't want to help you, it's that I'm not the right lawyer. I don't know criminal law. I'm a divorce lawyer."

"But you're a lawyer."

He nods.

"It's the same thing."

"No, it's not really."

"But you can do it. And the bottom line is that you're the only person I trust with this."

"Did you call any of those names I gave you?"

"There wasn't any point. Jake and I don't have that kind of money. Which doesn't mean we won't pay you—we will, but it might take some time."

"It's not about the money. It's about who can best represent Jess."

"And that would be you," I insist. He softens. I see it. His shoulders relax, and he leans back in his chair. Just then the waitress arrives for our orders, but I haven't even looked at the menu. It's expensive so I just order a salad. Kevin orders an appetizer and a full meal.

When the waitress leaves, he says, "You're sure about this?"

I nod. "Very sure. I am not sure about much else anymore, but about you being the person I trust to represent Jess–yes, very much. I'll figure out a way to pay you." I hold his eyes just a beat longer than necessary, trying to make my point.

"I have to be honest. When you called and asked me to dinner, I was hoping it was because you were interested in me, not as a lawyer, but as..." I watch him struggle to find the right word and land on "friend."

"Friend?"

"Well, maybe more than a friend."

This is the part where it gets dicey. Crossing a line I am not even sure he has drawn. I don't know how I feel about Kevin. I want him to help Jess, but is that help contingent on he and I becoming more than friends?

He is different than I remember him at Morningside. He is funny and charming, mostly when he stops trying to impress me. I guess I judged him harshly back then—his father was so proud of him and he took that for granted. I thought he was just some shallow guy who stuck his father in a home because he didn't want to deal with him. He never had time for his father, who only wanted his attention.

"You're such a smart woman. Why didn't you go to college?" he asks, startling me. I am not here to talk about me.

I shrug. "I tried a few times, but it always came back to money. In the beginning, right after Jess was born, Jake had this crazy dream about opening an auto repair shop. He was so certain he would make our fortune. He has always had a job in a garage, ever since I met him. When he said he wanted to use our savings to start the business, I agreed. He said he would make enough money I could quit my job and go to school. I believed him. He was so excited."

I smile at the memory of Jake flying Jess around the house like a little airplane and telling her all about the garage he planned to open and how we would move out to the country and he would build us a house.

"But that's not how it worked out?" Kevin asks.

I shake my head. "When the shop was barely breaking even, talk of us moving died down. Jake spent more and more time on the lake. He bought a boat and he would stay out there for hours."

"And you were still working?"

"Someone had to have a job with health insurance and a steady paycheck."

"Do you think you'll ever go back?"

"To college?" I smile. "It's probably too late for that."

"You should," he says confidently. "You are too smart to spend your life at Morningside."

"I don't know. I like it there. The residents are nice."

My phone rings, and it is Jake.

"I have to take this," I tell Kevin.

"Jake?" I say as the outside air hits me. It's hot—Indian summer, they keep saying on the radio. I walk toward a little stand of trees beside the parking lot.

"Hey Lizzie, got a minute?" When Jake calls me Lizzie it makes my skin crawl. There was a time when it made my stomach do flip-flops. I am not his Lizzie. I have not been for a long time. He is much too busy with all his bimbos.

"Is Jess okay?"

"She's fine. She's in the trailer with the boys."

The boys are the reason not only his trailer and truck stink like dog but he does, too, most days.

"She's pretty upset."

"I know she is, but I thought maybe being out there might help."

"Not so sure about that. While I was at work today, she smoked a bunch of Amanda's cigarettes."

"Jess doesn't smoke."

"Well, from the looks of it, she smoked nearly an entire pack. I asked her about it, and she said she didn't care if they killed her."

"What did you say?"

"Same stuff; it was an accident, people know that. It will get better."

I look back at the restaurant. I can see Kevin through the window talking with the waitress. She is laughing. He is such a nice guy, but can he save my daughter?

"What should I do about the smoking?"

"Get rid of the cigarettes. Spend some time with her. She needs a distraction."

"I'll try. She doesn't seem to care if I'm around or not."

"She does care. She's just a teenager; she can't show it. And keep her away from the newspaper. Have you seen the letters to the editor?"

"I read it. They're just spoutin' off."

"I hate that people are talking about Jess. No one even knows for sure what happened."

Jake sighs softly. "Remember what you said on our wedding night?"

Why is he bringing this up?

"No."

"Yeah, you do."

Our shotgun wedding was held on a Monday and not even written on the church calendar. A few of Jake's buddies, their current girlfriends, my simmering parents, and my sister, Kate were the only guests. Afterward, we spent a night in Dallas at the Motel 8. We got there late and the pool was closed, so Jake lifted me over the fence and we sat with our feet in the water and drank a bottle of sparkling apple juice.

"You said, 'We're more than they say we are.'"

That became our line. Jake would write it on an anniversary card every year. He said he was going to tattoo it on his chest, but he never did, as far as I know.

"Well, this is different."

"Not so much. People got a right to be mad. They're hurting. They need someone to blame. But she's more than all that talk."

"But Jess is just a kid."

"Doesn't matter. You gotta remember most people ain't as smart or as nice as you."

After I hang up, I pace the parking lot trying to decide if I should just drive out there and get Jess. Finally, I sit down on a curb and wipe my face.

"Hey, there," says Kevin. I didn't hear him come out. "Everything okay?"

I nod, wipe tears from my eyes. I look across the parking lot at the trash blowing and the little stray cat sitting by the dumpster. "The thing is, Kevin, you're really nice, and it's not that I'm not grateful, but, I can't, I mean, I need you to represent Jess, but this isn't going to be what you think it is." Tears stream down my face. It is all too hard. All of it. But I am not so desperate that I'll sleep with Kevin to pay him for representing Jess. I must be losing my mind.

"What is it I think it is?" he asks, sitting down beside me in his expensive suit, not even brushing the gravel away first.

"I am not going to sleep with you," I tell him.

He laughs. "Is that why you think I agreed to help you?"

I wipe my nose with the handkerchief he hands me.

"Well, if I'm honest I have to say that the prospect of sleeping with you is very appealing. But this," he hesitates. "This is about my dad. He would want me to help you. This would make him proud." He smiles at me.

I smile. "You really loved him, didn't you?"

He nods. "I did. I still do. Miss him all the time and wish I could get back all those years I spent chasing after success, thinking it would make him happy."

"It did make him happy."

"But I missed out. I missed out on him. So, this," he points to me and him, "This is for him. We will do this together. And maybe along the way, you'll stop thinking I'm such an asshole. Maybe I will, too."

16
JESS

Saturday night, I park myself on the couch with the dogs and watch really bad television, the kind you get with an antenna.

"So, you're all set, right?" Dad yells as he finishes shaving. "I hate to leave you, but I haven't seen Amanda all week, and I promised her a night out tonight. Her favorite band is playing at the Fishin' Hole."

"I'm good, no worries. Who's the band?"

I watch him comb the trailer for his car keys. "Bunch of cowboys whose name I can never remember."

I pick up his keys from the coffee table and toss them to him.

"Well, don't worry about us. I'm sure we'll have a fun night." I wrap one arm around Willard and prop my feet on Homeboy who's splayed out beside the couch, leaving a pile of drool on the carpet. I plan to make microwave popcorn and start reading the book for English, *The Catcher in the Rye*. Not that I'm going back to school anytime soon.

"I won't be very late." Dad's standing at the door, wearing his only pair of jeans without an oil stain and a neat plaid shirt. "And you can throw Homeboy back out on his chain if he starts farting."

Homeboy thumps his tail at the mention of his name.

"I can take it." I reach down and pat his pink belly.

"Well, keep the door locked and call me if you need anything. The Chocohaughs are next door if there's an emergency. Mrs. C doesn't hear so great, but Jim's a good neighbor and he'll help you if you need it."

"I'll be fine Dad, go! Say hi to Amanda."

Amanda works at the Dollar Tree and always smells like cheap plastic and stale food. But she's crazy about my dad, so that's good.

"Yep," he says and walks over to plant a kiss on my head like when I was little. I wave him away but don't say anything. I don't know why that little gesture makes me want to cry.

After he's gone, the trailer is even more depressing. It's homecoming weekend. Neither of my parents has mentioned it. Probably it isn't even on their radar. Tonight I should be at the game, walking on the field with all the other girls in the homecoming court, waiting to hear who is crowned queen. When I woke up in the hospital and found out about the accident, I thought the worst part about it was that they shaved my head and I would miss homecoming. How messed up is that? Tonight, that seems like a lifetime ago, before I knew it was possible to ruin your life and not even know how you did it.

I fall asleep on the couch watching *Saturday Night Live*. It's never funny anymore. Most nights I toss and turn sorting through my memories trying to put my finger on the one from Sunday, October 4. When I do dream, my dreams always lead me to the accident. Tonight, I see Coach Mitchell's face. He doesn't look scared, he looks confused, as if he's thinking, "Why is Jess Johnson about to run me over?" Then I hear a horrible screaming like someone in great pain, but it isn't coming from Coach Mitchell.

"Christ, Jess! What happened?" Dad shakes me awake.

"I saw him!" I yell.

"Saw who?" Dad looks around. He pulls the curtains aside; the sun is barely creeping over the sill. He looks back at me. "You scared the shit out of me."

"I saw Coach Mitchell."

Dad sits down on the couch next to me and sighs.

"In your dream? You saw Coach Mitchell in your dream?"

Dad cracks his knuckles. Willard wanders over and lays a paw on his knee. He wants to go out.

"In the dream, he looked right at me. He knew it was me."

"It's just a dream," he says and scratches Willard's back.

"I think I killed Coach Mitchell."

He stops scratching Willard and looks at me. “Jess, it was an accident. A horrible, fucked-up accident. Nothing more, nothing less.”

“Then why do I feel so guilty?”

He doesn’t answer, just hugs me. I cry into his strong shoulder. We sit like this for a few minutes until Willard starts barking. He really wants to go out now.

“Are you hungry? Let’s go get some breakfast,” says Dad.

— — —

Only in Harrison County can you ride your ATV to town and not seem odd. Dad pulls into Jeb’s Skillet and parks between a pickup truck and another ATV.

“I’m starved,” he says, hopping off. I don’t move.

Dad knocks on my helmet. “Hello, anybody in there? Let’s go get some grub!”

I shake my head.

“Aren’t you hungry?”

“I don’t want to go in there. People will stare at me. They’ll know what I did.”

“Not here they won’t. These people don’t read the paper and the only thing they listen to is the country station coming out of Dallas. They’ve never even heard of Jefferson High School or Coach Mitchell, trust me.” He offers his hand. I take off my helmet and hand it to him.

“Okay then,” he says and hangs my helmet on the ATV.

Dad is right. No one stares at us. Cindy’s our waitress. She’s been at the Skillet since I can remember. She says what she always says, “Jess Johnson, you are getting so big I hardly recognize you. And so pretty, you can’t be related to this old coot!”

Dad orders the Hungry Man Special and I watch him stuff himself.

“It’s not good to eat so much pork,” I tell him.

“It’s not pork; it’s scrapple.”

He smiles with scrapple in his mouth. Then he gets serious, as serious as Dad can get.

“I told your mom I’d talk to you about going back to school.”

"Maybe I could come live with you to finish high school." I hadn't thought of this until this precise moment, but if no one out here knows about the accident, then going to school here makes sense.

Dad almost chokes on his Texas Toast. "Wha....?"

"I can't go back to Jefferson."

He wipes his mouth. "Did you ask your mother about this?"

"No. I just thought of it."

"Sweetie, you know I'd love to have you here, but it's better if you're with your mom."

I look out the window. Why am I surprised? Dad is nothing if not consistent. "But I don't want to be there. Everyone there hates me."

"Jefferson is where all your friends are and your mom and school."

"I don't have any friends anymore."

He looks at his empty coffee cup, then waves to Cindy and lifts his cup.

"Sure, you do. You've always had lots of friends. They aren't going to abandon you because of the accident. Maybe they're freaked out a little now, but they'll come around."

I slam my hand on the table, and the silverware rattles. Cindy hustles towards us, but I don't care. "You and Mom don't get it! My friends will not *come around* because the few friends I had are all chasing after the guys on the football team. And in case you didn't know, I killed their coach. They don't want to have anything to do with me."

"It was an accident."

"That doesn't matter. Stop saying that." Tears roll down my face and my nose is already snotty.

Cindy appears with the coffeepot. She looks at Dad, raising her eyebrows. "Teenage girls," she mouths to him and smiles.

"Jess, you want me to bring you one of those orange-iced donuts? Jeb made them special for Halloween," she asks.

I shake my head and wipe my eyes with the napkin.

"You just let me know if you change your mind."

— — —

Later in the afternoon, Dad is tinkering with a boat motor and I'm playing fetch with Willard when a dirt bike comes flying into the yard, stopping in a cloud of smoke.

"Hey Fish, what brings you around?" Dad calls. Fish is the abbreviation for the more formal "Fish Finder" which is what everyone calls the kid who lives four trailers down and Dad says has an ungodly gift for knowing where the fish are biting on any given morning.

"Polly struck gold this morning and we're having a fish fry up at Catters Park tonight. Thought you might like some fresh trout."

"Jess' here." Dad nods towards me and Fish waves.

"She can come too."

I shrug and throw the ball for Willard. Homeboy watches from where he lies in the sun.

"Yeah, maybe we'll stop by for a little while," Dad tells him.

"Cool," says Fish. He hops back on his bike and spins out sending gravel shooting towards Dad who ducks and laughs as gravel hits the shed like tin rain. Fish grins over his shoulder as he turns onto the lane.

"Shithead," Dad mutters and goes back to his motor.

— — —

"A Fish Fry? You're serious?" I ask later when Dad actually suggests we go. "People really do that?"

"We don't have to go," Dad says. He's sorting through the dishes in the sink, looking for a clean glass. "We can just hang out here."

Another fun evening with farting hound dogs and no cable. "I think we should go."

"Hanging out with me is that bad?" He holds up a glass to the light, rubs the edges on his shirttail, and fills it with water. He drinks it down in one swallow.

"I'm going to grab a shower. What time does it start?"

"Probably started this afternoon when they pulled out the first trout. Which is why I should warn you some of these folks drink a little too much at these things."

"Like I've never seen that before," I tell him, and head for the bathroom.

"What does that mean?" he hollers.

When we arrive, the bonfire rises nearly two stories high. About twenty people sit around the park pavilion on picnic tables and folding chairs. Three grills are set up side by side. Next to them is a table loaded with bags of chips, crock pots full of baked beans, and a huge platter of cornbread. I pile three slices of cornbread on a napkin. Dad disappears, probably in search of the beer cooler.

"Hey Jess, you're looking so grown up," says Ernie, slurring his speech.

"Leave her be," says Maggie, who waves me over to her table. Maggie keeps like twenty cats in her trailer and writes romance novels that are actually erotica, but I'm not supposed to know that. How it is she has come to be accepted by this group still amazes me. Dad says it's probably because Maggie nearly always wins the local turkey shoot and makes amazing homemade brownies. I think it's more likely everybody who lives out here is an oddball, so they aren't the type to judge. It's not like Jefferson, where everybody's in your business.

Fish sits down on my other side and smiles at me shyly. He's got a dimple on his left cheek. It's kind of cute. I enjoy listening to him and Maggie cutting on each other. Dad sits down across the table from us. I wish he didn't feel the need to babysit.

"Jake," says Fish, nodding and touching the brim of his filthy ball cap. Dad nods and taps his beer bottle with Maggie's.

"Jess, did you get something to eat besides cornbread?" Dad asks, glancing at my plate.

"I'm not hungry. I just ran."

"Ran? As in with your two legs?" asks Fish.

I laugh. "I did about five miles. I would have gone further, but Willard was getting winded."

"Jess is the only person I know who can outrun a hunting dog," says Dad.

"Are you fast?" asks Fish.

"I almost made it to states last year in the 800."

"What's an 800?"

"A half-mile."

"Shit, I can run that far. Wanna race?"

I stand up. I'm always ready to race.

"Fish, she will smoke your ass in mere minutes. Besides, you're probably running on at least a six-pack."

Fish looks at Dad. "Nah, I only had five. Besides, she's a girl."

That is all the incentive I need. I look around for a good place to run. "How about we race from here to the entrance? That's about a half-mile."

Fish and I walk towards the road and when we're almost there I yell, "Go!" and take off. Fish whoops and runs after me.

I glance back over my shoulder when we pass Dad's trailer. It's only three lots from the entrance. Fish isn't as far behind as I thought he'd be. I run even faster. No way some redneck boy is gonna beat me.

I pull up at the entrance and collapse on the grass in front of the enormous boulder that has *Cache Creek Park* etched into it. A few moments later, Fish reaches me, heaving and holding his stomach. He holds up one finger as if he is about to say something, and then stumbles across the road and pukes in the grass.

When he finishes, he looks pale and shaky, but he smiles at me as he walks over. He pulls wintergreen Tic Tacs from his pocket and offers me one. I take one and he empties the rest in his mouth. He sits down next to me and leans against the boulder, crunching on Tic Tacs.

"I want a re-match."

"Anytime," I say.

Sitting so close to him is weird. I've met Fish before, but I remember a skinny kid doing stupid stuff on his dirt bike who went fishing with my dad sometimes. I sneak a look at Fish now. He's still skinny, but his shoulders are broad. The beginnings of a mustache are sketched in above his lip and his hair falls across his shoulders, dark and sloppy. He catches me looking and winks.

"So how old are you now?" he asks.

"Sixteen, but I'll be seventeen in January. How old are you?"

"I'll be twenty-one next month."

A pickup drives by and honks at Fish. He gives the driver the finger.

"You staying with your dad this weekend?"

I nod. "But I might move out here."

"Really? Why would you want to live here? It sucks."

"It sucks where I live more, I guess." I get up and dust off my jeans.

Fish looks up at me but doesn't move. "What makes it suck?"

I don't want to think about why it sucks so much at my house.

"Wanna race back?" I ask.

"Hell no," says Fish, getting to his feet. "But we ought to walk back before your dad comes looking for me with his 22."

We are almost to Dad's trailer, when Fish asks, "What would you do if you lived here?"

"I don't know. I guess I'd go to school."

"The high school is way the heck on the other side of the county. I used to go there. The bus ride was forty-five minutes and the people were stupid."

"Did you graduate?"

"Nah. I couldn't stand the assholes in charge, so I quit."

When we get to Dad's trailer, I say, "Give me a sec." I want to say hi to Willard and Homeboy. I scratch their heads and toss a stick for Willard. Fish walks over.

"They're great dogs," he says.

I sit on the picnic table and laugh as the two dogs compete for our attention. When I scratch Homeboy under the chin, Willard stands up with both paws on the bench to lick my face. Fish sits down next to me and rubs Willard's back. "It'd be cool if you moved out here. We could hang out."

"That'd be cool," I say. I watch him light a cigarette.

"Can I have one?" I ask. Fish looks around as if someone's watching. "Your dad would kill me if I gave you a cigarette."

"No, he wouldn't," I insist, reaching for the pack. Fish holds it away, just out of my reach, then jumps up. I get up and chase him around the table. He runs behind the shed, and I follow him. When we're out of sight of the road, he grabs my waist with one arm and pulls me to him, still holding the cigarettes up in the air out of reach, his own dangling from the corner of his mouth.

"God, I'd like to make out with you," he says.

"So why don't you?" I ask defiantly and stop reaching for the cigarettes. I want to do something I shouldn't. I reach for the cigarette in his mouth.

"Shit," says Fish, dodging my hand. He steps away. "C'mon, we got to get back. I need a beer."

I shake my head. "I'm going to hang out here. Tell my dad."

"Are you mad at me?"

"No."

He picks up a stick and scratches something in the dirt. It's a number.

"What's that?"

"My phone number. So you can call me," he says.

"Why would I call you?"

He shrugs. Smiles. "I don't know. Would you really have kissed me?" he asks. I look at him again, this time I see him as that scrawny kid wearing the Lincoln Park t-shirt standing over Dad as he tinkers with his dirt bike.

"You'll never know now, will you?" I say.

He smiles and lights another cigarette. "Maybe I will someday."

I watch him amble off. The seat of his jeans has grass stains on it. He doesn't look back.

I go in the house and find a pen and paper and copy down his phone number.

But I'm not gonna call him.

Not a boy like him.

17
LIZ

Kevin and I talk multiple times over the weekend. He has a lot of questions. He needs the names of Jess' friends, teachers, coaches. He asks which Assistant District Attorney used to hire Jess as a babysitter.

"Bill Monroe. Jess has been babysitting for his kids for at least three years, almost every Friday, but they haven't called since the accident."

"It won't hurt to have someone on Jess' side in that office. He might be somebody we could reach out to if we resume negotiating."

"They love Jess. She thinks of them as another set of parents."

— — —

On Monday, Kevin calls to tell me he talked to one of the ADA's (not Bill Monroe) and got their first offer. He asks if I want to call Jake so we can meet and talk about it.

"Just tell me what it is."

"It's not something we would seriously consider."

"Why not?"

"It involves jail time."

"Then it is definitely not something we would consider. Tell them no."

"I already did."

I smile at this. He gets it.

"But you should tell Jake about it since it's actually a decision the two of you have to make."

"I will, but I know he will agree. Jess cannot go to jail."

"Okay, here's the counter offer I'm writing up. Jess will plead to reckless driving and involuntary manslaughter, do six months of house arrest, surrender her license, and do 200 hours of community service. It seems like a lot, but we have to give them something significant to bring them back to the table."

"House arrest?"

"They would let her leave for school and work."

"What about track?"

"No. She'd have to be home otherwise. They'd probably give her an ankle bracelet to monitor it."

"Really?"

"Really."

"Do you think they'll take it?"

"Honestly? No. From what I can tell, the DA wants to make this a big deal, so it looks like he's cracking down on teenagers driving dangerously."

"What about adults driving dangerously? Jess is a better driver than almost anyone I know."

"I'll make that case, but I already told you, this isn't my area of expertise. You sure you don't want to call somebody else?"

I hesitate because suddenly it all seems too real. I trust Kevin; I don't know why, but I think he'll do everything he can to protect her. The fact that payment hasn't come up certainly plays into it, but if it meant making sure my daughter never sees the inside of a jail cell, I'd sell the house and forfeit every paycheck for the next twenty years.

"It was an accident."

"It was, but all the same, Jess is still responsible. I'll call you when I know something."

What is it with blame? For a country founded on Christian principles, the concept of forgiveness can be sorely lacking. I am as devastated as anyone about Robert Mitchell's death. He was a great man. But how does putting my daughter in jail make it better? I am willing to bet it is the last thing Robert Mitchell would want. Why does forgiveness require a sacrifice? That piece of Christianity never made sense to me. That sounds more like making a deal than offering forgiveness.

— — —

I wait all day for a call, and when none comes, I call Kevin.

"So no more word?"

"They are gonna play hardball for a while. We have to let them spin their wheels a bit. Meanwhile, I caught up with a buddy of mine who specializes in accident law. He thinks there are lots of holes in their case."

"Like what?"

"Like how much of the fault lies with Jess. If Mitchell was in the roadway, we could press that he carries some of the fault."

"Really?"

"Yes, and no. That will only work if we can cast enough doubt on whether Jess was texting. Sheila is our problem there. She's insisting that she was. She has even gone so far as to say she told Jessica not to look at her phone. It might come down to whether or not Jess was aware of the risk created by her conduct."

"Jess knows she shouldn't text and drive. She has been clear about that."

"Right. But if she unknowingly did or failed to do something that caused the accident, then it would be criminally negligent homicide."

"And that's better?"

"Yes! Same fines, but shorter sentence because it's a lesser charge."

"This sounds like verbal accounting."

"Pretty much."

"So you want to prove that Jess wasn't texting, but that she was distracted in some other way."

"Maybe not prove, but at least cast significant doubt."

— — —

When I call Jess on Tuesday, she says there is nothing to do at Jake's, but she won't go back to school. Jake takes her side every time. "Leave her be," he tells me. "Let a little time pass." When I ask him what Jess is doing out there, he says, "She's vegging." Vegging is something Jake can understand. He has made it his life's work.

When I hang up, I call the school counselor. It has been two weeks since Jess has been in school and I don't know what else to do. I have never met the school counselor, but I have seen her at back-to-school night. She always seemed nice.

"How is Jessica doing?" she asks.

"About what you'd expect."

"She's in a difficult position. I would like to help. Has she talked to anyone? A psychologist?"

Jess should see a private psychologist, her doctor suggested as much when he removed her stitches, but I can't afford that. Our health insurance is bare bones and I need every penny I have to pay Kevin, even though so far he has refused everything I have offered.

"No. It's not really something we can afford, and honestly, I'm not sure she'd talk to anyone."

"I can give it a try."

"I'd appreciate that."

"When is she coming back to school?"

"Thursday," I tell her, but I have no idea how I will make that happen.

"Tell her to come to my office instead of homeroom."

"Will she have to go to classes?"

"Not yet. Let me just see how she's doing. Is she working on the assignments she's missing?"

"Yes," I lie. I know she hasn't touched anything except her English work.

I call Jake at the shop.

"She has to go back to school on Thursday. I will pick her up tomorrow morning at eight. I'll go to work a little late."

"Have you told her?"

"No. That's why I'm calling you. You need to convince her. Has she done any of her homework?"

"I don't know."

"Of course you don't."

"I think math is the least of her worries right now."

I bite my tongue and don't say the things I'm thinking, like maybe if she started doing her school work she would spend less time watching TV and feeling sorry for herself. I need to keep the peace with Jake for Jessica's sake.

"Just talk to her. I'll be there at eight."

"Aye, aye, captain."

— — —

That night I meet Kevin for dinner ostensibly to talk about strategy and give him more of Jess' things—report cards, academic awards, and a copy of her clean driving record I got from the DMV. But instead of talking about Jess, I unload about Jake.

"It's just so frustrating! Why can't he act like a parent? Why does he always need to be the pal?"

"Not that it isn't pretty obvious, but how amicable was your split with Jake?"

"Basically, Jake just jumped ship. He didn't fight me on anything, we even used the same lawyer."

"So you two can play nicely sometimes."

I roll my eyes. "What about you? What happened with Jill?"

I learn that while Kevin and his wife Jill, have been separated for over ten years, he is not yet legally divorced. He says it's because he "hasn't gotten around to it yet," and I ask if that is like me 'not getting around to picking up my dry cleaning?' I have at least two orders still waiting, but I am hoarding every penny these days.

He laughs when I say this. "But it is like that for me," he protests. "I'll do it. I just haven't had time. I have all the paperwork. I just need to file it. Jill has her own life. She has plenty of money. She doesn't want anything. It's just a matter of doing it."

"Then do it," I tell him, but the more I get to know him, the more I wonder if he is dragging his feet for a reason. The man has a suitcase full of regrets he carries around.

"I will," he says and looks at me a moment too long. I look away. I can't go there yet.

"Maybe you haven't done it because you really don't want to."

He frowns at this. "Are you asking if I still have feelings for Jill?"

"That might explain why you're procrastinating."

"Do you still have feelings for Jake?" he asks.

We are dining at a schmoozy club Kevin loves. The walls are floor to ceiling bookshelves filled with vintage books. There is a lamp with a cut-glass lampshade on each table. The rest of the room fades away into darkness, creating the illusion of privacy. I imagine a lot of legal deals get made here.

Kevin sips his wine and waits for my answer. One thing I have grown to appreciate about Kevin is he listens well. He leans in and asks questions and genuinely focuses on what I am saying. I'm not sure I have ever spent time with a man like this. Jake was always fun, but in my mind, Jake is still the same guy who played football and wrecked his pickup truck and bought his mother plastic flowers on Mother's Day. Listening was never his specialty.

"I care about Jake because he is Jess' father, but I think what it comes down to is I've grown up and Jake never has. In some ways, I think he is happier than I am."

Kevin leans back against the leather booth. "Current situation aside, you aren't happy?" he asks.

I wave away his question. "I'm just saying Jake always seems pretty happy. He doesn't stress about anything. He doesn't worry about bills or what other people think or what might happen tomorrow."

"That's easy to do when you aren't responsible for anyone but yourself."

"Exactly," I say and drain my wine. "But back to my original question. Do you have feelings for Jill?"

"No," he says and refills my wine glass from the bottle on the table. "I do not. I rarely think of her unless I cross paths with her because of work. She is also a lawyer. We've been physically divorced for so many years, getting an actual divorce is almost an afterthought."

"Hmmm," I say. But I don't ask him the question I really want to ask—why is he divorced? From where I sit, he is every woman's dream guy. He is handsome, smart, charming, considerate, and successful. *What's not to like?*

18
JESS

After Mom drops me at our house, I take a shower. The shower at dads sucks and I can never get all the soap out of my hair, plus it's kind of like camping out there. I come home feeling like I'm wearing a layer of dirt. Standing in the shower, I contemplate my options.

Going by the comments on social media, it's clear that everyone hates me. Lying around with nothing to do has given me plenty of time to think and I have come to the conclusion that there is no good option. Door number one, I tell the police I'm guilty and they send me to jail, which is scary as shit. Door number two, I go to school, which is also scary as shit. And glorious Door number three, I off myself—the scariest of all which explains why I haven't done it and why, for now, it's not really an option. Sometimes when I'm running, I dare myself to step out into the roadway as a car approaches. Once, I even put a foot into the lane, which made the driver swerve and honk. The only thing that keeps me from doing it is that I figure I'll just be trading places with some other poor soul who won't remember what happened but will feel eternally guilty for killing someone, adding another name to the list of people whose lives I've ruined.

I just want to remember what happened. Sometimes I think I remember something, some little piece of it—a noise, a smell, a moment, but then I end up questioning whether I'm making it up. Or maybe I'm just afraid to remember. Because maybe I did what they're saying. Maybe I looked at the text from Casey and because of that, I hit Coach

Mitchell. Maybe I am that person. And if I am, how come I don't know it?

I'm so tired of thinking about all of it; I wish I could just shut my mind off. Killing myself would effectively do that. And yet I don't. I stare at passing cars and I tell myself to move, but I don't. So, really, why am I so set against door number two? Going to school can't be worse than living with myself alone all day.

I spend the day watching TV, which even though we have cable isn't a lot better than the crap at Dad's. The sound of the school bus lumbering up the street reminds me that I haven't touched my makeup work except for English. I have already finished *The Catcher in the Rye.* It seems like an appropriate read. I can relate. I've even wondered if I should pull a Holden and just disappear. Only where would I go and how would I get there?

Movement out the window catches my eye. Dylan, the kid next door, is climbing up a ladder to his pathetic tree fort. Sheila says he built it just so he can watch us sunbathe, but Sheila also says he's gay, so one kind of cancels out the other and I'm thinking maybe she's wrong on both counts. The last year or so, Mom has paid Dylan to cut the grass or rake the leaves in our yard. Sometimes I refer to him as Freddie because, besides an odd fashion sense, he likes to sing seventies music while he works and has a particular affinity for Queen's Bohemian Rhapsody.

I pull the slider door and walk outside. Dylan waves at me. I give him a half-hearted wave. Not sure if I should encourage him, but I'm tired of my own company. He's in eighth grade. I've hardly ever talked to him, even though back before I got my license we rode the same bus every day. He climbs down from the tree fort and walks up to the rusty chain-link fence that weaves between our houses. You can't lean on it because it sways.

Dylan is wearing skin-tight pants and a big purple scarf wrapped around his orange jacket. It's a look that makes people in Jefferson assume you're unstable, or at the very least, a Democrat. He smiles like I'm just the person he was hoping to see.

"Hey," I say.

"Hey," he says.

I wave him in, and he pushes open the gate.

"Are you ever going back to school?"

I shrug.

"Will you ride the bus again?"

I shrug again. I suppose so since my car is toast.

"So, what have I missed?" I ask and sit down on the edge of the concrete slab we call the patio as if it's a place we'd hold tea parties and not just where we put boxes before they go to the curb for recycling.

"You know, the usual. Assholes in the back of the bus were caught smoking and before the bus driver got to the back to catch them, one of the geniuses opened the emergency door and dropped the butts out. So they got kicked off the bus for opening the door instead of for smoking."

"Huh, has anyone said anything about me?"

Now he averts his eyes. I know the next thing out of his mouth will be a lie.

Only it isn't. He sits down a few feet away from me on the patio edge.

"Pretty much everybody."

"What do you think?"

"It sucks."

I'm glad Dylan doesn't say, "It was an accident."

"Yeah," I say. There's a lump in my throat, and the tears are coming. Luckily I'm saved by his mom who comes out to call him for dinner. They have this cheesy bell she rings, kind of like in the Little House on the Prairie books when Ma would call Laura and Mary. I loved those books when I was a kid.

"Gotta go," he says heading for the gate. "See ya at school tomorrow!"

I give him a half-hearted smile. "Sure."

19
LIZ

At work, I go through the motions, but my heart is elsewhere. All I can think about is Jess walking into that school tomorrow and feeling the same accusatory air that envelopes me everywhere I go in town – the grocery store, the gas station, even here at work sometimes I feel people staring.

Every day Jess sinks further into herself. I have tried to talk to her, but her answers are flippant, or else she ignores me. I wish she would tell me what she is feeling–anger, sadness, something.

I listen to Mrs. Buchanan complain about her new roommate, Mrs. Switzer, and I want to care about the difference between opening the curtains a crack and opening them a hand's width.

"It may be because her hand is so fat. That is probably it," she says. "When she asked if she could open the curtains a crack, I said no more than a hand's width. But every day, she flings those curtains open first thing. And then she leaves and goes to breakfast."

"You could ask her to close them."

"But I'm not awake when she leaves."

"But I thought the sunlight woke you up."

"It does."

I sigh. She wrinkles her brow.

"I'll speak with her," I say.

"Thank you, dear. I appreciate that. And I hope the police don't lock up your daughter for killing that man," she says as she walks out.

Later, I get a call from Aaron.

"So, is your daughter going to jail?" he asks.

"Not even a hello, how are you?" I joke, although I don't feel the least bit jokey.

"Liz, to be frank, I had a call from one of the residents."

"From who? Mr. Parker? He's just mad because I told his daughter he's been making crude comments to the nurses."

"It doesn't matter who, I just want to be sure you're still up to doing your job. You are under a lot of stress."

I say nothing. My pulse is racing. I cannot lose this job.

"Maybe you should take some personal time."

"And what is that? Unpaid vacation?"

"Pretty much."

"Is that a direction or a request?"

"It's just a suggestion. Maybe you need to focus on your family."

The afternoon does not get much better from there. Avery is out because she had to take Kimba to the doctor. Just a regular checkup, she assures me when I text her. Without her, I feel unprotected, unsure who to trust. More and more, I feel that way everywhere I go—the grocery store, pharmacy, even the gas station. It seems like everyone is staring, talking about my daughter, wondering what kind of mother I am. I want to shout at them, "Jess is a good kid! It was an accident! You people aren't perfect either!" Instead, I keep my head down and try not to make eye contact.

Jess *is* a good kid.

— — —

Kate has left several messages about my father. I have no answers for her, but I call his nursing home, not to talk to him, but to speak with his caretakers. I talk to the nurse manager. She tells me his kidneys are holding steady, but that he needs dialysis more often now. He has good days and bad days mentally.

"Has he asked for me?"

"No, but you know your dad. He won't ask for help even if he isn't sure what day it is."

Arlan Campbell would never ask for help. He has never needed it, not until now as his body betrays him. He only agreed to move into the nursing home because he didn't want to ask Kate or me for help. After we made the decision, he acted as if it was his idea. "I'm moving into some fancy apartment so I don't have to fuss after a lawn anymore. They even have a meal service." It wasn't until Kate ran into his doctor on one of her visits that we found out about his failing kidneys. Being Arlan, he never complained about the pain he had been having, and my mother was not there to speak for him.

When I hang up, I call Kate back.

"He's our father," she says. "Who knows how much time he has."

"The nurses told me he's doing okay. The dialysis is still working. They aren't sure if his disorientation is from the kidney failure or maybe early dementia. Either way, it is not an emergency. We have time. Renal failure doesn't happen quickly. He isn't that old."

"He's seventy-two."

"That's not old. He'd be a youngster at Morningside."

"Look, I know you don't want him there, but it would be a lot easier to manage him. And who knows, it might help him to be back in Jefferson."

Whenever I invited Mom and Dad to visit, Dad would tell me he could never show his face in Jefferson again, not after what his daughters did to him. As if Kate decided to be gay and I got pregnant just to spite him. Mom came for a few visits, but she never stayed long. She didn't say, but I am pretty sure those visits were a source of strife in their marriage. Growing up, I don't remember my parents ever fighting about anything. And even when they decided to move, and clearly Mom did not want to, she backed him up. Maybe that's one of the reasons Jake and I didn't make it. All we did was fight, and I had never learned how to disagree in a healthy way. I didn't understand that compromise is the language of relationships. If I disagreed with Jake, I dug in. I wasn't going to be the blindly obedient wife my mother had been. I know there is much more to it than that but witnessing what I perceived to be an unhealthy balance in my parents' marriage probably made me more combative than I needed to be. I'm sure Jake was not always the bad guy, but I was too immature to see otherwise. He was young and self-centered, but he wasn't the same stubborn, controlling man my father had been.

"Being in Jefferson might actually kill him if you take his word for it," I say.

"I think we're beyond that. Maybe he would never admit it, but I think he has a few regrets. And you will regret it if you never make up with him."

"Has he ever apologized to you?" I ask her.

"In his own way. He's not an apologizer."

I laugh. "Don't I know it."

"He wants to see you. And Jess."

"Now he wants to see us. He never wanted to see us for the last seventeen years."

"Just think about it. It might be good to get away from Jefferson. We could go over Halloween weekend. Do the schools still have that Friday off? It might help us make a decision."

I do not understand why Kate is so insistent, especially right now. I can't do anything to help him. And yet after I hang up, my unwillingness follows me around. *He is my father. How can I not help him?*

— — —

When Kevin calls, I am still thinking about my father and can't focus on his questions about our insurance company. He has to repeat himself so many times, he finally asks, "Are you okay? Did something happen?"

"It happened years ago," I tell him before explaining about my father.

"You should go see him," he tells me. "Don't wait until it's too late."

"I might," I say, but I wonder if it would do any good. In rare moments I wonder if one day he will apologize and say he regrets all that he missed in our lives. I imagine a Hallmark moment, but I know that could never happen. That would require him to admit he was wrong. And Arlan Campbell is never wrong.

20
JESS

I concentrate on the tiles beneath my feet and follow them to Ms. Schultzman's office. She's the guidance counselor. I have never met her before, but Mom says she wants to see me before I go to classes. I should not be here. I threw up three times this morning. I thought I could do this, but now I'm not so sure. Every nerve in my body is on high alert. If someone touched me, I would probably explode.

Ms. Schultzman is with another student, so I sit on a bench just outside her door, right next to the main doors. Every person who enters the building does a double-take as they walk by me. This is probably what it's like to be that beta fish in the bowl on the counter of the pediatrician's office. I pull out my copy of *The Catcher in the Rye*. I've read the same paragraph at least seven or eight times when the student in Ms. Schultzman's office finally leaves and she appears.

"Jessica! It's so good to finally meet you," she says, holding out her hand for me to shake. I hate it when adults do this, but I take her hand. It's tiny, just like her. She is barely over five feet tall. With her practical haircut and twinkling eyes, she looks sturdy, ready for anything. She smiles brightly at me and directs me to a couch in her office. She sits on a chair next to it. I have never been in the guidance office. I guess I never needed any guidance until now.

"So, I've looked over your files. You are quite an excellent student. And it seems you're also our best hopes for a state title in track and field!"

I shrug. I want to hate her, but it's hard. She's so perky.

"How're you feeling about going back to classes?"

"I'd rather not," I say.

"Well, maybe for today, we can hold off. I'm sure you have a lot of work to catch up on."

I shrug.

"I don't know if your mom told you, but I'm not only a guidance counselor, I'm also a licensed psychologist."

I shrug again.

"Which means that I'm an excellent listener."

I look at her blankly.

"So, if you need someone to talk to, maybe someone not in your family or your peer group, I'd be happy to listen. I imagine this is a pretty tough time for you."

"It is," I say and lean back on the couch but what I think is, *Great, a shrink, Mom must have told her I'm nuts.* We talk about nothing for a while—the new school logo, AP classes, the track team. She tells me to call her Ms. Ellen. She asks me what I enjoy doing. I shrug because I don't enjoy doing anything anymore.

"You don't have any hobbies? How about running?"

"I run sometimes."

"But you must enjoy other things?"

I shrug. "Not really."

"Okay," she says, and she squishes up her face like she's thinking. "How about you tell me one thing that makes you happy? It can be anything. Maybe frosted flakes or going to the beach? Anything."

Does she think I'm five years old? She leans forward, smiles at me like she can't wait to hear my answer. I haven't thought of anything happy in a long time. I sigh. Happiness seems like a foreign concept anymore, but I reach for it in my memory.

"Kids," I say, thinking of Sally and Stu and how I miss them and their family. Mr. Monroe works in the DA's office and I've heard Kevin and Mom talking about whether he might be involved in my case.

"Kids?"

"Well, not all kids, I guess. Sally and Stu."

"Who are Sally and Stu?"

"They're these kids I babysit. Or I used to babysit."

She nods and waits for me to go on.

"I love that they think everything is cool. And they say whatever they think and don't worry what anyone else thinks."

"Children are wonderful that way," Ms. Ellen agrees.

I look at her. She looks like a mom.

"Did you have kids?" I ask.

"Oh, I very much wanted kids, but we couldn't have any. It was hard for me and my husband to accept."

This is a weird thing for an adult to tell me. I don't know what to say.

"Is that why you work with kids now?"

"I like young people. I enjoy helping them."

Ms. Ellen doesn't say anything more. She waits for me to say something. I try to wait her out, but it goes on so long I can't stand it.

"It was a mistake to come to school today," I say.

"Maybe it feels that way, but I'm glad you're here."

"I can't go to class."

"It's understandable that you'd feel that way. For now, how about I set you up in one of my testing rooms and you can work on catching up. Then you can go to class when you're ready."

"What if I'm never ready?"

I study the bookshelves next to Ms. Ellen's desk, willing myself not to cry again. I'm so pathetic. The hallway buzz starts up between classes. Ms. Ellen gets up and closes the door. She sits back down and looks at me.

"Jessica, I'd like to help you."

"What if I don't need any help?"

"Maybe you don't, but it might feel better to talk about it."

I look at Ms. Ellen perched on the edge of her chair. What can she possibly do to help me? And why would she want to? I can't imagine they pay her enough to get involved in my nightmare. I sigh and lean back in my chair, picking at the tiny flecks of gold left on my nails from when Sheila painted them on the Friday before the accident. Back when things like manicures and homecoming nominations mattered.

I shrug. "There's nothing to say." I toy with the straps on my backpack. "I screwed up. Now everyone hates me. I don't blame them."

"You're still a good kid," says Ms. Ellen softly. "One mistake doesn't change that."

Ms. Ellen lets me spend the day in her office doing makeup work. She sets up meetings with each of my teachers for tomorrow.

— — —

Ms. Ellen doesn't make me go to class the next day or the day after that. In fact, she says I don't have to go back to class until I'm ready. She also doesn't make me talk, but somehow I end up talking. I tell her a lot about me and Sheila. When I say some of the stuff out loud, it doesn't seem nearly as cool as it did at the time. Ms. Ellen raises her eyebrows when I tell her about how much Sheila cuts class, and how she always gets away with it because she knows how to talk to teachers.

"You haven't been tempted to join her?"

I shake my head. "I'm serious about going to college, and the only way that will happen is if I do well in classes."

"Sheila doesn't feel the same way?"

"Sheila's family is loaded. Besides, she doesn't care about where she goes to school, as long as they have a good Greek system."

Ms. Ellen frowns.

"Sheila's a lot of fun," I say as if I should defend her. "She's not stupid, she just likes to play around." I don't specify what that means—sleeping with her boyfriend, shoplifting lingerie, cheating on tests (not because she needs to but just because she can), but mostly cutting up with me at other people's expense. I know that makes her sound like a horrible teenager, but she isn't. Not if you know her. She's my best friend. Or she was. In eighth grade, she gave me a necklace with half a heart and she has the other half. Or at least I assume she does. Mine is still on my dresser.

Ms. Ellen and I also talk about what I want to do with my life. Ever since I was little I've wanted to be a doctor. I want to be the one who puts people back together when they're broken.

"What kind of medicine do you want to study?"

I shrug. "Regular medicine. You know? Like work in an ER."

"Most doctors have a specialty. Although, you could be a general practitioner."

"I think I want to work on hearts," I tell her, although it's the first I've thought of it.

She nods. "That will take a lot of schooling."

"Which is why I have to do well in school."

— — —

"How would you feel about going back to some of your classes?" Ms. Ellen asks one day.

"This morning someone put a picture in my locker of me in a jail cell."

"What?"

"It was really badly photoshopped, but I get it."

"What's there to get about that? That's bullying."

Ms. Ellen is hung up on bullying. Her definition of it is far and wide.

"I think it was just someone expressing their opinion."

She frowns.

I shrug. "They might be right. I might have to go to jail."

"It doesn't seem likely that they would put you in jail for something you don't remember doing."

"Maybe I just don't want to remember."

"Is that true?"

I look away from her. Ms. Ellen has this way of looking right through you. I haven't known her long, but it sometimes feels like she can read my mind.

"I want to remember," I say quietly, almost whispering. "I don't know why I can't, but sometimes I think it's just my mind protecting me. Does that make sense?"

"There's actually a lot of scientific evidence that backs that up. Your brain contains chemicals that go to work when you're under stress or in danger. To protect you, sometimes it buries painful memories or loses them completely. Maybe the experience was so painful at the time that your brain won't let you remember it."

"Will it ever?"

Ms. Ellen hesitates. "Hard to say. Maybe it will surface, but maybe not."

"Great."

"You may just have to come to terms with that."

— — —

Every day after school I go for a run. Sometimes I think about the things that Ms. Ellen and I have talked about, but sometimes I just turn my music up loud and try not to think about anything. Most days I run past Coach's house. There's very little activity there these days. I've seen a guy raking up the leaves. He's probably Coach's son. I haven't seen Helen Mitchell, but she must be in there. I'm terrified I will see her, but I still look. I want to tell her I wish I had died instead of her husband.

If Mom asks me one more time, "How're you doing?" I might just have to tell her. She doesn't want to know how I really feel, so I always say, "I'm fine." But I'm not fine. In fact, some nights I lay in bed and hold my breath, wishing I could stop being and feeling. I will my heart to stop beating, but it just keeps going. Forcing me into another day as painful as the last.

The only person I can tell any of this to is Dylan. Which is weird, right? Dylan is just about the dorkiest kid you could know. He's in middle school and dresses like a freak. He draws earrings on his earlobes with a permanent marker. I've started talking to him on the bus, because, well, no one else will talk to me.

Turns out Dylan is pretty cool. He's smart and funny. We've hung out a few times now, mostly when I get back from my runs before I have to go inside and pretend I'm fine for mom. What I appreciate most about Dylan is that he listens when I tell him stuff that I'm thinking, but he doesn't try to fix me, like Mom or Ms. Ellen. When he has the chance to direct our conversations, he veers towards music or math or global warming.

I think if Dylan wasn't around, I might actually lose my mind and end up like Bridget Cantor. Bridget spends more time suspended than not. Sheila loved to talk about Bridget. Sometimes I think Sheila wants to be like her in some small corner of her brain. Some people think

Bridget has mental health problems (clearly) but other people say she does hard drugs; that's why her behavior is so erratic and extreme. She broke her hand once, slamming it on the principal's office door. They had to call the mall cop to come get her. Most everyone is afraid of her (me included). She disappears from school for a few months every year. Everyone says she goes to rehab, but when Bridget comes back, and she always does, she's even angrier.

I imagine there will be lots of girls like Bridget in prison.

21
LIZ

Every day when I ask Jess how school went, she says, "Fine."

"Really?" I ask on Thursday, one week after she went back. "Because your face doesn't say it went fine." I picked her up from school today because we have a meeting with Kevin. The DA rejected our counter, so it seems a judge will have to decide, which means a trial. Kevin has assured me it will not be like the movies because Jess is a minor. There won't be an audience, just us and the DA and whoever he calls to testify.

Jess flips down the mirror on the sun visor and studies her face.

"My face doesn't say anything," she says.

Ellen Schultzman told me Jess has yet to go to a class. She sits in the guidance office and does her makeup work, but Ellen told me that's okay for now. She says they talk, and Jess will go to class when she is ready. I have to admit, I'm jealous. I wish Jess would talk to me. She used to replay her entire day for me when I picked her up from after-school daycare. I hung on every word. Somewhere between when she stopped needing after-school daycare and when she got her driver's license, she morphed into a little adult busy doing her homework, running, going to football games, babysitting for the Monroes, hanging out with Sheila, but always busy. I would hear Sheila and her laughing behind Jess' closed door and I would wish I was in on the jokes. Single parenting consumes your every waking moment until the moment when they don't need you, and then it becomes the loneliest job in the world.

Before the accident, Jess was so confident, so independent, so sure about everything she did. Now, she hesitates before she speaks, guarding her thoughts. She is a shadow of who she was. I only hope when this is all over, whatever happens, I will see my daughter smile again and hear her laugh. I don't want this accident to dictate the rest of her life. Or mine.

I turn off Pershing toward the business park where Kevin's office is.

"How long is this going to take?" she asks.

"I don't know. Kevin just said he wanted to talk to you before we leave for your grandpa's."

Somehow I have allowed Kate to talk me into driving all the way to Arizona for fall break so we can meet with the staff at Dad's nursing home and make some decisions. As much as I hate the long drive, I do like the idea of getting out of Jefferson. It might be easier to breathe.

"What if I don't feel like talking to him?" Jess asks. I choose not to hear her.

When we get there, Kevin is on the phone but waves us in. Jess prowls the office, and then finally sits down in one of the leather chairs. I follow her eyes. She is studying the two pictures on Kevin's shelves, one of his father and one of his nephew in Florida.

"Is that your kid?" she asks when Kevin hangs up.

"Oh, no," says Kevin. "I don't have any children. That's my nephew."

"Are you married?" she asks. I try to catch her eye. She is not usually so rude. But this accident has changed her. It has changed both of us.

"Not really," he says.

"Either you're married or you're not," she says.

"Well, technically I'm still married, but we haven't been together for about ten years. Just haven't gotten around to getting the divorce." Kevin looks uncomfortable.

"But you're a divorce lawyer."

"I know, but it's still a lot of paperwork. I need to take care of it; I've just been really busy."

"Making lots of money," says Jess, studying the enormous fish tank beside his desk.

"That's enough Jess."

"Okay, let's get to it," begins Kevin. "I want to run through some questions I have about Sheila."

"Sheila?"

I sit down in the chair next to Jess and rest my arm on the back of her chair. She leans forward, away from my touch.

"As she is the prosecution's star witness, I'd like a better idea of who she is."

"She's Sheila."

"Right, but what kind of person is she?"

Jess shrugs. "She's popular. Everybody thinks she's cool. Her parents have tons of money and they pretty much let her do anything." She glances at me. She knows I have never liked Sheila. Call it a premonition, but I have never trusted her, never understood what Jess sees in her.

"Mom doesn't like her," she informs Kevin and I frown but say nothing.

"Besides, your mom, how do other adults react to her?"

Jess laughs. "Sheila knows how to work it. She can be charming—she's good with adults. She knows how to say what they want to hear."

"What's important to her?"

"Her boyfriend Jason, for sure. And being popular. She's really into fashion—that's what she wants to be—a fashion designer."

"How are her grades?"

"They're okay. She's not the best student, but she usually does pretty well."

"She's been caught cheating before," I interject.

"But they couldn't prove it," Jess says.

Kevin makes a note. I know he will follow up on that.

"What's her motivation for lying about this?" he asks.

"How do you know she's lying?" says Jess.

"I have a suspicion," he hesitates, then rolls a pencil between his palms before adding, "And I think you do, too."

Jess does not say anything. She rolls her eyes and looks away from us. Kevin makes another note.

"Bottom line," he says and waits for Jess to look at him again. "Do people trust her?"

"Sheila?" Jess smiles, but it is laced with sadness, or maybe regret. She has always believed in Sheila. Every time I have said anything negative, she has come to her defense. Even now as it becomes clearer every day that her friend is not her friend.

She shakes her head. "Not really. Most people wouldn't."

"Do you have questions about the process for me? How the trial will work?"

At this Jess sighs loudly and gives him the duh-I'm-not-three look. I know it too well.

"I realize we are still a few months away from this, but by the time it comes you need to be solid with your answers. The DA is going to try to shake you and you need to be unshakeable."

Kevin comes around and sits on the edge of his desk in front of us. His hands rest on either side of him, his fingers drumming the underside of the desktop. "You'll know the questions I will ask before I ask them, and we will practice the ones I think the DA will ask, but the important thing is to relax and just honestly answer the questions."

"But I don't remember what happened," she reminds him.

"Then you say that. I will try to make it clear that you have never texted while driving before. That is a fact, right?"

"Pretty much," she says.

"Define pretty much."

"I've looked at a text when I was stopped at a traffic light, but never while I was actually driving."

"Okay, but in this situation when you're asked about texting and driving it refers to texting while the vehicle is in motion and you're the one behind the wheel."

Kevin asks questions about her driving habits—how much she drives, whether she has ever had an accident, even a tiny fender bender in a parking lot, whether she talks on the phone while driving. Jess answers clearly and concisely.

He goes through what happened on the day of the accident and she tells him everything she remembers, but then he asks about the text.

"Do you remember how you knew the text was from Casey?"

"I guess because I was expecting it."

"You were expecting a text from him specifically?"

"Well, I guess I didn't know it would be a text. It could have been a phone call. But he was supposed to contact me."

"To ask you out?"

She nods. Blushes.

"Do you remember specifically what it said?"

"No." She shakes her head.

"Then how can you be sure you read it?"

She does not have an answer for this.

"Maybe your friend Sheila told you. Or you heard it online. I presume you've been following the scuttlebutt in the comments section of the online edition of the paper."

I know she has, but Jess never talks about it. I told her once she shouldn't read it, but I can't stop her. I read it, too. It is like some sick compulsion, showcasing the underbelly of public opinion.

"There's another thing, probably nothing, but I wanted to mention it."

"What?"

"The local press has been bad enough, but now there is some national attention. There is a group from Dallas sticking their nose in. They are trying to make you the poster child for texting and driving. I would like to avoid that. They shouldn't have any real influence on the case, but their presence here will raise the drama a bit. I will work to contain it."

"National attention would be good for business," says Jess. She fingers the silver letter opener on Kevin's desk.

Kevin looks at her. "I'll level with you. You don't want that attention and I don't need it."

Jess looks up from the letter opener. Places it back on the desk. "So, what do we do?" she asks.

"You don't engage with them. Not on the phone. Not at school. Not online. Hopefully, no one from the DA's office will give them the time of day."

"Will I go to jail?"

Kevin has said if that were to happen, which he doubts, it would be a minimum-security kind of place. Jess wouldn't be with real criminals, but I don't know how he can know that. Aren't all criminals real? Why else would they be in jail?

"We are a long way from that. Let's just take this a day at a time."

22
LIZ

"Did you lock the door?" I ask as Jess climbs into the car. It is still dark, but I want to start early. We are headed to Arizona. Tomorrow we will see my dad.

Jess doesn't answer me. She rolls her eyes and puts in her earbuds. The first few hours are quiet. I watch the sun come up and Jess drifts back to sleep, her head against the door. We stop for breakfast and eat in silence. It is a long drive across west Texas. I have not seen my father in person since my mom's memorial service, and those days were a blur of meeting people and keeping Jess busy. She was only six and not much about the trip or the service was child-friendly, least of all my dad. Before that, I don't remember a civil conversation since before I was pregnant with Jess. After they left Texas, my mom said to give him time, but time stretched from months to years and silence was easier.

And yet, I am tired of being angry.

Maybe I understand a little now. He had such hopes for me, and I disappointed him. When I was three, I won a poster contest at our church for my crayon drawing of Jesus and his disciples. The disciples had overly large heads and enormous smiles and I had numbered them one through twelve. That fading picture hung above our kitchen table for years. My father always pointing out that I had been able to count to twelve and 'write the damn numbers too.' The smile he bestowed on me each time he told a visitor about the contest was one I worked hard to earn throughout my childhood. Science fairs, honor society, honor roll, and academic awards followed. He loved to tell me I would probably be the 'damn valedictorian.'

But then I met Jake and being with him felt even better than winning my dad's smiles, especially after Kate came out to the family just before she left for college. My father told her not to come home until she had come to her senses. Watching how easily he cut Kate from our lives made me suspicious of the praise he gave me; one false step and it would evaporate like summer heat rising from the pavement after a storm. Maybe I was looking for a way to disappoint him or maybe I was just testing my theory or maybe... maybe I really was in love with Jake Johnson like I told everybody.

I missed my sister. Our house seemed somber without her jokes and her teasing. Jake was my escape. He was fun. He drove fast and laughed hard. He didn't care about grades or college or even what he was doing next week. When I was with him, I could breathe. I was no longer holding my breath, waiting for my prize. Waiting to be good enough, to have done enough. With Jake, I could just be Lizzie. *Lizzie and Jake.* I suppose when my father banished my sister, I realized I could be next. Maybe I wanted to be next. So why was I driving fifteen hours to visit him now? What was I looking for?

When I told him I was pregnant, I knew he would be upset. I knew he would be disappointed, but the silent, seething anger I was not prepared for. "Just because I'm going to have a baby, doesn't mean I can't go to college," I protested.

He shook his head, would not even meet my eye. My mother patted my hand and then got up and started supper. No one talked any more about the baby or college, only the wedding that needed to happen immediately.

At the time, I was so filled with righteous anger—*how dare my father condemn me*? But now, as I think about Jess' accident, I realize I broke his heart. He had such hopes for me; he was counting on my bright shiny future. And to him, it was gone. In my darker moments, I fear Jess' future is gone too. And I am angry. *She knew better. How could she have done this*? But my anger does not affect my love for Jess. I love my daughter *no matter what*. My father's love was a powerful force in my life, but until I felt its absence I did not realize his love was conditional.

I will not let this situation drive Jess from me. I will not condemn my daughter for making one mistake, no matter how big it may be. Even if it changes the trajectory of her shiny bright future.

When my parents moved to Arizona, I missed my mother desperately, especially when Jess was a baby and again later when Jake drifted away. I called her, but it wasn't the same. I begged her to visit. "Your father and I are busy making our new life here," she would say. "You can handle this, Lizzie. You're the mother now."

She didn't say it like she was rubbing my nose in my mistake; she said it because she believed in me. Losing her was like losing the compass for my world. I guess I always thought there would be time. My father would soften. We would have time to reconnect as a family. When my father called to tell me Mom had died in her sleep from the pancreatic cancer I didn't even know she had, I was furious and told him so. "So much for your God!" I sobbed.

"She's in a better place," he assured me, and while my years as a Sunday School superstar should have allowed me to, I just could not believe that.

— — —

It is late when I turn into the hotel parking lot. Kate is sitting on the bench outside the lobby with a coffee cup full of wine. She sets the cup down and wordlessly gathers Jess in her arms. I unload our bags and follow her to our room.

It is too late for talk, all of us are exhausted. Kate's flight was delayed, then canceled, and she had arrived only an hour before we did. We go directly to bed. Kate and Jess in one bed and me in the other, alone with my sad heart.

— — —

In the morning, Kate and I let Jess sleep and go downstairs for the Continental Breakfast of mushy apples, rock hard bagels, and cereal in little boxes.

"The meeting at Rockridge is at one. We'll go over the doctor's notes and see if we can get Dad to understand his situation. Then we'll take him to a restaurant with an all-you-can-eat buffet."

I look up from my coffee and nod.

"We can't speak with the doctor?"

"He's on vacation in Tahoe with his family."

"Oh," I say.

"He needs a Healthcare Proxy."

I look at her and frown. I do not want that to be me.

"Look, I know you don't want to be the one to make the decisions, but it makes more sense for it to be you. In his saner moments, he still trusts you. And besides, you understand these situations. You work in a nursing home. You know more. And you're closer."

I roll my eyes.

"And if it drags on, Morningside may be the only option we have."

I look up, startled. How do I tell Kate it is not just the money? I don't want him so close. Despite his numbered days, I am not ready to forgive a man who doesn't even think he needs to be forgiven.

"Moving him now isn't a good idea. It might aggravate his dementia."

She is quiet for a moment. If anyone can understand my hesitation, Kate should. Finally, she says, "It seems sad for him to be here, all alone. He could die alone."

"It's what he wanted. And Arlan Campbell gets what he wants."

"You know it's not what he wanted."

"But it's what he chose. Why do you care so much?"

She shrugs. "We're all he's got."

"Right, and he threw us away."

"And throwing him away now makes us no better. It makes us like him."

Maybe Kate is right. Maybe we are just like him.

23
LIZ

At one, Kate and I meet with Dad and Ms. Klinefelter, a case manager at the home. Dad's greeting is not any more familiar than Ms. Klinefelter's. I hug him, but he looks startled.

"It's me, Lizzie," I say.

"I know who you are."

After we are all seated, Ms. Klinefelter goes over the doctor's report, noting Dad's complaints about abdominal pain and back pain. She says the nurses reported he has been having occasional bouts of diarrhea.

"None of their business," scowls Dad, embarrassed to have us discuss his bowel movements over coffee.

"So, the other matter we wanted to discuss with you, Mr. Campbell, is the matter of a living will."

"No need," says my father.

"Well, since both your daughters live a distance away, it might be best to have something in writing about the measures you'd like the staff to take in the event your health takes a downward turn."

"If I sign that damn paper and my ticker stops, you'll just let me die then?"

"Dad," I say. "She's not talking about a heart attack. She's talking about whether you want them to keep you alive on a ventilator with tube feeding."

"Like if I become a vegetable?"

Kate says, "Exactly," with a nod.

"Well, I don't want to be a damn vegetable."

"Why don't we go over all the different directives," says Ms. Klinefelter, as she scoots her chair closer and uncaps her pen.

"Just write if I become a vegetable, shoot me."

Kate laughs. I shake my head.

"We can't do that, Mr. Campbell," Ms. Klinefelter insists.

In the end, Dad does not agree to much, and he only grows more irritable. Ms. Klinefelter asks about a healthcare proxy. Kate and I exchange glances.

"I guess, for now, I can be it," she says.

Dad is looking out the window, not even paying attention.

— — —

At dinner, Dad is much better than I expected. He talks animatedly to Jess about track and her college plans. Several times she shoots me a look that says, "What the heck?" She only knows what I have told her about him, which is not much. He has never been so interested in her. She is polite and answers his questions, even asks him some of her own.

"What do you do for fun around here?"

He smiles. "Well, when I really want to go crazy, I ask the ladies for extra desserts," he says with a wink. The ladies are the nurse's aides who bring him his meals.

Dinner is pleasant, benign. No one says what they are really thinking. I linger in Dad's room afterward. I don't know what I want from him. Maybe it is what Kate has—his affection, even if forgiveness is not part of the package. He has been formal with me, saving all his smiles for Jess. Kate and Jess have gone in search of microwave popcorn to go with the movie Kate brought to watch with him.

It is just the two of us, and I wait while he gets ready for bed. He waves off my offer of help. He pokes first one withered leg, and then the other, into his pajamas, holding the railing that lines the room to keep from losing his balance. I note the swelling of his ankles and feet; they look like saggy nude-colored socks. He sits on his bed, scoots back against the pillows, and pats his stomach. "Think I overdid it tonight," he says. I watched him at dinner. He ate a half slice of roast beef and a few spoonfuls of mashed potatoes before nibbling a small piece of apple pie.

"Would it be better if we left you to sleep?" I ask.

"No, no, I like having you girls here." He pats the spot on the bed next to him and I sit down.

"Daddy?" I am hesitant; I don't even know what to ask. He turns his light blue eyes on me. They stand out against his impossibly pale skin and ghost-white hair.

"Hmm?"

"Are you still angry with me?"

Confusion skitters across his face. "Why on earth would I be angry with you?" He waves his hand as if shooing a gnat.

"About Jess."

"Jess?" He narrows his eyes at me, trying to remember. "That was a long time ago," he says. "You have to let that go."

I am stunned. *Me? Let it go?* How can he so casually talk about it like it did not completely change the course of my life?

"But I can't," I say. I will not let him off that easy. He condemned me and my daughter and then took my mother from me right when I needed her most.

"You still mad at me for not walking you down the aisle?"

"No. I didn't care about that. I just..."

He looks at me, a hesitant smile, leans towards me, waiting for me to let him off the hook like all he did was refuse to walk me down the aisle as if that could generate a lifetime of pain.

"What?"

Impatience colors his voice. I hear Jess and Kate in the hall talking to the nurses, smell popcorn. I have to say it now. I may never have another chance.

"You've never apologized. What you did was wrong."

"What did I do?" he asks. "So, I wasn't a perfect father. That's what you're upset about?"

"No, that's not it," I say, but Jess arrives in the room with three bags of microwave popcorn and a six-pack of coke. Kate slips in behind her and flashes a wine bottle at me from her purse. The moment is gone, but I watch him all evening, trying to catch his eye. I never do. Why do I need this? Why do I need him to admit he was wrong? Will that make any of it right?

"Did you talk to Dad?" Kate asks when we are alone in the hotel again. Jess is snoring at about the same decibel as her headphones. I slip off the headphones and adjust her covers, she opens one eye, then rolls over and is asleep again instantly.

"I tried. He acted like he didn't know what I was talking about."

"Because he probably doesn't."

I scowl. "He's not that far gone."

"What do you want from him?" Kate asks.

"I just want him to say he's sorry."

"Why?"

"So I can forgive him."

"Why does you forgiving him depend on him being sorry?"

"That's how it works!" I insist.

She shakes her head. "That's making a deal. That's not forgiveness."

I toss and turn for hours, mulling over Kate's words and my father's lack of words. I have waited and waited for him to acknowledge that he was wrong so I can forgive him, but can I forgive him without that acknowledgment? As if his apology would release the resentment I have carried for so many years, like a weighted vest strangling my heart. Without it, would I see him differently? Could I love him? It is clear now that his decision to abandon me and take my mother from me is not one that has haunted him as it has me. The pain is mine, not his. Maybe that also means it is me who has the power to remove it, not him.

24
JESS

The words painted on the sidewalk in large messy black letters are impossible to read. I can only make out the words *BITCH* and *DIE,* but the message is obvious. When Mom sees them, she goes ballistic. It's great to be home. Maybe we should have stayed in Arizona with my crazy granddad.

"Who did this?" she screams as we stare at the blurry letters. She storms into the house to call Kevin or the police, she wasn't sure where to start.

I sit down on the stoop and stare at the words scrawled in black paint, each letter at least two feet high. For once, I don't cry. Maybe my tears have finally run out. Or maybe whoever wrote this has plans for me. Plans I can't seem to carry out myself. I imagine a car going by and a gun raised in my direction. I watch the movie play in my head over and over.

Kevin and the police pull up at the same time. I lock myself in my room, put in my earbuds, and blast The Violent Femmes. Wait until they all go away.

Later, when Mom calls him, Dad says he'll come by and paint over the words tomorrow. He told Mom he was in the middle of something, but she said he was obviously drunk.

"I'm going for a run," I say. I need to stretch my legs after the long drive. But more than that, I need to see Helen Mitchell's house. It draws me like a magnet. No matter what route I take, every run leads me there. I pull up to a walk as I pass the picket fence, sometimes I run my fingers along it. There is rarely any movement at the house, but once I saw her sitting in a chair by a window reading. When she looked up, I sprinted away. I don't know why I go there or what I'm looking for, but after being gone for two days, I need to see the house and look for Helen Mitchell.

"You can't go outside," Mom says. "What if whoever did this is still around?"

"I kind of doubt it. Not after the police were here. Besides, they did what they came to do."

She sighs and sadness settles like a cloak on her shoulders. I've always liked that I have a 'young' mom. She has never looked like the moms of my friends, but tonight she looks a decade older. "I wish you wouldn't," she says.

If she had told me flat-out that I couldn't, I'd still go, but the weariness in her words pins me down. I can't leave her.

"It's okay. I don't have to run. Let's watch something instead."

Periodically all evening, we hear the police drive by, windows down and scanner running. We watch a movie, but neither of us can follow the plot and we turn it off before ten o'clock.

"It's okay, Mom; go to bed."

"I can stay up a little later," she offers.

I look at the circles under her eyes, her hair needs a cut. She isn't sleeping much more than me. Most nights, I hear her in the kitchen making chamomile tea well after midnight. I think about getting up and talking to her, but what would I say? All of this is my fault. I know I have been horrible to her. I can't help myself. She's an easy target. She always bounces back. "I'm sorry," I tell her now. I want to say more, but I can't. Mom puts her arm around me.

"We'll get through this," she says.

I frown but don't say what I think. There is no getting through this. Not in Jefferson. It's not like people will ever forget, and forgiveness is just something people talk about on Sundays. In Texas we make people pay for what they've done. That's why we kill more people than any other state. Forgiveness is for Yankees and weak people. What I have done isn't forgivable; it's a brand I will wear my entire life.

She touches my arm, takes a breath like she's going to say something, but then doesn't. We sit like that, and I pretend to watch the TV. "I'm sorry," I say again, but this time it's a bigger sorry, one that encompasses everything that's happened since that awful Sunday. She nods but doesn't speak because she's crying. She pulls me to her and wraps her arms around me. I stiffen. If I hug her back, I will cry.

"Maybe we should move," I say into her shoulder.

She lets go of me. "This is our home! We have lived here all our lives. We aren't going anywhere."

"Couldn't we go live with Aunt Kate?"

"We are not leaving. We will figure this out. Kate has her own life. She loves you like her own, but there is no room in Minnesota for us. Besides, it's cold as hell there."

"Hell isn't cold."

"Smartass," she says, but she smiles, reaches out and touches my face.

I get up and go to my room. I pull out *The Catcher in the Rye* and read back over the parts I highlighted. I copy some of them into my journal.

"Mothers are all slightly insane."

"It was that kind of a crazy afternoon, terrifically cold, and no sun out or anything, and you felt like you were disappearing every time you crossed a road."

"This fall I think you're riding for—it's a special kind of fall, a horrible kind."

"It's such a stupid question, in my opinion. I mean, how do you know what you're going to do till you do it? The answer is, you don't."

I lay down but can't sleep. I listen to mom closing up the house, making her tea, talking softly to someone on the phone, probably Aunt Kate, making sure she got home okay. A full moon lights up the street. I open my window and lean out, looking for the words on the sidewalk, but all I can see are large black blobs as if someone has painted over the words. There's a movement outside, and my heart freezes. A light flashes at my window. It's coming from Dylan's house. On and off. On and off. It has to be Dylan. I turn my light on and off twice, too. In a moment, Dylan stands under the window. He hoists himself onto the sill.

"Hi!" he says and grins at me like it's not the middle of the night and I didn't just find him prowling the street.

"Are you crazy? The police have been up and down our street all night," I tell him.

"I'm not worried about them," Dylan says, still smiling.

"Well, if they see you sitting on my window ledge, they will arrest you."

"Nah," he says.

"You painted over what they wrote, didn't you?"

"My mom has all kinds of shit in her craft cupboard."

"Thanks."

"Don't mention it."

Dylan is all right. Obviously, I underestimated him. "What's the deal with the purple hair?" Dylan has a new purple streak down the side of his head, it shimmers in the moonlight.

"Do you like it?"

"I don't know. I guess."

Dylan laughs. "It pissed my mom off."

"I bet."

"I still have some dye left; you want me to do your hair?"

"Nah. Not my style. People already stare at me."

"Then give them a reason to," suggests Dylan.

You just never know about people. The night is clear; the stars as bright as they can only be in Texas. Dylan points out the constellations he knows. I've heard of most of them, but then he tells me about Cygnus, the Swan.

"Sometimes it's called The Northern Cross, too. Anyway, Cygnus was racing with a friend across the sky and they flew too close to the sun. Their chariots burned up instantly, and they fell to the earth. But Cygnus' friend was trapped at the bottom of a river and died."

"That's a horrible myth!"

"I'm not finished."

"Well?" I prompt him.

"So Cygnus asked Zeus to help him, and Zeus told him he could turn him into the form of a swan so he could dive in the water and get his friend's body and give it a proper burial."

"Did he do it?"

"He did. The only catch was that he'd stay a swan."

"Wow. That's a good friend."

"That's what Zeus said, so he placed an image of Cygnus in the night sky to honor his unselfishness."

"Cool."

I love the stories in the sky. They beat the ones down here.

"I've got to get some sleep," I tell him.

He looks at me very seriously. "If anybody else gives you a hard time, I'll have your back," he offers.

"That's sweet," I tell him, "Thanks."

I have no more faith Dylan can protect me than that his parents would applaud a few more streaks of color in his hair. He's sweet, though. Just then a police car comes up the street. Dylan drops to the ground and sprints for his house. I close my window. In my journal I write,

"It's easy to judge someone you don't know, but much harder once you know them."

— — —

On Monday, I go to all my classes for the first time since *the accident*. (Mom always lowers her voice when she says those words, so now I've begun doing the same thing in my mind.) It has been over a month and it's like stepping into another dimension. I walk down the halls, braced for the onslaught of anger, but I'm met with stares and silence. When a guy bumps my shoulder in passing and mutters, 'Bitch,' it almost comes as a relief. My teeth hurt from clenching them and I have perfected the ability to look without seeing, staring right past people and never making eye contact.

I enter my Calculus class, creating a noticeable pause in conversation. Like a marionette operator, I force my legs to move and my body to take a seat. Most people in this class are seniors or nerdy underclassmen, so they are more focused on the board than my reappearance. Sheila always made fun of the 'parade of freaks' in

Calculus, but I'm beginning to appreciate them. The bell rings, and I take my time organizing my stuff, letting the other students leave before me.

"Good to see you, Jess," calls Mr. Cafferty when I'm almost out the door. I give him a grateful smile.

I catch a glimpse of Sheila before Latin, but she purposely ignores me. Kayla and Jamie circle her, her faithful disciples. They've worshipped Sheila for years, following her lead on everything, but Sheila always kept them at arm's length, unless she needed them for something, like a ride to Johnny Mac's before she got her license. Kayla sees me but looks away and doesn't return my wave.

"Whatever," I say out loud to no one in particular.

The few people who speak to me don't mention *the accident*; they just say it's good to see me, although none of them are people I'm particularly glad to see. Casey is in my Latin class. When I walk in everyone watches to see if I will speak to him. Thanks to Sheila, it's common knowledge Casey sent the text that caused *the accident*.

When I walk by his desk, he glances up at me and then looks back at his homework. My regular seat is right behind him, but I find a seat in the back and pull out my work.

At lunch, I go to Ms. Ellen's office. I can't bring myself to go near my locker, so I carry all my books everywhere.

"That's quite a load," she says when I drop my bag in her office. "How'd it go?"

"It sucked, but I did it."

"I'm here if you'd like to talk."

I pull my lunch out of my backpack. The sight of my sandwich makes me nauseous, so I shove it back in the bag and open my water bottle instead.

"Talking about it might help," says Ms. Ellen, her open face ready, she leans back in her chair.

Talking about any of it seems pointless. How I feel doesn't change anything. Coach Mitchell is dead. It's still my fault. "Everyone either stares at me or tries not to stare at me."

Ms. Ellen nods. "They're curious."

I shrug. "I think it's better if people stare at me than if they ignore me."

"Why is that?"

"Because if they stare at me, at least they see me. Ignoring me makes it like I don't exist, or maybe they wish I didn't." Like I do.

She nods.

"And what about this boy who sent the text?" asks Ms. Ellen.

I look away. "He's nobody," I tell her. I don't know what I feel about Casey anymore. Mostly, I try not to think about him.

"But you said he asked you out in the text. Did you ever answer him?"

"It's kind of impossible now."

"What makes it impossible?"

I bite my lip. I look out the window. She doesn't get it. "It just is."

It's a windy day and leaves are falling from the trees lining the sidewalk. I watch a leaf fall to the ground and tumble along until it gets caught under a bush.

"Why would the accident change this boy's mind?"

I look at Ms. Ellen. *Is she that dense?*

"Because it was his text and now Coach Mitchell is dead?"

Ms. Ellen sighs. I pack up my things. When I get up to leave, she says, "I want you to do something for me."

"What?" I just want to get away from her and all her caring about me, but she's so earnest, I wait.

"I want you to go home tonight and imagine if someone else, say Sheila or this boy you like, or me, had been driving the car when it hit Coach Mitchell. I want you to think about what you would say to that person."

"That won't help."

I pick up my backpack, and as I walk out the door, Ms. Ellen says, "I'm serious about it, Jess. Think about it."

But that's stupid because no one else was driving that car.

— — —

In chemistry, I have a new lab partner. Jennifer is a quiet girl I've never really noticed before. She gives me a half-smile and scoots her stool over to make room for me at her counter. She says, "Sheila asked Mr. Farenz to switch partners." Then she smiles and whispers, "But I'm glad because Mitch has the worst BO." I glance over to where Mitch sits in my old seat at the bench he now shares with Sheila, who isn't there yet.

I pull out my chemistry notebook and open to a clean page. Mr. Farenz calls roll. Sheila comes in late and doesn't acknowledge me.

"Ms. Richards, I hope we aren't keeping you from something more important," says Mr. Farenz.

"Of course not, Mr. F. I love chemistry," purrs Sheila as she takes her seat next to Mitch. When the class ends, Sheila glides out the door without a backward glance.

The next class is American History. Several soccer players in the class are friends with Casey. I take my regular seat behind Erik and Jay.

When I sit down, Jay turns to me and says, "We missed you. There's been nobody to copy off of." He grins and turns back around as the teacher begins her lecture.

The rest of the week goes by much the same. I go through the motions of being a high school student. A few people talk to me, but it's always awkward. I tell Ms. Ellen about it at lunch.

"They're figuring out you're not made of glass," says Ms. Ellen.

"It's funny, though, because most of the people who speak to me now are people I've never talked to before."

"Maybe you're more approachable now," she suggests.

"Why?"

"They know you're human. You've been through something terrible. You're hurting. It makes you human. You're not just one of the in-crowd."

I roll my eyes. Sheila would be glad to know even the guidance counselor she's never met considers us the 'in-crowd'.

25
LIZ

Jess goes to Jake's the weekend after we get back from Arizona. I think we have both had enough of each other. She said she made a friend out there. I am not sure whether that is a good thing, but I know she could use some friends, so I drive her out after work on Friday.

Early Saturday morning, before it is even light, I wake up with the feeling that someone is in the house. A chilly breeze blows across my face like a door or window is open. I lay still and listen to the silent house. I think about the people who painted my sidewalk last weekend. Would they also break into my house? I sit up, slowly. A car door slams next door, and I hear the muffled sound of Van Halen from my neighbor's car stereo.

I creep carefully to the closet and pick up Jake's baseball bat he never took with him when he moved out. He told me I might need it someday. I inch to the bedroom door, my arms shaking but the bat in the ready position, not that I have ever hit a softball, let alone a person. All I can hear is my heart galloping. I creep into the living room in search of my phone, charging on the counter. Nothing looks out of place. The silence is eerie.

I growl, "Who's there? I'm calling the police!" The quiet screams back at me. As I make for the front door, I notice the slider is slightly ajar, only a sliver near the bottom, but not locked as it should be. It looks like someone yanked it closed in a hurry, the way Jess does sometimes. I have asked Jake to look at it a million times.

I can't decide if I should put the bat down and call 911 or run out of the house. What if I am just being paranoid? I can't hear anything except leaves blowing across the cement pad out back. The nice thing about an open layout house is I can see the entire space except for Jess' room and the bathroom. I take a tentative step towards her room. Her door is ajar; I flick it open with the baseball bat. It rattles against the wall and causes Jess' computer to light up. I scream.

And then I realize there is no one here.

There is no one in my house except me—a crazy, paranoid woman with a baseball bat. I set the bat down and turn on the lights. There is no point in going back to bed now. I have never been a nervous person, but lately, everything makes me jump. Every person looks suspect. I am wary and I no longer meet a stranger's eye or offer a smile on the sidewalk. That is what this is doing to me.

I wrench the sliding door shut and lock it. I lay the board on the track that Jake gave us to use until he fixes it. I sit down on the couch and let myself cry. Not just cry, but sob, releasing the pent up pain I have held at arm's length to protect my daughter. As my grief fills the empty house, I see this from the town's point of view. Whatever happened in that car, it is clear Jess was careless. And her carelessness cost Coach Mitchell his life. She never intended to take it; she never even knew it was in her power. We all assume that what we say and do and think means nothing to anyone but ourselves, when in reality it can alter lifetimes, change history, even snuff out a soul unknowingly. Our lives intertwine in invisible and impossible ways. We take that for granted, or maybe we don't believe it until we have no choice. Everything we do matters to someone.

I let myself cry for Coach Mitchell, for Helen Mitchell, for their children, for my community, instead of just for my daughter. I understand the anger. None of this is fair or right. None of it. But I can't make it right. And neither can Jess. And neither can the court.

Later, Kevin calls with a question about Sheila. Her testimony has him the most worried. I answer his questions, but repeatedly suppress yawns. My early morning freak out has rendered me slow and sleepy.

"Did I wake you?" he asks after I yawn through another answer.

"Tough night."

"Anything I can do?"

I almost say, "Nothing. I'll be fine." That is my standard line for seventeen years now whenever anyone asks if they can help. I have always handled everything as if I had something to prove—Jake leaving, holding down a job and juggling childcare, Jess' tantrums and moods, practices and lessons, birthdays, and braces—all of it. But I am tired. Tired of always being the one to handle everything. I tell Kevin about my early morning fright.

"It's understandable. You've been under a tremendous amount of pressure."

"I'm not a wimpy person, though. It seems a bit ridiculous."

"Not at all, considering the circumstances. How about if I come take a look at that sliding door?"

I hesitate. I don't want to take advantage of him, but there is a part of me that was dreading the weekend alone. I would like to see him. Even if it is only to have him fix my door.

"Sure. That would be great."

"Be there in an hour," he says.

— — —

I run the vacuum and wipe the worst spots on the worn kitchen linoleum, gather up dishes abandoned in the living room, and fold the afghan. Kevin's been here before, but this is different. He is coming here as my friend, not my lawyer.

He shows up at eleven carrying a toolbox.

"I didn't realize you were a handyman," I say.

"My dad made sure I grew up knowing my way around a power tool. Every weekend I was with him, he had another project for us to work on."

I smile thinking of his father.

"I'll just get to work," he says, refusing my offer of coffee. He moves furniture out of the way and examines the slider. Then he shakes his head and pulls out a tape measure.

I sip my coffee and admire him in blue jeans. I have never seen him in anything but a suit. He looks more vulnerable in his sweatshirt without the armor of his coat and tie. Younger. Friendlier. I decide I much prefer the casual Kevin. He catches me staring and I am certain he blushes before saying, "I think the best option is to replace the thing. All the weatherproofing is shot, and the track is rusted."

"Oh," I say. "Really?" I haven't got money for a new sliding door.

"I'm going to run to the hardware store and see what they have."

"Kevin," I say beginning to protest, but he holds up his hand.

"I don't want to worry about you. We can figure out the cost of the door later. For now, you need to be safe."

"You don't have to do this. I can ask Jake again."

He pauses at the door. "Do you want to ask Jake?"

Jake's name hangs there in the air between us, like an intruder.

I shake my head. I know asking Jake will not get me anywhere. He will just remind me to put the stick on the track for security and tell me the old door is fine.

"Then let me do this. I want to do this."

— — —

So, I let him. It takes Kevin the rest of the day to remove the old door and install a new one. While he works, I go to the grocery store and buy the ingredients to cook a puttanesca sauce with mussels, my specialty. On the way home from the store, I call Kate and tell her what is happening.

"So, let me get this straight. You have decided you like your lawyer after all, so you're cooking him puttanesca?"

"Yes."

"Don't you want to kiss him?"

"What does that have to do with it?"

"Is there any dish that renders your breath more unapproachable than puttanesca?"

My heart sinks. She is right. On the seat beside me, in addition to mussels, tomatoes, and pasta, are cloves of garlic, a bag of onions, plus bottles of capers, anchovies, black olives, and green olives. It is my favorite and possibly best dish, but it is also powerfully pungent.

"I guess I've been single too long," I laugh.

Later, after we are well into our second bottle of red wine, I confess my conversation with Kate to Kevin.

"Does that mean you don't want to kiss me?"

"No."

"No, you don't want to kiss me or no, you do?"

I shake my head and get up to clear our dishes. "Maybe I can loan you a toothbrush," I tease and hardly recognize myself. But later, when Kevin says goodnight, I do kiss him.

After he has gone, I test out the new slider. It glides open easily, and I step outside and look at the stars. I feel more hopeful tonight than I have felt in a long time. All the time I knew Kevin when his father was at Morningside, I was cynical, skeptical. Not just of Kevin, of all men. I pushed aside his compliments and questions, assuming I knew who he was and what he wanted. Have I always done this? Are Jess and I alone because I always think people want something from me I don't want to give? I gave everything to Jake—my family, my reputation, my future—and he walked away from it; but he was only one man, and really he was just a boy.

26
JESS

Saturday morning, Dad is up early. He has some colossal job to do. Which is fine with me because yesterday when Mom dropped me off, he told her we would go fishing today. I wasn't looking forward to an entire day stuck on a boat pretending everything is fine. When he got a call for a tow late last night, I was relieved.

"I'll be home around eight. I hate to leave you, but I need this job. I could use the money."

"I'll be fine," I tell him, as I follow him out of the trailer to feed the dogs.

"Watch Homeboy; he keeps running off."

I eye Homeboy; he's twirling in circles at the sight of his breakfast, completely tangling his line. Willard sits by his bowl patiently.

"Call if you need me. I'm only ten minutes away."

"I won't need you."

"Roger that," he says and pulls away.

After he's gone, I spend the morning watching not-cable television, but by the middle of the afternoon, I can't take it anymore. I clip a leash on Homeboy and let Willard run loose. It's turned into a nice day and I don't want to spend it in a smelly trailer. I grab my copy of *The Catcher in the Rye* and set off to hike along Cache Creek.

After twenty minutes of Homeboy yanking on my arm, I've had enough and stop to take a break. I wind his leash around a tree, pick my way down the bank, and climb out on some rocks in the middle of the creek. Willard whines from the shore for a few minutes and then circles out a spot in the leaves to lie down.

Out here in the middle of the creek, with the noise of the water, it's easier to breathe. I push Jefferson and Mom and Kevin and school and Helen Mitchell off to the side of my mind. I read for a while. I like the way Holden talks. He says whatever pops into his mind. I totally get what he means when he says everybody is fake except for little kids. I wish I could see Sally and Stu. They would treat me like they always have.

I pull off my shoes and socks and dip a toe in the icy water. It's hard to believe it's been only a month since the accident. It seems more like years. I can hardly remember who I was back then. Back when all that mattered was Homecoming Court and a letterman jacket and hoping Casey Miller would ask me out. Now that all seems like another lifetime when I was someone different. The sunshine sparkles across the water and slides around me like a warm blanket. A bird screeches from the branches above.

The creek isn't deep, but there's a spot closer to the trailer park where I used to go swimming with Dad. It has a branch with a rope over it. I loved to swing out over the water on that rope, but I never let go, never let myself drop in. It made Dad laugh that I would ask him to give me a push, but then scream for him to pull me back safely to the bank. I touch my heel to the freezing water now. I've always been such a baby.

The water is clear as glass. I can see right to the rocks on the bottom. The water bugs from summer have gone wherever it is they go in winter. When I was little, Dad and I used to catch crayfish and race them on the rocks. They scuttled into the water like wind-up cars, swimming backward until they disappeared. I set my book next to my shoes on the rock and stand up, starring at the water until I feel dizzy.

I lean towards the water and then the Jess who always does the right thing, who never does anything stupid like jump in an icy creek or text while she's driving, stops me.

"AGHHHH!" I scream and smack my legs with my fists. "I'm so sick of me!"

Willard lifts his head to watch me. He thumps his tail and whines. I look at him and yell, "Screw it!" and then I leap into the creek.

My feet hit an angled rock on the bottom and go out from under me. The cold water swallows me up and I scramble to my feet. The freezing water takes my breath away. I crawl back on the rocks.

"What the hell are you doing?" yells a familiar voice.

On the shore Willard is dancing in circles, barking beside Fish. "Are you fucking nuts?" he asks.

I am nuts, aren't I? I am fucking nuts. You can't drown in three feet of water. I smile weakly at Fish. He shakes his head. I hold my shoes and book against my chest and wade towards him, my entire body shaking with the cold.

I reach the side and Willard jumps all over me.

"You'll fucking freeze to death. Come up to my place and get a blanket or a coat or something."

I nod because my teeth are chattering so hard I can't speak. Fish pulls off his sweatshirt and gives it to me. After I put on my shoes and his sweatshirt, Fish grabs my hand and pulls me up the bank. We walk towards his place, but then I remember Homeboy.

"Where is he?"

"I tied him to a tree back there."

"I'll come back for him. You need to get dry first."

I'm too cold to argue, so I follow him to an RV close to the bank. It's a gooseneck trailer, the kind you tow with a pickup truck. The front is propped up on a stump and most of the windows are covered with plastic.

"Nice place," I say as Fish opens the door.

"Shit hole is what it is," he says, and I follow him in.

The inside is dark. Fish kicks a path through the clothes and papers littering the floor. There's a bed up on the gooseneck part of the trailer and empty beer cans line the window above it.

"You live here by yourself?"

"Ever since my old man threw me out. He lives up the hill in the white trailer. My mom split when I was a kid."

Dad told me Fish had a tough life, but I had no idea. I let Fish wrap me in a blanket from the bed.

"There's not much heat in here. I use a propane heater in the winter. I'll get it going."

"You don't have to do that. I can go back to Dad's."

He shakes his head. "Not yet. You need to get warm first. How about I build a campfire?"

"That'd be cool," I say.

Fish starts a fire in a matter of minutes and then sets off to find Homeboy. Willard runs after him. I sit so close to the fire my clothes steam. My body shakes from the cold even as my face burns from the heat of the fire. I rotate myself every few minutes like a human rotisserie shivering in Fish's smelly blanket.

— — —

Twenty minutes later, Fish and Willard return. He holds up Homeboy's leash.

"Damn dog slipped his collar. Willard and I looked for him, but he's gone. Maybe he went back to your place."

"Crap. I told Dad I would keep him on a leash."

"You did; he just didn't keep himself in his collar." Fish grins. "You hungry?" Fish climbs in the RV and hollers back, "What time's Jake get off work?"

"He said he'll be home around eight."

Fish reappears with a pack of generic hot dogs and a six-pack of beer.

"Fine dining," he says, with a wink. He pulls out two well-used wire coat hangers and threads a hot dog on each. He crouches next to the fire and holds the hot dogs to the embers.

"You doing okay? Drying out?"

I nod. Fish opens a beer and takes a long swig.

"So why the hell did you jump in the creek, anyway?"

I blush despite the cold. Now I feel stupid. "I don't know. I just felt like it."

"That's cool. I do stuff because I feel like it all the time. Gets me in a shit-load of trouble, though."

Fish offers me a coat hanger and I nibble at the hot dog. I haven't eaten in hours. Nothing has ever tasted this good.

"You wanna beer?"

Two beers later, I remember Homeboy. "I need to take Willard back and see if Homeboy is there." When I stand up, the world sways. Fish reaches out and takes my arm.

"Let me give you a ride home."

"What about Willard?"

"He can run behind. I'll go slow."

We climb on Fish's dirt bike and I wrap my arms around his narrow waist. He feels solid. He doesn't smell so bad today. When we get to the trailer, Homeboy is curled up by the door. I clip him back on his chain and put Willard inside. Then we get back on the bike and go to the package store for more beer.

It's only 5:00.

— — —

By six-thirty, I am completely plastered. I can tell Fish is growing nervous. He knows my dad will kill him if he finds out. I keep hoping Fish will kiss me, but he doesn't. I climb on a tire swing that hangs from an old oak near the RV. Fish says his uncle hung it for him the last time he saw him. That was probably ten years ago.

Fish gives me a push and the branch creaks as the tire swings in a big arc. At first, it's fun, but then my stomach catches up. "Stop! I'm going to puke!"

Fish steadies the swing and helps me out. I stumble around like a kid who's just been turned loose from Pin the Tail on the Donkey. Miraculously, for once my stomach holds.

"Guess I better get back," I say. "I'm totally loaded. My dad will freak."

Fish takes my hand and we walk towards the trailer. Halfway there, Fish says, "Maybe you shouldn't go back. We could tell Jake I took you to a movie or something. Leave a note."

"Would you really take me to a movie?"

"Nah. I don't have any money and I'm too drunk to drive, but we could watch something on cable."

"Would you kiss me this time?" I ask. I hear myself say this, my words slurring. I sound like a cartoon version of myself.

"I would do anything you wanted," says Fish moving closer and pressing his hand into the small of my back. I think he means it. I know I should go home right now. I'm drunk and I might do something I regret. But then, regret is all I've got these days.

Fish pulls me to him. He glances towards the road and Dad's trailer as if someone might be watching. Then he leans down and kisses me gently. It's nice, and I lean into him. He kisses me harder. I can feel his warm skin through his thin T-shirt. I'm not cold anymore. Fish leads me out of the road, pushes me up against a tree, and kisses me urgently.

"Oh God, you're killin' me. Can we go back to my place?"

"No," I say. I don't want him to stop kissing me.

"Why not?"

"Because it smells in your trailer."

Fish works his hands under my sweatshirt. His hands are icy against my skin. He places one hand over each breast. I feel a warmth coming from deep inside. I sigh and hear myself moan.

"We got to go back to my place," he insists.

"Not yet," I say. I don't want to move. It feels good to be held—to be wanted. Fish isn't worried I'll lose it and he doesn't hate me for killing the coach. I close my eyes, but I can't stop the tears. They run down my cheeks and spill on to his face as he kisses my neck.

Fish pulls his hands away.

"Why're you crying? Shit, I thought you liked this."

"I do. I don't know why I'm crying," I say. "I don't know what I'm doing anymore."

"Maybe this is like jumping in the creek."

"I think this is different."

"Nah. You just do what you feel like doing. What do you feel like doing?"

I shrug and sit down in the leaves. Fish sits down next to me. His stringy hair probably hasn't seen a shower in weeks. Zits cover his forehead, and his eyes are bloodshot. I watch him reach into his pocket and pull out his cigarettes. He offers one to me and I shake my head. He lights it and leans back against the tree.

"I think I better go home," I say and climb to my feet.

He doesn't move. "Okay," he says.

When I get back to the trailer, I feed the dogs. Then I shower, brush my teeth, and climb into bed. When Dad gets home, he opens my door and whispers, "You asleep?"

I lay still in the dark, feigning sleep. He shuts my door, and I open my eyes because each time I close them the room spins and Helen Mitchell's face appears above me. She's disappointed, too.

27
LIZ

"Hey, babe," I say when I finally reach Jess. I have been calling all morning, and no one answers. Jess says she and Jake went to Jeb's for breakfast. She is in a foul mood, irritated at just the sound of my voice. My world has shifted so much in her absence I half-expected her to feel different, too.

When it is clear she has nothing to say, I ask, "Hey, when you left the house on Friday, do you remember if you locked the back slider door?"

"Oh, crap!" she says. "I didn't. Did something happen?"

"No," I tell her. "Nothing happened. I just wondered."

Jess didn't close the door properly. That was all it was. I am becoming paranoid, terrified of strangers and suspicious of friends. It is not just the door; my heart races when I walk from my office to the car after dark. I'm afraid to stop for gas, especially since twice now I have been harassed at a gas pump by some guy who used to play for Coach. It is like people think she murdered him. I know they have a right to their anger, but why can't they see this tragedy for what it is—a tragedy?

"That door was in terrible shape. Kevin installed a new one this weekend," I tell Jess.

"Guess he's a full-service lawyer, huh?" she says, but I don't take the bait.

"So what do you and your father have planned for today?"

"He wants me to go with him to look at some boat."

"He's buying a boat?"

"I don't know."

I swallow my fury. Jake has been clear that he is not paying for Kevin's services. "He's *your* friend," he says. I had hoped once he saw that Kevin would be the best person to represent Jess, he would get on board, but so far that is not the case.

"Okay, well, your father will get you to school in the morning."

"Uh, huh."

"I love you."

"Same."

The best part of Jess being out there is that she can't see today's paper or the comments online. When she is at Jake's she is unplugged. It used to be a source of frustration for me because I felt so out of touch with her, but these days I think it's a reprieve for Jess. A much-needed one. When she is here, I know she reads all the hateful comments online that pop up like foul mushrooms after every article about the case.

Today's paper had a big piece about the group from Dallas. The MADD women were here for a rally for tougher texting laws. One woman gave an interview about how her son was killed by a distracted teen driver. She was eloquent and convincing in her argument that the law needed to change. She never said Jess' name, but she said that Jefferson County has an opportunity to save future lives by sending a powerful message with an upcoming case.

"I want to live at Dad's," Jess says à propos of nothing.

Her words feel like a physical blow and I reach out for the wall to steady myself. "Did your father ask you to live there?"

Her voice is steely. "He didn't say I couldn't!"

"Your father will not want you living out there. He has his own life."

"How do you know? Maybe he'd be fine with me being here! Then you could have your own life, too."

"I don't want my own life. I want us here, together, like always."

"It will never be like always. Why can't you see that?" Her shrill words echo in my head long after we say goodbye.

— — —

Every day Jess seems further away from me. Sometimes I am not sure my heart can hold the churning emotions; love, fear, and anger swirl through me like a river raging forward and then back on itself. I have never felt so helpless. When she was little, it was so much simpler. She was an easy kid. And once Jake left, she was my best friend. We did everything together. She was always my date for parties or my buddy to go to the movies, but now I feel a disconnect. Even before the accident, there was a distance. I was no longer her go-to for what was on her heart. That honor went to Sheila, and I never trusted that girl. But even I never dreamed she would desert Jess so blatantly because of a boy. If that is what this is about. I know that no matter what I do or how much I want to help, Jess has to go through this by herself. Her actions, whatever they were, got her into this situation. I can love her and love her and love her, but my love can't protect her. Not from what happens in February at her trial or what happens at school or even from herself.

28
JESS

The next morning, Dad is unusually cheerful for 6 am on a Monday. After we looked at the boat yesterday (which he didn't buy), we met Amanda for lunch. It was awkward as always. She tried to engage me in conversation, but it was a half-hearted effort and she spent most of the lunch looking at her phone.

"So, do you like school?"

"No."

"Do you have a boyfriend?"

"No."

"So, like, what's your favorite class?"

"None of them."

"Jess," Dad chided me. "You like some of your classes."

"No, I don't."

He gave me a look that said, *be nice*. But I didn't feel like being nice. Not to a girl only a few years older than me who clearly was not wearing a bra, has a pierced tongue, and is shagging my dad. After we finished eating, Dad dropped me off at the trailer and went to "help Amanda with something." Obviously, I know what he was helping her with. When he got back to the trailer it was late. I didn't get the chance to talk to him about moving out to Gillam. I just need him to see that my being here wouldn't change his life at all. He can still screw his girlfriends and spend his days fishing. I wouldn't mind. But before I can figure out how to say that, we pull up in front of the school.

He offers to walk me in.

"You don't need to," I assure him.

"Does your mom walk in with you?"

"I'm not in kindergarten." I open the car door before he can insist on making my life even more miserable.

— — —

I feel the accusatory eyes follow me as I make my way to Ms. Ellen's office.

"Hello, Jess!" Ms. Ellen greets me, always cheery, always thrilled at the sight of me, or at least she's very convincing. "How are you holding up?"

"I'm okay." I settle onto her couch. The guidance office is now my homeroom. It's our chance to 'check-in' she says.

"So, how was the weekend?"

"It was."

She smiles. "Mr. Cafferty says you're doing great in Calculus. He says you haven't missed a beat. And your English teacher told me your class is reading *The Catcher in the Rye*. What did you think of it?"

"It was good."

"What did you like about it?" Ms. Ellen leans back in her chair and gives me a knowing look.

"I liked Holden."

"Uh-huh. He is an interesting character. What did you like about him?"

"I liked how he talked. It wasn't like reading a real book." I thumb through the worn pages and unstick a few that have dried together. "And I totally got how he said people were phonies."

Ms. Ellen nods.

"They pretend they like you, only they don't really, they just don't want you to know they don't. Turns out, most of my friends were phonies."

"What makes you say that?"

I shake my head. "Everybody is siding with Sheila. Which is the way it always is. Even though Sheila treats them like shit."

"Do you have any other friends besides Sheila?"

"I thought I did, but I guess they were really Sheila's friends."

I shake my head. Even I can't believe not one of these people who were so important a month ago, have called me. But I wonder what I would do if the tables were turned.

Ms. Ellen doesn't say anything, but she makes a note.

It's not surprising I have no friends now that Sheila isn't speaking to me. Being in Sheila's circle was like being high school royalty. I liked being popular. Sometimes I didn't like things Sheila did, but it was easier to go along. She'd cut people down because of their clothes or hair or for no reason at all, and I just laughed. Like it was a big joke. I think I knew at the time it was cruel, but it was fun to be Sheila's friend. She wasn't always mean. Sometimes she was hilarious.

Ellen looks at her watch. "Guess you better get to class."

"Yup."

"And Jess?"

I poke my head back into the room.

"I'm still waiting for an answer to my question."

"Question?"

"The one I asked you before the break. What you would say to someone else if they were in your situation."

"Oh yeah. I'll work on that." I had hoped she'd forget. Especially because I have no answer for her. It's a stupid question.

I go to my locker to drop a couple of my books. I'm sick of carrying everything around with me. I've been avoiding it because Jamie and Sheila have lockers in my row. It takes me two tries to get the combination right. Homeroom hasn't let out yet, so there's no one to witness when I finally pull the latch up and open the door. A cascade of papers falls at my feet. Each one printed in red block letters. *KILLER*. I slam the locker, catching some of the papers half in, half out.

— — —

On Friday afternoon, Mom drops me off at the Monroe's. Mrs. M called earlier in the week and talked to my mom. She told her since Mr. M was involved in the case, they weren't sure whether it was okay for me to babysit, but that the kids missed me so they'd decided they couldn't worry about that. I'm a pariah everywhere, it seems. Still, I'm touched that they called and excited to see Sally and Stu.

Sally comes running out in an elf costume. She and Stu are in some pageant coming up at their school.

"Stuey is a Christmas tree," she tells me. I follow Sally inside, listening to her running commentary of what everyone else in her class will be.

Mrs. Monroe appears, already dressed for dinner. She looks gorgeous, as always. She's wearing the perfume I love. I'll never smell lilacs and not think of her.

"Wow, you look great," I say.

Mrs. Monroe tears up and pulls me into a hug. "Oh, Jess," she says. "I'm so sorry. Bill's office was involved, and he didn't want us to..." She stops, looks down at Sally, and steps back. "I'm just glad you're here." She smiles at me and I have to look away and blink back tears.

Any further talk is interrupted by Stu dragging an enormous piece of cardboard behind him. "Jess! I'm a kissmas tree!"

"He wants to add real ornaments," explains Mrs. M. "But his teacher said it isn't necessary."

He beams up at me in all his five-year-old adorableness. God, I love this kid.

"I'll help you," I tell Stu.

Mrs. M kisses the kids and pulls on her coat. "I'm meeting Bill so I have to run, but I ordered dinner for you."

"Awesome. I hope it's the Proverbial Panda."

"It is. Enjoy. We should be home around eleven-thirty."

Fifteen minutes after Mrs. M leaves, the doorbell rings. I hurry to the door with my mini-entourage in tow, still holding the glue gun I was using to help Stu affix ornaments to his tree costume. When I open the door, Tucker Mobley is standing there.

"Hey!" he says, then glances at the glue gun in my hand. "Don't shoot!" Tucker is one of Jason's best friends. Sheila tried to fix me up with him last summer. He's the kicker on the football team and deals pot on the side.

I laugh and set the glue gun on the tiny table beside the door. "I didn't know you worked at the Panda," I say, taking the food from him.

"Yeah, well, I needed the cash. Got busted a few weeks ago."

"I hadn't heard."

"Yeah, most people were too freaked out about Coach to pay attention." Tucker looks away when he says this.

"Huh. Well, that sucks, I guess."

"Yeah."

I hand him the money Mrs. M left. Sally yanks the bag out of my hand and runs back inside.

I close the door and ask, "How are Sheila and Jason? Has she said anything about me? About the accident?"

"Huh? Oh, yeah, she's said a couple of things about it."

"Like what?"

"Like you were texting and didn't have your hands on the wheel when you hit Coach." Tucker looks down at the ground, asks, "Is that true?"

"I don't think so, but I don't remember much about the accident."

"Yeah, well, Sheila's a piece of work. She could be makin' that shit up. Jason's crazy about her though. She is a nice piece of ass." Tucker looks to see if he's offended me, and then continues, "Ninety percent of what comes out of her mouth is bullshit. Jason knows that too, but he thinks it's funny. Anyway, gotta run. Couple more deliveries."

Tucker shoves the money I gave him in his pocket as he walks back to his car idling at the curb, filling the street with black smoke. His jeans hang low on his hips, and he walks on the cuffs.

— — —

It's a struggle to keep my eyes open reading my American History homework. Mrs. M comes in a little after midnight. She overpays me and says Mr. M is waiting in the car to take me home.

"Good to see you, Jess," he says when I get in.

"Yeah, you, too," I say and look out the window, away from his kind face.

"I'm sure it's been a tough couple of weeks."

I nod but say nothing. He backs down their long drive, narrowly missing the garbage cans. I don't want Mr. M to have to talk about the trial, so I tell him about Stu's costume and how well Sally is reading. Eventually, though, I run out of commentary.

We drive in silence for a few minutes. As we follow the curve on Elm Drive, Mr. M says, "This is where it happened, isn't it?"

"Uh-huh."

"It's tragic, really. I wonder what Bob was doing on that turn. He should have crossed to the other side. There's no real shoulder there."

I hadn't considered the curve. It never entered my mind Coach could have been at fault in any way.

"Most people, runners anyway, know better than to follow a blind turn, especially running into the morning sun like that. A driver might not see you."

Mr. M's a runner, like me. He went to college on a track scholarship. He came to watch one of my meets last year. He doesn't say anything else. A few minutes later, we arrive at my house.

"Thanks for the ride," I tell him as I get out.

"Jess," Mr. M says so quietly I almost pretend I don't hear him, but then I lean back in the car and look at him. "We missed you," he says.

I nod and turn to run into the house before Mr. M can see my tears.

29
LIZ

Jess tells me nothing. She is a robot doing her homework, going to school, and running in the afternoons. She barely speaks at dinner. It is a relief to drop her off at the Monroe's on Friday. I'm not sure I can take another evening of her stony silence.

Kevin picks me up not long after I have dropped Jess at the Monroe's. He greets me with a kiss on the cheek and asks, "Where would you like to go?"

"Hawaii?"

"That could be arranged," he says, and I bet he is half serious.

"Sushi?"

"Sounds like a plan."

When we stop at a light, he smiles at me and it doesn't seem like an I'm-glad-we're-having-dinner-so-we-can-talk-about-the-case kind of smile. It is a smile that sends the thrill of possibility up my spine.

But as the light changes, a memory flashes through my mind. I'm in Jake's pickup truck. He is wearing his ball cap backward and They Might Be Giants is on the radio. We are parked up at the lake and I have just told him.

"*You're pregnant?*" he asks, a grin splitting his face. I thought he would be as upset as I was. But, no, he thought it was the greatest news ever. It meant I would stay in Jefferson instead of leaving him for Baylor. Jake was never going to college. He never wanted to leave Jefferson, and he never wanted me to either.

"I'm glad you agreed to go to dinner," Kevin says, he raises his eyebrows at me as he smiles, and I blush. This is more than dinner. This is our first actual date.

"You know, I should check on Jess," I say. I reach into my purse for my phone.

Everything okay?

Peachy, she texts back, with a little peach icon.

At the restaurant, they seat us at a corner booth in the front window; it is elevated above the other diners. I feel on display and say as much.

"I'll ask them to move us," says Kevin.

"It's fine," I say. "Really."

We order wine and appetizers, and I relax. All week I have been trying to sort out whether dating Kevin is a good idea. I have been over it in my head a million times. I like Kevin, but if we pursue this relationship and it doesn't work out—what then for Jess? My relationship with Kevin and his defense of Jess are intertwined. If one comes apart, would it take the other down with it?

And yet, when Kevin's leg touches mine beneath the table, a warmth spreads through me. He smiles at me, and I press my leg against his and smile back. Just then, a woman appears at our booth. I know her. She is the mother of another student in Jess' class. I think we chaperoned a field trip back in elementary school together.

"Isn't this cozy?" she says. Big, pink lip-glossed smile at Kevin.

"Do I know you?" asks Kevin.

"Jill is a friend of mine. We work out together at the gym. You're defending Jessica, right? Hello, Liz, how are you holding up?"

I can't remember her name. I mumble, "We're doing okay."

"I imagine this is an awful time for you. I don't know how you're surviving. Just devastating. I don't know what I'd do if it was my daughter. I couldn't do it; I'd probably have to move. You're amazing."

I don't know what she expects me to say, so I nod and try to smile.

Kevin stands up to shield me from her, and she takes a step back. "I'm sorry to be rude. This is a business dinner," he says. *Is that what this is?*

"Oh, I'm leaving. I was just picking up some takeout for my family. Say hi to Jill for me. I missed her at spin class this morning."

Kevin sits back down. "Guess that kind of breaks the mood," he says.

"Why did she mention Jill to you? I thought you never see each other?"

He shrugs. "We don't."

I drink my water, try to relax. But it occurs to me I have taken everything Kevin has told me about Jill at his word. Why isn't he divorced? Is it really because he has been too busy, or is it because he doesn't want to be? What if all of this really *is* about sex? What if Jake is right after all?

After that, dinner is strained. I can't find my way back to that feeling of possibility. Instead, I watch the other people in the restaurant and wonder what they are thinking. Are they all having the same thoughts but afraid to voice them?

When we get in Kevin's car to go home, I tell him, "I think you need to divorce Jill, legally."

He nods. "I know."

"So why don't you?"

He shakes his head. Then he sighs. "I will get to it."

"Maybe you should do that sooner than later."

We ride back to my house in silence.

"Do you want me to come in and make sure everything is okay?"

I look at the dark house. "No, I'm okay."

"Let me walk you to the door."

"I can go in by myself."

"Well, flash your lights once you're in and everything's okay."

This is the part when I should lean over and kiss him. Let him know everything is all right when clearly it is not. "Thanks," I say and touch his arm. He leans towards me, but I jump out of the car and hurry up the walk.

— — —

When Jess gets home, she doesn't want to talk.

"I'm tired," she says and leaves me alone in the living room with the popcorn I made for us to share.

I pour a glass of wine and call Kate. I know she will be up.

"I just freaked out," I say after telling her about my aborted evening.

"Poor man, dating you. He has no idea."

"But what if he's lying about the divorce?"

"Why don't you ask him?"

"I did."

"So why don't you believe him?"

"I don't know. Because he's a man?"

Kate laughs.

"I like him. A lot. It's just bad timing."

"I still think you should just sleep with him if only for the stress-relieving aspects. As they say, 'You could use some.'"

"Sex isn't the answer," I say, then laugh, "But it's not a terrible idea."

"You do like this guy; I can tell."

I take a long drink of my wine. "This feels bigger than I'm ready for. Kevin is....he's real. He's a good person. And he likes me and believes in me. He thinks I should go back to school when this is all over."

"You should."

"I don't deserve him."

"You don't," she says, laughing. "But maybe for once, the universe is tilting in your favor, Lizzie."

"I just feel so guilty."

"You? What have you done?"

"If Jess hadn't had the accident and Coach Mitchell wasn't dead, I would never have gotten together with Kevin. I would never be feeling this."

"Why are the two things connected?"

"Because they are."

"That's like saying Coach Mitchell died because he walked his dog."

"It's not the same."

"It is."

30
LIZ

Even though it is Saturday, I have to go to work. Today is our big Fall Festival and with the way Aaron has been riding me, I need to be sure everything goes smoothly. When I arrive at Morningside, Avery follows me to my office.

"You're here too?" I ask. Avery has been here long enough not to have to pull weekend shifts unless she wants to.

"The newspaper is coming to the festival. Edna Mae's daughter wants me to do her hair. Ever since her big party, she's a celebrity."

I laugh. "And Kimba must be with her other grandparents."

"That's not the only reason." She shrugs. "So, how's Jess?"

"Same."

My desk is covered with piles of work and post-it notes. It has never looked this bad. Normally, I clear my desk before leaving every evening, but now I can't get caught up. Everything takes me longer to do. My mind jumps around and I am never fully present. It is hard to be here when my heart is still in the lobby of the hospital listening to Jake tell me there has been an accident. It is as if everything that happened prior to that moment was leading me to it. Was my father right? How can I even think that?

Last week, my report to the Board was full of typos, which Aaron was quick to point out. Several times, I have found myself distracted while listening to a co-worker or resident, missing whatever it is they are saying to me, lost in my fears for Jess.

Avery's daughter, Kimba, is only three. Cherub-cheeked with a honey gold complexion. Her world revolves around her as surely as mine revolves around Jess. She understands how much I am hurting, yet I don't tell her. Am I ashamed of Jess? Ashamed of what she has done? I am carrying around all this pain and fear like a thousand-pound gorilla made of glass—I don't dare mention it, but I couldn't possibly put it down. I am waiting for someone to say to me what they are saying online or out of earshot. *Your daughter killed a man. It was her fault.* Something happened in that car and I may never know exactly what, but it does not change the fact that Jess is responsible. And I am responsible for Jess.

"How's Kimba?"

"This morning she got herself all worked up over the wrong cereal and all she wanted was Meemaw. Guess that makes sense. She spends more time over there than at my house."

"It's a phase. She knows who her mother is."

"You know, I'm here if you need me," she says, as she stands in the doorway.

"Thanks," I tell her, but I know there is nothing she can do. She can't change what's happened. And Avery has her own issues. Single parenting is not for the faint of heart. Kimba's daddy has been locked up since before she was born. Avery left the drugs behind, but not the pull of that man. She still visits him, but at least she doesn't take Kimba.

When Avery leaves, I stare at the spreadsheet in front of me. I need to double-check the numbers for my part of the budget, but they blur together. I look at all that money. Put all those department lines together and it is literally millions. How will I ever scrape together the money to pay Kevin what we will owe him when this is all over? If it is ever over. Morningside spends more than ten times my salary on lawn care.

"Liz?"

Carmelita appears in the doorway.

"We have a problem. No one ordered any porta-potties for the festival."

"Who usually does that?"

Carmelita frowns. "You?"

I don't remember ordering porta-potties for last year's festival, but there is no time to quibble.

"Can we designate the bathrooms in the lobby for non-residents to use?"

"We can, but it might get messy and loud."

Our fall festival attracts lots of visitors, mostly relatives, but some people come from town looking for free food and cheap crafts.

"I'll supervise," I tell her and head to the lobby. *Bathroom attendant*—my latest title.

Everything goes well until lunchtime when the line grows long. As I am making small talk with a few residents, a scruffy guy approaches me.

"Hey, ain't your daughter the one that hit Coach?"

My pulse quickens, and I force a smile.

"I'm sorry, sir. Is there a problem?"

"Only that your asshole kid was too busy talking on her damn phone and she killed the greatest man in Jefferson football! You should have taught her better, but don't worry none cause the state'll do that for you—put her away in jail where she belongs. Electric chair, if it were up to me."

He is loud and gruff, and his words blast me backward. I reach for the reception desk to steady myself. Avery appears at my side. "Boss, we need you in the medical wing. Emergency."

She pulls me away before I can say anything, but the man continues to ramble.

"What happened?" I ask as we hurry out of the lobby.

"Nothing happened. You just needed to get the hell out of there."

I stop and grab for a wall. "I can't do this."

Avery takes my arm, leads me along. We head to my office. "You can do this because you have to do this. That guy doesn't know Jess; he doesn't know the whole story."

"Neither do I," I confess.

Avery leaves me in my office and returns to the lobby to deal with the bathroom line. I can't stop shaking and my vision blurs. I call Kevin. I don't know who else to call. My anger last night was unfair. All the man does is help me, and here I am once again calling him. I know I shouldn't call him, but I also know that when I do, he will come.

"Can you come get me?"

"Has something happened?"

"I need to get out of here and I don't think I can drive my car."

Kevin shows up twenty minutes later. He asks if I have eaten and I tell him no, so he stops to grab fast food for me and we park in an empty lot where he watches as I eat french fries and sip a soda. He talks about nothing. The crack in his windshield. The truck that kicked up gravel and then drove away. Where he might go to get it fixed.

I squirt ketchup out of a packet onto my fries. Wipe the grease off my chin. He transitions to his childhood. His failed plan to play major league baseball. Piano lessons. Fishing with his granddad.

I crumble up the fry package, lean my back against the passenger side door, and drain my soda. I take a deep breath and almost feel normal again. And then he tells me how he and Jill struggled to have children and how that was the first crack in their marriage. A crack that splintered and grew until it was an impassable gorge. Four failed in-vitro attempts and too many fertility experts. It was his job to get her pregnant and he couldn't do it. He felt responsible for her sadness. She blamed him and said she didn't. They grew apart. Jill had an affair. Kevin tried to work past it but couldn't. Finally, they separated. Jill re-focused on her career. She is doing well. They don't talk often. He needs to get around to filing for divorce. As he tells me all this, he looks out the windshield, closing his eyes occasionally like a kid swallowing a pill.

I know he is only trying to distract me, but I see him differently now. He is not a lawyer on the make. He is broken, like the rest of us.

31
JESS

On Monday, Ms. Ellen wants an answer to her question. "It's not that tough. I just want you to imagine what you would say to me if I was the one who hit Coach Mitchell."

"I don't know."

She waits. She's a good waiter. Finally, I blurt out, "This is stupid. I'm the one who hit Coach Mitchell."

"No, I did," she says and takes a sip of her tea. "I hit Coach Mitchell," she insists.

"And his dog," I correct her.

"And his dog."

I take a bite of my sandwich, stalling for time. Ms. Ellen waits. I know she'll sit there and say nothing all day if necessary.

"I'd tell you you're fucked."

Ms. Ellen doesn't even raise her eyebrows at my language. She just watches me, her blue eyes not giving away anything.

"I'd say you shouldn't have touched your phone. You're an idiot."

"I shouldn't have," says Ms. Ellen pretending to be me.

I put down my sandwich because the bite I took is still stuck in my throat.

"People around here hate you. You should find another school or be homeschooled. Or better yet, get out of town, out of this state, away from anywhere anyone knows about Coach Mitchell."

"Is that what you want?" asks Ms. Ellen.

I can't say anything because I'm crying and there's food stuck in my throat and I'm just so damn mad at Ms. Ellen for making me cry.

"Wouldn't you?" I finally say.

"Maybe," says Ms. Ellen. "But I'd think about all the people here who love me and who need me."

"Nobody needs me," I tell her, crossing my arms.

"Your mother needs you."

"No, she doesn't. She would have had a life if it weren't for me. She got married and stayed in this crappy town because of me. Did you know that? And this is the thanks she gets."

"Jess, your mother loves you and I'm certain she'd make the same choice again."

"She gave up college for me, how stupid is that? And now she's sleeping with my lawyer to pay for his help and she might lose her job."

"Your mother is an adult, and she is doing the best she can. Sometimes that's all people can do." Ms. Ellen looks at the clock.

"I have to go," I say and pile my books into my backpack.

"We can talk more about this tomorrow," Ms. Ellen tells me. She stands to give me a hug, but I turn and leave before she can reach me with her pity.

In Chemistry, Sheila actually looks at me. I smile and she rolls her eyes and turns back to the person she's talking with. Jennifer is as friendly and chatty as ever. I try to tune her out and focus on the lab.

"Jess, did you hear me?"

"What?"

"Did you really write that e-mail Sheila is showing everyone?"

I sit back and take off my safety goggles. Is this what Tucker was talking about? "What e-mail? Sheila never answered any of my e-mails."

Jennifer looks around, leans towards me, and whispers, "She's showing people an e-mail you wrote. It says you think people are overreacting and that Coach Mitchell was old anyway and you have some big hot-shot lawyer who will get you out of the charges."

My head spins and I reach out and hold the counter to keep my balance.

"I didn't write that."

"I figured, but Sheila's been sending it to everyone. It does look like you sent it."

"I didn't."

"I'm sure people will figure that out."

Mr. Farenz appears at our table. "How're we doing, ladies?"

Jennifer launches into a play-by-play of our results. I stare at Sheila who does not look up. *How could she do this? What happened in that car?*

32
LIZ

I look through the requests from the dining room manager. She is planning quite an elaborate Thanksgiving feast. The holiday can be hard for some of our residents—the ones whose families don't take them home for the holiday and the ones who have no family left to go home to. I approve all six kinds of pie she would like to order.

Around ten, a shadow appears above my desk, and I look up to see Aaron.

"To what do we owe the honor?" I ask him.

"We need to talk," he says and pulls my office door shut behind him.

I close the folder on my desk but say nothing. He paces in front of my desk.

"I heard about the scuffle in the lobby on Saturday."

"There was no scuffle."

"Well, whatever you want to call it. I think it would be best for the residents if you took some time off until this thing with your daughter is settled."

"Jessica's situation has nothing to do with my work here."

"I disagree. It's affecting your work and more importantly, the residents."

"Are you telling me I *have* to take a leave or still just suggesting?"

"Just suggesting. I can't make you, but I may find it necessary to limit your interaction with the residents which will probably require I reduce your hours so I can afford to bring in someone else."

"Someone more male?"

"Please don't start banging that drum again. My only concern is the security of our residents."

"And me being here jeopardizes that."

"I believe it does. I also believe it might be good if you spend more time supervising your daughter."

Fury rages through me and I have an irrational urge to throw the stapler in my hand at his shiny forehead. He is like those people you see rioting after a natural disaster. Where there is chaos, there is opportunity.

I set the stapler down and open the folder of invoice requests. I don't look at him.

"Get out of my office," I tell him.

"Excuse me?"

"I said, get out of my office."

I will not look at him. I will control my fury. I will not give him the excuse he is looking for to fire me.

"I don't appreciate your tone. If I were you, I would tread carefully, not many people in this town will be inclined to hire you, even *with* my reference, but definitely not without it."

I say nothing. He lets out a long sigh. "You have a good day," he says as if having a good day is within my control.

— — —

"I know he didn't fire me, but if I leave, it will seem like he did," I tell Kevin when I call him at lunchtime.

"He can't do that. He has no grounds."

"I don't know what to do. I need the money. Now, more than ever."

"You want me to get involved?"

"No! The last thing I need right now is another lawsuit."

"You could come work for me," he says.

"Doing what?" I laugh. Kevin is already doing so much for us; I can't take his charity.

"Being a clerical assistant. My secretary is out more than she's in. She's pregnant and the morning sickness seems to be an all-day problem. I could use someone to handle the phones, do some filing, open the mail. I know you are way over-qualified, but it would allow you to take a break from Morningside. Just until the case is resolved."

"Seriously?" I ask. Once again, I question his motives. Is he being kind? Or is he just trying to ingratiate me to him? And why am I so suspicious of every move he makes?

"They might realize what they're missing if you took a leave. And if your job isn't waiting for you when you're ready to go back, I'll help them understand the legal ramifications of that decision. Meanwhile, I need the help. It's not fun work, but if you don't take it, I'll have to call a temp, anyway."

"I can't type very well, and English was not my strong subject."

"I'm not worried. The job is mostly dealing with people. You're good at that."

"I will think about it," I say, but after I hang up, I pack a few things. No one would argue with my decision. *My* decision. Lately it feels like no decision is mine. Avery will be mad, but she will understand.

And then I have a brilliant idea. An opportunity out of the chaos I could seize.

I dial Aaron.

"I'll leave."

"You will?"

"On one condition?"

"I'm not sure you're in a place to make conditions."

"I'm not sure you're in a place to make me leave. My lawyer informed me I have grounds for wrongful termination."

"I'm listening."

"Avery Bennett has worked here almost as long as I have."

"Yes."

"And she knows how to do my job as well as I do. I will take a leave of absence if you let Avery backfill my job."

"Ms. Bennett doesn't have a college degree."

"And neither do I, as you so frequently remind me."

"I don't think it would be appropriate to give her your job."

"You wouldn't be giving her my job, remember? This is a temporary leave; you said so yourself."

Aaron is quiet for a few moments. Finally, he says, "Done. But if she can't handle the job..."

"She can handle the job," I assure him. "I'll train her myself and leave on Friday."

"I don't think that will be necessary. I'm sure you can teach her all she needs to know before you leave today."

I hang up the phone. "Asshole," I mutter.

I have had this job for eight years and put in more hours than anyone. It is hard to imagine not seeing these people every day. I wrap the pictures of Jess in paper from my recycling bin but leave my drawer full of chocolate, Tylenol, and Tums for Avery. I put the box in my car and then find Avery in the supply room.

"Guess what?"

"What?" she asks with a pen in her mouth and a case of tissues open on the shelf.

"You're getting a promotion!"

Avery is furious that I am leaving, but she can't hide her delight at getting my job. And she is a quick study. We spend the rest of the day going over every file and form and responsibility. I don't tell anyone else I'm leaving. I don't want anyone to make a fuss.

"That's it," I say when we have covered everything.

"Nope. It isn't."

"What did I forget?"

"The part where I buy you dinner to thank you for doing this for me."

I laugh, but then I realize that I was so focused on making sure I told Avery everything that I forgot to pick up Jess.

"Crap! I was supposed to be at the school an hour ago!"

33
JESS

After I finish taking my history test, Mom isn't waiting outside for me. I told her I was staying after for the test. She should be here. I call her, but it goes to voicemail. I pace around for a while and then sit down on a bench trying to decide if I should call my dad or Mrs. M. Either of them would probably come to get me.

As I'm considering this, Casey comes out of the gym and heads up the sidewalk towards me on his way to the student parking lot. He walks past me but then turns around.

"You okay? Do you need a ride or something?"

I can't look at him. Instead, I look towards the parking lot and mumble, "My mom was supposed to be here, but she isn't."

"C'mon, I can give you a ride. You live on Beckett, right?"

I pull on my backpack. "Uh, yeah, Beckett." I sound like an idiot.

We walk to the student parking lot in silence. When we get to his car, I ask, "Are you sure you want to give me a ride?"

"It's not a problem."

As we pull into traffic, Casey clears his throat. It occurs to me he's nervous too. He probably doesn't want to be seen with me. I sink low in my seat.

"I'm sorry about everything," he says.

This makes me sit back up.

"You have nothing to be sorry about."

I swear he winces.

As we sit at the next stoplight, Casey says, "Once, I was driving home from practice and I was fiddling with the stereo. My dad had just gotten me Sirius Radio, and I was trying to find a station I heard about. I wasn't paying attention to the road. It was only a few seconds, but when I looked up, I was in the other lane."

I know what he's trying to say, but it doesn't help.

"I guess, I mean, I was lucky. I could have hit someone."

My heart is pounding so loud I can hear it ringing in my ears. I can't look at him, so I lean against the cool glass of the window. I watch the other cars go by. A tear slips down my cheek and falls on the door of Casey's car. I watch it melt into the upholstery.

When Casey pulls into my driveway, he shuts the engine off and turns to me.

"I'm sorry this happened to you. It could have been anyone. Maybe people are freaked out because they know that, and they're just glad it wasn't them."

I nod and wipe my nose with my sleeve. Such a lovely picture I make, but I don't care.

"That crap Sheila's saying - most people know she's full of shit; they don't take her seriously."

I nod again. I just want to get out of the car. I can't breathe.

"You okay?" Casey asks.

"Thanks for the ride," I mumble and open my door, hiding my face from him.

"Anytime."

As I hurry up the walk, Casey calls out the window, "Jess!"

I stop and turn back to him.

"People will get over it. They just need time."

I nod again and hurry into the house and make it to the toilet just in time to unload that sandwich that has been lodged in my throat all day.

I pace the house, caged. I can't stay here. Casey's wrong, Sheila's lies will become truth. She's making sure of that. People believe what she says because they want to believe her. As if just her words on your lips make you cooler or more popular or whatever it is you think she has that you wish you had.

There is no place for me at Jefferson High. And it's not "just going to take time" like Ms. Ellen and Mom and now Casey say. They don't understand. They act like I'm a little kid whose boo-boo will eventually heal. How could it? It cuts right through to my soul.

My phone rings. Mom.

"I'm so sorry! I completely forgot!" she cries.

"It's okay. I got a ride."

"You did? With who?"

"A friend. It's okay."

"Do you think you can get yourself dinner if I go out with Avery?"

"Sure," I tell her, and then I see my opportunity. "I'm going to call Dad and see if I can go out there."

"Oh? Why would you do that?"

"I kind of want to hang out with my friend out there."

"Oh, okay, but how will you get to school tomorrow?"

"Dad can take me."

Avery leans into the phone and yells, "Hi Jess! Your mom is awesome!"

"You're sure?" Mom asks, but I can tell she's relieved. She hasn't hung out with Avery since this whole nightmare started.

I hang up and consider my options. Casey did say he could give me a ride anytime when he dropped me off. But wishing on Casey is what landed me in this nightmare. I dial Fish's number.

"Hey," he says. "I didn't think you would ever call me."

"Well, I did. Can you pick me up?"

"Right now?"

I load my backpack with extra clothes, granola bars, and all the cash I can find in the house, which is only thirty-six bucks. I have no idea where I can go. All I know is I can't stay. Anybody who doesn't hate me already will hate me after Sheila's e-mail makes the rounds.

Less than an hour later, I hear Fish's bike turn on our street. I grab my backpack and run out without a backward glance.

"Where to?" asks Fish when I climb on the bike behind him.

"I don't care, just away from here."

"Shit, I hear that," he says and tears out of the driveway.

November in Jefferson can get cold. The days are still in the seventies, but nights hover in the fifties. After about an hour, I'm too cold to ride any longer. Fish pulls the bike into a rest area.

"I know this place," he says. "C'mon."

I follow him behind the bathrooms to a small concrete building. I watch while he jimmies the lock and opens the door easily. I've chosen the right accomplice, it seems. He waves me inside. It smells like gasoline. Fish turns on a light. Tools hang from the walls, and paper supplies for the bathrooms are stacked everywhere. An old newspaper, empty soda bottle, and half-full pack of cigarettes lay on a small desk. Fish moves aside a pile of boxes and finds a thermostat. I hear the heat click on.

"How'd you know about this place?"

"I did a stint on maintenance for the highway department."

Now that we're here, away from Jefferson, I feel scared. I always thought when I left Jefferson it would be for college with a future solidly in my hands. But this feels flimsy and dangerous. I lean on the desk and hug my arms around myself, trying to get warm.

"You cold?" asks Fish.

I shake my head.

"Yeah, you are," he says. He takes off his jacket and wraps it around me. "I gotta go take a leak," he says and slips out the door.

I look at my watch. It's almost nine. Mom must have gotten home by now. I just hope she doesn't call Dad to check up on me.

Fish reappears with a package of cheese crackers and some M&M's from the vending machine.

"Dinner?" he offers.

As we share the crackers, Fish asks, "So what's the plan?"

"No plan," I tell him. I wish I had a plan, a place to go, anything. All I know is I can't go back.

"Well, how 'bout we catch a little sleep then. We have to be out of here by five when the guys open up."

Fish finds some canvas jumpsuits and spreads them out on the floor. I'm too keyed up to sleep, but I take a sweatshirt out of my backpack and roll it up for a pillow. Fish lies down beside me. He puts one arm around me, and I freeze up.

"Don't worry. I'm not gonna try anything. It's just warmer this way."

I scoot back against his chest. We snuggle like spoons. I whisper, "Thank you," as tears roll down my cheeks.

"Anytime," Fish mumbles and hugs me closer. He's asleep in minutes. I lay awake for hours. I listen to the big rigs drive into the rest area and idle while their driver's nap. I imagine hiding in the back of one and letting it take me far, far away from Jefferson, Texas, where Helen Mitchell is a widow because of me and Sheila Richards is determined to make sure the whole town knows it.

— — —

Fish shakes me awake. "Hey, we gotta get out of here. It's almost five."

It takes a minute to remember where I am. Fish lies beside me, propped up on one elbow. He smiles. His breath is terrible.

"C'mon, let's hit it," he says, getting up and offering his hand. We put the jumpsuits away and turn the heat off. Back on the bike, it's cold and Fish says we should have nicked a couple of jumpsuits. It's too cold to ride for long, so we stop at a diner for breakfast.

"It'll be warmer in an hour," Fish assures me.

After we order, Fish says, "Look, I don't need to know all the details, just a general idea. How far are we going? Are the cops going to be looking for you? Is your dad gonna kill me?"

I laugh. "My dad will definitely kill you."

The waitress brings us coffee. I watch Fish dump nearly the entire pot of creamer in his cup.

"That looks more like a milkshake than coffee."

Fish smiles. "So, what's the 911?"

I don't know what to say. I look out the window and then check my watch. It's only six. With a little luck, we still have about nine hours before anyone misses me.

"You know that accident back in October? The one where that guy, the football coach, got hit by a car?"

"I mighta heard something about that. I don't get the paper. Yeah, I think a guy at Mikey's said it was some girl who ran him over. She was texting."

I look out the window, watch a trucker filling his tank, a cigarette hanging from the side of his mouth. "I was that girl."

Fish leans back in his seat. "Holy shit," he says as he spears more of his pancake and chews thoughtfully. "So, are you running because they want to put you in jail?"

"No. I mean, I don't know if they will put me in jail. My lawyer says they won't, but it's not up to him."

"So what's the problem?"

I look back at him and sigh. "The problem is the whole town hates me. My mom follows me around asking me how I am, thinking she can fix this nightmare, and my dad acts like everything is just great. No one speaks to me at school. And even if I get thrown in jail, the Coach's family will still sue us for millions. If I just disappear, then there's no one to sue and maybe my mom wouldn't have to grocery shop at midnight at the Walmart off the interstate just to avoid seeing anyone she knows." I don't mention Helen Mitchell and how even here I can see her sad face from the photo in the paper about Coach's service. She has one hand on his casket and the other on her heart. She looks a million years old even though the paper said she is seventy-two.

"Huh," says Fish. For once, he seems speechless. He has no clever come back for such a fucked up situation.

"Everything will be better if I'm just not there."

"I think your dad's gonna freak out."

"Maybe at first, but then he'll be relieved."

"Look, I don't know what it's like to have a mom or dad who gives a shit about you, but I've seen you with Jake. I don't think you being gone is gonna make him relieved. You should at least let him know you're okay." He pulls a cigarette out of his pack and rolls it between his palms, shaking his head. "Christ, Jake is gonna skin my ass."

"He doesn't have to know you're here. You can always leave. I'm not going back, but you can go back anytime."

It's slow going. We have to avoid the bigger highways because the mini-bike has a top speed of 45. We stop at a state park to use the restrooms and I study the map hanging on the side of the building. I wish we were further away. Out of Texas, at least.

Fish appears. "Were you really texting when you hit that guy?"

"I don't know."

"Then how can they sue you?"

"Even if I don't remember, Sheila does and for whatever reason, she's telling everybody I did it and I don't even care that I killed Coach Mitchell. His dog, too."

"There was a dog?"

I nod. I'm crying now, I can't help it. I thought eventually I'd run out of tears, but it never happens. Maybe if we get far enough away, I'll feel better. Or maybe I'll feel like this for the rest of my life. There's one old lady at Morningside who cries all the time. Her face is chapped, and her eyes are ringed red. Mom says nobody knows why she cries. Maybe some kind of pain never goes away.

Fish looks at the map and says, "I guess we'll just keep going southwest until it gets warmer."

— — —

We stop outside San Antonio at a biker bar, and I splurge on dinner. Fish orders a beer, and I ask for water. We watch a sit-com on the bar television. Fish has several more beers and chats up the locals.

I go to the ladies' room to wash the day's grime off my face and watch the last of Jefferson swirl down the drain. By now they know I'm gone. I think of Helen Mitchell and wonder if she is alone in her old house. I see the windows lit up—two downstairs and one upstairs—the way they've been when I run past at this hour. Mom and Dad and even Casey say everyone just needs time, but what about Mrs. Mitchell? How much time will she need?

When I get back from the restroom, Fish says, "The bartender said we could crash in the old rig parked out back."

He wheels his bike around to the back of the building and parks it behind a big rig with a flat tire next to the fence that separates the bar from the highway. He climbs up and tries the door. It opens with a creak. Fish looks around inside, and then he reaches down and pulls me up. Fish takes off his jacket and puts it on top of the filthy mattress behind the seat and we lay down on it.

He is asleep in minutes. I try not to think of my mom and dad. I try not to think of Helen Mitchell. I try not to think of anything. Even with Fish pressed up against me, I've never felt so alone in my life.

34
LIZ

My head is buzzing the next morning as I get ready for my first day in Kevin's office. It was fun to be with Avery. Ever since the accident, I have held her at arm's length, even though I needed her more than I knew, but that is the thing about a genuine friend—no judgment. Our friendship persists no matter how crazy our lives get or how much we take each other for granted. For a few hours last night, it was like it has always been. My cheeks are sore from laughing.

When I got home to the empty house, it all came rushing back. The mortgage papers for the house were still sitting where I left them on the counter. Kevin says we don't have to pay him, but I am determined I will. And yet, if I go through with the second mortgage and squeeze what I can out of this house—which is admittedly not much—there will be no money left for college. I left that decision and everything else behind last night, for just a few hours. And it was heavenly.

I am tempted to call Jess. Just to be sure Jake will really get her to school on time, but I stop myself. I am not ready to shoulder everything again just yet. I take my time and dress with care for Kevin's office, my nerves already jangling at the idea of spending my days in such close proximity to him.

Kevin is out when I get there, but I meet Tracey, his current secretary, who is four months pregnant and so eager to be a mom, she has her ultrasound photo framed on her desk and asks me what I think of the name Natasha for a girl before I have even taken off my coat. Kevin thinks she is coming back after her maternity leave, but Tracey tells me she has signed up for Gymboree on Thursday afternoons next fall. She is nice, but I learn more about the decorations for the nursery and where she has registered than I do about handling Kevin's office. I will figure it out though. It does not seem too complicated.

Despite doing nothing more taxing than proofreading contracts and making a pot of coffee (for me, Tracey is avoiding caffeine during her pregnancy), I am exhausted when I finally leave the office to pick up Jess.

When I get to the school, she isn't there and the school secretary says Jess didn't come to school today. Damn Jake.

"What do you mean Jess didn't stay with you last night?"

"Just what I said. I haven't seen her."

"She told me she was going to your place. She said she wanted to spend time with you."

"That should have been your first clue."

"Then where is she?"

"Did you call Sheila?"

"Where've you been, Jake? Were you not at the courthouse? Sheila hasn't spoken to Jess since the accident."

Still, when I hang up, I call Sheila. She is laughing as she answers.

"Up?"

"Sheila, this is Mrs. Johnson, I'm looking for Jess. Have you seen her?"

"No," she says flatly. I can hear other kids and music in the background.

"Was she in school today?"

"How would I know? I'm not the attendance keeper."

"Sheila?"

Silence.

"You're a lousy friend."

I hang up. I call the school; Ms. Schultzman does not know anything either. "She was upset, but no more than what's become normal for her. We talked about how hard it is to be in school. What about the boy who wrote the text? Casey? Maybe you should try him."

She gives me his number even though we both know it is against policy and she could get in trouble for it.

"I haven't seen her since I dropped her off at your house," Casey tells me when I call.

"She said nothing about running away?" I ask. It is the first time I name what could be happening here and I find tears catch in the back of my throat. *My baby has run away. Where is she? Where is she? Where is she?*

"She was upset. I tried to tell her people will get over it. She didn't say much."

I hate myself for not picking her up yesterday. I hate myself for being preoccupied with my life instead of being where my daughter needed me to be. I don't know who else to call, so I dial Kevin. He says we need to fill out a police report. It has been over 24 hours. He will meet me at the station. I call Jake, and he says he is on his way.

At the police station, Kevin is talking to an officer when Jake comes flying in.

"How the hell did this happen?" he asks.

"I told you. I thought she was with you."

"Jesus, Liz, how stupid can you be?"

"Wait a minute," says Kevin, stepping between us. "This isn't her fault."

"Stay out of it! What's he doing here, anyway? This isn't his business!" Jake pushes Kevin aside roughly and the police officer stands up.

"None of this will help us find your daughter. I need you all to calm down," he says.

Jake shakes his head, but steps back. He glares at me.

"You're her father?" the officer asks.

"Yes," he says.

"I need to get some information from you. Have a seat," he says and points to a chair beside his desk. "I've got all I need from your wife."

"Ex-wife," he mutters as he sits down.

Kevin takes my arm and leads me to a break room where we drink burnt coffee and swallow our words. I study the MOST WANTED posters and wonder who left a whole pizza minus one slice on the table. What emergency called them from their dinner?

"God, what happens now?" I ask.

"We let them do their job."

— — —

When the officer calls us all back together, he says, "You all need to go home so you're there if Jessica comes back. If you hear anything from her, let us know. Call anyone you can think of who she might contact. And then just sit tight. We will find her. In my experience, kids like Jess, come home. She doesn't have a record of drug or alcohol abuse and it sounds like you both have a good relationship with her. She's a smart kid. Hopefully, she'll make a smart decision and come back. Meanwhile, we've got her picture and information in the system. Everyone will be watching for her. If she doesn't come home, we'll find her."

I wish I could believe him. I want to believe him.

In silence, the three of us walk outside. Jake's truck is parked in front of the station in a no-parking zone. Kevin politely backs away to let us talk.

"I'm sorry," I say.

"This isn't your fault," Jake says, "I know that. I was just mad and scared."

"I'm scared too."

He shakes his head. "Why would she run?"

"I don't know." I shiver in the chilly air, shake my head.

Jake leans on his truck and looks up at the darkening sky. "Jess is smart. She'll come back. She'll be okay."

I nod through my tears. Jake kisses my forehead and pulls me to him, wrapping his powerful arms around me. "We'll find her," he says. "I promise."

I don't want to let go. I want him to be able to fix this. Finally, he releases me.

"I'll call you if I hear anything," he says.

"Me too," I tell him.

When I get to my car, Kevin is there, waiting. "I'll follow you home," he says.

I nod, glad for his company, checking for his headlights the whole way home. At home, I call Kate. I call Avery. I even call Sheila's mom, who is unsympathetic. "I can understand why she'd run away," she says. "From what Sheila tells me, all the kids are upset with her."

Kevin makes coffee and checks in periodically with the police. There is no news. At midnight, I call my father. Kevin is sleeping on the couch, and I am drinking my fifth cup of coffee. I do not want to be sleeping if the police call. I don't know why I call my dad. I really want my mom, but she is gone, so he is the closest thing.

My mother could always help me figure out what to do. When schoolwork overwhelmed me or something didn't go my way or I was upset about anything, she would say, "Let's set the emotion aside, and make a list." We wrote down the good and the bad, the possible next steps, and what I could control and what I could not. Even if the answer was not immediately clear, I felt better. She was so practical, never accepting my tears or my tantrums. I can imagine her now saying, "There is no point to all these tears, Elizabeth. Let the police do their job and you do yours. Save the tears until you need them."

The night I told them I was pregnant with Jess, my father voiced his fury and retreated to his wood shop, and my mother shook her head and cleaned up dinner. I sat at her spotless kitchen table and asked, "What do I do?"

"You marry Jake and you raise a good child," she said. There was no list of the pros and cons. There were no options to weigh. I knew from her face it devastated her, but true to form she held her tears. She knew my father would insist they leave. Kate coming out had been hard enough, but my pregnancy drove him further away. Looking back, I don't know why she went with him. Did she love him? They never fought, but then they never loved, either. Night after night they sat side by side watching television. The only time I saw them touch was when we prayed at dinner—hands held around the table. "The husband is the head of the household," she reminded me when I asked why she had to go. "We're a different generation."

She came to our rushed wedding in the church basement and tried to put on a bright face, but I remember glancing back at her just before I said my vows. I saw the sadness on her face.

The day they left, she told me, "You can do this. You'll be a good mother."

But am I?

Or am I too preoccupied with Kevin and the court case and my job and dealing with my dad? How could I not know Jess was so devastated she would leave? I thought we were past the worst of it. She was back at school; she said it was fine. Obviously, it was not fine.

I am startled when my dad answers his phone. It has probably rung twenty times by then. There is no answering service for the room phones. Most patients' families give them cell phones. Dad didn't want one. "This one's fine," he said when Kate tried to press a cell phone on him. He patted the big, boxy phone that was probably installed thirty years ago, its cord tangled irreparably.

"Hello, daughter," he says.

He sounds clear, alert, awake.

"How did you know it was me?"

"Who else would call me at this hour?"

He doesn't sound angry or surprised, just matter of fact.

"How are you, Daddy? Are you still having stomach pains?"

"Now and again, but it's nothing."

"Maybe your doctor needs to change your meds."

"Maybe, but that's not why you called I imagine."

I shake my head, try to form the words.

"What's the matter, cat got your tongue?" he asks.

"Jessica is gone."

"Is that right? Where to?"

"She ran away. I don't know where she is."

"Why'd she do that?"

And that is the real question. Going back to school has not been easy, but she has insisted she is fine. I had no idea it was so bad that she would run away.

"I don't know."

"Seems to me, if you knew why she left, you'd know where she'd gone."

"I wish Mom were here."

"I do, too, every day. She was always good with you girls. You never listened to me."

"I'm sorry I didn't listen to you more," I say.

"Yeah, well, sorry doesn't do us any good, now does it? Don't change facts. You'll find your girl."

"How do you know?"

"Your mother said you raised her right. Better than I did with you."

I catch my breath. I have never heard my father express any remorse for how he raised Kate and me, or for how he deserted us. But he sounds clear, not confused tonight.

"I better be getting some sleep. Gotta go into work early tomorrow," he says and my heart sinks.

"Daddy?"

He has already hung up; the dial tone rings in my ear. My mother never told me she thought I was doing a good job with Jess. She was not one for compliments. I hold on to those words all night long. Hoping they were meant for me.

35
JESS

It's still dark when I wake up. I've been dreaming of the accident like always, but fresh pieces of the memory broke loose—Sheila laughing, the sun so bright I flipped down the visor, "Hey Soul Sister" by Train was playing on the radio. It's all clear for a moment, but then it's gone again. I crawl up to the passenger seat and roll down the window, gulp in the night air trying to steady my heart. The night is clear and dark, and even with the parking lot lights, I can still see the stars. I wish I had a friend like Cygnus the Swan to come and rescue me.

I wish I could start over or be someone else. It all feels out of control like I'm a player in someone else's film, God's puppet with no idea how I got here or where I go from here. And yet I know I am not a puppet. I did something so horrible that my own brain is keeping it from me. The pain bears down on me; searing the breath out of me.

I am all alone.

I crawl back to where Fish lies, slip my arms under his shirt, pull him to me, and crush my lips on his as if I want to swallow him alive. He kisses me back and then helps me slip off my shirt, unhook my bra.

"We don't have to do this," he whispers.

"Yes, we do," I say because it's true. I need someone to love me. Right now. Love away all this hurt. I dig my fingernails in his back and burrow my face into his chest.

He takes my face in his hands. "You sure about this?"

I nod, but tears stream down my face. "Nah," he says, "You ain't." He holds me tight while I sob. When I finally stop shaking, he says, "It's gonna work out."

I nod numbly, but I don't believe him.

"I need a smoke," he says.

He sits on the bumper of the rig smoking a cigarette and I pull his jacket tight around me and inhale the sour stench of the mattress and Fish's cigarette smoke. How did my life come to this? I did everything right. I was going to get out of Jefferson, and not on the back of a mini-bike. How can you lose so much in only a moment? I wish there was some way to rewind my life. I'd do it differently. Life is a collection of moments, one after the other, you don't think one matters more than another until it does. I'm trying so hard to remember, but why? It doesn't change the outcome; it doesn't help me one bit. And just because I don't remember doesn't mean I'm not guilty.

— — —

The next morning, I spend the last of my money on breakfast and gas. We finally get on the road, and a cold rain pelts us. Fish pulls the bike under an overpass and we scramble up the concrete embankment to get away from the splash of the passing cars. Fish smokes a cigarette and recites the graffiti on the underside of the bridge to pass the time.

"'FUCK EVERYONE,'" he reads and laughs. "Now, there's a life goal. 'YOU SUCK.' Wow, this bridge is just full of cheerful shit." He looks back at me. I'm holding my knees to my chest, trying in vain to get warmer. I watch car after car go by and worry I'll never be able to get far enough away. Fish sits down beside me. He wraps an arm around me.

"You okay?"

I shake my head; my teeth are chattering.

"Can I help?"

I shake my head again.

I put my face down on my arms and say, "I did it," to my knees.

"Did what?" asks Fish.

I lift my head and look at him. The tears come quickly now and I know snot is running out of my nose, but I'm too cold to wipe it away. "I had to have read that text. I knew what it said before the police told me."

Fish looks confused, and maybe a little scared. He rubs my back. The only sound is the splash of the cars echoing off the concrete walls.

"What did it say?"

"Casey wanted to meet at Jacardo's and play pool on Wednesday."

"Huh," says Fish. He takes a long drag of his cigarette. "You any good at pool?"

Just then a police cruiser pulls in behind the bike.

"Shit," says Fish. "It ain't registered."

"What isn't registered?"

"The bike."

"Why isn't it registered?"

"Because I don't drive it anywhere 'cept around Gillam and to the fishin' holes."

"But it has a license plate!"

"Expired," Fish says. He stubs out his cigarette and walks down to the cop who stands behind his bike talking on his radio.

The police officer talks to Fish but keeps looking at me. He walks Fish back to the cruiser, handcuffs him, and puts him in the back. I can't believe they will arrest him for an unregistered bike. I jump up and run down the embankment.

"You can't arrest him just because his bike isn't registered!" I yell.

"I'm not. I'm arresting him for kidnapping and corrupting a minor. I imagine you would be...," he glances down at his notepad, "Jessica Johnson?"

"You can't do this!" I yell and try to open the door. Fish frowns. Shrugs his shoulders. "He didn't do anything!"

The police officer shakes his head and steps between me and the car. Two other cruisers pull in behind us.

"Your parents are very concerned about you," says a female officer. She leads me to one of the other cars and I get in only because I'm freezing. The heat feels wonderful and I hate myself for being glad I'm off the bike because it also means I'll have to go home.

— — —

When we arrive at the police barracks, I demand to know where they've taken Fish.

"That's none of your concern, young lady," says a grandfatherly officer. I give him the finger when he looks the other direction. A social worker and a nurse arrive. They're full of questions.

"Were you being held against your will?"

"No. I asked him to drive me."

"Did Mr. Tanaletti assault you?"

"No. I already told you. We're friends. I asked him for a ride."

"Where was he taking you?"

"He wasn't taking me anywhere."

"Then what are you doing in New Mexico?"

"Trying to get away!"

"From whom?" asks an attractive black woman I didn't see come in. "I'm Detective Aronson. From whom are you trying to get away?"

She's young and has perfect features, like a cop on television.

"Me," I tell her.

"Okay ladies, have we established Ms. Johnson has not been physically harmed?" Detective Aronson looks at the social worker and the nurse.

"I'm not sure," says the nurse.

"She's not been very cooperative," says the social worker.

"Well, give me a few minutes." Detective Aronson nods toward the door, and the women leave.

"Fish did nothing wrong. You can't call it kidnapping if I asked him to drive me."

"Well, you are a minor. So technically it would have been better if he had asked your parents for permission to transport you over state lines."

"Oh God," I wail, "I just keep fucking up everyone's life."

Detective Aronson dials a number and hands me the phone.

"Jess?" It's my mother's frantic voice.

"Hi, Mom."

"Are you all right? Did he hurt you?"

Now she's crying and I can hear Kevin next to her asking to speak to the detective.

"Fish only gave me a ride because I asked him to."

"Thank God you're safe. You'll be home soon. We will get you the help you need. Your father is on his way to get you."

"I don't want him to." I wish she would listen to me. I can tell she's in fix-it mode where she just barks out orders and can't hear anything I say.

"You just need to come home. Then we can sort this out."

"I don't need to come home! I don't want to come home!"

Kevin gets on the phone.

"Hey Jess, your mom's just worried. Let's get you back home safe and then we can talk about what happened."

I hand the phone to the detective. I have to pee and I do not want to talk to Kevin or my mother. I need to find Fish. I have to tell him how sorry I am. God, I am so sick of telling everyone how sorry I am.

36
JESS

I spend the day eating candy bars from the vending machine and watching stupid cable shows muted on the waiting room television. A steady parade of human regret and frustration cycles through the police station.

When Dad arrives, he pulls me into a bear hug and doesn't let go. "Don't you ever do this again." He has tears in his eyes and I feel like a jerk in too many ways.

"You could have come to me," he says, still not letting go.

I shrug him off. There is nothing I can say that will improve this situation, so I sit back down on the bench to wait. Luckily an officer shows up to talk to Dad before he can get all mushy and say shit that he only thinks he means. The officer takes Dad to sign some papers. By the time he comes back, I've fallen asleep upright on the bench.

"Time to go home," he says, squeezing my shoulder. He takes my hand and pulls me to my feet.

"What about Fish?"

"I bailed him out. He can ride his sorry bike back home."

"I'm not leaving him here!"

"Your mom will kill me if I show up with him, too."

I sit back on the bench and cross my arms.

"Jessica, I have just about lost my mind thinking about you alone with Fish for two nights. I'm not sure I can be near him without hurting him right now."

"Well, I'm not leaving without him."

He shakes his head and glares at me, then mutters, "Shit," and goes back to the desk.

Fish doesn't say much as we load his bike in the back of Dad's truck. The drive is ominous. The silence punctuated by the rhythmic slashing of the windshield wipers. With every mile that brings us closer to Jefferson, my chest grows tighter and the lump in my throat grows bigger. We stop for food, but I can't eat.

I watch Dad and Fish eat their burgers. I pick up a salt shaker and slowly empty it on the table, watching the crystals pile up. Finally, Dad breaks the silence.

"So, where were you headed?"

Fish says nothing, just examines his burger. I look at my father and mentally tell him to SHUT UP. He doesn't.

"Well?" he asks.

"Nowhere," I say.

He looks at Fish. "You must have been headed somewhere."

Fish shrugs. "I was just doing what I was told."

When we're back in the truck, Dad says, "Your mom's real upset."

"It wasn't about her."

"This has ripped her up. She would do...." He stops and shakes his head. His voice cracks as he finishes, "She is doing everything for you."

"I didn't ask her to." I can't help it if my mother is a sucker for lost causes.

Fish sighs and leans against the window, his hip pressed against mine. My thoughts wander back to the night before. I lay awake on that filthy mattress for hours trying to figure out how to fix things. That I almost had sex with Fish—with anybody—made me think of Sheila. She tried to get me to get rid of my virginity all last year, picking out guy after guy for me. She teased me about how much I was missing. I don't know what I was waiting for; I guess I just thought it should mean more than bragging rights. I wanted it to matter. Not that sleeping with Fish would have been the right thing either. My life is over. Maybe I was just trying to prove that point. Or maybe I just wanted someone to want me, someone who didn't care what I'd done.

— — —

Dad clears his throat. He has probably been thinking about what he's going to say for the last few silent hours. "Look, there are a lot of people trying to help you."

"I wish they'd stop."

"What is so awful about people wanting to help you?"

"Maybe I don't want their help."

"You've got to stop this. It was an accident, for Christ's sake! You don't even know what happened in that car."

I slam my hand on the dashboard and turned to face him.

"But it wasn't an accident! I hit him! *I* did that! That was no accident!" I want to keep screaming but now I'm sobbing loud, like a little kid. Fish blocks my hands when I reach for the door handle. I have to get out of this truck.

Dad pulls the truck to the shoulder and flips on the hazard lights. He grabs me and hugs me tight. I fight to get free, but he's too strong.

Fish jumps out of the truck. "I'm gonna catch a smoke."

"Let me go! I can't go back there!" I punch Dad's shoulder uselessly.

He holds me tighter and finally, all the fight goes out of me. I cry into his sturdy chest until I have no tears left, then I slump back against the seat, numb. Fish appears at the window and Dad lowers it. Cigarette smoke wafts in the window along with the damp from the cars splashing by.

"Fish, look I don't know what..." Dad says.

"I'm sorry man," says Fish cutting him off. "I shouldn't have given her a ride. But she was pretty torn up."

"I can see that."

Fish takes a drag of his cigarette. "You can beat the shit out of me if you need to," he says dropping his butt and crushing it out with his heel.

"I'm not gonna beat the shit out of you, but once we get back to town, you stay the hell away from my daughter."

"Shit, Jake. You don't gotta be like that."

"Get in the truck."

I want to argue, but I have nothing left. My heart is exhausted.

We pull into the driveway at three in the morning. Mom comes running out and when she sees Fish, she yanks him out of the way and crawls in the cab with me.

"C'mon baby girl," she says and pulls me out of the truck. She holds me so tight I practically trip over her as we walk to the house. For once, I don't mind. I want her to take care of me.

"Thank you," I hear her say to Dad before she shuts the door in his face.

37
LIZ

After Jess is in bed, Jake turns up again.

"You didn't need to come back."

"I did."

"Why?" I ask, but then my tears of exhaustion come, and before I know it Jake is holding me. And then he is kissing me, and I kiss him back, our tears blending. When he leads me toward the bedroom, I stop him. Instead, we go outside and sit on the concrete pad that never became the porch we dreamed it would be. We sit side by side, and I lean my head on his shoulder.

"I'm sorry," he says.

"Why?"

"Just sorry I wasn't here for Jess, more. Sorry I wasn't the dad or husband I should've been."

I put my hand on his knee, and he puts his hand over it. "You did the best you knew. I wasn't such a prize."

"But Jess was perfect," he says.

I nod. "She was."

"She still is," he says.

"How do we make her see that?"

"I don't know," he says. "But I'll do whatever it takes."

I shake my head and look up at the stars. "I feel like we're losing her."

"I'm gonna get my shit together. I broke things off with Amanda. Driving down there, all I could think was, I'm gonna do better. If she's okay, I'm gonna do better."

"It was my fault. I should have been here. I should have picked her up."

"What happened?"

"I was with Avery." I fill him in on leaving Morningside and giving Avery my position. When I tell him I am working for Kevin, he frowns. "She had to get a ride home from school with Casey on Tuesday. If I'd been here..."

"She would have just done it on a different day."

"But she might not have gone so far, been gone so long, been with that... that... boy. Kevin says we can push the DA to press charges if we want."

Jake shakes his head. "Nah, we can't. Fish ain't a bad guy. He's just stupid is all."

"Do you think they had sex?"

"I don't know, but I hope Fish had more than the little bit of sense God gave him."

We sit in silence. His hand still on mine. Finally, he pulls it away. "So, this is serious—this thing with the lawyer?"

"I don't know," I tell him, but I know it is. Kevin has kept me sane over the last thirty-six hours, especially once Jake left to get Jess. I would never have survived it without him. If I had doubts about my feelings for him, they are gone; but I know I have to be here for Jess now. Jess has to be my focus. "It doesn't even matter. What matters now is our daughter. I will not screw up again, I promise."

"You didn't screw up. Besides, I'm the last person to be telling you how to parent." Jake stands up. "I wish things had gone differently."

I think he is talking about the last few days, but it almost feels like he is talking about us.

"Me too," I whisper. He leans down and kisses my forehead. And then he goes inside and lies down on the couch. I call Kevin and tell him Jess is home safe. He offers to come over, but I tell him Jake is here, and I am okay.

— — —

In the morning, Jake and I are having breakfast when Ellen Schultzman shows up.

"I'd like to talk to Jessica," she says.

Jake offers her a seat and I wake Jess.

"Like, here? In our house?" she asks.

I pull her robe from the hook on the bathroom door and toss it to her and she follows me back to the kitchen.

"Good morning," says Ellen. Jess makes a beeline for the coffeepot.

Jess looks at her father, at me, and then at Ellen. "It's not like I need a babysitter."

"No, you don't, but I'm guessing you could use a friend," says Ellen.

Jess puts bread in the toaster.

"I bet you're exhausted," says Ellen.

Jess sits down across from her. She sighs heavily, her every movement and feature colored by teenage annoyance.

"I will not mince words. You have run out of time, and soon you will run out of sympathy. If you don't make an effort, you will fail out of high school. People, teachers, administrators, feel horribly for you. They want to help, but they can't help you if you don't help yourself."

Jake and I look at each other. He tenses, but I put a hand on his arm. Maybe Jess needs some tough love at this point.

"What if I don't want to help myself?" Jess asks.

"I don't believe that. So, here is the deal. I've brought the classwork you have missed the last few days, you can catch up over the weekend. Starting next week, I will expect you to attend all of your classes and then stay after school for Study Buddies."

"I don't need a Study Buddy."

"Maybe not, but I will be there and that way I will know you're working."

Jess says nothing. Her toast pops, and she gets up and puts it on a plate. Ellen sits politely, waiting. Jess carries her toast to the table. She takes a bite and chews. The house is quiet. Just the sound of Jess chewing and the nervous bouncing of Jake's knee.

Finally, Jess speaks. "Why do you care so much?"

Ellen cocks her head and looks at Jess, smiles. "You're a smart young woman with a bright future. I don't want you to give up on that future, so I am not giving up on you." She picks up her jacket, stands up.

"I thought you said I was running out of sympathy," says Jess.

"I don't feel sorry for you. I just like you. I think you will get through this," she says, pulling on her jacket.

Jake gets up and walks Ellen to the door. He follows her outside. Hopefully, he is saying what I am feeling—*thank you, thank you, thank you for caring this much.*

38
JESS

After Ms. Ellen leaves, Mom goes to work and Dad offers to stick around. "Maybe we could go look at some cars," he suggests. I tell him I'm okay and he doesn't need to hang around. I don't tell him he is whacked if he thinks I am getting behind the wheel ever again.

"Maybe I want to," he says.

"It'll be boring, I have to study. Besides, Willard and Homeboy are probably starving."

"They'll live."

"So will I. Go," I tell him.

He gets up to leave. "You scared the shit out of us. Don't do that again, okay?"

He pulls me into a hug. "I love you. I might be an idiot sometimes, but I am here for you."

I can't help but smile. I do love him, but all I can say is, "Thanks."

After he leaves, I go for a long run. It feels good after the day in the truck. I think about how Fish isn't the kind of guy my parents would want me to date. He's actually a guy Sheila would term a 'loser.' But he listened to me. He didn't judge me, which is amazing considering how everyone else judges him. I'm kind of worried about seeing him again. Will he think I still want to have sex? It probably doesn't matter though, because there's no way my dad will ever let me see Fish again.

I run past the Mitchell's house. It looks empty, and there is only one car in the driveway. I slow to a walk. I don't know what I'm looking for. I don't even know why I'm here. One shutter is broken, and there's a path worn in the grass from the front door to the driveway, probably a shortcut made by kids who couldn't bother with the front walk. In the side yard, a tire hangs from a branch, the ground underneath it bare from years of feet skimming the grass away.

After a few minutes, a car comes up the road, slowing as it approaches me, so I sprint off. When I get back to my house, Dylan is sitting on the stoop.

"What are you doing out of school?"

"I'm sick," he deadpans.

"Like crap you are."

"I saw you get home last night, and I wanted to see if you were okay."

"Wow, everyone's all concerned about me today."

Dylan blushes.

"Thanks," I tell him. "Want some lunch?"

"Sure," he says and follows me inside. He sits at the counter while I fix sandwiches.

"So, where did you go?" he asks.

"I just went for a ride."

"Oh."

I guess I owe him the truth. If anyone around here might understand, it would be Dylan.

"Actually, I was leaving. Or trying to. But my dad dragged me back."

"Really?"

I nod and take a bite of my sandwich.

"Where were you going?" Dylan asks.

"I don't know. I just had to get out of here."

"I feel like that sometimes. I only do my homework so I can get into a college that's at least a plane ride away from here."

"Cool."

"Where do you want to go to college?" Dylan asks.

"I don't know if I'll go to college."

"Why wouldn't you go to college? You're smart."

"Depends on whether I can afford it. And if I graduate."

"You'll graduate," Dylan assures me. "You're smart."

Dylan takes off after lunch. "Gotta go play the sick kid for my mom when she gets home at two."

I take a shower and then pull out the work Ms. Ellen left for me. Maybe Dylan has a better plan. Maybe what I need to do is bust my butt in school so I can get into a college far, far away from here. Away from this town that hates me and away from the silent Mitchell house and its sadness. I glance at my running shoes where I kicked them off near the front door. Those shoes might be my only ticket.

— — —

When Mom comes home, I know she has a well-rehearsed lecture prepared. There is no point in trying to make her understand why I need to leave Jefferson. All she cares about is proving Jefferson wrong, proving I'm not guilty. But I'm not so sure. I mean, I was behind the wheel. I know what that text said. The car hit Coach Mitchell. How can I not be guilty? Besides, there is no place for me here anymore. I will always be a snag in the fabric of this town. People might be polite, but they will always know. They'll whisper to newcomers, "That's the girl who killed Coach Mitchell." The accident will never be over.

When we sit down to dinner, Mom says, "I wish I'd known how unhappy you were. I wish you'd talked to me."

"I'm sorry," I say and hand her the salad bowl.

She looks up. She expects a protest, an excuse, something, but she isn't ready for my apology.

"Well, I'm not happy about you leaving with that kid from the trailer park, either."

"I know. Bad choice. Sorry," I say and concentrate on buttering my bread.

"Are you just saying what you think I want to hear so you won't have to hear what I have to say?"

It's impossible not to smile. "Sort of."

She glares at me, but she's teasing.

"I *am* sorry. I didn't mean to make you worry. I thought it might be better if I left."

When I say this, she drops her fork. "Jessica, it will never be better if you leave," she says through tears. "Ever."

Sometimes it's hard for people to accept what's best for them. It's like when Mom had to have our cat put down. I begged her not to, but she knew the cat was dying. She didn't want her to suffer. It was the best thing to do, only I couldn't see that.

39
LIZ

Jess seems almost angry when I tell her I am working for Kevin. I tell her it is temporary; I don't want her to think it has anything to do with the accident, but I doubt I am fooling her.

"I'm curious about paralegal work and Morningside allowed me to take a leave of absence. Avery is filling in for me."

"That makes zero sense," she says. "You love old people."

"Well, maybe I'll love this more!" I tell her in as cheery a voice as I can muster.

"I'm not that stupid," she says but I pretend I don't hear her.

The work at Kevin's is easy—answering the phone, greeting clients, opening the mail. He gets a few calls from MADD, the group from Dallas, but he always tells me to take a message. He says there is no point in talking to them. There are letters too, some from MADD, but others from people right here in Jefferson. Letter after letter. I have opened a few since many are addressed to me or Jess, care of Kevin's law office.

The letters in one form or another say he shouldn't defend Jess. That she should go to jail. That the law needs to change. They are right about the law needing to change, but they don't know Jess. Their judgment strikes at my heart. One letter was from a mother whose child was killed while texting and driving, her pain was so palpable it clung to my hands after I had folded the letter back up. For a brief moment, I imagined if Jess had died in the accident, that she had struck a tree or another car, but the thought of it took my breath. I stopped opening the letters after that.

— — —

A month passes with no plea offer. Jess and I have found a truce. Jess keeps to herself, does her school work, even helps out more at home. She does not mention the trial. Her solemnness worries me.

Jake is all he said he would be. He comes to see Jess every chance he gets. He is here most weekend nights, usually with pizza, and he and Jess watch movies. I try to give them that time and find things to do, like meeting Avery for drinks or a movie. Sometimes I go to her house and help her with Curtis and her mom. I find it oddly comforting to watch cartoons with Curtis. We sit side by side on the couch and he rocks back and forth, laughing joyously each time the roadrunner tricks the coyote. Sometimes he will turn to me and smile as if he is saying, "See?" And his smiles and laughter are genuine every time, even though it is the same set of movies over and over. Any minor change in Curtis' routine can take weeks to make, but if you follow the prescribed order of activities, he is happy. In some ways, it seems like Curtis has it easier than the rest of us. His joy is simple and predictable. I help Avery prepare Curtis for bed. Her mother needs help too, and I do whatever I can, although many times that means simply offering company and sympathy. Each time I leave, I am astonished at the load she carries.

Working with Kevin every day has given me a greater appreciation for him. He is respectful with everyone, the philandering husbands who claim their shrill wives drove them to it, the weepy women who sit on his couch and pour out the contents of their broken hearts, even the clients who arrive angry and blame him when he explains how the system prevents them from taking every penny from their soon-to-be ex-spouse. The dismantling of so many marriages should make him jaded and skeptical, but he is earnest in his pursuit of me. For weeks we have kept things chaste and danced around the idea of sleeping together. It is a commitment I am not ready to make or ask for.

It would be so easy to fall into him. Let him take care of me. Take care of Jess. It is clear he wants to, and I am tempted to let him be the white knight and me the helpless princess. But I need to rescue myself. If not for me, then for Jess. I cannot give in to whatever this is that is happening with Kevin. Not now. Jess is too important. When I try to tell him as much over yet another dinner together at a restaurant I can't afford, he protests.

"I care about Jess, too," he says. "Why are you being with me and taking care of her exclusive?"

"They're not. I just can't do this right now. I need to focus on her. I wish I'd met you sooner."

"You did," he points out.

He is right and I wish when I met him years ago at Morningside, I had given him the chance he deserved. I wish our relationship was not tainted by Jess' accident. I am so grateful for all he is doing for Jess and I have to wonder—is this just the patient falling in love with the doctor?

"I need to focus on Jess, now. I can't get distracted by whatever this is," I say, waving my hand back and forth between us.

He takes my hand in his, runs his thumb across my palm, sending shivers through me. "Let's just take it slow. I'm in no hurry. I'm not going anywhere. I'll be here no matter what happens."

"You're amazing, you know that, right?"

He grimaces, uncomfortable with my flattery, but he *is* amazing. More than I deserve.

— — —

Thanksgiving is a small affair; Jess and I have an early dinner with Avery and her family, then we stay for the rest of the day. Jess plays with Kimba, and I watch cartoons with Curtis while her mother naps. Avery drives down to the state prison to visit Kimba's father.

"Don't even say it," she says when she returns. I still cannot fathom her devotion to a man who does not reciprocate it, even when confined behind bars.

Spending my days with Kevin tests my ability to keep things platonic. Most days he buys lunch and brings it back to the office to eat with me. I pack my lunch, still counting all my pennies. We talk about a lot of things, but the tension between us is distracting. My body operates on a different level around him—it is as if there is a magnetic pull that I spend my days resisting. He is kind and funny and so very smart. He diligently builds his case for Jess, and in so doing is stealing my heart.

The holidays come before we know it. We go to Christmas Eve services with Avery to see Kimba sing in the Cherub Choir. When we get home, we Skype with Kate. Dad's condition doesn't change, and Kate, thankfully, doesn't press me to decide about moving him.

We struggle to find our footing, resume a life that is the same, and yet completely different. The MADD people have come to town a few times, mostly trying to drum up anger. I brace myself and insist Jess stay in when I know they are around.

"No sleepovers?" Jake asks one night when I am home early after dinner with Kevin.

"It's not like that," I tell him, but I know the only reason it is not is Jess.

— — —

Finally, in the first week of the new year, the district attorney offers another plea agreement. It is not what we hoped for. They refuse to budge on jail time. Jake picks up Jess and brings her to the office to meet with Kevin. We sit in the conference room at the enormous table that takes up the entire room but puts space between arguing spouses. I pull water bottles from the fridge, and we crowd around one corner of the enormous table. Kevin explains the deal they have offered. He has been unsuccessful in arguing them down very far.

"Why are they so insistent she go to jail?"

Kevin shakes his head. "I imagine it's political. That's probably why they've waited so long to start these proceedings. They wanted to see whether the public reaction would die down."

The public reaction has not died down. If anything, it has amped up. The MADD people are like a mob who want Jess' head. I have taken to shopping a few towns over and ordering anything I can online. Someone regularly dumps their trash can on our front lawn. Jake sat out there every night for a week after it first started, but the culprit didn't come back. The first night he wasn't there, the trash was back.

"I find it hard to believe that one man's political ambitions will dictate my daughter's future." The entire experience has taught me that our legal system is not nearly as fair and just as we believe it is.

There will be a pretrial conference in one week and Jess will enter her plea. The prosecution will drop all the charges if Jess pleads guilty to criminally negligent homicide and goes to jail for 180 days (the minimum) and we pay a fine of $10,000.

"It's not a bad offer," says Kevin. "I can try to argue down the jail time, see if some of it could be served in house arrest."

"It already feels like we live in house arrest."

"What will happen at the pretrial conference?" Jess asks.

"It will be relatively informal. We will meet with the DA in front of a judge, he will ask if we have come to an agreement. If we have, the DA will explain that to the judge. If we haven't, charges will be read again, and then you'll enter a plea."

"She'll plead not-guilty," Jake says.

Kevin turns to Jess now. "It's up to you, Jess, not your parents."

Her eyes give away her terror, but she says nothing. Kevin keeps saying it is up to Jess, but it is obvious he thinks she should plead guilty. With only Sheila's account of the accident, he worries that no judge will believe she isn't guilty.

Jess asks, "If I plead guilty, will it be over?"

"Well, it depends on what you mean by over. If we take their deal, the judge will look over the deal and agree to it or not."

"What do you think he'll say?"

"I have no idea, but likely he will do what the DA recommends." He sets his elbows on the table, steeples his fingers, and looks at Jess. "But here's the thing. If you plead guilty and we make a statement of some sort—about your exemplary record, your remorse, maybe the judge will go easy. But if you plead not guilty and at the trial, she decides you are guilty, the judge might not be so easy."

"What are you saying?" I ask him. "You think she should plead guilty?" I try to read his face—does he think I am foolish to believe my daughter is not responsible for Robert Mitchell's death? But causing a death and being responsible for a death aren't necessarily the same thing, are they? Isn't an accident, just that—an accident? No one meant for this to happen, no matter what happened. It is clear, though, from the radio talk shows, the messages on my phone, the notes left under my windshield wiper, and the trash on our lawn, that this town holds Jess responsible. They are just waiting for a judge to officially lay the blame on her.

"I'm just saying it's an option." He leans back, adjusts his dress pants when they pull at the knee, doesn't look at me. "I told you early on that a case like this would be wide of my area of expertise. If we go to trial, you would probably be better off with different representation."

Jake acts like he doesn't hear Kevin.

"If Jess don't remember what happened, I don't think she can plead guilty. That makes no sense."

While I agree with him, I also see what Kevin has been trying to tell us for the last few months. We need a different lawyer. A lawyer we cannot afford. And beyond the money, I also understand what Kevin's saying. There is a good case for getting this over with. Jess needs to salvage what is left of her high school years instead of letting this case steal them. In all likelihood, it already has, no matter which way this thing goes.

"Can you just plead for me? Do I have to be there?" asks Jess.

"You have to be there. And no, I can't enter your plea. It's up to you."

It seems like the only thing in this entire situation that is up to Jess is how she pleads and neither of her options is good.

"Pleading guilty and taking this deal doesn't mean you are," I say and realize the ridiculousness of my statement as I say it.

"But she's not guilty, so why would she say she was?" asks Jake again.

Jess sits up. "I must be. Everybody says I did it. Sheila says I did."

Jake frowns, mutters, "Sheila says a lot of things."

"Well, it's not like an alien took over my body and drove my car. Just because I don't remember doesn't mean I didn't do it."

Nothing is decided. Kevin tells Jess to think about it and Jake takes Jess shoe shopping for new running shoes and spikes. I know he just wants to distract her. Like me, he wants to believe there will be a track season, that Jess will not miss it because she is in jail. I hug Jess, but it is like wrapping my arms around a board. "See you at home," I tell her.

40
JESS

I can almost see the question hanging in the air—a gray thought bubble with my entire future in it. The moment goes on impossibly long.

The courtroom for our pretrial conference is dark and foreboding, with lots of dark paneling. The rain outside lends an ominous air. The judge has explained the charges to me and now everyone is waiting for me to tell them whether I did this. But I don't know if I did. The conversation in Kevin's office yesterday felt like a poker game—everyone hedging, trying not to tell me what to do while telling me what to do, and then saying over and over that it's up to me. Which it is. Right now.

Pleading guilty would be the smart thing to do. When Kevin pulled me aside this morning after my parents were seated, I told him I would. It makes sense. Then I can just be the bad guy, everyone can hate me, the MADD women can go back to Dallas, I go to jail or whatever, end of story. I no longer have to be this person no one knows what to say to or how to deal with. There will be no need to defend myself to anyone. They can all be right—the kids at school, the MADD women, the person who keeps throwing trash on our lawn, and Sheila.

I know Mom and Dad don't want me to plead guilty. They don't want me to take a felony charge with me when I finally leave Jefferson. Mom says it will hamstring my future as if I still have a future. They don't want to believe I could have done this, but every day it seems clearer that I did. Mom keeps saying to trust her, to trust the process, to trust Kevin. But of those three things, she is the only one I trust. I have absolutely zero faith that my mom can figure a way out of this, but in all my life she's the only person I've ever been able to count on. I know that recently we haven't exactly agreed about a lot of things. She wants me to be her, but *not* be her. She wants me to be the exemplary student, the happy, joiner girl she was. I've seen the pictures—she was in every club, every cause, everywhere at Jefferson High. She wants me to be the girl she was, but not the girl who slept with some guy and got pregnant. Not that girl. Not the girl who made her dad so angry he moved away and still doesn't talk to her. Not the girl who didn't take the scholarship ticket out of town, who instead stayed here and had a baby and then had a divorce and now works with old people who can't remember what they had for lunch, let alone what she might have been.

I look at the judge. She's staring at me over her glasses, eyebrows raised, pen in hand. Kevin whispers, "Jess, you need to answer."

I glance back at mom in her suit and nylons; her face implores me to speak, to deny that I did this. She is holding Dad's hand, and he is all cleaned up, no remnants of his trailer park life clinging to him. He winks at me and smiles like I'm in a school play or something instead of about to confess to killing or not killing the coach he's looked up to all his life. All those years when I was little, I tried to be good, so they would get back together and now I do something seriously bad and they're finally getting along. Go figure.

The Mitchells are here today because they believe that this is the end. They have come to see me locked up. The parking lot was jammed with the crazy MADD people and reporters. If I can just tell them all I'm guilty, then they can put this one in the books. They can say, *"See? She was texting and driving. She killed Coach. It was her fault."*

I can't look at Helen Mitchell, so I turn back around and face the judge.

"Not guilty," I tell her.

41
LIZ

"It really may come down to what Sheila says. It will be hard to refute as long as Jess can't remember what happened. We can say we don't think she'd text and drive all we want, but when the only eyewitness says otherwise..."

Ever since the pretrial conference, Kevin has been different. He is working hard on the case, but he also seems scared. And that scares me. We spend every waking minute together, even though we cover the same ground every time.

"Sheila's lying," I say.

"Even if she's lying and I can cast some doubt on her, we don't have another logical explanation. Jess was driving."

He is right; I know.

"I will do all I can to paint Jess as a good kid and to muddy the waters of what might have happened, but I'm just being honest here. I told you I'm out of my league."

I touch his arm. "And I appreciate all you're doing for us."

We both look at my hand on his arm. Every time we touch there is electricity. I can't deny that, and I am certain if what we were discussing was not how to keep my daughter out of prison there is no doubt where all this flirting and conspiring and time together would lead.

"Just dinner," I tell him every time he asks me out. And when he invites me to his house, as he always does, I tell him I can't, but sometimes I think, "I can't—yet." Avery says I am just being cruel, but I have had unplanned sex turn my life on its end once, I can't do it again. If I sleep with Kevin, it will be after careful consideration.

"That's boring as shit, you know," she teases.

"That's me, though, boring as shit."

She laughs. "Don't I know it. Your job is too." She says that but I know she is enjoying the position and she is good at it.

It would be too easy to let my relationship with Kevin become all-consuming, but right now Jess is my priority. There is no room in my life or my heart for him. I hope there will be someday I tell him, and I hope when that day comes he will still want me. Every time I try to explain this, it comes out wrong.

One night in frustration I say, "Maybe if you had a child, you'd understand."

He looks at me long and hard, and I brace myself for the words I deserve, but he looks away, tells me I am probably right.

I know Kevin can only be patient for so long. It is not that I'm not interested; I assure him; I am more than interested and each time he kisses me goodnight, it takes all my willpower to get out of his car and walk back into my house. I assure him I just need more time, but mostly I don't go to his place because I am afraid if I go to Kevin's beautiful home I will want to stay. I will want what he is offering—security, love, an escape. We talk about everything, but what we don't talk about is what will happen if they send Jess to jail. I can't entertain the possibility. It has only been a week since the pretrial conference when Kevin says, "Jess doesn't want there to be an appeal."

"Why would there be an appeal?"

"If they find her guilty."

"But they won't."

He sighs. "It's possible they will."

"Then there has to be an appeal. She just doesn't understand."

"Actually, it's not up to you."

We are sitting in a restaurant near the office. It is a rare lunch date for us. Kevin insisted. I pick up my water glass and fish out an ice cube, place it in my mouth. He watches me. I look away.

"I'll talk to her."

"And there's something else."

I raise my eyebrows, clutch the ice cube between my teeth, say nothing.

"The Mitchells are exploring a civil suit."

I gasp involuntarily, and the ice cube lodges in my throat. I try to cough it out and finally do, but now my eyes water and I can't speak.

Kevin tells me he has already spoken to my insurance company, but it doesn't look like they will be a whole lot of help. Jake and I bought insurance from a local outfit years ago because it was all we could afford. We have never given a thought to our coverage. Every time the price went up, we dropped another benefit and raised our deductible to keep it affordable.

"Some of the fine print also gets the company off the hook if they charge Jess with a felony."

"Of course it does," I whisper. Panic threatens to engulf me, and I try to picture myself sitting beside Curtis, rocking back and forth. I am the roadrunner, running in thin air, moments from smacking into reality. I barely listen as Kevin says he is hopeful he can get them to take part in a settlement if it comes to that.

"Let's not worry about that until we have to," he says, but I feel the cliff disappearing beneath my feet.

42
JESS

Mom and Kevin are together all the time, but whenever I ask her what's up with that, she says, "We're just friends." Only it's clear they are way more than friends. Friends don't make such an effort to assure everyone they are 'just friends.'

"Are we finished?"

"For now," says Kevin. He has just finished asking again about Sheila. I don't know why he is obsessed with Sheila. I told him, once more, that she's lying, but maybe he doesn't believe me.

We're sitting in the living room. Kevin looks at Mom, and she nods. I groan and look away. For people who are 'just friends' they sure act like a couple.

"I know you're opposed to an appeal, but if things don't go the way we hope, there's an argument for appealing. If Sheila is lying..."

"She is lying," I remind him.

"Well, lies tend to unravel over time."

"Or maybe she will come to her senses," Mom interjects.

"She might not be able to keep up the pretense through an appeal."

"You don't know Sheila," I tell them. "She always wins."

I get up and leave them there to make googly eyes at each other. I don't want to think about Sheila or the trial that is a little more than a month away now.

A little while later, Mom knocks on my door. "Jess? I'm going to dinner with Kevin. You want to come?"

"No."

"Can we bring you something back?"

"No," I tell her. I shouldn't be angry. She has a right to this. I get that. I have seriously screwed up our lives; I really can't begrudge her being with Kevin. Even if he is a serious dork. I don't think she's nice to him only because of me anymore. I think she might be in love with him, which is totally inconvenient now that Dad is back in our lives.

"I won't be late."

After they go, I make myself a peanut butter sandwich and work on my English homework. It's an essay about one of the three novels we've read so far this school year. I'm writing about Holden Caulfield. I like him, even though I know he has problems. He doesn't operate in reality. And he expects way too much of people. People disappoint you. I could have told him that. I remember the moment I figured that out as a kid. I was all hopped up about going to see the latest Harry Potter movie and Dad had promised to get tickets for opening night. I bragged to all my friends I was going. And then he forgot. "We can go see it next weekend," he told me and didn't understand why I was upset. That was only the beginning, though. Dad is an Olympian when it comes to disappointers. So I get Holden's frustration with the adults in his life.

— — —

The next few weeks are a blur of homework and training and helping Dad design the screened-in porch. He has this crazy idea that he and I can finally build the porch-that-never-was, as mom has always referred to the concrete pad on the back of the house.

My birthday happens, and Mom and Dad try to make a big deal of me turning seventeen. We celebrate with a cake, and Aunt Kate sends me movie passes. I take Dylan to see a horror movie, and we scream like girls and throw popcorn at the screen. It's probably the best night I've had in months.

— — —

January 25 is the first meeting for track; my stomach is in knots all day. It's not actual practice, just an organizational meeting. The coach will hand out paperwork, give us a preseason workout plan, and we'll elect a captain. When I walk into the gym for the meeting, only a few students are hanging around on the bleachers. Coach Fines looks alarmed when he sees me and says, "Jess, can you come to my office for a minute?"

I follow him to his office, wondering if he will ask me to run for captain this year. He closes the door.

"Here's the thing. There's some concern about you representing the school this spring."

"What do you mean?"

"I don't agree, but the school board thinks until after the trial, it would be best if you weren't on the team."

"What?" I blink away shocked tears. "But I've been training."

"If it was up to me, you know what I'd say. We need your speed. This just came to my attention today."

I shake my head. This can't be happening. I stare at him, holding back tears. I don't want to cry in front of the coach, but if I can't run for Jefferson, I don't have a chance at a scholarship. I will be trapped here forever.

"Hopefully, next year it'll work out."

"But I need to compete this year. This is the year colleges look at for scholarships."

Coach Fines sighs. "I will speak to the school board, but it doesn't sound as if they'll change their minds."

"I have to run, Coach." I feel the tears starting.

"Believe me, I want you to. But for now, you'll have to sit it out. I'm sorry. I've got to get the meeting started."

Coach Fines walks with me to the door of the gym. No one says anything, but I know everyone is watching me. I can't look at any of them, so I don't know if their looks are pity or condemnation.

"It'll work out, Jess. I'm sure it will," Coach Fines assures me.

The door closes behind me with a hollow thud. I slam both my hands against it so hard I yelp in pain. And then I run, sprinting away from the school. Tears streak into my ears. My backpack bounces against my back. My lungs burn. Finally, I slow to a walk. It is four miles to my house. I try to adjust the shoulder straps, cursing at the nylon as it twists in the buckles. Finally, I throw the whole damn backpack on the gravel at the side of the road and sit down on top of it.

"AGGGGHHHHH!" I yell as loud as I can. I cover my face with my hands and sob until I have nothing left. Cars pass, but I don't care what it looks like.

"I'M TRAPPED HERE FOREVER!" I yell to the sky.

A small car pulls to the side of the road. I don't acknowledge it. I don't want anyone to help me.

"Jess?"

I look up and it's Casey. I laugh out loud. My most humiliating moment and who should witness, but Casey Miller. Figures. I put my head down. I can't look at him.

Casey sits down beside me. "I heard about the track team."

I snort. "Great. I'm sure the entire school knows by now."

"It's not fair."

"Doesn't matter," I mutter into my arms.

"Yes, it does! They can't do this. I don't even think it's legal. You need a lawyer."

"I have one."

"Oh, yeah. Well, you should talk to him about this."

"You really think it'll matter?"

"You want to run, don't you? It's worth trying."

I raise my head and look at Casey. "Thanks," I say. Finally, a glimmer of light.

"You want a ride?" Casey stands and extends a hand. He pulls me to my feet and grabs my backpack.

43
LIZ

"I waited at the school for thirty minutes. Everyone had left!"

My relief at finding Jess at home gives way to fury. All the scenarios that flashed through my mind as I raced home, slink away to the far corners of my mind for another day. I should probably call Kevin and thank him. He was the one who told me to come home and see if she was here before calling the police.

"Oh crap, Mom, I'm sorry. I got a ride."

"I saw Coach Fines, and he told me what happened. I was scared to death. I didn't know where you had gone. You couldn't have called me?"

Jess points at her phone on the counter. "It's dead. I think it needs a new battery."

"Next time borrow someone else's!"

She nods sheepishly and turns back to the pasta sauce she is cooking. I go to my room to change out of my work clothes and call Kevin, but he doesn't answer. I text him to tell him Jess is here. He texts me back, "K," but doesn't call.

Lately, he seems preoccupied. I wonder if he is having second thoughts about how he feels about me. To be fair, Kevin's been caught up in a crazy civil trial between two of his former clients and they have been monopolizing his time, competing for his opinion. He has also been meeting with Jill about some legal matters. He is very vague about it, but clearly, it upsets him. When he hangs up after talking to her, he seems distant and distracted.

Sometimes he almost seems jealous of Jake. We were having a rare lunch together, and I told him about Jake finally getting wifi service at his garage and how some of the guys who hang out there thought that was 'high faluttin.'

He laughed and said, "You and Jake seem to be getting along a lot better these days. He's at the house a lot."

"I don't know why it took a disaster to bring us together, but I think it's helping Jess."

He nodded and didn't say any more, but something hung in the air, an awkwardness that neither of us acknowledged. I didn't want to accuse him of being jealous, because he had no reason to be, and he probably didn't want to admit to being jealous, so we sipped our water and examined our menus. Eventually, the waitress turned up, and we moved on, but it still felt like Jake was there at the table with us for the entire lunch hour.

When I return to the kitchen, the table is set, and Jess dumps pasta in the strainer. We have been sharing the cooking duties since I started working at Kevin's. It has been a nice change, even if on her nights we always have one variation or another of pasta.

"It's horrible what they did. Coach Fines said he doesn't think it's fair. Apparently, it was a couple of members of the school board who say they're looking out for Jefferson's reputation. It never seems to end." I know she is upset at not being allowed to run this season, but part of me is grateful she will not be such a public target.

Jess sets a plate of spaghetti in front of me and sits down with her own. I scan her face for the devastation I expect to see. She doesn't look upset as much as determined. She adjusts her utensils, takes a gulp of water. "How are you doing?" I venture. Talking to her about the case is a landmine of late. I am never sure if she needs me to be a sounding board or a punching bag.

She stabs at her spaghetti. "Do you think Kevin can help me?"

"Of course, he can," I say. Is she doubting him?

She waves her fork. "Not with the case, with the school board."

I frown. "Why would he get involved in that?"

"The school board has no right to kick me off the team. There is no rule about it. I checked the school handbook."

I sigh and look at her, fork poised, spaghetti twirled, so hopeful. I don't want to call Kevin. He has enough on his plate, and I am tired of asking him to save the day. "I can't ask him for help right now. He's overwhelmed at work and he's done enough for us already."

"You can at least ask him. Let him decide if he wants to help."

"I can't ask him to get involved with the school board. I'll talk to the principal, see what I can do."

"You can't fix this! The school board will not listen to you! I need a lawyer, not a mom!"

"Did you not just hear me tell you I can't ask him to get involved? I need you to drop this. I'm not dragging Kevin into our mess once again."

"That's what I am, right, a mess?" she shrieks before jumping up from the table and racing for her room.

I know I should follow her, comfort her, but I am all out. Racing home from her school, certain she had left again has emptied me of motherly compassion, so I call Kate.

"What should I do?"

"Well, the first thing I would do is call Kevin."

"But I don't want to drag him into this. He's done enough."

"Jess is right. She needs a lawyer, not a mom right now. If you look at it from her perspective, the entire world is out to get her. Don't be another person out to get her. Just be ready to catch her if she falls."

"How come even though you've never been a parent, you always know what I should do?"

She laughs. "Long-distance parenting is easy. And it helps that my only responsibilities are to my landlord and my kitty."

After I hang up, I call Kevin, and he is furious.

"Why didn't you call me sooner? It's nearly nine. Okay, let me see if I can get something over there first thing in the morning."

"I'm sorry," I say.

"For what?"

"For once again asking you to help us."

"Liz," he says, softly. "I *want* to help you. When will you accept that? I'm not doing this out of obligation or because I expect anything. I am doing this because I like Jess. She's a good kid. And this is wrong. Get some sleep. I'll take care of this."

"Kevin?"

"Yes?"

I don't know how to ask this, but I need to know. "You've done so much for us, and you keep doing more and more and more."

He says nothing, so I plow on. "I'm grateful, beyond grateful, and I know you say you're doing this for your dad or Jess or me, but what do I do for you?"

"Liz," he says, and I can hear a smile soften his voice.

"I'm serious. I take and take and take, but what am I giving? Secretarial help? I just feel like a needy jerk and I think soon you will get tired of me."

"I won't get tired of you."

"Yes, you will. I get tired of me."

He laughs softly. "You make me better."

"You've said that before, but it makes no sense."

"All my life I've been surrounded by people who have everything. Heck, I've had everything. And I never appreciated it. I just grabbed for more. I didn't think about the people I walked over or the people who never had what I've had. They were suckers there for the plucking. And then you were so kind to my dad, and you weren't impressed by my cases or suits or success. And now, you still aren't. You ask me about my mother even though you've never met her and you miss my father with me. You remember the names of my clients. Heck, you don't even have to re-read their files before they come in because you know the details. You know which woman is broken-hearted because she's going to lose her dog in the divorce. You know who they are, not just what they need. And that is amazing. I watch you and I want to be better. I want to care. I want to be the kind of man you'll fall in love with."

I am crying as I listen and when he stops, I'm afraid to speak. I love this man. I do. If ever there was a time to tell him, it is this moment. And yet I don't. I hold it back.

"Are you still there?" he asks.

"Yes."

"Does that answer your question?"

"Yes."

"Good. I'm going to hang up now, I've got to get a letter ready for the school board."

"Thank you," I tell him, but it comes out a whisper. I hang up and walk outside. I look up at the stars.

"I love you," I tell the darkness.

— — —

In the morning, Jess pours herself a cup of coffee and sits down beside me. I have already talked to Kevin. I know the school board will be served this morning with papers Kevin has been up half the night preparing. I can't wait to tell her, but before I can say a word, she speaks.

"I know," she says.

"What do you know?" I pick up my coffee cup and lean forward.

"I know I can't ask Kevin to get me out of this. He's already helped me enough." She picks at the Formica where it's coming away from the corner of the table.

"That's what you don't know," I say.

She stops picking and looks up.

"Kevin Sharp is such a good man that he's already sent a letter to that stupid school board, threatening them with a lawsuit if they don't allow you to be on the team."

"Wow."

"I know. Wow."

She smiles and gets up to leave, but then she comes back and plants a kiss on the top of my head. "I love you," she says.

"Not as much as I love you," I tell her.

44
LIZ

The board members sit around a horseshoe table, matching laptops propped open and complimentary water bottles scattered in front of them. Ellen sits with Coach Fines at a table labeled *Staff and Administration* facing the horseshoe. We sit behind them–Jess, Jake, Kevin, and me. A smattering of parents, plus two student representatives, are also present.

I hold Kevin's hand. He is coiled anger. I have never seen him like this.

"It's just bullshit," he has said again and again during the day when the subject came up.

I hold his elbow as if I can contain him. He seems like a tiger ready to pounce. On the drive over he recited all the ways the school board is violating Jess' constitutional rights. It is a new side of him I have not seen. He is really pissed off, and I can't help but be grateful.

Jess whispers in my ear, "I'm beginning to understand what you see in him. It's kind of nice you have a shark-lawyer for a boyfriend."

I scowl at her. "He's not my boyfriend."

"If you say so."

Inside, I smile. I don't know why it makes me so happy that Jess likes the idea. *Kevin is my boyfriend. That is my boyfriend right there, the handsome lawyer who is about to explain the law to you idiots.* Jake sees me smiling and gives me a questioning look. I shake my head, set my face back to neutral.

The meeting is gaveled to order, and the board president introduces the board members who each smile in acknowledgment. I have never seen any of them before. They are mostly older people—too old to have children in school. Then the president tells us the proceedings will be live on the district's cable channel and they do not allow questions or comments unless they have been previously scheduled. He talks to us like we are three-year-olds. Then he turns back to the people sitting around the horseshoe.

"We're meeting tonight to discuss the action we took last week at our monthly meeting. At that time we decided to bar a student facing felony charges from participating on our track team."

When he says this, Kevin stands up quickly and raises his hand. The President glances at him but continues.

"The student has been informed of our decision and has retained legal counsel with the intention of suing the board and the district in the amount of ten million dollars if not allowed to participate on the track team."

Kevin clears his throat loudly and continues standing, hand upraised, like a dutiful student.

Finally, the president sighs heavily and looks at Kevin. He speaks in a tight voice that makes it clear he is pissed.

"We do not permit the public to comment on these proceedings unless previously scheduled. You are here only as a courtesy."

"I understand that, but I thought the board should remember that Jessica is innocent until proven guilty and barring her from the team would violate her constitutional rights."

"Again, this isn't in order. I must ask you to sit down."

"I have made the press aware of the situation," Kevin says nodding to a man seated behind us. I had no idea he had invited a reporter. He told me he didn't want the press involved. He didn't want to do anything that might stir up public reaction so close to our trial date.

"Please sit down sir, or I'll have to ask you to leave."

Kevin sits down. "Idiots," he mutters.

"That's bullshit," says Jake, loud enough for everyone to hear him.

Another board member clicks on her microphone.

"Mr. Chairman, I propose the board go into a closed session to deal with this matter."

The president and the board members look visibly relieved. "All in favor?" he asks. It is unanimous.

"We ask everyone other than faculty and administration to leave," he says triumphantly.

As we get up to leave, Ellen turns to us. "I'm so sorry about this," she says.

"It's not your fault, Ellen," I tell her and we leave.

— — —

When we get home, I make coffee. Kevin and I sit at the kitchen table. Jess turns on the TV. Jake sits with her and watches a sit-com.

Kevin scrolls through his phone looking at his email, but occasionally he blurts out comments like, "It's ridiculous this is taking them so long," or "They're just trying to figure out how to cover their butts because we could still sue them for defamation of character." I touch his hand each time and give him a knowing look while nodding in Jess' direction. He goes back to his e-mail. More than once, I catch Jake watching us. I pretend to read my book.

"Who was that guy behind us?" I ask Kevin. "Was he from the paper? I didn't know you'd contacted them."

Kevin looks confused for a moment. "Oh, him? No idea."

— — —

An hour later, my phone rings. It is Ellen. Jess clicks off the TV. Jake comes into the kitchen, takes off his ball cap.

"Excellent news! The board rescinded its earlier decision. Jessica can return to track for now," Ellen says.

"That's great news!"

"And could you tell Jess how sorry I am she had to go through this? I feel like everything with her is two steps forward, three steps back."

I glance at Jess. "Yes, I'll tell her. Thank you so much for your part in this."

"Oh, I didn't do much. I think bringing a lawyer into it was the key. Everyone's afraid of money."

I thank her again and hang up.

"So they reversed their decision?" Kevin asks.

"Bunch of idiots," says Jake. He puts his ball cap back on.

"Of course they did. They know they'd be liable if they didn't," says Kevin.

"But at least they did," I say. I am relieved and happy and so very grateful to this man who has once again rescued my daughter. I look to the living room, but Jess has already gone to her room.

"I'm gonna head home," says Jake. He turns to Kevin and extends his hand. They shake and Jake says, "Thanks, man."

"Happy to help," says Kevin.

After Jake leaves and Jess goes to bed, I ask Kevin, "If Jess is found guilty, will they bar her from the team?"

"If that happens, track will probably be the last thing on her mind."

"But you don't think they'll send her to jail?"

He hesitates a moment too long before saying, "I'm doing everything I know to do to keep that from happening." He looks defeated as he says this, but I need to believe that he can save her. That he can save us. What if he can't?

Kevin says, "I guess I better get going."

I take his hand and walk with him to the door. Before he opens it, I stop him.

"What?" he asks.

I put my arms around him and press myself into his chest, breathing him in. "Thanks," I murmur into his shirt. "For everything you're doing for Jess, for me."

He cradles my cheek in his hand. Then he kisses me softly, slowly on the lips, and says, "I just hope it's enough."

45
JESS

I still expect the phone to ring and it to be Sheila asking me to go get our nails done at Sylvie's. We did an experiment in Chemistry to test how fast liquids evaporate. Nail polish remover was fastest, water second, and vinegar last. My friendship with Sheila, Jamie, and Kayla was more like nail polish remover than vinegar. Gone in moments, even though we'd been friends for years. I guess they were never real friends. I thought Sheila was different, though; I thought that was real.

I still don't understand why she said what she did or sent that awful email, but I've tried to accept that they were things she needed to do to prove to everybody, or maybe just Jason (they're still together) that she had nothing to do with Coach's death. I know I should hate her (Dylan says he would), but I can't. Even after everything.

Kevin says it will be her word against mine at the trial. Which means I'll lose because Sheila never loses, plus I have no idea what really happened. Whenever I say that he gets angry. I know he wants to win the case and save the day and get the girl (my mom), but I'm pretty sure that's not what's going to happen.

It's the first Sunday of February. The month of the trial. Twenty-four more days. It's barely dawn as I take off on a run. I love the power of my legs propelling me, carrying me out of my head, away from my life. On the silent streets, the world seems kinder, softer somehow. It doesn't seem possible that in three more weeks I could lose this easy freedom. A judge could put me in jail. Mom is freaked by the idea; Kevin says it won't happen, but I'm coming to terms with it. I think it's just this that I will miss—this time of day when the world is mine and no one else exists and the only thing I can hear is my breath blowing hard. Track is the only good thing in my life at this point. Maybe I won't ever get to run a race this year, but damn if I won't be ready.

I loop back for my last mile and pass the Mitchell's house. It looks like it always does except that tennis balls polka-dot the lawn and there's a bright red dog bowl near the porch. Mrs. Mitchell's newspaper is in the street. I pick it up and lay it carefully on the sidewalk so it won't get run over.

When I walk in the house after my run, Mom and Kevin are sitting at the table drinking coffee. Kevin this early in the morning is never a good thing.

"Hey," I call and make for the fridge.

"Hey. Can you sit for a minute? Kevin has an idea."

"What is it?" I ask without looking away from the open refrigerator. Kevin always has an idea.

Kevin clears his throat. "I thought maybe if we looked at the accident scene together, it might trigger something. I'd like to go over there with you this morning."

My stomach drops and I close the fridge door. "I don't think so."

"I keep getting stuck on the chain of events. Sheila's story doesn't make sense to me."

"A lot of time has passed," Mom says. "Maybe you'll remember something if you go back to where it happened."

She knows I haven't been there. I specifically avoid that road. I make Mom detour around it when we're driving.

"I won't."

"Well, you won't know unless you try."

I close the fridge. "No."

"You don't even have to get out of the car if you don't want to," Kevin says.

"You need to do this," Mom says.

Kevin stares at his papers and says nothing. I bolt for the bathroom.

— — —

Mom knocks on the bathroom door.

"Go away," I tell her.

"No," she says.

The way the two of them are so unified on this crazy idea pisses me off. It's a stupid idea. If I was going to remember anything else, I would have by now. "Seeing it won't make any difference."

"Then it shouldn't be any big deal for you to go over there with Kevin."

"Are you coming?"

"He asked me not to."

"Why?"

She leans closer to the door and says in a quiet, but steely voice, "Kevin is doing all of this for nearly nothing because he cares about you."

"No, he's doing this because he cares about *you*," I tell her.

"You need to stop being a child. This is your case!"

I open the door. I walk past her to where Kevin is still sitting at the table. I sit across from him.

"I will not remember anything by going over there. So, while I'm grateful for all your help, this I won't do."

"Jessica, you can do this," Mom says, but she can't possibly know that. If she really understood what she is asking, she would never ask me to do this.

"How would you know?" I study the yellow marks on the table in front of me. They're from the permanent marker I used to draw smiley faces on an envelope when I was about five. It bled through, and Mom was furious. Faint yellow traces are still visible after all these years. Nothing really ever goes away.

"This is going nowhere," says Mom, with a heavy sigh.

"No, it's not," says Kevin. He stands up. "Come with me, Jess."

"I told you I'm not going." I cross my arms.

"If you don't get your ass out of that chair and get in my car, I'm done representing you." Kevin walks towards the door.

"Kevin!" Mom exclaims.

"If you want to give up now, then fine. I will not keep trying to help someone who doesn't want help."

Mom looks at me, pleading. "I know you're scared, but please...."

I stand up. "This is stupid! It won't change anything!" I yell at her, but I grab a jacket off the coat rack and storm out the door.

"Trust me on this," I hear Kevin say to Mom before he follows me to his car.

"Put on your seatbelt," he commands. He drives slowly, following the same route I took the day I hit Coach Mitchell. I wait for him to say something, but he doesn't. We round the corner where Coach Mitchell was, and he pulls to the side of the road. I look at the small wooden cross planted on the bank overlooking the road. Dead flowers and note cards are tangled in the weeds beneath it.

Kevin puts the car in park and turns on the hazard lights.

"I'm here. I don't remember anything," I tell him. I know it's no use no matter where I am.

Kevin flips through his notes but says nothing. Maybe he thinks if we sit here long enough it'll come back to me. Finally, I say, "This doesn't seem like a safe place to be sitting. What if someone hits us?"

"This is the spot where they found Coach Mitchell."

"So?"

He keeps reading. "After making contact with him, your car hit the embankment and rolled on its side, fifty feet from the body."

"Get out," he says and opens his door.

I scramble out after him. "Are you crazy?" I yell as another car speeds around the curve and has to cross into the other lane to avoid us.

He has me stand in front of the car and hands me the end of a tape measure, then he walks out to some point on the tape and looks back at me. "Here is where the car was."

"So?"

He looks at his notes again and then waves me to him. I let go of the tape and follow it as it recoils like a lethal, metal snake at high speed. When I reach him, he hands me the tape again and starts walking further away. Finally, he stops and looks back at me. He is maybe two car lengths away.

"What's that?" I ask.

"It's where your phone was found after the accident."

"So?"

"It changes everything," he says.

46
LIZ

Fickle February has turned cold again. It is Wednesday, three weeks before the trial and Jake is sitting at the kitchen table with Jess going over his sketch of the long-awaited screened-in porch. The trial is all I can think about, but Jake only talks of the screened-in porch.

"What kind of money are we talking about?" Jake asks when I tell him we need to get money together in case we have to appeal.

"I don't know, ten thousand? We cannot keep expecting Kevin to do this for free." Now that I have seen the money his other clients pay him, I am hyper-aware of the value of what Kevin has been doing for us. If Jess is found guilty, we have to appeal, but we can't expect Kevin to continue to represent us for free. Lately, he has been working ridiculous hours trying to keep up with his other clients while Jess' case is taking the bulk of his time. He is obsessing over every detail, even hired an accident recreation expert, and he has spent heaven knows how many hours trying to understand cell phone transmissions. He looks tired all the time. When I express my concern, he says he is fine. It will all be decided soon. But what if it isn't decided in Jess' favor? He cannot keep going like this.

"We don't have that kind of money."

"No, but we can borrow it."

Jake frowns; snaps his pen down on his clipboard. "Let's not worry about it until we have to."

Typical Jake. When I sigh in exasperation, he winks at Jess, and she grins. Lately, I always seem to be on the outside of their inside jokes.

In the end, Jake refuses to co-sign on a loan and he refuses to talk about the civil suit until it happens. Never mind that a civil suit could mean bankruptcy for both Jake and me. It could mean Jess does not go to college. It could mean I spend the rest of my life paying Jess' debt. I don't know if Kevin has that kind of money. I know he is wealthy. But I would never ask for money from him. He is doing enough. And that is one more reason I can't sleep with him. It feels too much like a bribe. Jake rarely says anything about Kevin's money, except to admire his BMW. He says it costs more than our house did.

Tonight Jake hangs around even after Jess has gone to bed. He tells me about his plans for the porch but also his plans to rebrand his business. "Bring it into the twentieth century."

"Twenty-first," I mutter and he pinches his eyebrows.

Jess is excited about the new porch. I don't hold my breath; Jake has made plans before, but I am hopeful. I do like that things have become very peaceful with Jake. I think that has been good for Jess. I wish we could have been these two people who talk civilly and worked together when Jess was little. I tell Jake that and he says, "Nah, we were too young. We didn't know what we had."

"Why now?" I ask him as he carefully rolls up his drawing for the porch. "You don't even live here."

"I want it to be nice for you and Jess. I said I would build it, and now I am."

— — —

Jake starts work on the porch two days later. He is here almost every night. I am surprised by how much I enjoy having Jake around. Jess sits outside, and they talk as he works. He teaches her how to use power tools and in less than two weeks there is the skeleton of a porch out there. He is the dad I had hoped he would be when I imagined our life together. Ironic that it is happening now when in just another week they could rip our daughter from us.

It is good that he is here so much though since I have been staying late most nights at Kevin's office. I feel guilty if I go home and he is still working. And he is always working. One of his cases must involve his ex-wife Jill because she calls a lot. When I ask about the case, Kevin looks surprised.

"What case?"

I shrug. "I just assumed that's the only reason Jill would call so often." I don't mention that she is almost always rude to me. I don't ask if he has explained to Jill that he is kind of dating me.

"Oh that," Kevin says, but he looks at his cell phone and then says, "I've got to make a call. You should go home. It's been a long day."

He disappears into his office. I have no right to be suspicious, yet I am. But why would I be jealous of Jill? I busy myself filing and wait in vain for Kevin to finish. Finally, I do leave. I need to get home for dinner. We have had a string of warm days and Jess wants to eat outside on the partially finished porch.

As challenging as I find the work at Kevin's, it is not what I want. I miss the residents, and I miss Avery. She keeps me up to date on the happenings at Morningside, but I feel my future there slipping away. The trial date races towards us. I want to believe that soon we will all have our lives back.

— — —

"Well, then you have to believe him," says Kate when I tell her Kevin denies keeping something from me. "He has been working late every night, and he's just been so weird lately."

"Weird how?"

"I don't know. A little distant, distracted maybe. And his ex-wife has been calling a lot."

"What does that have to do with Jess' case?"

"Nothing," I say.

"Why are you worried about him talking to his ex-wife?"

"I don't know. I just get the feeling Jill doesn't like me. She's rude to me on the phone and she always refers to Kevin as 'my husband.'"

"But they're divorced."

"Yeah, I know, but it's weird isn't it?"

"Maybe, but why does it matter?"

"It doesn't. Forget about it. Anyway, what's happening with Dad?"

"No real change in his physical symptoms, but he's even more lost in space mentally. Let me worry about him though, you deal with Jess."

"Thanks, but you'll let me know if you need me."

"Of course."

I know I am obsessing, but I can't help myself. "Do you think I should be worried about Kevin?"

"If you're worried, why don't you just ask him what's going on?"

"Because that seems paranoid."

"No, that's being an adult."

47
JESS

The weekend before the trial, I go to Dad's for the weekend. I know he's just trying to distract me. Ostensibly I'm there to help him hook up an extra monitor for his work computer. Dad and computers have never mixed, but lately, he's full of surprises. I'm worried I might see Fish. I don't know what I'd say to him if I did. That crazy trip across Texas seems like another lifetime ago.

The first night Dad and I watch our favorite movie, *The Incredibles*. When it ends, I get up to fix some tea. Dad's asleep, but when I click off the TV, he yawns and rights his recliner.

"I'm gonna check on the dogs and then hit the sack."

I take my tea and American History homework to my tiny bedroom with the Hello Kitty comforter and the rickety dresser full of Barbies and Beany Babies. In this room, time never passes. The reading is dense and boring; I've been slogging away for about an hour when a knock on my window makes me jump and I spill tea on my textbook. Another soft knock convinces me it isn't the wind, so I set down my tea and look out the window. There's almost no moon, but I think I see a shadow moving and then the unmistakable flare of a cigarette. Just before I let out a scream, I realize it's Fish. I'm relieved, but my heart hasn't stopped racing. What does he want? And do I want him to want something? I open the window.

"What are you doing? You scared the shit out of me!"

"Is your dad awake?"

"I doubt it."

"Can I come in?"

"That's not a good idea." I listen for Dad but don't hear anything. "Give me a minute," I tell him. "I'll come out."

Homeboy whines, but Willard only watches as I walk past them. Fish waits in the road smoking a cigarette.

"Hey," he says.

"Hey."

"Want a smoke?"

"No, thanks."

I pull my hood up and stuff my hands in my pockets, trying not to meet his eye. He stands close and the smell of him—diesel and stale clothes—brings back the maintenance shack where we spent that first night. His hard chest pressed against my back, his arms wrapped around me while I lay awake that long night wondering how far away from Jefferson I could get.

Fish kicks at the gravel in the road. "So, how's it going?" he asks.

"All right. I mean it's going, you know. Did anything ever happen with the police?"

"Nah. They had nothing on me. Just a fine for the bike, but Jake paid it."

"I'm glad." We walk down the road away from the trailer. I don't know what to say but whatever I say, I don't want to be within earshot of Dad. "I'm sorry I dragged you into all that. I didn't mean for you to get in trouble."

"I'm used to it," he says, grinning and reaching for my hand. I let him hold it for a minute, but it feels like a lie.

"Look," I say, dropping his hand. "We don't really know each other."

"I think we know each other," he says with a smile.

I walk faster, so he won't see me blush at the memory of asking him to have sex. I was out of my mind and I'm super grateful Fish refused, and I know that makes him an honorable guy, but now I don't know how I feel or what to say. He's a good person despite the greasy hair and the cigarettes, but he's not someone I could be with, not in that way, but I don't want to hurt his feelings either. I don't have many friends to spare these days.

He catches up, touches my arm to stop me.

"My dad will kill me if he sees me with you."

"He doesn't have to know." He looks away, kicks at the gravel. "I like you. I thought you liked me."

"I like you, but things are different now. If the judge doesn't throw me in prison, I'm getting out of Texas."

"I'll go with you. We'll make it this time."

"Not like that. I'm going to college."

Fish lights another cigarette. "So that's it. I mean nothing to you."

Honesty seems like the best option. "I'm sorry. I thought I wanted you, but.... I think I just wanted a way out and you were that."

"So you don't want to have sex with me now?"

A nervous laugh slips out, but I don't want him to think I'm laughing at him because I'm not. "That....that was just me trying to find someone to love me and I was pretty messed up."

He sighs. "And I'm not someone you want to love you?"

"We're too different. But we could be friends. We are friends."

"Right. That bullshit."

"It's not bullshit."

"What does Jake think? Does he think we slept together?" he asks, rubbing out his cigarette on a tree.

"I don't know what he thinks. We don't talk about you."

Fish shakes his head, focuses on something up the road. I think he's trying not to cry and I feel like a supreme jerk for making him feel that way.

"I will tell him we're friends and I want to see you sometimes."

"Right. That'll go over well."

"It's my life."

"But you're his daughter. He's already told me two ways to seven that I can't see you."

"So you're afraid of him?"

Fish tilts his head one way, then another. He taps his finger on his chin.

"I ain't afraid of Jake Johnson."

"Good. Then it's settled. We're friends." I hold out a hand.

He looks at me for a long time, then he leans in and kisses my forehead. "I wish things were different," he says.

"I do too," I whisper.

Walking back to the trailer alone, I wonder if I'll ever see Fish again.

48
LIZ

On Sunday night, when Jake arrives with Jess, I am kneeling in what is left of our front garden. I used my nervous energy to clean the inside of the house and then came out to get the stray bits of trash Jess missed when she picked up after this week's deposit. Bizarre that it has become a weekly chore—pick up the trash that a stranger throws on our yard. Once I gathered the trash, I spotted the dead flowers left from last summer, forgotten in the chaos of our fall. So, I got my gloves and the wheelbarrow and pulled them out. I guess I am trying to put our house in order.

Jess slams the door to Jake's truck, glances my way but says nothing and then spots Dylan in his backyard and heads in that direction. Jake approaches me where I am kneeling in the dirt.

"How'd it go?" I ask.

"It went." He shrugs. "She got the monitor working, we did some fishing, nothing biting."

I pull off my gloves and sit back on my heels. His dogs lean out the truck window. Drool hangs from the snout of the bigger one. I watch it drop to the sidewalk.

"So, you and Kevin....," says Jake, raising his eyebrows. "Have a good weekend together?"

I ignore his comment. Kevin and I did not see each other at all. He was too busy. "Did she say anything about the trial?"

He shakes his head. "I thought about what you said, the appeal, I mean. I think if that happens we ought to go with a new lawyer."

"Kevin is an excellent lawyer."

"But he said that trial stuff isn't his specialty. If we lose, well, maybe we should get a recommendation."

"I think Kevin is doing a good job." At least I am hoping he is. I have the same doubts as Jake the closer we get to Wednesday, but what choice do we have?

"You don't think him having the hots for you is clouding his judgment."

I frown, roll my eyes. I know what is coming. "What are you trying to say, Jake?"

"Nothing," Jake says. "Hey, whatever. I just don't think we need him. I can find the money."

"Right! Sure you can!" I stand, toss my gloves on the ground with the pile of dead flowers. "You are always going to take care of it, fix everything, only it never happens, does it? You never actually come through with any of your promises."

"That's not fair. I'm building the porch. I'm here for Jess."

"Better late than never, right?" He can't get back all the time he missed when she was growing up. There is no do-over in raising your kid.

"What does that mean?"

"I'm so tired of having this argument with you. Just drop it. Whatever Kevin and I have is none of your business."

Jake turns to his truck and I think he will leave it at that, but then he says, "Shit, Lizzie, I never promised to be any more than I am. I'm sorry it's never been good enough for you."

I lean down and scoop up the pile of weeds, watch him get in his truck and leave. He doesn't look back.

"Asshole!" I mutter as I fling the weeds in the wheelbarrow. Where was the grown-up Jake when I needed him?

49
JESS

On Tuesday, Ms. Ellen calls me down to her office. She says she just wants to check-in, see how I'm doing. The trial starts tomorrow.

I shrug. I don't want to talk about it. I don't want to think about it.

"You ready for tomorrow?"

"No."

She smiles. "In some ways, you must be relieved that it will finally be over."

"It won't be over."

"No, but the legal part will be."

"That depends on whether the Mitchells bring a civil suit."

"Do they plan to?"

"I don't know. Mom never wants to tell me anything about that."

Ms. Ellen scrunches up her face like she does when she's considering something I've said. I like that she listens so hard. I wait.

"I've known Helen Mitchell a long time, and one thing I can say for sure about her is that she is a forgiving woman."

I picture Helen Mitchell yesterday. I saw her on her porch yelling at a brown and white dog running around the yard barking. I almost stopped. "I don't think I can ever expect the Mitchells to forgive me."

"Forgiveness is complicated," she says and then opens her planner like she's finished talking.

"Why would the Mitchells ever forgive me?"

She sets down her pen, temples her fingers, and looks at me all serious. "You know, Jess, they may need to forgive you as badly as you need to apologize."

Ever since I was little and my mom made me apologize to Billy Higgins for running over his foot with my bike, I've hated to say I'm sorry. He had it coming, and it's not like I really hurt him. But after he told on me and his mother called, Mom drove me over to his house and made me stand on his porch and tell him I'm sorry. And then she and his mom drank lemonade, and I had to spend my Saturday afternoon at Billy Higgins' house. I wasn't sorry. I told my mom that later, and she said, "That's how life works. You hurt someone; you say you're sorry. The sooner you figure that out, the happier your life will be."

It's not that I don't feel sorry. I've never been sorrier for anything in my life than I am for whatever happened in that car. But saying I'm sorry doesn't seem like it would ever be enough. Not for the Mitchells or this town.

— — —

I skip practice and text Mom I'm going home early to get ready for tomorrow. On the bus, Dylan is surprised to see me and waves me back to his seat.

"What're you doing on the bus?"

I shrug. "Can't I ride the bus?"

"So what gives?" asks Dylan. "Isn't track, like, *every* day?"

"I didn't feel like going today."

"Cool," says Dylan. I put my earbuds in so he'll stop talking, but he doesn't. "You wanna hang out then?"

"I'm going to go for a run."

"You make no sense. Anyone ever tell you that?"

I turn up the volume on my music and lean against the window and close my eyes. I wonder if there is any way I could skip the trial. Kevin could just say I was sick. Seeing Coach's family up close again. I don't know if I can do it.

Mom is crazy stressed about tomorrow. She's constantly asking if I'm okay. I'm not okay, but there's nothing my mother, or anyone else, can do about it. Aunt Kate said not to worry, she'll be praying all day tomorrow. Our family has never gone to church, but sometimes I imagine there's this really great dad-type guy who's up there looking out for people. But then I wonder why he didn't look out for Coach Mitchell. Still, it's kinda nice that Aunt Kate will be praying.

As soon as I get home, I change into my running shoes and head out. There's somewhere I have to go. I can't explain it, but ever since I talked to Ms. Ellen I feel like I have to do this before tomorrow happens. Before someone *makes* me apologize.

When I get there, I stand by the mailbox and study the house. It has a stillness about it like it's waiting for someone. I follow the stone path to the door. If I don't do this now, I might never do it. Before I can ring the bell, a dog barks. And then Helen Mitchell opens the door.

"Jessica," she says, then holds up a finger and disappears back into the house. A moment later she reappears and has the source of the barking on a leash. The dog has short hair, like Homeboy and Willard, but he's less substantial. His short ears bend over crookedly.

Ms. Helen opens the door and hands me the leash. "Could you walk him for me?"

"Uh, yeah," I stammer.

"That would be so helpful. Thank you, dear," she says and closes the door.

I look down at the quivering dog beside me. He can't contain his excitement and launches himself off the porch, dragging me with him. We complete two laps of the block and still, the dog pulls at the leash. Has no one walked him in a month?

When I return to the house, Ms. Helen is sitting on the porch with a book. She smiles when she sees me.

"Oh, good. Did you tire him out?" she calls.

"I don't know. He still has a lot of energy."

"Have a seat." She gestures to a bench against the wall. Miraculously, the dog lays at my feet.

"Mrs. Mitchell, I—"

"My son Robert Junior got me that dog. He thought I needed the company. He wears me out." She smiles and shakes her head. "The dog, not my son. Or maybe my son, too." She chuckles softly.

I don't know what to say. I pet the dog and try to form the apology on my lips again, but I seem to have misplaced it. I take a deep breath and look at her. She's staring at me and smiling.

"When my husband came home at night, first he'd walk his dog and then we'd sit on this porch if it was nice or in the kitchen if it wasn't. He always wanted to talk about the boys- the football players," says Ms. Helen. Now she stares out toward the road to where the daffodils line the picket fence like brightly colored socks. I follow her gaze and watch a rabbit hop between the flowers, nibbling on a few of them. I glance at the dog sleeping by my feet, oblivious to the rabbit's presence.

"He loved the boys. Do you know I found a prayer journal of his in the stuff they brought over from the school? There were hundreds of prayers in that book for boys who are grown men by now. I wonder if they ever knew he prayed for them."

My heart begins to hammer. I have to say it, but now I feel like I'd be interrupting. I can't tell if she expects me to respond or if she's just thinking out loud.

"Everyone misses him," I finally say. "The track team dedicated their season to him."

Ms. Helen turns to look at me. She stares so long I grow uncomfortable. Finally, I say, "I'm sorry," but the words sound small and insignificant. Like dandelion fluff, they vanish and I wonder if I really said it.

"You'll come and walk Sherman again," says Ms. Helen as she gets up. She reaches for the leash and pulls on the sleeping dog. "C'mon, Sherman," she says, and the dog follows her inside.

Walking home, I'm convinced I never really said I was sorry. That I only imagined it. It was crazy to go there. She seems crazy too. But maybe it's grief. Maybe her grief made her crazy.

50
LIZ

On Tuesday, Kevin shuts himself in his office all afternoon, telling me to hold his calls. And then Jill calls. When I tell her he isn't taking any calls, she says, "He'll take mine."

I knock tentatively on the door before opening it. Kevin is leaning over his desk, one hand rubbing his temple, the other staring at his computer. He says nothing.

"It's Jill," I tell him.

He looks up like a startled deer. "Here?" he asks.

"No, on the phone."

He looks at the phone like it might bite him. "Okay, thanks."

He waits for me to leave before answering the phone.

A few minutes later, he reappears and says, "I need to talk to you."

Something about him is off. He has been distracted and distant for days. I figured he was just worried about the trial. He locks the front office door and sits down on the loveseat in the waiting area. I sit beside him.

"I need to tell you something."

"Okay," I say.

He doesn't look like he has happy news, whatever it is, he can barely speak the words. "Say it, whatever it is, please."

He looks at me. Terror on his face. "Jill is having a baby."

"What's that got to do with anything?" Relief floods my body followed by confusion.

"It's *my* baby."

"Huh? How is that possible? You told me..."

"It's possible because she did another in-vitro treatment."

"But why?"

He shakes his head. "She wants a baby. The sperm bank contacted her to say we had to decide what to do with our remaining embryos. I told her we should consider donating them, but she got this crazy idea that now that she's healthier, now it might work."

"But you're divorced. Why would you agree to that?"

"This all happened right about the time I first started seeing you."

I nod. Afraid to speak.

"And when I insisted on the divorce, she said she'd sign the papers as long as I signed consent for her to try in-vitro again."

"Why would you do that?"

He sinks back against the cushions, defeated. "Because I wanted the divorce. I wanted to be with you, and I was sure she was wasting her money. It hadn't worked before. She's over forty now. What were the odds?"

"Apparently, quite good."

Kevin shakes his head and frowns.

"So, what does that mean?"

He shrugs. "Jill told me I can walk away. I don't have to be part of the baby's life."

"Do you want that?"

He looks at his hands, shakes his head ever so slightly. "It's what I've been trying to figure out ever since she told me. At first, I thought she was making it up. Some kind of crazy scheme because she was jealous of you."

"You didn't answer my question."

He looks at me. "It's what we wanted so desperately and could never have. How could I not want this baby?"

I bite my lip, will myself not to cry.

"This doesn't change how I feel about you, but I realize it changes everything."

I nod. "It does."

"But it changes nothing with Jess' case. I'm ready for tomorrow."

"I think I need some time."

"Of course. We can talk about it after the trial."

"No. I think I need a lot more than that."

"Oh." He turns to me and reaches for my hand. I let him hold it, but all of me just wants to get away from him. Far away.

"When did Jill tell you?" I ask.

"In December, she told me she had done it. She didn't know yet if the pregnancy would be viable. That's why I didn't tell you. I thought she was crazy. She'd never get pregnant."

"But miracles happen," I say, trying to smile. *Just not to me.*

He smiles, despite himself. "It is a miracle."

The office echoes with our silence. How can I be angry when he is talking about a new life? His child? How can I resent that? And yet, I am angry. Angry and hurt.

"I think I'd better get home. Jess needs me there," I tell him.

"Liz, please, I can't lose you."

"Can I ask you one question?"

"Anything."

"Do you still love her?"

"It's not that simple. Your relationship with Jake is complicated, too."

"Except, I'm not committing to spending the next eighteen years raising a baby with him."

He sighs.

"Have you even thought about that? Having a baby with Jill, even if you are divorced, still means your life is tangled up with hers *forever*."

I stare at him. I cannot believe this is happening. I wanted him to be the one. I wanted him to be the good guy. The right guy.

We talk in circles for another half hour before I insist I have to go. I promise we will talk again, after the trial, but I know we won't.

51
JESS

I laid out the clothes Mom bought for the trial before I went to bed. The high-collared shirt and neat sweater are supposed to make me look innocent. The last time I dressed in clothes I'd laid out the night before, I was in second grade. There's probably a picture somewhere of my outfit—purple cowboy boots and jeans with stars embroidered all over them.

I was innocent then. *Am I now?* If only my clothes could make it so. If only I could.

It seems impossible that all these people—lawyers, policemen, judges, even Mr. Monroe in his job at the district attorney's office will be there just to talk about what I did, something I don't even remember doing. Sometimes it feels like I'm in a dystopian novel being controlled by a cosmic author who makes the characters do things no one would ever dream they would do—especially themselves.

Kevin says Sheila is the prosecution's star witness. I can already tell you what will happen. Sheila will look perfect. She'll dress the part of the innocent friend. Her makeup will be flawless; her peachy skin will sparkle in the light because of the expensive foundation she drives to Dallas to buy. People cannot look away. That's the way it always is with Sheila. I've watched her turn boys to putty and make teachers question themselves. So no matter what Sheila says, whether it's the God's honest truth or a tale she made up about aliens landing on the road in front of us, everyone in that courtroom will believe her. I don't have a chance. No matter what I wear.

These are the things I think about as we sit in the tiny alcove off the side of the courtroom, waiting to go in. Once again, they have to clear the courtroom because I'm a minor. I'm seventeen now, so they could try me as an adult, but Kevin says they go by your age at the time of the alleged crime. Everything with him is alleged.

Finally, we're escorted into the courtroom. It's a bigger room than where the hearing or the pretrial conference were held. The windows are tall, and the chair rail that lines the room is dusty. I drag my finger down it as we enter.

There's no jury. Kevin made that decision. He said we could ask for one, but that we'd be better off with a judge. It would be hard to find an impartial person in this county. To find twelve of them, they'd probably have to move the trial. We drew Judge Harkins. He says she's fair. She sits at a tall desk up front. I watch as she writes something, pushes her glasses up the bridge of her nose, and then listens as the DA explains the case they're about to present. Kevin says they get to go first, again.

Once again, the police officer and the accident specialist have their say. It's the same information, only this time Kevin asks them a lot more questions. It's mostly technical stuff. Stuff about my cell phone, the position of the car in the roadway (on its side), how much room there was between the white line and the bank (2.7 inches and the line was obscured by overgrowth). He repeatedly asks about the exact time the text was opened and the exact time of the accident. The experts believe it to be nearly the same time. Why he keeps hammering at that I don't understand. Doesn't that just make me look more guilty? It takes the entire day. The cell phone information is especially tedious and I don't understand most of it. At four, the judge says we're done for the day. Kevin said the trial will only take a day or two, but at this rate, it could be weeks.

We leave out a side door to avoid the crowd of MADD demonstrators out front. Dad goes ahead of us to be sure there's none of them at the house, but they aren't there. He and Mom sit at the kitchen table. He has a beer, and she drinks coffee. They talk through the entire day's testimony. I slip out the door, and go to Ms. Helen's. She wasn't there today, but her three kids were. They sat all in a line in the back. Dad and

Mom know them. They all went to school together. I bet they never imagined they'd have a reunion like this.

There's a movement behind the curtains and by the time I reach the door, Ms. Helen has Sherman on his leash. He bounds outside, knocking into the screen door and nearly toppling me. Ms. Helen smiles and gives me his leash without a word. Sherman and I make several laps around the block.

When we return, Ms. Helen is sitting at the top of the steps. She pats the place beside her, and I sit. I don't know what Ms. Helen wants from me, but I don't think it's just to walk her dog.

"He was better today," I tell her.

"He needs exercise," she says. "Robert Jr thinks Sherman will force me to get out and get some exercise, too, but he pulls too much for an old woman."

"You don't seem that old."

"Bless you, dear."

I want to ask her why she wasn't at the trial, but I don't.

We watch Sherman dig up the edge of the yard.

"When Robert and I were first married, he told me he wanted twelve children. Can you imagine?" She laughs and shakes her head. "I told him three was my limit. He loved having kids around. One time we had a player who was going through a rough time; his mother was sick, and his dad wasn't around. Robert brought him home to stay with us. This was thirty years ago. They'd never allow that now."

Ms. Helen sighs. "Things were different then. James was his name. Likable kid, very bright. Do you know he graduated top of his class at Stanford?" Ms. Helen pauses, probably thinking about James. "Children made him happy. Sometimes he'd get sad, but kids would always lift his mood. Robert tutored him. Helped him fill out college applications. James went to Stanford on an academic scholarship. He never was very good at football, barely made the team at Jefferson."

Ms. Helen pats my knee and then gets up and takes Sherman inside. I wait a few minutes, but she doesn't come back.

— — —

When I get home, Dad is gone.

"What's up with you and Kevin?" I ask Mom.

"Nothing," she says and asks, "How're you doing?"

She wouldn't even look at Kevin today. It was weird at the courthouse. He kept trying to talk to her, and she kept avoiding him. Since she's lying to me, I lie right back.

"I'm fine."

"Do you know what you will wear tomorrow?"

"Clothes."

"Jess...."

"Don't worry, I'll find something innocent looking," I tell her and go to my room before she can ask any more.

52
JESS

On Thursday, they bring Sheila in. The DA goes through her original testimony, line for line. When it's Kevin's turn to cross-examine her, he doesn't ask her who answered the text, he asks, "What did the text say?"

Sheila glances at the DA, looks confused. The judge tells her to answer the question.

"It was from Casey, this guy Jess has had the hots for since, like, forever." She smiles, laughs a little. "He asked her if she wanted to play pool on Wednesday."

I sit up. *How does she know what the text says if I was the one who read the text?* That's Kevin's point. Mom catches my eye and smiles.

"And you know that because you read what was in the text message?"

She nods.

"Could you answer that question for the record?"

She smirks. "Yes."

"So, when exactly did you read the text message on Jessica's phone?"

Sheila shrugs. The DA scribbles furiously on his notepad.

"Did you read the message on Jessica's phone before or after the car hit Coach Mitchell?"

"I don't know," she says and smiles at the judge, like *Duh*, but the Judge furrows her brow, straightens her glasses, and makes a note.

"If the crash happened moments after Jessica supposedly read the text, you couldn't have read it before. But then again, I can't imagine in the aftermath of that awful crash, that you took the time to locate Jessica's phone and read the text."

She looks at the DA, who says, "Is there a question?"

"So, should we assume that you read the text after the crash?"

Sheila shrugs. "I read it whenever. I guess after."

Kevin steps back to the table where I am and pulls out a police report. He hands it to Sheila.

"Could you read the highlighted portion?"

She looks confused. Before the DA can object, Kevin explains to the judge that he only wants to show where the police found my cell phone.

Finally, after much arguing between Kevin and the DA, she reads, "A cell phone belonging to Jessica Johnson was located fifteen feet north of the car, in the roadway."

"And if Jessica's phone was fifteen feet from the car, from which paramedics had to extract you, I find it highly unlikely that you could have read what was in that text message."

"Again, is there a question here? Judge? Judge?" asks the DA. The judge doesn't look up from the notes she's writing. I almost smile because he sounds just like that scene from Ferris Bueller's day off. *Bueller? Bueller? Anyone? Bueller?*

The judge tells him he can redirect. He tries to ask Sheila about the common knowledge of the text message and could she have known what was in the text because everyone at Jefferson High School does?

For the first time, Sheila's confidence falters, but she smiles and nods. "Yeah, that's probably how I know. Everyone knows about the text Casey sent." She looks at me pointedly, tilts her head, raises her eyebrows. Kevin is right, though. I don't remember reading the text message, but I know what it said, and I didn't tell anyone except Fish, so if the entire school knows what was in that text message, they only know because either Sheila or Casey told them. And I'm betting it wasn't Casey.

But if Sheila was the one who opened my text, why would I have hit Coach Mitchell? And why would she say I did it?

53
LIZ

We break for lunch. Jake brings us sandwiches, but neither Jess nor I can eat. My body is reverberating like a tuning fork.

"It's going well, isn't it?" I ask Kevin. It is the first time I have looked at him. I am still heartsick about the end of our relationship, but I push that aside. I focus on Jess.

He is calm but quiet. "So far, so good," is all he will say.

He leaves us to go check his messages. Jake is all smiles now, so different from the man who called me this morning to suggest we ask for a mistrial and look for a different lawyer. Some ridiculousness about Kevin not being up to the task and there being a conflict of interest because of my relationship with him. He is singing a different tune.

"Man, he got her!" he says. "Sheila is lying and now everybody knows it."

Jess sips on a water bottle, says nothing. I know her heart is breaking. Despite everything that has happened, she still misses her friend. Jake goes on and on like he does after a football game, recapping the highlights for us, even though we were there.

Back in the courtroom, we take our seats. Jess sits next to Kevin at a table up front. I sit behind them, a railing separating us. Jake sits beside me. He is wearing clean jeans, a wrinkled shirt, and an out-of-date tie. He glances at me now and raises his eyebrows, silently asking if I am okay. I shake my head and look away. I will my heart to slow down and my tears to stay inside. I have to keep it together for Jess. She is about to testify.

When the door opens, I can hear all the people outside who want to come in but are not allowed because Jess is a minor. Gone is the assurance I gave Jess yesterday that things would go well today. Today I am gripped with terror. I wish I could sit next to her, but I trust Kevin to protect her. I know he will, no matter how angry I am with him.

As if he senses me thinking of him, Kevin glances back at me and winks. I nod at him and watch as he whispers to Jess. Probably some last-minute advice, but she leans away from him. She is nervous and snappy like she is before a big meet or an oral report. She threw up her breakfast in the ladies' room as soon as we got here this morning and refused to eat any lunch.

Jake gets up and reaches across the barrier separating us to hand something to Jess. She smiles. It is a roll of lifesavers—butterscotch. She loved them when she was a kid. Jake used to leave them everywhere for her. It was sweet. I don't think I have stumbled across a roll in years. I reach over and squeeze his hand. He leans his shoulder into mine. I am glad he is here.

This morning Jess woke up surly and far, far away. I wanted to wrap her in my arms and tell her it would be okay, but she stepped away from my embrace and I couldn't find the words to say it will be okay, because surely I don't know that it will be. She would not talk to me as we sipped coffee in the dark kitchen. Kevin wanted us at the courthouse two hours early to avoid the press. I changed my clothes at least three times before we left, finally settling on my navy suit, even though Jess told me I looked like a sausage in it. She is right; it is a little tight. I bought it for a job interview fifteen years ago.

The side door of the courtroom opens, and the Mitchells walk in. I remember many nights drinking with Bobby Mitchell at the reservoir. It was hard to be Coach's kid—everyone expected a lot, and Bobby was only a mediocre player. He was not the star that his brother Brian had been or that Jake would be. I don't remember Karen that well. She was younger than me, only a freshman when I graduated.

I watch Jake nod to Bobby as they pass. Karen and Brian follow him. Jess doesn't look up. She swallows hard. I pray she will not throw up again.

The door opens, and the judge enters. She is an older black woman with a creased face and tightly curled hair dusted with white who doesn't look any happier to be here today than she did yesterday. Everyone stands when she enters, and she waves at us to sit. Then she opens a folder and puts on her reading glasses.

Jess is visibly shaking when she takes the stand. Kevin tries to calm her with some questions about how long she has been driving, her school records, the track team. He asks her what she bought me for Christmas and she says a headset because she doesn't like it when I talk on the phone while driving. I brace for the questions he has warned us about—how much she loved Coach Mitchell, how well she knows that road, her friendship with Sheila.

The other lawyer breaks in, sounding like an impatient child. He wants to know what any of this has to do with the case. Kevin explains he is providing context. The judge tells him to move along with his questions, but she is not unkind when she does.

Kevin guides Jess through the day of the accident, asking her about when Sheila arrived at the house and how she got there, skirting around the DA's objections. When he gets to the actual accident, Jess struggles.

"What do you remember about driving Sheila home that morning?"

"I remember getting in the car and arguing about what to listen to on the radio. But after that, I don't remember anything clearly. I remember hearing sirens, seeing flashing lights, but I think I was in and out of consciousness."

"The hospital record says you suffered lacerations to your face and head and had a severe concussion."

Jess nods.

"But you don't remember hitting your head or anything else about the accident?"

"I don't."

He moves on to her relationship with Sheila.

"She's my best friend," Jess says. I look over at Sheila who glances up at Jess quickly, then looks away.

"So it's fair to say you know her better than most people?"

Jess says, "Yes."

Sheila rolls her eyes, but a moment later she wipes a hand under one.

"And in the time you spent with Sheila, did you ever witness her lying?"

The DA objects to the line of questioning. The judge sustains it.

"Would you say that Sheila lies easily?"

Jess says, "Yes," at the same time that the DA objects again.

The judge reminds Kevin that there isn't a jury and we are dealing with juveniles here.

Kevin asks Jess about Sheila's boyfriend, the captain of the football team. He asks questions like, "How would the student body react to the news that Coach Mitchell was killed in a car accident caused by a student?" The DA objects and objects over nearly every question Kevin asks, but I know he is only asking them to plant doubt. He said that was his goal for today—to plant doubt. So that the judge—and this town—understand that many factors beyond the text message contributed to Robert Mitchell's death. He wants to point out that Sheila is very capable of lying and had a motive to lie, to absolve herself from blame.

Next, the DA questions Jess. He is gentle with her, talking softly, but his questions are tough.

"Just before you left to drive Sheila home, did you receive some news?"

Jess squints at him.

"Did Sheila tell you that her boyfriend had informed her that Casey Miller would ask you out?"

"She did," Jess says.

"Were you excited about the potential text message?"

"Objection!" says Kevin. "Jess had no idea the question would come in a text message."

"Let me rephrase," says the DA before the judge can rule on Kevin's objection. "Were you excited about the possibility of Casey Miller asking you out?"

Jess nods.

"Is it fair to say you were *very* excited?"

Kevin objects, the judge rolls her eyes, nods.

"Jessica, have you ever texted while driving? And remember you're under oath."

"No," says Jess, glancing at Kevin. She remembers his definition of texting while driving.

"You've never taken a quick peek when you're on a familiar stretch of road?"

"No," says Jess firmly.

"Admirable," says the DA. "But your friend Sheila says you read a text message this one time. Is it possible that in the throes of your excitement over this boy, that, just this one time, you loosened your own standards?"

I want Kevin to object, but he is still, waiting.

"Jessica?" asks the DA again.

Jess is crying. She is looking down at her hands. Her shoulders shake. Finally, she says, "I don't know."

The DA asks again, but Kevin objects and says he is badgering. The judge tells him to move along, but the DA says he has nothing further.

It is over. Because this is a juvenile case and not a jury trial, Kevin has told me the closing statements will be brief. He will try to weave an alternative story, to be certain there is room for reasonable doubt.

The judge writes something, then takes off her glasses before looking at Jess. Her look is hard, but on the very edges, I see sadness. She is probably someone's grandmother. Maybe a girl like Jess. A good girl who is not infallible, who is only a child.

The judge lifts a heavy folder, all the papers and character references Kevin has gathered. There is one from Jess' track coach, a few of her teachers, Ellen Schultzman, Avery, and Mrs. Katz across the street.

"I have had to do more than my share of reading for this case. You have both laid out your cases concisely and I appreciate that. I would ask that you also keep your final comments brief. This case has gone on longer than it should have considering it involves a minor. I would like us to bring it to its conclusion today."

I cannot tell from the judge's face whether that means she is eager to get Jess behind bars or she is tired of hearing about it or if, maybe, she thinks Jess is innocent.

The DA goes back through the facts. He says Jess is obviously a good kid, but sometimes good kids make dumb choices. It is the nature of a teenager to put herself before others, he says. As he says these things, fear grips my heart. He is smooth, persuasive; he is paving the way for the judge to decide Jess is guilty of this crime without saying she is a terrible person.

"Robert Mitchell deserves justice and everyone, regardless of their age, must be held accountable for their actions."

He nods at the judge and takes his seat without looking at Jess or me. Bill Monroe has been here the entire time, sitting like a statue beside the DA, taking notes, rarely looking up. The last time I saw Bill Monroe was in July. I ran into him in the produce section of the grocery store and helped him find cilantro. He was doing the shopping for Linda for a dinner party they were hosting. He would have gone home with parsley if not for me.

Now it is Kevin's turn. He stands, buttons his jacket.

"Your honor, I am not arguing that Jessica Johnson did not hit Robert Mitchell with her car, causing his death. But I would argue that she did not hit Mr. Mitchell because of her recklessness. She was not texting and driving. Her passenger was the person who opened and read the text. Jess was not distracted. As she approached the bend in the roadway where Mr. Mitchell was walking his dog, a series of unforeseeable and perhaps unavoidable circumstances came into play.

First, at that time of day, the sun was hitting her windshield at an angle that makes it difficult to see, even if she was wearing sunglasses, which she was. The lacerations on her face attest to that fact. Second, the bend of the roadway prevented Jess from seeing Robert Mitchell far enough in advance to move her car further into the roadway to avoid him. And third, Robert Mitchell was walking his dog in the lane of traffic because there was not sufficient room on the shoulder.

Jess is not at fault here. If we must assign fault, it would have to be on the county that did not provide a shoulder on this busy road or on the victim himself. Had there been a sufficient shoulder or had Robert Mitchell moved to the other side of the roadway to avoid the blind turn, this tragedy could have been prevented.

I would ask that you not allow this tragedy to have more than one victim."

Kevin sits, and the courtroom is quiet. The judge looks through her paperwork, occasionally making notes. She does not look up for what seems like an eternity. Kevin has told me she may make her ruling right away or she may take a day or longer to think about it.

"Before I make my ruling, would anyone from the Mitchell family like to speak?"

We all turn to look at the Mitchells in the back of the courtroom. Bobby, Brian, and Karen sit in a row with Karen's husband.

I look at Jess, tears are brimming her eyes. Kevin hands her a tissue, and she blots her eyes. Karen Wilcox stands and walks to the front of the room. She is shaking as she unfolds a piece of paper. She turns to address Jess.

"I'm sorry," she says. "I wanted to say a lot of things, but now I can't." She wipes her eyes. The judge hands a tissue to a police officer who takes it to Karen. She blows her nose.

"Take your time," the judge says.

I look at Jess. Her eyes are on Karen, but I see her fingers moving through the same nervous routine they have had since she was little. She pinches them together in succession. First thumb and pointer, then thumb and middle finger, then thumb and ring finger, and last thumb and pinky. Then she starts over. She used to do this whenever Jake and I started fighting.

Karen looks at her paper and then up at Jess. She smiles through her tears. "When I heard how dad died, I was mad for a long time. Furious, really. But then my mom said to me, 'What would your father say if he was here?'" Her voice cracks, and she has to take a moment to wipe her eyes again. She takes a deep breath and then looks at Jess. "He would say you're just a kid who made a mistake."

Karen looks back at her paper. Jess is crying now.

"My dad was the most amazing man," Karen reads. "Not just at your school, but in my life. He dressed up as Santa for my kids last year. He loved people, especially young people. He would never want to ruin your life."

"But I ruined his," Jess says and her words seem to echo through the courtroom.

"Counselor," says the judge, nodding at Jess and Kevin whispers to Jess. She is not allowed to speak.

Now Karen seems to soften. She addresses Jess. "No, Jessica, you could never ruin his life. He had a wonderful life. And it would ruin his life if this accident ruined yours. I know if he were here, my dad would want us to comfort you. And I want to do that, but I'm not sure I'm ready to do that yet. I'm still comforting my own kids and trying to help my mom. But I need you to know I don't condemn you."

She folds up her paper and walks back to where her brothers sit.

"Anyone else?" the judge asks, but both men shake their heads.

She clears her throat, takes off her glasses, looks at Jess.

"This has been a hard case for me. There is much of me that sees you as just a little girl—unformed and uninformed, and yet when we give young people the right to drive, we must hold them to the same laws that we hold adults to. Jessica Johnson, regarding the charge of reckless driving, I find you not guilty. Regarding the charge of criminally negligent homicide, I find you guilty—while it is clear that you had no intention of doing harm in this situation, your actions resulted in harm.

However, there are many, many contributing factors here. I believe you were not the only one at fault. Because of that, I don't believe it warrants jail time. Instead, you will be on probation until you are twenty-one, you also may not drive a motor vehicle until that time. You will serve one hundred hours of community service in the form of educating others regarding the dangers of distracted driving." She nods and gives Jess a tight smile. "Let's see if something good can come of this."

The breath I am holding releases. I want to shout for joy, but I know that would be inappropriate considering the Mitchell's pain. Karen's words and their presence have been a glimpse into the nightmare they have been experiencing. There has been no room for it in my heart.

None of us move as the judge leaves, followed by the DA and his people. The Mitchells are next to leave. As they walk past us, Bobby nods at Jake. We get up, but Jess remains seated, frozen. I crouch down beside her, look her in the eye, and take her hand.

"It's over," I say and she nods. I pull her to her feet and wrap an arm around her. Jake takes her other hand. Kevin leads us out the side of the building again to avoid reporters.

Standing in the parking lot, Jake asks, "Now what happens?"

"Now we wait to see if there's a civil suit. Frankly, I'm a little surprised they've waited this long to file one. All we can hope is that this guilty verdict will be enough," says Kevin.

54
JESS

For some reason, I assumed that when the trial was over our lives would be different. I mean, for months it's all Mom has talked about, but afterward, we just go home and eat leftovers. Dad stays over on the couch because while they don't say it, both my parents know this town won't be satisfied with the judge's decision. Sure, she said I was guilty, but she isn't putting me in jail or in the electric chair like some people hoped. It's like I got away with something, only I didn't. It's cool, really cool, that I will not go to jail, but talking in front of high school students about the accident seems scarier right now. Jail might be better. I have no idea what I will say. When I mention this, Dad says, "You'll think of something." Seriously, not helpful.

Nothing happens Friday except I don't go to school and Dylan comes over in the afternoon. We play scrabble in the living room because Mom doesn't want us to be on the new porch. We're still kind of in lockdown. I wonder how long we can live in this bubble before it bursts. Mom goes to her room, and Dad watches basketball. When the phone rings, which it does all day long, no one answers it. When there's a knock at the door, we ignore it. Only a handful of protestors show up, and the reporters don't hang around long. The plus is that whoever dumps trash on our yard won't do it with an audience, so no trash this week. The internet is all in a flurry and the newspaper has plenty to say, but at our house all is quiet. Mom and Dad are painfully polite to each other and no one mentions Kevin. I'm bored out of my skull and jonesing for a run. I haven't mentioned Helen Mitchell or her dog to anyone, not even Dylan, but I wonder if she was expecting me.

Saturday morning after Dad finally leaves, Mom goes on a cleaning tear. She sorts out every drawer and closet and cleans the house to within an inch of its life. The phone still rings, and we still don't answer it. The newspaper columnists are happy that I am guilty, but they are mixed in their feelings about my sentence. Several are still calling for my head. I try not to think about the judge's words, "find some good in this." I still have no idea what I will say if I really have to talk to other kids.

Mom says, "Let's not think about that yet, okay? Let's just be happy this weekend." As if she is happy in any way, shape, or form.

Dad brings pizza over on Saturday night and we play poker with peanuts (his invention). When Dad finally asks about Kevin, Mom says, "I don't want to talk about it." He wiggles his eyebrows at me, and I laugh. I think Dad has a crush on Mom, but he is blind if he can't see that she is miserable without Kevin. Not just miserable, but maybe a little nuts too. I don't know what the man did, but I sure wish he'd apologize.

After all the lead up to the trial, it feels foreign not to have it hanging over our heads and odd not to hear from Kevin. It's almost as if it was all one long, terrible dream.

On Monday, school is no different. I don't know why I thought it would be better. People still stare, there is some fresh graffiti on my locker, and Ms. Ellen still wants to know how I feel. After practice, I ask Mom to drop me off at Ms. Helen's house.

"Why?"

"I have to walk Sherman."

"Who's Sherman?"

"Mrs. Mitchell's dog."

"Why do you have to walk Mrs. Mitchell's dog?"

I shrug. "I just want to."

"Is she expecting you? Jess—what is going on?"

"Nothing. It's nothing. I just told her I'd walk her dog."

"Does Kevin know about this?"

"No. Why would Kevin know?"

"We need to ask him about it. It might jeopardize the civil suit. Let's clear it with him first."

"Fine," I tell her, but when I go out for my run, I go directly to Ms. Helen's.

— — —

When I'm with Ms. Helen, it's on her agenda, not mine. I'm willing to do anything she asks, but so far all she wants is for me to walk her dog and listen to her stories. Mom says no more about it, but she doesn't ask Kevin about it either. With no trial, there's no reason to talk to him, and she goes back to work at Morningside.

Each day Ms. Helen is waiting for me on her porch. She tells me more about Coach Mitchell. He volunteered to go to Vietnam but got turned down because of an irregular heartbeat. One year there was no money in the school budget, so Coach Mitchell bought the jerseys for the team. The school board president asked Coach to consider going to graduate school so he could earn the qualifications to be a principal, but he said no, he liked coaching football more. Coach Mitchell drove a snowplow in the winter to make extra money when his kids were in college. He loved model trains, and he set up a train display at the retirement community where Mom works. I've seen it. The residents love to tinker with it. I wonder who will take care of it now.

Ms. Helen never mentions the civil suit, the trial, or the accident. I asked her once why she didn't come to the trial and all she said was, "Why would I do that? It doesn't change anything."

— — —

I meet with my probation officer, an older grumpy woman with close-cropped hair. I can't tell if she likes me or not, but it doesn't matter because she seems to have outsourced my probation supervision to Ms. Ellen. She says I'll need to meet with Ms. Ellen regularly and that she will set up my speaking engagements (plural!). I'm so wigged out to be sitting in the police station again, that I can't protest, but there is no way I can stand up in an auditorium and talk to other teenagers about the accident. I want to explain to this nice woman in the wrinkled uniform with a slight mustache that it's not like kids will listen. Everybody knows you shouldn't text and drive, but they still do. How is my pathetic story going to convince other kids not to do it? I don't say that; instead, I agree to whatever she says and let mom lead me out of the station.

When I was little, I always tried to be good. I thought if I was good enough, my parents might get back together, even though they fought all the time. Little kids are idealists. I remember sitting in the car while my parents fought outside the door—my mom's face so red with anger and Dad puffed up, defying her. They were the same age I am now when they got pregnant with me, just kids. But I wanted them to be the mom and dad in the storybook. And when they couldn't be that, I tried to be the daughter in the storybook. And now look. No one would think I'd be the kid who runs over the football coach because she's texting. But I am. I may have banked a lot of goodness, but that didn't exempt me from doing something monumentally awful. For the millionth time, I think, *If only Coach Mitchell wasn't at that particular spot in the road at that precise moment or if only I wasn't.*

If he hadn't been there, I would have gotten to Sheila's house where we would have squealed about Casey and figured out what to text back. And my life would be completely different. I'd still be popular and have friends. Sheila and Jason and Casey and I would have double-dated. I'd have been on the Homecoming Court. I'd have my letterman jacket.

My mom would still be the day manager at Morningside and Kevin would be doing whatever it was Kevin was doing before he horned his way into our lives.

Ms. Ellen would still be that sweet guidance counselor who spoke at the fall assembly and signed my college applications. So much would be different if Coach Mitchell hadn't taken his dog for a walk at that precise moment or if I'd waited another ten minutes to take Sheila home. It's like those choose-your-own-adventure books I read as a kid or the video games Dylan talks about where you enter different worlds depending on which door you open. *One moment, one stupid decision you don't think even matters.* It becomes a hinge in your life, swinging you in a different direction only you don't know it at the time and there's no way to undo it.

— — —

The next day, Ms. Ellen asks, "Have you thought of what you might say in your presentation?"

"No," I tell her.

"I know this won't be easy, but it might help you reframe the accident. See if you can help another young person avoid this situation."

"As if," I say.

"Well, you've got to start somewhere. Let's just start the conversation. What would you want them to know?"

I sigh, lean back on the couch, and throw one arm over my eyes. "Never drive a car. Never."

Ms. Ellen ignores me as if I haven't spoken. She won't play along.

"Maybe start with the day of the accident. How it was like any other day. It was, wasn't it?"

"I don't remember much about that day."

"Well, maybe you can talk about the impact it's had on your life."

"Oh, that will be tons of fun."

She sighs. I hate that she cares so much. It's just one more thing for me to feel bad about.

"I know I need to take this seriously, but I really don't remember anything. Why doesn't anyone believe me?"

She says nothing. She opens her planner and ignores me.

"The one thing I do remember about the accident is that horrible thump when I hit Coach Mitchell."

She sets her pen down and looks at me. Her eyes are shiny, like maybe she's the one who is going to cry this time.

I look away, focus on the stupid teddy bear holding an apple on the corner of the desk.

"I can hear that thump over and over and over. Hollow and solid, like when the football players hit those padded bars at practice. I can hear the screech of brakes and the crash of glass showering the pavement. And then an awful quiet. That's it. That's all I can remember, except the EMT guy telling me, "It will be okay," which is what everyone kept saying. Only it will never be okay.

Now, I have no friends except my neighbor, a nerdy eighth-grader whose parents don't let him watch TV. Everyone else hates me. And there's nothing I can do about it. No way to fix it."

"Oh Jess," says Ms. Ellen.

I drop my arm and look at her, tears streaming down my face. How is it I keep coming back to this same place on this same sorry couch?

"You're right. It won't ever be okay that Coach Mitchell died. But I promise you someday you will feel okay."

I want to believe Ms. Ellen more than anything else in the world. But the pain inside me feels permanent; anything good or happy seems temporary—band-aids that momentarily cover what is really wrong, which is me.

"I think no matter what I say or don't say, it'll never be 'over.' No one believes me. No one believes I wish it had never happened. No one knows how much I wish I was the one who died." Ms. Ellen hands me tissue after tissue. When her phone buzzes she ignores it. When the secretary pokes her head in the door, she waves her away.

"I want to ask you a favor," says Ms. Ellen. "I want you, just for today, to leave all this guilt and pain right here on the couch. I don't want you to carry it out of the office. Tomorrow, if you need it, you can have it back, but for right now, I want you to leave it here. It's too much for you to keep carrying. You need to put it down for a while. Can you do that?"

"I don't know," I mumble.

"Can you at least try?"

"Okay," I tell her because I really want to leave this all here, more than anything.

"Why don't you use the bathroom and freshen up? I'll write a pass to get you back into class."

When I walk into Latin class, I keep my head down. When I reach my seat behind Casey, he turns and whispers, "You okay?"

I nod and open my book.

The teacher holds me after class to go over what I missed, which saves me from having to speak to anyone, but Casey is waiting for me outside the door.

"You okay?" he asks again.

"I'm fine. Don't worry about me." I realize my voice is laced with hysteria. I take a deep breath and scan the ceiling, try to gain my composure. Then I say, "Yes, I'm fine. Thanks for asking." I drop my Latin book in the locker and grab my Calculus book. "I've got to get to class."

Casey follows me. "Jess?"

"What?" I ask without slowing down or looking back at him.

"Did I do something to piss you off?"

I snort. "This has nothing to do with you."

Casey grabs my arm and stops me. His touch is like a branding iron. I stare at his hand on my arm, and he releases it.

"I'm late. I can't miss any more classes," I tell him.

"Can I drive you home after practice today?"

"Fine," I say and hurry to class.

— — —

Practice exorcises some of the emotions dredged up by Ms. Ellen. I want to do what she said. I want to leave all the pain in her office on that couch. But I don't know how.

Casey is waiting when I walk out of the locker room.

"Thanks for the ride," I say and follow him to his car. It seems to be the only place he wants to be seen with me. Which is fair. I get that.

"Sure," he says.

When we get to the car, he unlocks my door and opens it. An awkward silence descends.

Finally, after we've gone a few blocks, he says, "Look, I know you're still pretty messed up about the accident. I'd probably be, too. But does that mean we can't be friends? I know there's all this..." he takes his hand off the wheel and waves it around and then frowns and puts it back on the wheel. "I know everything is different now, but does that mean you never want to go out with me?"

I bite my lip to keep from smiling. He still wants to go out with me! I don't know how to answer. I want to go out with Casey, but I can't. Can I?

When we stop at a light, Casey turns to look at me.

"I like you. I thought maybe you liked me. The accident doesn't change that, does it?"

I shake my head. I don't know what to say. The light changes. Casey doesn't say anything else until we pull up in front of my house. He turns off the engine. Neither of us moves.

"Okay," I say.

"Okay, you will go out with me?"

"Okay, we can be friends, but it feels weird."

Casey looks at his phone where it lies on the seat between us. "Because I sent that text?"

"I don't know. Maybe."

"I can't change that."

"I know."

"So maybe we have to just start over."

"That would be good," I tell him, wishing it was that easy.

"Casey Miller," he says, holding out his hand.

I shake it. "Jess Johnson. Thanks for the ride."

"Anytime," he says, flashing his dimples at me. I jump out of the car before I say anything stupid. I wish starting over were that easy. I wish I could really leave all the memories and pain and regret on Ms. Ellen's couch.

55
LIZ

After the trial, I go back to Morningside. In an ironic turn of events, I apply for Avery's old job and she hires me. Aaron is apoplectic when he finds out.

"Yeah, he pretty much lost it when he heard," Avery tells me when she catches me in the break-room. "But I reminded him it was my job to hire a qualified person, and that's what I did. Although you are way over-qualified, and I feel kind of bad. You should have my job."

"Nonsense. You're doing a great job, and I don't want it. I won't have time for it if I go back to school."

I have been spending hours on the community college website pouring over the possibilities trying to imagine a new future, despite the threat of a civil suit that hangs over us. I had assumed I would have Kevin in my life after Jess leaves for college. But now, I realize how stupid that was—how can I be thirty-five years old and still believe in a fairytale? I do not need a man to take care of me. I have taken care of me and Jess for years. And now that means imagining a new future for both of us. No matter what happens with this civil suit. I will make sure she goes to college, and I will figure out how to pay for it. Which means I need a job that pays real money, so I also need to go to college.

"How's your dad?" Avery asks, knowing better than to bring up Kevin.

"Same. Kate is going to visit him for her spring break. She's the family martyr."

"Lucky you have one."

"I know." We are the only ones in the break-room, so she sits down and catches me up on the latest gossip. Aaron is dating one of the nurses, which should technically be against policy except she is not an employee of Morningside. The medical staff is contracted. Still, it has lots of people worked up. I forgot what a bubble exists at Morningside. Everything is a big deal even when it isn't and everyone knows everyone else's business.

I am happy to be back at Morningside, but it is not nearly as exciting as Kevin's office. No more teary calls from angry wives or juggling visits from fighting spouses, just wheelchair scuffles, complaints about the soggy green beans, and a family member wondering why we don't have HBO on the resident's basic plan.

Kevin is still calling me nearly every day, and it has nothing to do with the civil suit. Each time I see his number my heart leaps, but then I remind myself. It is over. It has to be. I never accept his calls and his voicemails are piling up.

"Please, Liz, I'm losing my mind. I need to see you."

"Please call me back. I'm so sorry. Can't we talk about this?"

"I feel like I'm losing you before I ever had you and I know it's been crazy but I know you miss me too. What we have is special. (long pause) *I love you, Liz. You love me too. I know that. We can figure this out, can't we?"*

"You need to call the man back," says Avery two days later when she catches me listening to his latest message on speaker. "You're torturing the poor man."

"What could I possibly have to say to him?"

"How about, 'I realize you're not perfect like I thought you were?'"

"I never said he was perfect."

"Uh, huh." She rolls her eyes and plops in one of the extra chairs in the office I share with the other aides near the Alzheimer's wing. Avery says it is a great place to be—no one will remember anything you do wrong.

"I haven't."

"Not in as many words, but you're holding him up to some crazy standard. Not everyone is as perfect as you." Avery slurps the very end of her milkshake and sets the empty container on the corner of my desk and gets up.

"I'm not perfect," I protest.

"Don't I know it," she laughs. "None of us are, including Kevin. Give the poor man a second chance. Besides, you love babies."

"I don't know if I can."

"Then be prepared to be alone for the rest of your life, because making any relationship work depends on second chances. And sometimes third chances, too."

I look at her and raise my eyebrows. She knows exactly what I am thinking. She has already given Vinny about two dozen chances.

"Don't say it. Vinny and I are different. Kevin probably won't need quite so many chances. He's more evolved."

"Avery," I begin, but she cuts me off.

"I know, I know, but I'm working up to it. Just cause I don't take my advice, doesn't mean I can't give it."

I think about her words that night and almost call Kevin. Instead, I call Kate and tell her about all the messages and what Avery said. "Do you think he deserves another chance? Is there any point in trying to salvage this? I don't want to raise someone else's baby and I still don't understand what's going on with him and Jill."

"Never mind whether he deserves another chance, give him one anyway. Talk to him. You're just being cruel by ignoring him. So, he's having a baby with his ex-wife, it could be a lot worse."

"How?"

"He could be in love with the woman, but he's not. For some crazy reason, he's in love with you."

"How would I ever trust him again? What if being around the baby and Jill all the time makes him want to be with her again?"

"Just like being around baby Jessica all the time made you and Jake want to be together? Lizzie, forgiveness has never been your strong suit, but maybe it's time to try it on. Give the man another chance."

"I don't know if I can forgive him."

"That's because you've never tried. This one's easy. Maybe after that, you might work up to forgiving Dad or the whole friggin' town of Jefferson. Call the poor man back."

But I don't call him. Instead, that Saturday I take my placement exams and do much better than I expected after almost eighteen years out of school. And the following week I apply for the nursing program at the community college. The admission counselor says that with my scores and my transcript, and my income, I will be eligible for financial aid. I hope it will be as easy when it is Jess' turn.

One night, Jess observes my ringing cell phone on the counter while I am making a stir-fry for our dinner. She has a meet tomorrow, so I'm packing in plenty of protein.

"You know this is kind of high school."

"What is?" I ask.

"You not answering his phone calls."

Later I think about it and realize she is right, but more than that, I realize I miss Kevin. I want to tell him about school. I know he will be excited for me. When I told Avery, she said, "Why would you go to school? You're already qualified to be a manager." And when I told Jake, he said, "You're crazy, why would you go back to that hell?" Jess seemed proud, though, even though it is only community college. With each hurdle passed, my fingers itched to dial Kevin. He would have wanted to celebrate.

But still I don't call. I cannot seem to let go of my fury. I am not going to once again let a man get in the way of my future.

56
JESS

March settles in with a string of days that repeat themselves. I go to school, to practice, and then to Ms. Helen's to walk Sherman. I talk to Casey most nights. We talk about school and track and even sometimes the accident. He tells me that Sheila never talks about the accident anymore. She even told Casey she's glad I didn't go to jail.

"You're making that up," I say.

"No, I'm not. I think she might even feel kinda bad for her part in this."

I assume a reporter's voice, "And in the end, Sheila comes out smelling like a rose." I smirk. "She has a gift for that."

Sheila has always had a wind at her back. She can walk a much thinner line than the rest of us and never lose her balance. Casey tells me I want the world to be fairer than it is.

"Some people are just lucky," he says. "Nothing sticks to them."

I'm not sure if that's true, but it does seem like people have already lost interest in the accident. I wonder if Ms. Helen thinks people have forgotten about Coach. Maybe that's why she talks about him so much.

And then one rainy day, Ms. Helen tells me about the time Coach Mitchell talked a young woman out of having an abortion.

"She was the girlfriend of one of his best players. The two of them had gotten into a situation. Now, back then folks around here were opposed to abortion, I suppose they still are. But they also weren't willing to educate young people about birth control, as if talking about sex meant kids would be more likely to have it. But what they really didn't want to deal with was a high school student walking around pregnant. Most girls who didn't have an abortion just quit school, but this young woman refused. She wanted to finish high school and go to college."

She looks at me for a long moment. I know she is talking about my parents, but she doesn't say it.

"He asked this young couple if they loved each other and they said that they did. So, he asked them why they would want to abort a baby they'd created out of that love. They were scared and there were a lot of tears that night, but Robert convinced them to tell their parents. That wasn't easy, and those parents didn't necessarily handle it well, but Robert supported those kids. And he went to bat against the administration to make them allow the young woman to graduate from high school. There were some on the school board who fumed over that for years—as if there was anything wrong with educating a young woman who was pregnant. A woman in that situation needed her diploma more than most. It's not easy raising a child, especially when you're still a child yourself."

A car in need of a muffler roars up the street and we both watch it pass. Sherman doesn't even lift his head. The street is quiet after the car passes, only the birds above us arguing over the feeder that hangs on the corner of her porch.

I've gotten used to Ms. Helen's pauses, but this time she hesitates so long I wonder if she's forgotten what she was going to say, but when I look at her, there are tears on her cheeks.

"I know I make Robert sound like a saint. He was a good man, but he wasn't perfect. He let me down plenty. He put his work before me, and sometimes he put the team before his own kids. And sometimes when he was here, his mind and his heart were elsewhere, fixing someone else's problems instead of ours. Oh, he tried to make up for it with flowers or a card or ice cream for the kids. When I was young, it made me angry. I almost left him once!" She laughs under her breath and then continues. "I can't even remember why now—isn't that something?" She shakes her head, puts both hands on her knees as if she's about to get up, but she doesn't. "But then I realized I was only angry because he didn't live up to *my* expectations. And I'd never even told him those expectations! As I grew older, I realized I didn't want a perfect man; I just wanted a man who loved me. And, oh, Robert loved me. We worked hard at loving each other. It's work, you know, loving another person. The songs and movies make it look easy, but it's not."

Ms. Helen wipes her eyes and gets up to leave. Each night she's told me a story and left without another word, but tonight she hesitates on the doorstep.

"He wasn't perfect," she whispers, "He knew that people make mistakes—even good people."

I walk home in the rainy darkness and I feel a little lighter.

– – –

Track is going well; I'm winning a lot, even break my PR in the 400. Casey never misses my meets, even the away meets. My parents don't come to watch me run—Mom always has to work and Dad can't get here from Gillam in time. I don't mind, though, because Casey is there, cheering for me. He walks me to the bus. Sometimes he holds my hand. I'm not sure exactly what we are. We're friends, but we're more than friends. Life feels a tiny bit better.

Mom is home every night cooking dinner; she even takes me shopping for new clothes and a dress to wear to the track banquet. I feel happy, but that seems wrong. Will feeling happy always feel wrong?

"Earth to Jess," Mom says. I roll my eyes at her. I hate it when she says that.

"I'm going back to work. There are leftovers in the fridge."

"Have fun."

Mom frowns at me. I watch her leave. She still hasn't told me what happened with her and Kevin, but whatever it is, I hope it's over soon. I can't take much more of sad mom. She's way too invested in trying to make me happy. She should worry about herself.

57
LIZ

Jake calls after I am already in bed. My first thought when I see his number is the civil suit, but I know Kevin would call me first—wouldn't he?

"What is it?" I ask when I pick up the phone.

"Hey, Lizzie," he says in a warm voice coated with liquor.

"What's the matter?"

"Nothing's the matter. I just wanted to see how you were."

"I'm fine. It's late, Jake. Why are you calling?"

"I just," he starts, but then his thoughts sputter out.

"You just, what?"

"I wondered what happens now?"

"What do you mean? We wait to see what happens with the civil suit. Get some sleep."

"I'm not talking about Jess or the accident."

"Then what are you talking about?"

"What happens with you and Kevin now?"

"Why does that matter?"

He laughs softly. "I guess it doesn't. I just wondered."

I glance at my clock. "You just wondered at eleven-thirty at night?"

"Yeah."

"Why do you care, Jake?"

"I think things have been pretty good with us. Jess is doing better. I'm doing well with my business."

"And that means?"

"You're not making this easy, are you?"

"What do you want me to say?"

"I want you to say you feel the things I do. That we're good together. I want you to say we should give this another shot. We should try being a family again."

"Jake," I say, but he cuts me off.

"No! Hear me out! This has been good. You know it has. Don't just dismiss me like some school kid. I still love you, Lizzie. And I'm sure you still love me. It's not gone."

"I do still love you, but it's different. I love you because you're my friend and because you're Jess' father, but what we had has been gone for a long time."

"But the business will make real money this year. I know I've been a screw-up for a lot of years, but I'm getting it together. I can take care of you and Jess."

"That's not what it's about."

He snorts. "Then why are you chasing after a lawyer?"

"I'm not chasing after Kevin. And what I feel or don't feel for him has nothing to do with the fact that he's a lawyer." I hear the words come out of my mouth and they sound hollow to me, too. If Kevin wasn't a lawyer. If he hadn't rescued Jess again and again, would I have fallen for him?

"Just give me another chance."

"I can't do that, Jake. I'm sorry."

"We could be good again."

"We're different people."

"Exactly! I'm different. I'm not the same screw-up you married. That's what I'm trying to tell you!"

"But I'm not that girl either! I want more than this!"

"More than what? More than life in Jefferson? Move out here. That's what I'm trying to tell you. We can start over. Here in Gillam. You won't have to work."

"I don't want that. Don't you hear me? It has nothing to do with where I live. I'm going back to school. I'm going to make the life I want."

"Why can't I be a part of that?"

"Because you can't. You're moving on, too, don't you see? You're growing your business. You're stepping up as a dad. It's only a matter of time before you find the woman you're meant to be with."

"What if that woman is you?"

"You're wrong. And you've been drinking. And tomorrow morning you'll probably realize how right I am."

It takes another fifteen minutes to get Jake off the phone. I almost hang up on him several times, but I know he needs to salvage his pride. I am touched by this call, but I can't go back there. I am not that girl he thinks I am.

I am also not the girl Kevin thinks I am. All I know is that right now, I need to be the woman I am. So, for the next few weeks, I focus on doing a good job at work and taking care of Jess. I try very hard not to think about what may or may not be happening in some lawyer's office across town where the Mitchells hold our future in their hands. Kevin stops calling, and Jake is too busy with his business to turn up much. Jessica spends hours on the phone with some boy. I think it is the boy who sent the text and I don't know how I feel about that. At least, so far, there is nothing more to it than phone calls. No dates. No declarations. We need a few weeks without drama. For a while, I think I can hold off the inevitable with normalcy. And it works.

— — —

The third week of April, it happens. Kevin leaves a message he has met with the Mitchells' lawyer. He has news.

After Jess is in bed, I call him.

"Thanks for calling me," he says. "It's great to hear your voice."

"What did the Mitchell's lawyer say?"

"No civil suit."

"What?"

"Just what I said. They aren't planning to bring a civil suit. Legally, they still could, but he's certain that won't happen."

My heart unclutches. A future—mine and Jess'—is possible now. Anything seems possible now. The fear that I have been clutching so tightly to my heart, the one that startles me awake at night, that steals my breath as it runs through me in ordinary moments every day—in line at the grocery store, wiping the counter, pausing to chat with a resident—it lifts so instantly and completely I feel as though I am breathing for the first time in months. The world brightens impossibly and spins just for me. If I was standing, I would probably collapse in a dramatic heap like a woman on a soap opera. Instead, I rock like Curtis on the edge of my bed, hold my hand over my mouth and cry silent joyful tears. I can't speak; no thoughts form on my lips. Kevin laughs softly; I can feel his smile. He has done this, given me this tremendous gift. Briefly, I think of the Mitchells and I wonder if they are also relieved.

"Liz?"

I nod, but still can't find words.

"Are you okay?"

"Yes," I finally squeak out. "Thank you. We will find a way to pay you for everything. I am back at Morningside, and Jake will pitch in too. I know we can't afford what you charge, but maybe we can work out a payment plan."

"You don't need to pay me."

"I do."

"You don't. Please, I won't take your money. I would do it again, even if it meant we still landed in this place."

"Why?"

"Because you're a good person Liz. A really good person. Much better than me."

"Kevin—"

"Can we just talk? In person, not over the phone? If I could just see you..."

I ignore his question and remind myself, and him, what stands between us. "How is Jill?"

"The baby is fine. It's a boy."

"Congratulations."

"Look, I know I messed up in too many ways, but I need to see you."

I don't know why I agree to see him. Maybe it is the news that there won't be a civil suit or his insistence that we don't have to pay him, but I feel I owe him this much. We make plans to go for a walk on Saturday.

58
JESS

They don't make balloons that say, "Congratulations you aren't going to be sued!" but Mom and Dad and I still have a little celebration when we get the news that the Mitchells will not sue us. It seems weird not to have Kevin here since it's probably because of him we're ducking this lawsuit. Or maybe it's Ms. Helen. She doesn't seem like the suing type. I've never asked her if she's told her kids I walk Sherman. We go out to dinner at Jeb's Skillet because it's our safe zone, and no one mentions the accident, not even any of us at our table, because it's hard to celebrate anything about the last seven months. Except maybe Casey. Whatever it is we've become feels right. Talking to him is the only time I feel okay, except maybe walking Ms. Helen's dog. Our celebration dinner is kinda good, too, because Mom and Dad get along like they like each other, which lately it seems like they do.

— — —

Track season is over for everyone except those of us going to Regionals, and hopefully States. I'm running the 800 and 1600, plus the relay. There are twenty-two of us going to Regionals, which is more than Jefferson has ever sent. The team took the dedication to Coach Mitchell seriously, but no one more than me.

Even though he's not on track, Casey drives me home most nights so I don't have to ride the activity bus since Mom is back at Morningside and can't pick me up. Casey and I never seem to run out of things to talk about. I've talked to him about the accident and about how scared I am about the upcoming 'talks.' He's an excellent listener. Sheila would laugh to know that we've been 'hanging out' for weeks and he has yet to kiss me. But it's none of Sheila's business anymore.

— — —

Casey asks me to prom, which changes everything, even though the thought of prom makes my stomach drop because it's the day after I give my first community service speech. I still have no idea what I'll say. Everyone, and by everyone I mean Ms. Ellen and Mom, think I'm working on it, but mostly I just stare at my blank computer screen until I can't stand it and then I either call Casey or watch YouTube to distract myself. There really isn't anything to say. Every time I write anything down, it just sounds stupid, so I delete it. Why would anyone listen to me, anyway?

— — —

One Friday night after practice, Casey says, "Want to come over tonight? My parents are out of town."

I shake my head. "I'm having dinner with my dad and his new girlfriend."

"Can't you cancel?"

"She's cooking. I think she's trying to demonstrate what a great mom she'd make."

"Would she?"

"If I was five."

"So cancel. Hang out with me."

"I promised my dad I'd give her a chance, plus I have to walk Sherman."

"Oh yeah. I could help you with that."

"Thanks, but it's something I have to do by myself."

I ride my bike to Ms. Helen's. I'm cutting it close. Dad is supposed to pick me up at six. When I knock, Ms. Helen appears with Sherman already on the leash.

When I'm walking Sherman, my life feels better, different, not so ominous. It's crazy to think walking someone's dog could make up for killing her husband. Or maybe it's Coach Mitchell's spirit hanging around. Crazy.

When Sherman and I turn onto Maple Street, I hear a car pull up behind me. It idles for a while but then follows me. My heart races. Maybe it's the crazy person who still periodically throws trash on our lawn. I glance at Sherman. He offers little in the way of protection. I look over my shoulder at the car and freeze in my tracks when I recognize Sheila's Mustang. I stop walking.

Sheila pulls up beside me and lowers her window, casting her perfectly made-up eyes on me. "Hey," she says. She looks past me at Sherman who is yanking my arm backward, trying to chase a squirrel teetering on the picket fence behind us.

"Hey," I say.

"I heard you made Regionals."

I nod.

"That's cool."

I nod again. I can't think of anything to say. How can she act like the last seven months never happened? There's no point in asking once again what really happened in that car. By now she's solidified her lies not just in this town but likely in her heart. That's what happens when you tell it enough.

"A bunch of us are going up to the reservoir tonight. Maybe you could come with Casey."

"Really?" I ask. It would be easy to cancel on Dad. He'd understand. This is my chance. Sheila inviting me back into her good graces. Just like that. I never thought she would be my friend again, not in a million years. I wonder if it's because of Casey or if she misses me, too.

"I don't know. I've got plans with my dad."

Sheila laughs. "Oh, C'mon, you can blow him off."

I remember that laugh. I used to crave it. When Sheila moved to Jefferson, my life went from black and white to color. Without Sheila, I would have been consigned to the Math Olympiad after school and fishing with Dad every weekend. After the accident, sometimes it seemed like I hurt as much from the loss of Sheila as from the knowledge I'd killed Coach Mitchell. It was another aspect of my guilt.

Sheila checks her phone, waiting for me to agree to come. As if nothing happened. As if she didn't lie. As if she didn't ignore all my phone calls. The late day sun sparkles off her hair. She smiles up at me, raises her eyebrows—asking. I know there will not be another opportunity. This is it. I'm in or I'm not. I know Casey would be happy to take me up to the reservoir. I can almost smell the smoke from the bonfire and hear the laughter and music echoing across the water.

Sherman barks and makes a lunge for a squirrel. The leash slips from my hand. He bounds over the picket fence with more athleticism than I thought him capable of. I turn back to Sheila. She guns her motor. I take a deep breath, and then I set down the picture in my mind. I am not that person anymore. I don't want to be.

"Thanks, but I can't cancel. I made a promise. He's counting on me." For a moment, sadness flickers across Sheila's face. But then she snorts.

"Suit yourself!" she says and squeals her tires in her rush to get away.

I retrieve Sherman and hurry back to Ms. Helen's. She is waiting as usual.

"I can't hang around tonight," I tell her. "I have to meet my dad."

She nods but looks disappointed, so I sit down on the step, anyway.

"You look different tonight," Ms. Helen says.

I smile. "I feel different."

"Well, it's good. You look good, so I'm glad."

Is it fair I get to reach for happiness when Ms. Helen is so sad? What is her life like, stuck here with her memories and Sherman?

"Well, you go on and meet your dad now. I wouldn't want you to be late on account of me," she says. She takes Sherman inside.

I sit unmoving on the porch step. I'm trapped between the happiness I want and the guilt I can't let go of. Why does every step forward hurt so much?

59
LIZ

"Thanks for seeing me," Kevin says as he gets out of his car at the park where we agreed to meet. The park is hosting some kind of dog event; dogs and Frisbees fly all around us.

"I didn't know this was happening," I say, indicating the pandemonium just beyond the parking lot.

"Should we go somewhere else?"

I shake my head. "It's fine. If we stick to the path, hopefully, no one will hit us."

He waves me in front of him as we head to the narrow gravel path that rings the park. An awkward silence ensues, but the barking dogs and yelling people are a convenient distraction. I watch a small wire-haired dog leap into the air and completely miss a Frisbee that sails past him and lands just feet from Kevin and me. Kevin picks up the Frisbee and tosses it back to its owner who has the dog under his arm like a package.

"I've never had a dog," he says.

"Jake's dogs were always a big draw for Jess to visit when she was younger. She calls them her fur-brothers."

We walk to the far side of the park, away from the dogs. Kevin stops next to a bench. "How about if we just sit?" The dog event has started and whistles sound.

It feels good to be with Kevin; he is easy company, plus I can't wait a moment longer to tell him. I grin as I say, "I have news!"

"You do?" His face lights up. I love that he is already excited, and he doesn't even know what it is. Happy because I am happy.

"I'm registered for community college! I'm taking Bio 101 this summer and two more courses in the fall."

"Oh, Liz, that's great!"

"I'll probably be the oldest student."

"And the smartest." He smiles and touches my arm.

I laugh. "Hardly!"

He turns serious, his voice choked. "These weeks without you have been awful."

"I've missed you too," I tell him because it is true.

"Before you, my life seemed fine. I wasn't necessarily unhappy, but I didn't realize what I was missing." He looks at me, his eyes searching for forgiveness. "After we started seeing each other, everything changed. I changed. And now with the baby... I just want to share that with you."

"Not Jill?"

"Look, I know it's a weird situation, but I swear my relationship with her is strictly about this baby."

"That's easy to say, but Jake and I have lived that. It's difficult to do."

He nods. "You're right. I have no idea what will happen. I just know you are the person I want to talk to about it. Jill sent me the ultrasound picture and all I could think was how much I wanted to show it to you."

"How's this going to work? Have you talked about shared custody?"

"We're lawyers, remember?" He smiles.

I laugh. It feels so good to be with him. He takes my hand and says, "I can't imagine this life without you. I should have told you what was happening with Jill from the beginning, but our relationship seemed so fragile. I never thought she would really get pregnant. I didn't want to risk losing you, but now... I can't walk away from a life I created. I promise I won't ever keep anything from you again. I will always be honest with you."

He has said all of this before in one way or another in his messages, but I needed to see it in his face. I believe him, but that doesn't change how much it hurts. Really hurts. I hate that he kept it from me, but more than that, I hate the idea of him sharing the miracle of birth with someone other than me. I know it is not fair, but I am ready to start my life. Jess will graduate; my nest will be empty. I could go anywhere, be anyone. Being with Kevin would mean being a part of another child's life. Maybe even a stepmother. I sigh. I don't know if I want that. A baby? Another child whose life will take a piece of my heart, carry it with him through good choices and bad ones. Another being with the power to inflict devastating pain and unbelievable joy.

"Just say something, please," Kevin begs. "Just tell me there's still a chance here."

I watch the dogs leaping and running. I look back at Kevin, pain etched in his face. It is hard to believe I mean this much to another person. Once upon a time, I wanted to mean this much to Jake, but Jake meant too much to Jake. Every part of me wants to go back to where we were, but I can't. Now I understand the potential for pain. I know how much power he has to hurt me. And even as he says he never will, there is a tiny voice inside saying, "You can't be sure."

"I want there to be a chance," I say. "I do. I just don't know if I'm ready to take it. I need to focus on me." My words are bitter on my tongue, but I steel myself because this is the right decision. This I can control.

We settle into silence. We watch the dogs. Finally, I squeeze his hand. Then I get up and walk to my car. I leave him there on the bench with my future.

— — —

A week goes by and Kevin doesn't call. I don't call him. I look at the phone in my hand and every ounce of me wants to call him and let him back into my life, but this hold-out part is stronger. I will not set myself up for pain. I am tired of letting a man be in charge of my heart. I tell myself all these things and yet my heart lifts when the phone rings, hopeful it is him. Instead, it's Kate.

"So, have you let him off the hook yet?"

"It's not that simple."

"I know," she says.

"The baby changes everything. Jill will be a part of any relationship I have with him."

"She would be anyway."

"I hate how much this hurts. How do I know he won't hurt me again?"

"Hate to break this to you, Sis, but he will."

"Which is exactly why I need to end this."

"Right," she says. "Forgiving him and trusting him is a terrible idea."

"So, I'm doing the right thing."

"If you say so."

"Kate! I hate when you do this I'm-just-humoring-you-bullshit!"

"What do you want from me?" she asks.

I sigh. "I want you to tell me what I should do."

"That's what you're waiting for?"

I know what my heart wants to do; I am just afraid to trust it. But I trust Kate.

"You can figure this one out yourself," she says.

"But what if I can't? And what if I am making a huge mistake? I can't think about it. Jess has her first speaking engagement next week. That's all I can think about right now."

"I wish I could be there, but finals week is coming up." Kate is a sociology professor. She is beloved on her small college campus. And happy. She dates occasionally but nothing ever seems to last long. She was dating someone in Minneapolis a while back but has not mentioned her in a while.

"That's okay."

"I'd come, except, I'm kind of seeing someone and we made plans to go to Yellowstone as soon as I get my grades in."

"Good for you. Is it serious?"

"I'll tell you after Yellowstone."

60
JESS

My speech at Elm Grove High School is only a week away. I haven't written a single word. Every time I imagine speaking to an audience about the accident, my stomach heaves, and I break out in a sweat. So, instead, I think about Casey.

At practice, I can't focus and Coach Fines grows frustrated warning me I won't do well at Regionals if I don't pull myself together.

When Casey drives me home from practice, I tell him, "I can't talk tonight. I need to work on my speech and you're too distracting."

He smiles. "I like that I'm distracting you."

I roll my eyes. "You distract me a lot."

I don't even know when we morphed from friends to more than friends, but we are. Nothing has happened—not kissing or anything like that. I don't know if crossing the friendship barrier is too hard, but I'm okay with things like this. I'm okay with being pretty sure he likes me and I'm excited about going to prom with him. If it weren't for the impending speech, I'd say that my life is better than I ever imagined it would be only a few months ago. I hear mom tell Aunt Kate that kids are resilient, but I don't think I've 'bounced back' as she put it, I think I'm just moving forward instead of staying where I was. I've let go of the hope that Sheila and I will ever be friends again. I'm okay with that. And I'm still trying to let go of not knowing what happened in that car. Whatever it was, like Ms. Ellen says, my brain must be protecting me from it. Maybe that's the problem with this entire speech—I don't want to look back anymore. I don't want to remember.

Casey smiles at me. "You okay?"

I nod. He smiles the whole drive home.

When we get to my house he says, "I know you can't talk tonight, but I'll still be thinking about talking to you."

I laugh. "Now that's just distracting."

Mom pulls in next to us in the driveway. I shake my head when she starts towards the car. I know she only wants to get to know Casey, but I'm not ready for that. I don't want her questions or her enthusiasm. I don't want to have to define this for her. She makes a face at me but turns for the house.

"I promise I won't call, but feel free to call me," says Casey as I get out of the car. "You know," he winks, "if you need a distraction."

"Maybe," I say.

Twenty minutes later we're talking on the phone.

"Do you think we'll get sick of talking to each other soon?" I ask.

"I'll never get sick of you."

I note that he said he'd never get sick of me, not sick of talking to me.

"I gotta go," I tell him.

Is 'I'll never get sick of you,' the same as 'I love you?'

— — —

The next day, when I return Sherman to the house, ominous clouds have moved in and rain chases me up the walk. Ms. Helen says, "Come inside and wait out this storm. I'll make us some tea."

I towel off Sherman and sit at the worn kitchen table scarred from a lifetime of dinners. There is a calendar on the wall with numbers counting backward towards Thursday, May 5th. That is the day I give my speech at Elm Grove High School. *Is Ms. Helen counting the days too?*

She puts the kettle on and then sits down across from me.

"The day Robert died, I was in the kitchen putting up applesauce. He came in and kissed my cheek. He said, 'We've made a wonderful life.' I told him to have a nice walk and got back to my applesauce. It was odd how he told me that before he left. It was as if he knew what was about to happen." She pauses, twisting the ring she still wears on her finger. "Sometimes I wonder if I just imagined him saying that."

She shrugs and then asks about our walk. "Is he still pulling so much?"

"He's getting better."

"I don't know what my son was thinking." She shakes her head.

"Ms. Helen, what is your calendar counting down to?" I ask and nod towards where it hangs on the wall, the numbers counting down in bold red letters.

"Oh, that! Big day, my dear. Big change!"

The tea kettle whistles, and Ms. Helen removes it from the burner.

"Ms. Helen..." I need to tell her in person, not in a big auditorium in front of hundreds of kids. I said it once before I knew her, before I knew who Coach was and what he meant to her. "I... I need you... to know..." I want her to know how sorry I am, but pain fills my chest, stealing my words. I shake my head, frustrated with my tears.

Ms. Helen sits down next to me and takes my hand. Her own is papery and soft. She looks at me, waiting until I meet her eye. "It's okay, Jessica. I know. And I also know that Robert would not want you to suffer because of his death." She leans towards me, squeezes my hand. "There was so much goodness in him, and I can't help but think now some of it is in you."

She pats my hand as if that is that and gets up to pour water over the tea bags. She smiles as she works as if some mystery has just been solved. It cannot be that easy. You can't just give the goodness of one person to another like an heirloom handed down through generations.

Tears stream down my cheeks, but I can't say another word.

We drink our tea, and Ms. Helen tells me about her latest quilting project. The rain finally stops, and I walk home in the dripping silence.

— — —

"Jess, I asked you a question," says Mom, jarring me out of my thoughts. I'm struggling with my speech. Helen Mitchell's words still echoing in my heart. I have only two days to figure out what I will say.

"What?" I ask with more annoyance than I mean.

"Can you make yourself dinner if I run back to work for a few hours?"

"Uh-huh." I stare at my words on the page. They seem so inadequate.

She sits down across from me. I try to ignore her, but she's staring at me. Finally, I put down my pen and look at her. "I'll be fine."

"How's the speech going? Want me to look at it?"

I push what I've written to her side of the table and get a glass of water and drink it, leaning on the counter, watching her face. She bites her lip as she reads, then frowns.

"Maybe you need to focus more on the Coach's life than his death," she says. "Maybe instead of thinking about how he's gone now, maybe you should talk about what he left, how you're different. You are different, you know?" She gets up and walks to me. I hug her hard, nod into her shoulder, and swallow my tears.

"Maybe," I say, but she's right. Writing all this sadness will not inspire anyone.

Finally, she releases me. "Are you ready for tomorrow?"

Regionals are tomorrow.

"I have to be. There will be scouts there. If I don't get out of Jefferson..." I set my glass on the counter, look out the window instead of at her. "Getting out of here is my only chance to have a normal life."

Mom touches my arm. "Sweetie, no one has a normal life. And whether you stay in Jefferson or win a scholarship on the other side of the country, you'll take yourself and your memories with you."

She's right. I know that, but I've put so much on this race. I need to win. I need to leave. And if I don't win, I can't leave.

— — —

At Regionals, I'm still distracted by my upcoming speech. I still don't know what I will say on Thursday. I run my 800 in a daze and finish fourth. I push the thoughts out of my head for the relay and help our team finish first, breaking a track record.

My last shot is the 1600. I set my feet for the start. I lift my hips at the ready call and push off at the starter's pistol. A moment later we're called back. False start. One kid from Central jumped the gun. Now we have to start again. Another chance. This time we get a clean start and soon I'm running near the middle of the pack. At the quarter-mile, I'm third, tucked behind the two frontrunners but close enough to take them when it's time. Out of nowhere, a memory forms. I'm in the car again with Sheila. She's laughing and holding my phone. I shoo the memory away and concentrate on my hips, pushing my legs to reach further.

The next quarter flies by, and my lungs burn. *Can I keep this up?* I pump my arms hard; I'm almost to the other girls. We make the turn, and we are running directly into the setting sun. It's blinding. Suddenly I'm back in that car again. The light glares brilliant, the morning sun glitters off Sheila's earrings. Beside me she laughs, singing and teasing. I see my phone. And then a door in my mind opens. The memory is so clear, I almost stop. I remember it all.

A runner zips past me, and I chase after her. At the start of the last lap, I ignore the pain in my legs and lungs. I ignore the memories pouring into my mind. I pass the struggling second-place runner and catch the front-runner. I have to outrun her, outrun the memory that is chasing me. We run next to each other, stride for stride as we head for the last turn.

Images fill my mind. Ms. Helen's weathered face. *I can't help but think some of Robert's goodness is in you now*. Sheila laughing. When I round the turn, Coach Mitchell is waving at me, urging me on. I glance at the stands as we pass them. Mom is there. She has her hands over her mouth. Dad is jumping up and down with his fist in the air. Casey runs along the railing in the bleachers. He's screaming, but I can't hear him. All I can hear is my heart pounding...... because I remember.

61
LIZ

It is almost midnight when I dial Kevin. I can't sleep. Tomorrow Jess will have to stand in front of an entire auditorium and talk about the accident. I don't know what she will say or if she knows what she will say. She went to bed at 8:30 so she would be rested. I have spent the entire evening pacing and drinking red wine. Almost an entire bottle.

When Kevin answers, I say, "I need you."

Ten minutes later he is at my door. As soon as I see his face, the tears come. He holds me and listens as I talk through all my fears. Not just for Jess and the judgment of her peers, the pressure to right a wrong somehow with words, but for me and this future I want. "What if I fail? I haven't been to school in so long."

"You won't fail," he says.

"What if Jessica doesn't get a scholarship? I'll have to put off school so I can work more, get another job. I think I want this, but maybe I don't. Maybe I am just trying to prove something. Months ago, Jessica wanted to move from Jefferson. Maybe she was right. Maybe the only way we get a fresh start is somewhere else."

"Do you want to move?" he asks.

I shake my head. "I just want my daughter to be happy. I'm so tired of worrying about her and my job and my father and Jake and what this stupid town thinks and..."

"And me?" he asks.

"And you."

"Don't worry about me. I'm here. I will always be here."

He leads me to the bedroom and I tell him I'm not ready for that, but he shushes me, pulls back the covers, and tucks me in like a little child. Then he kisses my forehead and says he will see me in the morning.

— — —

Jess and I drive the thirty minutes to the school in silence. Ellen Schultzman meets us at the door and takes Jess backstage. The principal walks me to the auditorium. I stand in the empty hall, watching a custodian sweep the stage. Kevin shows up. He squeezes my hand, and we find a seat near the back while the students file in. It feels so right to have him here. In moments the hall is noisy, hot, packed.

Ellen peeks out from the side of the stage, she finds me in the crowd and nods. Thank God for that woman. The principal quiets the students and warns them about being respectful of the speaker. Then he introduces Jess. He says she is a student from Jefferson High School who has a very important message for them. There is a smattering of hesitant applause.

Ellen holds the curtain back for Jess, who moves towards the podium stiffly, eyes fixed on the microphone. She doesn't look at the crowd, but I do. A lot of kids are whispering or checking their phones. This is any other moment for them.

Kevin squeezes my hand, nods towards the exit door, where Jake has just appeared. That is when I notice Casey standing almost behind us. I did not see him come in. Jake nods at me and takes a spot next to Casey. I wonder if he has met Casey, wonder if Jess knew Casey was coming. She didn't tell me.

The spotlight is on Jess. She swallows and adjusts the microphone, clears her throat, and lays her notecards carefully on the podium, rearranging them several times. The noise in the auditorium grows and the principal steps back out on the stage and waves at the kids to keep it down. He nods at Jess and retreats.

Finally, she begins.

"My name is Jessica Johnson. I'm here today because..." she stops and squints at her note cards. Then she looks up, fear grips her face. She glances towards Ellen off stage then back at her notes. I hear a few kids giggle and others shush them.

Jess looks up at the audience; the silence is paralyzing. I will her to speak, to say something. Finally, she says, "I'm sorry. I'm not very good at this." She looks back down at her notes. Takes a breath. "Seven months ago I was in an accident. A man named Robert Mitchell died."

I look around the room, gauge the reaction. Mouths stop whispering and heads turn at her words. Every eye is on Jess.

"It was my fault. And there is no way to apologize or make it right, so what I hope is, that by telling you about it, you will be different."

She looks up, pauses, and says, "I also hope that *I* will be different."

Jess looks in my direction. I don't know if she can see me, but I smile, nod, try not to look as terrified as I feel.

"She's doing great," whispers Kevin.

Now she sets her shoulders and leans forward and seems to find her voice. "My life changed on Sunday, October 4. Before that day, I was just doing whatever, hanging with my friends, going to school, not taking any of it seriously. Not thinking anything I did really mattered to anyone but me. Now I know different."

She looks back at her notes.

"Until just a few days ago, I couldn't remember the accident no matter how hard I tried. Everyone said it was because I hit my head on the windshield, but I think I didn't want to remember. I was afraid to. I didn't want any of it to be my fault."

"On that Sunday, just before we got in the car, my friend Sheila told me a guy I'd had a crush on for years was going to ask me out. I was excited about it—happy."

Now she blushes and glances towards Casey. Of course, she knows he is here. Lately, they are always together. I have been almost jealous, and also grateful, for the way she confides in him. I look back at him; his eyes are fixed on Jess.

"For a long time, I didn't remember much else about that day. Just getting in the car and then waking up in the hospital. Which made it easier to believe that it wasn't my fault, even though I was driving, so it had to be. But two days ago, it came back to me—everything that happened in my car on that day."

"On the way to Sheila's house, I got a text. Sheila knew I wouldn't look at a text while driving. I'm kind of militant about that ever since my mom almost wrecked our car looking at her phone." She pauses. There are a few whispers.

"I told Sheila not to read it, that I would wait until we got there, but she grabbed my phone and read the text."

I can see the tears welling in her eyes, she blinks them away.

"I asked her what it said. She said, 'Read for yourself' and handed me the phone. And then she put her hand on the wheel to steer. It was a road we've both driven a million times. I remember looking back at the road. There was nothing there. Just the glare of the sun and the empty road. What was the harm? Sheila had the wheel. So I looked at the text."

I am stunned. Jess has told me none of this. I had no idea she remembered what happened.

Her voice cracks as she says, "I just thought..." She pauses, searching for words. She shakes her head but continues. "I never thought there would be anyone there." She wipes at her tears, swallows. Her tears bring mine. "Sheila was laughing, watching me, not the road and when I looked up, I saw Coach Mitchell, but it was too late."

There are a few gasps. Jess continues, her voice choked with tears.

"I can't stop hearing the car hitting him. It made this awful thud. I hear it in my dreams. I can't stop hearing it."

The auditorium has grown silent. No one whispers or checks their phones.

"I wanted to blame Sheila, to think this was her fault. But it wasn't. I was driving the car. I decided to look away. And because of that one moment, I've hurt so many people I love and so many people who I don't even know." She pauses, unable to speak for the tears, and then whispers into the microphone, "I'm sorry."

She looks up at the audience. They are rapt. "I wish you could have known Coach Mitchell." She smiles through her tears.

"I've gotten to know his wife, Ms. Helen. She has told me so many stories about Coach Mitchell. I knew what everyone else knew—he was a brilliant coach who led our football team to win states six times. I think we beat you guys a couple of times." There is cautious laughter and Jess smiles.

"Coach Mitchell believed in people, even when they made mistakes." As Jess says these words, I am transported back to Coach Mitchell's office and Jake nervously explaining that I'm pregnant, that I wanted to have an abortion, but we don't have the money. Jake never wanted the abortion, but I knew my family would never accept a baby. And I needed to get out of Jefferson, almost as bad as Jess thinks she does. Adoption was not an option. I knew if I had that baby, I would keep it and if I kept it, there would be no college. No getting out of Jefferson.

Instead of Jess, I hear Coach now. "The two of you created a life. That life is your responsibility and every decision you make must be in the best interest of that life. It is not just about you anymore; now there is someone more important." He paused to let those words become real. And then, almost as an afterthought, but quite possibly the largest truth of my life, he said, "I'll tell you this, no matter what you decide, your lives will never be the same."

Jess is still talking, telling them about her visits with Helen Mitchell, how Helen told her about Coach, and all the people he helped. I wonder if Helen told Jess that if not for Coach, she might not be here. I say a grateful silent prayer and shoot it up to Coach.

"I thought because of what happened, because of this one huge awful mistake, I was a terrible person." Jess stops, wipes a tear. "It was a bad decision, the worst of my life, but that doesn't mean I'm bad; it means I'm normal, not perfect."

I look at Kevin, his eyes fixed on Jess. She is right, I realize. A bad decision doesn't make you an awful person. It makes you human. I have been waiting for this town to realize that for seventeen years, and I can't even offer the same forgiveness to this man who I love, or to the father who created me, or to Jake who gave me Jess standing up there right now. I squeeze Kevin's hand. I love him. That is all that should matter. I lean into him, and he smiles at me.

"After the accident, I felt so alone. Sometimes I wished I was dead. I didn't think I could ever be happy again. Coach Mitchell's daughter Karen said something that changed everything. She said, 'My father would never want your life ruined because of his death.' That's so huge." Jess hesitates, her voice raw. "Who forgives like that?"

She wipes at her eyes, and a startled look crosses her face. I follow her gaze and recognize Coach Mitchell's children, Bobby, Brian, and Karen seated near the back. They are crying too. Jess seems to address them, now. "I can't ever make up for taking a life, but I can take responsibility for it. For too long I have taken too much for granted—I was more important to me than the people around me. I am not that person anymore. I promise. Ms. Helen told me she believes that some of Coach is now in me. I want to believe that.

The state of Texas wants me to tell you not to drive distracted, but what I really want to tell you is not to live distracted. I don't plan to take another moment or another person for granted. I hope you won't either." She steps away from the microphone. Then steps back, leans in, and says, "Thank you."

The sudden silence in the room makes the sniffling audible. I am not the only one crying. The clapping starts from the back near the door and fills the auditorium. My tears come in torrents. I watch as Ellen comes to the podium and guides Jess off the stage so the principal can dismiss the students. It occurs to me my daughter is a lot more grown-up than I am.

When I find Jess afterward, I pull her into my arms. "I have never been more proud, Jessica. Never. I love you."

"I've never been more scared," she says as she clings to me.

I whisper in her ear as I hold her tight. "You are amazing, you know that, right? You will be fine. Me, too. Both of us. We will be just fine."

She nods and whispers back, "I love you, Mom."

"Outstanding job, Jess," says Kevin. Casey and Jake are walking towards us. Casey smiles shyly at Jess, but Jake grabs her in a bear hug. "You rocked that place!"

"Thanks, Dad." I watch as she looks over his shoulder at Casey whose own eyes look a little wet. "I guess you met Casey."

"I did. Who do you think started your standing ovation?"

Casey grins.

We say our goodbyes and leave Jess with Ellen. She has to stay for a visit with the driver's ed class. We walk out with Casey.

"So we'll see you Saturday night?" Jake asks Casey when he turns to go.

"Yes, sir," he says.

"Thanks for coming," I tell him.

He blushes and says, "Sure," before hurrying up the hall.

— — —

I walk out of the school with Jake on one side and Kevin on the other. Jake and I have never spoken of his drunken phone call. It is too late for us, and I am sure when he sobered up, he realized it, too. Because of Jess, who has not only his freckles but his kind heart, Jake will always be a part of my life. But I am finished judging him. Jake is who he is, no apologies. He has made plenty of mistakes, but I have too.

His truck is parked in the loading zone, and we pause to say goodbye.

"She did it," he says to me.

I smile. "She did." Then I hug him. He winks at me and climbs into his truck.

"See ya Saturday," he yells out the window as the engine roars to life and diesel fumes fill the entranceway.

"Are you bringing the new girlfriend?" I ask.

"Who?"

"Your girlfriend."

"Nah, we split up. It'll just be me," he says and pulls out.

— — —

Kevin walks with me to my car.

"You should be proud," he says.

"Thank you," I tell him, but it is a monumental understatement for the debt I owe him. "I couldn't have made it through this without you."

"Oh, I don't know." He nods towards Jake. "You had friends with you."

"No, Kevin, not just today. All of it. You saved her. You know that, right?"

He shakes his head. "Jess saved herself. You and Jake raised a tough kid, a smart kid. That accident could have happened to anyone. But your kid, despite the few rough patches, handled it like a champ. You raised her well. So, this one is on you. I just did what I always do."

"What's that?"

"Look for the truth under all the mess."

I smile. "Well, thanks."

He kisses my forehead. "It has been my complete pleasure."

He walks away, but then I call to him. He stops and turns to me, his face a question. I close the distance between us, put my arms around him, and kiss him. "I want to try this again. See where it takes us. I think there's a lot of truth under all this mess."

"I promise no one comes before you from now on."

"I seriously doubt that," I tell him with a wink. He gives me a questioning look. "You are going to be a dad, so there will soon be one person who will."

He smiles, even blushes. "I can't wait to be a dad."

"I can't wait to see you be one," I tell him.

62
JESS

It felt good to say all that stuff out loud. Maybe none of those kids will do anything differently because of what I said, but saying it helped me. I needed to do it. I wasn't sure exactly what I would say until I started talking. I had notes, but that was all the stuff I'd written before the track meet, before I remembered exactly what happened in the car with Sheila. And I don't blame Sheila. I don't. It wasn't her fault; it was mine. I need to tell her that too, and maybe I will someday.

Tomorrow night is prom. *Prom!* My dress is one I borrowed from Avery, but I like it. Mom wanted to take me shopping for a real prom dress, but I know she needs to save her money for college. I am so proud of her for going back to school, even if it means I'll be doing more of the cooking next year.

I head to Ms. Helen's house; I haven't been to see her all week. It was too crazy getting ready for regionals and my speech and figuring out prom. I feel bad about it, but I didn't know what to say. Now I do. There is an enormous truck blocking the driveway and Ms. Helen is sitting on the porch with Sherman at her feet.

"Jessica! How wonderful that you're here!"

"I'm sorry I haven't been over to walk Sherman lately."

Ms. Helen waves away my apology. "No matter. I am glad you're here now."

I sit on the bench next to Ms. Helen. Sherman wags his tail, but for once remains still.

"I need to tell you something."

"Oh?" She runs her hand over Sherman and then glances at a man carrying a box past us across the porch. "What dear?" She smiles her grandma smile that makes her eye twinkle.

I thought she would be there at the school for my speech, but she wasn't. "I know I already told you I'm sorry and I know that changes nothing, but what you said about part of Coach being in me now... that's what I hope.... and I just want you to know that I don't expect you to forgive me."

"Oh Jessica, you don't need my forgiveness," Ms. Helen whispers. There are tears on her cheeks.

"Yes, I do," I insist.

She shakes her head. "Oh, dear, I forgave you a long time ago—for Robert. He would want me to." Ms. Helen takes my hand and pats it. She smiles through her tears. "Now, comes the hard part—forgiving yourself. I know that won't be easy for a young person like you. I can see that now. But it's important that you do." Ms. Helen releases my hand; she looks at me very seriously. "You need to remember that it was one careless mistake."

"It was more than careless."

"It was human," says Ms. Helen. She looks at me with such obvious affection that I have to look away. "You are human. A beautiful human from what I can see."

My words stick in my throat, and I shake my head. I want to say she's wrong, insist I am not, but I also want to believe her. I want to be the person she thinks I am. I know if I open my mouth to speak the tears will come and she must know that too because she pulls me into a hug and says, "There now. I'm an old person; you have to believe me."

She laughs and as she lets me go, she eyes Sherman who has gotten up. He's ready for his walk. "Now I have a serious question to ask you."

I wipe the tears away with the back of my hand and nod.

"Can you take Sherman?"

"What?"

Ms. Helen gestures around her. "I'm moving. I don't need this enormous rambling house. I'm moving to a condominium in a development just for old people like me. I plan to take water aerobics and join the knitting guild."

“Really?”

“Really. I’m ready to take it easy. But I can’t take Sherman. Even if I could, I wouldn’t. He’s too much dog for me. He needs someone who can keep up with him. Someone like you.”

I look at Sherman who regards me with his deep brown eyes.

“I guess I can take him. If my mom won’t let me have him, he can live with my dad’s dogs.”

“Splendid!” Ms. Helen claps her hands.

I walk home clutching the bag of Sherman’s belongings and the leash attached to Sherman. For once the dog doesn’t pull. Sherman walks contentedly beside me.

63
LIZ

When I get home from work on Friday, Jess is in the backyard with Helen Mitchell's dog. I look around for Helen, half expecting to see her sipping lemonade on the porch. When Jess first started walking her dog, I used to follow her. I was suspicious. It seemed an odd request. But she only walked the dog around the block and returned to the Mitchell's house. Then she would sit on Helen's front porch for a bit. I have wondered what they talked about, but I trusted Helen. When I told Kevin what Jess was doing, he said I should stop worrying. He said Helen Mitchell was the only reason there would not be a civil suit. She had to fight her children about it.

When I asked Jess about her time with Helen, she said, "She just needs me to walk Sherman. He pulls a lot."

"Why is Sherman here?" I ask now.

"Ms. Helen gave him to me," Jess says and the dog jumps on me, smearing mud on my dress pants.

Jess pulls him off. "Sherman, no!"

"What do you mean she gave him to you?"

"She's moving and she can't take him."

"Why does that mean you have to take him?"

"I want to take him."

"You agreed to take this dog without even asking me?"

She looks down at Sherman, frowns. "I didn't think you'd mind."

"You'll be going to college in another year and then who takes care of him?"

"He can go to Dad's. Willard and Homeboy will love him."

I frown. I don't want to be the bad guy. I am tired of that role. I look at the dog. He seems to smile at me.

"I need to do this. I need Sherman."

"You don't *need* a dog."

"Yes, I do. He'll help me remember what I said in my speech about being different now."

Her smile gives her away; she is playing me. Jess has always wanted a dog, but I have held out. I am responsible for enough. "I don't think you need a dog to help you remember."

"Still," she says, looking up at me hopefully.

I sit down on the porch steps and she sits beside me. Sherman lies down at her feet and rolls over for her to rub his belly. I realize she *is* different, with or without the dog's help. I am different too. I am finished withholding forgiveness and clinging to my anger and fear like some kind of sick armor to shield my heart.

"So, are you and Kevin back together?"

I nod.

"I'm glad," she says.

"You are?"

"Yeah. He's good for you. Plus, I like the idea of having a shark lawyer for a step-dad."

"Nobody said anything about marriage, but just in case, what would you think about a stepbrother?"

"For real?"

I nod. "Kevin's ex-wife is having his baby."

She wrinkles her forehead. "I thought he was divorced."

I nod. "It's a long story, but yes, he is divorced."

She shrugs. "I guess that would be cool. I like little kids. It'll be good for you to have Kevin and a baby when I leave for college."

"It will be," I say.

Jess tosses a ball for Sherman and we watch him chase it. Instead of bringing it back, he lies down in the grass and chews on the ball, making a steady squeak, watching us.

I put my arm around her, pull her close. "Just so you know, I'm not picking up dog poop."

She grins at me. "Thanks, Mom."

"I bet your granddad will love him."

"When is he moving to Morningside?"

"After Kate gets back from Yellowstone, she's driving him here."

"He likes dogs?"

I nod. "Loves them."

"I knew there was something about him I liked!" She grins at me, then claps her hands. "C'mon Sherman! I want you to meet Dylan!"

I watch them disappear through the gate into the neighbor's yard. Is forgiveness that easy? Is it that hard? I think of Jake today. I picture his easy smile. He is a good guy. He loves his daughter. He has stayed that same solid, what-you-see-is-what-you-get guy I knew when we walked the halls of Jefferson. He never pretended to be anything else.

As if he knows I am thinking of him, Jake materializes around the side of the house. He is carrying a bottle. "I brought champagne! It's time to celebrate!" He grins his double-dimple grin. I laugh as he pops the cork, and it flies into the backyard. The bottle spews champagne, so he chugs it. *Jake*. I smile.

After I retrieve glasses, he fills them both.

"To Jess," he says and we clink glasses.

"To us," I say and he gives me a questioning look. "For surviving this and coming out of it friends."

He smiles. "I've always been your friend, Lizzie. Always will be."

"I know," I tell him. "It's just sometimes I forget."

Jess comes back across the yard with Sherman in tow.

"Dad! Meet Sherman!"

— — —

Saturday morning, I take Jess to have her nails painted. On a whim, I get mine done too, even though I will have to take it off before I go to work on Monday. They do not allow aides at Morningside to wear polish.

Jess looks like a fairytale princess after Avery has twisted her hair up into impossible knots that give Jess another two inches (on top of the three she will add with the heels Avery loaned her), she sprays it with glitter and arranges a few daisies to hide the pins.

"Wow!" says Jess when she sees herself in the mirror in my bathroom.

"Serious wow," I agree.

Jess perches on the counter in her robe and lets me apply eye makeup and blush. She could easily do it herself, but I like that she is indulging me. In so many ways, I feel like I have my daughter back, but she is not the little girl who followed me like a shadow or the surly teen who couldn't lose me fast enough, she is a beautiful young woman who is teaching me the art of forgiveness.

Jake arrives, and Jess goes to put on her dress.

"I think I should have a little talk with Casey when he gets here," Jake tells me as we wait on the new porch. Avery ran to pick up the boutonniere we forgot to order for Casey.

"No, you don't," I tell Jake. "He and Jess are a lot smarter than we were."

"It has nothing to do with the brain," Jake says.

And then Jess appears, and he has no words. She twirls for us and Jake coughs to hide his tears.

Avery returns just in time to see Casey pull up.

"Damn, girl," she says to Jess. "I'm impressed."

Jess blushes.

He appears on the step with a beautiful corsage. His curly hair has been tamed by a professional, and his expression when he sees Jess is one of a boy who realizes just how lucky he is. He is handsome in a tux with a cummerbund in the same shade of blue as Jess' dress. They pose for pictures in the backyard. Dylan even crashes our little gathering and gets in on a few of the shots. My favorite is the one where Jess has an arm around each of them and Casey is looking at her with sheer admiration while she and Dylan are cracking up at some inside joke.

"They look like us," Jake whispers beside me.

"But they are not us," I reply.

"Being us wouldn't be so bad."

I lean my head against his shoulder. "Nah, it wouldn't."

"You ready to have your dad at Morningside?" Jake asks.

"It will be easier to take care of him, and maybe it will mean we see more of Kate."

"And what about your lawyer? I'm guessing we haven't seen the last of him?"

"Probably not."

"Good for you, Lizzie. I'm glad," he says, and I can tell he means it.

We watch Casey escort Jess to the car. He holds the door for her like a gentleman, and she laughs at his efforts. They are so young; they do look like Jake and me at that age. I wonder if he will hurt her and know inevitably that he will. But I think my daughter is way ahead of me. She knows that forgiveness is the bigger part of love.

After they leave, Avery takes off too. She has a date with a new guy she met at church. "But he's no Casey Miller, I'll tell you that," she says. "He's gonna need some training."

Jake whistles for Sherman. "I'm going to take him to meet his new fur brothers."

I roll my eyes. "Just so long as he doesn't come back smelling like them," I tell him.

My phone lights up with a text from Kevin.

"Be there soon."

I smile. My heart is happy.

THE END

NOTE FROM THE AUTHOR

Word-of-mouth is crucial for any author to succeed. If you enjoyed *Blind Turn*, please leave a review online—anywhere you are able. Even if it's just a sentence or two. It would make all the difference and would be very much appreciated.

Thanks!
Cara

AUTHOR THE AUTHOR

Cara Sue Achterberg is the author of several novels and memoirs, including *One Hundred Dogs & Counting: One Woman, Ten Thousand Miles, and a Journey into the Heart of Shelters and Rescues*. She is a blogger, foster dog mom, and the founder of Who Will Let the Dogs Out. Cara lives on a hillside farm in Pennsylvania but pines for the mountains of Virginia.

For more information visit CaraWrites.com.

Facebook – https://www.facebook.com/CaraSueAchterberg/
Twitter – https://twitter.com/CaraAchterberg
Instagram – https://www.instagram.com/carasueachterberg
Website/Blog – http://www.carawrites.com/
LinkedIn – https://www.linkedin.com/in/cara-sue-achterberg-7858976/

CPSIA information can be obtained
at www.ICGtesting.com
Printed in the USA
BVHW052341101122
651392BV00009B/11